FINDING LOVE'S WINGS

FINDING LOVE'S WINGS

Zoey Derrick

Cover completed by Olivia Rivers with permission from www.fotolia.com. Olivia can be found on Twitter @RiversOlivia. Cover material and photos (c) Fotolia.com

This book was edited with the help of Sione Aeschliman, Owner of Sione Aeschliman LLC out of Portland, Oregon. Sione has been my rock, my constant and the light that has kept this project moving forward, without her, this book would not be in your hands. You can visit her on Twitter at www.twitter.com/writelearndream or on her website http://sioneaeschliman.blogspot.com

ISBN-13: 978-0990326410

The following is a fictional novel and the characters represented here are not only over the age of 18, but full consenting adults who have only coincidental resemblance to real live people. The location of this story is called Tarah, and please know that this location exists only in my head.. Or at least this version of this location, any resemblance of someplace real is coincidental and if you know of a place like this, send me an e-mail, I need a vacation.

For Mom, without your undying support, this would not be possible.
Thank you, for everything.

ONE

CAMI

I have this distinct feeling that something is off, but I can't put my finger on what it is. As I pull into the parking spot near Reed's condo, the dreaded "something is not right" feeling courses stronger through my body. His car is here, right next to me, so I know he's here. And I can hear music coming from the window, which is wide open despite the ninety-five degree temperature. Typical weather for June in Phoenix, but most people would have the house closed up and the A/C blasting.

Reed is about five feet six inches tall. Not very tall, but about two inches taller than I am. He is very broad shouldered and muscular, with that perfect V at his hips. He just has an air of sexiness about him.

I met Reed at a bar about six months ago, and we hit it off pretty well. Really well, in fact. We ended up in bed together that same night. We've been seeing each other casually since then, but it's strange: we very rarely ever go out; it's usually just he and I in bed together. I'm not sure that we can be considered a couple, but we've been exclusive to one another since we met.

As I step out of the car, I take a deep breath. Pulling myself together, I head for the door. It's unlocked, which isn't unusual when he's expecting me, even though I have a key to his place. But when I enter the house, I hear a strange noise. I listen carefully, and over the beat of the music there it is again: a weird mewling noise that I can't immediately place.

"Killer Queen" by Queen is crooning through the bedroom stereo system. Reed loves his rock music, and Queen is a bit mellow for him. "Reed?" I call out. The music drones on, so I start singing quietly to myself as I make my way toward his bedroom. As I climb the stairs the music changes, though the song isn't over yet. It switches over to Adele's "Rumor Has It," but not before I catch the sounds again.

Are you fucking kidding me? I think. This rat bastard is sleeping with someone else. The woman moaning is a dead give away. I should turn around and walk out the door.

Instead I make my way further up the stairs, but I stop when I see that his bedroom door is wide open and catch an eye-full of the woman with him. She is mounted on top of him, riding him. Moaning like a cat in heat while she rubs at his chest. He has his hands on her breasts and is rolling her nipples between his thumb and forefinger. She throws her head back and moans again.

I would stomp up the stairs and barge in except I feel that familiar warming between my legs as I watch this display. I feel frozen in place. After a couple of minutes I realize I'm in danger of being caught, and I decide that discretion is going to be the better form of valor, so I turn around and get the hell out of the house.

As soon as I shut myself back in my car I start cursing and screaming at the top of my lungs. "That asshole. Why am I not surprised? He has no regard for anyone or anything. What the hell? Well I guess this explains the funny feelings. UGH!!!!! I'm so mad I could spit nails. What in the hell was he thinking? What in the bloody hell was I thinking? Oh, fuck this shit!" Driving myself the ten minutes back to my apartment is uneventful as I contemplate what to do next.

After about an hour of pacing, ranting, and trying to decide what to do, I grab my little carry-on suitcase and throw in a few changes of clothing. I need to get out of this town. Somewhere tropical. With beaches. Dammit, I need a vacation.

On my way to the airport, driving down forty-fourth street, I come across a billboard for the upcoming *Love Is Burning* movie. Up there, in all his twenty-foot tall glory, is the beautiful face of Tristan Michaels.

Looking up at his beautiful face is slowly washing away all the angst of the last couple of hours. For the last five years, I've been staring at his face in the magazines that grace the grocery store aisles. Looking at him gives me the strangest sense of security, protection, and need, but what that need is, I've never been able to figure out.

"I bet you'd never cheat on woman with another woman while the first one is on her way over, would you?" I ask his image. Those eyes seem to see right into my soul.

The car behind me honks. The light has changed.

At the airport I email Mick and Beau from my phone, letting them know that I'm headed to L.A. I know they will worry when they don't hear from me tonight. Beau is my best friend and a personal assistant to me. Mick is my financial genius, and the closest thing I have to a dad.

I received a text from Reed while I was en route to the airport, asking where I was. I decide that I should reply to him. My text is dripping with an anger that I'm pretty sure I no longer feel.

I turn off my phone as soon as I know my text has been sent to Reed. I know that leaving it on will mean I will start getting calls or emails from Reed, Beau and Mick. I need to make my escape without anyone convincing me otherwise.

I know that before I even land at my final destination – wherever that is – Mick or Beau will have tracked the ticket. It's fine if they know the where, but I don't want them to know why. Not right now at least. Because if I'm completely honest with myself, I'm not even sure I know why I'm running.

I make my way to the US Airways counter. After twenty minutes of shuffling through the options, I have a first class ticket on a flight from Phoenix to Los Angeles with the intention of spending the night. I'm really looking forward to going on vacation, but I have business in L.A. that needs to be dealt with first.

From L.A. I'll be heading to Honolulu, where I will connect with a flight to Tahiti. I've been in Tahiti before — it was the summer after my mom passed away and I loved it – so when I found out the option was available I took it. However, I have no intention of staying in Tahiti, either.

While I was there the last time, some of the locals told me about the island of Tarah, located about a four-hour boat ride or a thirty-minute helicopter hop from the Tahiti airport. Tarah is a very small, and very private, island. The island is frequently visited by celebrities and many others seeking anonymity. Someplace, I'm sure, I have no right to hide, but I'm going anyway. The island is tropical year-round and mostly inhabited by English-speaking French Polynesians and Australians, which is a huge bonus in my book.

Walking past all the magazine shops, bakeries and coffee shops on the way to my gate, I notice one thing in common all along the way: Tristan Michaels is everywhere I turn. Whether his image is splashed all over promotional magazines for his upcoming movies or on the raunchy tabloids citing the unnecessary and nasty rumors that make their way through the world of entertainment, he is beautiful as ever and I cannot pull my eyes away from him.

TRISTAN

"Tristan, you have to help me." I roll my eyes toward the vast, wide-open space of Nokia Theater in downtown Los Angeles. Layla, my girlfriend – well a loose interpretation of the word girlfriend – is arguing with me off in the corner of the reception area. Having just come off of the red carpet, I'm extremely irritable, and she decides that now is the perfect time for an argument.

Thank God that everyone is converging at the bars on the other side of the room. I can see Travis, surrounded by women and fans. Thanking my lucky stars that where Layla and I are standing is devoid of any other people. Though it's a bit conspicuous.

Layla is angry. Downright pissed, if you want the truth of it, and her face is starting to turn red.

"I need to do no such thing, Layla. This is your damn mess, you fix it." My voice is a harsh growl. We are in the lobby of a theater, at Travis's premier for God's sake. Of all the places in the world that she can bring up this mess, she decides to do it here, tonight.

"Tristan, I can't. They've tried and the magazine wants nothing to do with what I have to say." She is breathing heavy, her temper starting to flare. Her pupils are dilated and I have no doubt that she's high on something. This seems to be the new normal for her.

"Well, I'm not the one in the pictures, so why should I stop this story?"

"Because you love me? Because it affects you? Because you care about me? I don't care, pick a reason. Why would you want to see me destroyed?"

Words fail me. As little as a year ago, I would have done anything for Layla. I would have bent over, broken, and picked up the phone right this second to have Trinity working at getting this story stopped. But no, not this time. I'm not going to defend her anymore. I can't. "There is no logical reason for me to fix your mistakes. You made it, you lay in it." I turn to walk away and she grabs my arm. I turn back to her. "Let go of me." My anger is becoming palpable. Her grip sends a shiver of disgust through my body.

"Tristan, please." Her voice is low, pleading.

She looks so pathetic, broken, and for a minute I start to feel sorry for her. But it takes only a moment for her own history to go flying through my mind. She's the product of being coddled by her parents. She was handed everything in life that she ever wanted. They're extremely wealthy, and she lacks for nothing. She has never had to fight for the things she wants; she has been handed them. She doesn't know what it is like to be alone in the big bad world, and because her parents fix everything for her, she doesn't have Clue One about how to fix her own mistakes. "Why don't you go running to Daddy? I'm sure he can find a way to fix this for you."

Her face falls immediately, and she knows exactly what I'm referring to. She knows what my life was like, and she knows that I got to this position via a single, hardworking mom. I would have graduated college with a mountain of debt had it not been for getting my role in *Love is Burning*.

"Tristan, that's not fair."

"Not fair! Not fair!" My temper flares up. "Don't you dare talk to me about fair. You have evidence of your having a good time, surrounded by I don't know how many men, one of which is the producer of your last movie. Do not ever talk to me about fair, ever again." I slowly unclench my fists and start to turn. I take a long look at her ruddy face. The woman I once thought of as drop-dead gorgeous now has my stomach acid rising, making me want to vomit. I rub my hand on my chest in an effort to soothe the ache caused by this woman. I could claw my heart out of my chest and it wouldn't feel any better. "I've had enough of this shit," I growl at her. "If you want this story stopped, you will find a way and it will not be by my hand or my people." I turn on my heel and take two steps away from her.

"Tristan, I'm pregnant."

In an instant my heart swells and I start to turn toward her, wanting to embrace her. Then it hits me like a lightning bolt. Oh for fuck's sake, is she serious? The acid grows higher. "If you think that is going to bring my arms around you in a comforting, everything-will-be-all-right embrace, forget it. I'm not stupid, Layla." I lean into her ear and nearly growl at her. "For the love of all that is holy, Layla, get your shit straightened out. That goddamn article is the least of your problems."

I back away from her. Tears are streaming down her face. A look of defeat. I turn and walk away as quickly as

I can manage. I pass Tyson on my way to the door. I hold my hand up. "Don't." I walk out the door and turn to the left. I put my head down and walk as quickly as I can manage toward the back entrance of the J.W. Marriott. I'm walking at such a pace that by the time it registers on people's minds exactly who I am, I'm lost in the next crowd. I hear several girls calling my name, but I don't so much as flinch.

Fucking Layla. She has a damn orgy with God only knows how many men, gets pregnant, and she expects me to fall to bended knee and rectify her problems. Well, Layla, have Daddy or Mommy fix your latest problem, because I could care less.

I feel my phone vibrating in my pocket. No doubt it's probably her. Or Travis wondering where I've gone. I take a brief look and see that it's Tyson. I hit send and put the phone to my ear. "Meet me at J.W."

"Trist—" He starts to say, and I hit end. I refuse to have this conversation while walking down through the L.A. Live area of downtown.

I need to call Trinity to give her a heads up about this story. I'm not sure what the implications will be for me, and I'm not sure that I really care. Over the last five years it has become painfully obvious that an actor's career in Hollywood can be marred by his associations as well as the stories that are written about him. Frankly, I'm to a point that all this Hollywood nonsense is old, and I'm a bit tired of it.

My thoughts are random and scattered. I can't stay focused on one subject or another. Layla has me scrambling into hiding because I can't or won't deal with this. Why should I?

God, she's pregnant. And for a second I was ready and willing to embrace her. To show her that it would be okay, that I would make it okay. Then, for another half a second after the lightning bolt struck, her drug use was flashing through my mind. She was high, even tonight. The premiere is the reason why. We had talked about it a couple of days ago, and I was adamant that we were going separate. She and I hadn't been seen arriving together in over six months. In fact, I cannot remember the last time we went anywhere together.

Once I found out about her drug use, I slowly pulled back from my association with her. Some of the tabloids had even started questioning whether or not we were together. Layla's people denied any such allegations, and then they'd leak some random story about Tristan and Layla being seen somewhere together. They were so determined to keep us together, and it is finally time to break free. The pictures she showed me on her phone are their concrete proof, and there is nothing out there that can deny the newest accusations. For this, I'm grateful.

I make it to the hotel about five minutes later. I walk in and the concierge recognizes me, and I'm immediately ushered straight to the penthouse. It's my usual room, but tonight I would have taken anything. On the way up he asks, "How many nights, Mr. Michaels?"

"One, I think. Tyson will be along shortly. Send him up, will you, please?"

"Absolutely. Will you be needing anything right away?"

"No, the bar will suffice. Thanks."

I turn to my BlackBerry and text Tyson that I need my stuff from Layla's – all of it – and that I'm in my usual room. Yes, I've stayed here a few too many nights.

Layla has a house over in Beverly Hills. It was originally suppose to be 'our' house when she bought it about a year ago, but I didn't like the house, and Layla insisted it was what she wanted. I let her buy it herself. I guess this was the start of my knowing full well that our relationship was going nowhere.

I enter the suite and beeline straight to the bar. I grab the bottle of Laphraig and pour about two fingers' worth into the crystal glass. Once I pour, I stare at it like it's going to bite me.

"No more," I grumble out loud, and down the scotch. Immediately I pour another glass and make my way to the terrace. The hotel room has a retro feel to it. With a lot of orange, red, brown, and yellow, of all things. All put together, it really works. The streets of downtown L.A. are bustling with people going this way and that. The searchlights are still going in front of Nokia Theater and people are still milling about. No doubt waiting for all those who entered to leave again. The premiere isn't even for one of my movies. I felt no obligation to stay, and I refused to stay with Layla milling about. I turn my phone back on and text Travis to let him know that I've left. I had agreed to attend Travis's *Rebound* premiere more than a month ago. He never actually asks me to attend such events; it's kind of implied, when it comes to him. We met about four years ago at a charity event and we have been nearly inseparable ever since. He's been my rock since all of this Layla crap happened, including my escape and a place to crash.

His response to my text has me laughing. I stare at the "Fuck Layla!" replay and shake my head. If he only knew.

I sit down and rub my chest. While I wait for Tyson, I look to the stars and whisper. "Please, Mama. Send me a sign – something, anything – that this is all going to be right."

TWO

CAMI

Upon my arrival in L.A., I head downtown to the JW Marriott, I want to stay at the Hollywood Hotel, but my late arrival has me seeking something quick and guaranteed. If the JW fails, the Ritz is right next door.

Once I check in I take the elevator up to a suite on the eighteenth floor. The room looks like Ikea barfed on the decor: brown walls, orange furniture, and white linens. The furniture is eclectic, but strangely it all goes together.

I dump my luggage next to the bed, pour myself a glass of white wine, and flop into a white, high-backed club chair. While pulling my iPad from my knapsack I notice a strange light peeking through the closed curtains. Hmm, I wonder what that's all about? I get out of my chair and walk toward the window. Peering out, I notice a few spotlights floating around. My eyes follow the lights to the top of the towers located in the center of L.A. Live, then look down to see the red carpet and the crowd milling about. It's hard to make out what exactly is going on, but it appears to be a premiere.

I stare down at it for a moment, shrug and return to my chair. I email Beau and Mick to tell them that I'm in

L.A. I just leave it at that for right now. I'm sure the initial reaction is that I'm in town for business, which is now true: Trinity has emailed to ask me to come to a board meeting tomorrow. I guess since I'm here, I might as well.

I shut down the iPad, light a cigarette, and sit back. Taking a deep breath, I let the tears of frustration flow.

I'm not hurt, per se, regarding Reed. I'm angry with myself and – interestingly – with my parents.

Bobbie, my father, and Evelyn, my mother, were the definition of what a parent shouldn't be throughout my childhood and even into the early stages of adulthood. When I was only six, my parents sent me off to England with a personal matron to keep tabs on me until I was old enough to enter into a full boarding school.

I stayed in England until I was sixteen. I was brought home by Bobbie because Evelyn had passed away. I found out later on that she had been sick for some time. It was another thing to add to the long list of what my parents failed at.

After I graduated from high school and moved away to Phoenix for college, Bobbie started to come around and warm up to me. The emails were few and far between in the beginning. As time passed, his emails became more frequent. When I entered into my degree program, my schedule was such that my responses became shorter, and I sent them less often. But the emails from Bobbie got longer, and the more emails I got, the better I got to know him. I made a few trips out to California over the next couple of years, and, to my surprise, Bobbie made time for me. The lunches and dinners were awkward, but we managed to muddle through.

Last year, which was my senior year of college, my thesis kept me busy and left me little time for much fun. I did, however, make a point of returning his emails, though my replies were often short. I thought we had time. Just as I realized I was looking forward to having a better relationship with Bobbie, he passed away.

From my parents I learned to be insensitive, a bit of a bitch, and, most of all, shallow and empty. I know nothing of love, or what love is supposed to feel like. I constantly find myself in the arms of men that treat me as though I'm nothing more than a good fuck.

I'm so angry at myself for being susceptible to the weakness Bobbie and Evelyn have instilled in me that I can't stop the tears from flowing.

The next morning I wake up around six, shower, and put on jeans, a tank top underneath a lacy button-up shirt, and sneakers. I head downstairs and grab a cab, instructing the driver to head to Westwood Memorial Park in Hollywood.

When we arrive I ask the cab driver to wait for me, and I make my way to Bobbie and Evelyn's grave. As I approach their headstones my anger grows to uncontrollable proportions, and I walk up and kick Bobbie's headstone right in the name.

"Ow! Ow! Dammit." I fall to the ground, sobbing. "I hate you, you son of bitch! Why did you do this to me? I don't understand. If you never wanted kids, why the fuck did you have them? Because, believe me, right now, I'm sure I would be better off." For a moment the tears are so overwhelming that I can't speak anymore.

I have never understood why my parents saw fit to let us be raised the way that we were. Why did we never have parents, but only house staff and guardians at school to take care of us?

"Because of you, I'm dead on the inside. I can't love or be loved," I continued to sob. "You were never there for me. You were never supportive or loving. You left me to care for myself at an age when I needed you most." I wipe the tears from my cheeks. "I've never been anything more than a throw-away toy, a sexual object, and for that I hate myself. I just wish I knew better how to handle myself and my emotions, or even something as simple as a relationship. Instead I give in to someone so fast they see a way to use me for their own satisfaction."

The anger that pulled me here quickly turns to loneliness and isolation. I shift my position, pulling my knees up to my chest and wrapping my arms tightly around my legs, and stare at my father's grave.

He's been gone for a full year now. Despite all his God-awful flaws, I'm really starting to miss him. I need someone to be there for me on an emotional level. I need someone who has holes in their head that fit all the rocks in mine.

Bobbie and I were never a father and daughter; it was more like ward and warden because he was always cold and unyielding when it came to expressions of love. I am so angry at the fact that I feel so lost and I have no one to turn to.

After a few more minutes, the cab driver approaches me. "Ma'am, we need to go if you want to make your meeting."

I wipe the tears from my eyes and stand up. "I'll be right there," I tell him. Take one last look at the headstone.

As much as I want to hate him and be angry with him, it's no use. There's only this bronze-colored headstone.

"Good Morning Rayne," I say to my assistant. She starts, then quickly puts her hand dramatically over her heart. I can't help but smile at the fact that she looks so guilty, but all I did was scare the hell out of her. Rayne's presence in the office, while helpful when I'm here, is ridiculous if you want the truth of it. She ends up doing ridiculous office duties when I'm not around and it's unnecessary. I watch as she quickly composes herself.

Rayne is about my height, with blond-highlighted, chestnut colored hair and brown eyes. She is very pretty in a simple-kind-of-girl way. Her makeup is subtle, but present. A curvy yet slim figure. She's downright gorgeous, if you want the truth of it. Her outfit today is a black suit with an electric blue camisole underneath.

"Good morning, ma'am. I assume that Trinity doesn't know you're here?"

I smile. "No, I didn't see her email until last night. I had already come back to L.A., so I figured I'd come in."

"Fair enough. Trinity is here, in her office. She seems a bit out of sorts this morning. No doubt it has to do with one of her clients." Rayne giggles. She knows how worked up Trinity can get. She definitely sees it more than I do.

I nod to her. "Can you bring me some coffee, please?"

"Sure thing." And off she goes. I walk past my office to Trinity's. Her door is ajar, but only by inches. I tap lightly and push it open.

"Holy shit, Cami, don't scare me like that." She smiles.

I giggle. "Then maybe you shouldn't be doing something you're not supposed to do." I watch her face fall and the stress return to her features. "Why are you so tense?" I ask.

"I've been up half of the night, trying to track down one of my clients. He took off from a premiere and no one has seen him since he left so abruptly."

Trinity Parish is the Vice President of Public Relations at Bold International, Inc., and the glue that keeps this company functioning. Founded by my father back in the late seventies, Bold International is an agency that offers all manner of services to a wide variety of clients: actors, athletes, artists, authors, and the like.

Compliments of my father, Bobbie, I inherited this gig. When he passed away he left me half of his fortune and all of Bold International, Inc. It's a job that I don't want – well at least at the time I didn't want it – but that I was required to take. Bobbie had written his will so that I had no choice to take over. If I hadn't, the company would have been sold off in tiny pieces to the lowest bidders.

Trinity's panic is almost comical. "I'm sorry, I guess I am failing to see the urgency in the situation. Its been what, eighteen hours? Give him a break. He probably ran off with some random woman and is holed up in a hotel somewhere."

Her face visibly relaxes. "I suppose you're probably right."

"I usually am." I give her a cheeky grin and she smiles. Trinity really is pretty, with her blond-, brown-, and red-streaked pageboy haircut. Her eyes are a warm green, her lips are thin, and she's pleasantly plump yet elegant. She's not the typical type you see around Hollywood, but she is definitely a powerhouse. She stands about five feet eight and is always in heels, pencil skirts, and silk blouses. She keeps a wardrobe in the office, full of jackets of various colors and lengths. Ready at a moment's notice.

"Thanks for telling me you were coming." She says sarcastically.

I glare at her. "For the record, Ms. Parish, I was already back in L.A. – don't ask – and I figured I would drop in for a surprise inspection."

She knows full well that this isn't really the case, but she laughs. "Surprise inspections only work when you're an active CEO."

"Yeah, that I suppose would be about the truth. Then again, look at me. Could you see me coming into the office every day dressed like this?"

She laughs again. "You are the CEO. You can dress however you want. Are you coming to the board meeting?"

I nod, but I'm looking around Trinity's office at all the head shots of her clients, past and present. The south wall of her office is full from baseboard to ceiling with various photos, all arranged around a single, overly large headshot. The last time I was in here there wasn't a picture in that space. In fact it had never had a picture until now.

My mouth drops open and I feel a familiar desire deep in my core. The image is about twenty by twenty and contains a very professional headshot of none other than the gorgeous face of Tristan Michaels.

The next thing I know Trinity's shouting my name. "Cami!"

"Huh?" I slowly peel my eyes away from the image and look at Trinity.

"Wow, girl, you got it bad."

I shake my head in a desperate attempt to clear it. "Since when has Tristan Michaels been a Bold client?" I ask.

She scowls at me. "Since the very beginning of his career. Bobbie picked him up when he was cast as Dakota in *Love is Burning*." She looks at me, puzzled. "How, as CEO, did you not know this?"

"I'm not CEO," I mutter.

"Yes you are, you just fail to realize or embrace that fact. Think about it, Cami. You attend board meetings pretty regularly. Despite whatever brought you back to L.A. yesterday, here you are instead of running off to where ever it is that you were planning on going." I scowl back at her. "Don't give me that look. I know you better than you think. One day soon, you will have to step into your role here, and now is the best time to do it."

I let out a very strained chuckle. "No, Trinity, it's not. You and Vincent have things under control. The board members are not ready to have me take on an active role, and I don't have a clue about running a business."

She laughs. "Cami, as CEO of Bold, you're a face. Your job description is pretty pale when compared to the things that Vincent or myself do on a daily basis. You sit behind a desk, sign checks, meet with clients, and woo the crowds."

"You make it sound so easy."

"Believe me, it is."

"You saw how dumbstruck I got over a damn picture of Tristan Michaels. For God's sake, how I am I supposed to sit there on the other side of that desk from other celebrities?" I was trying not to get angry. "The title of CEO was bestowed upon me compliments of my father's will and not for hard work and dedication. Do you have any idea how hard it is for me to just step in and sit behind that desk when I haven't earned it?"

I watch as her face falls. "I see your point, but it was given to you by your father, who obviously believed in you and your abilities—"

I cut her off. "Do not go there. My father knew nothing of who I am, what I am about, or what it is I want out of my life. He gave me the CEO position as a punishment, and he set me up for failure."

Trinity crosses the room toward me and puts her arm gently around my shoulders. "Do you honestly believe that Vincent, Mick, Rayne, any of the staff, or I would let you fail?"

I'm fighting back the tears. The last twenty-four hours have been so maddening, frustrating, and overwhelming. I shake my head. I need to get out of here.

"See," Trinity says. "Once you fully realize that, you will be fine and you will step into this office as our CEO and you will be magnificent at it. Now come on. We have a meeting to attend."

With that she releases me and strides back to her door. I look back up into the eyes of Tristan Michaels, a god among men.

I enter the boardroom to find the entire board already assembled, along with Trinity and Vincent. Vincent is your typical Hollywood looker: suit, tie, jacket, and matching cufflinks. His head is shaved bald. Or maybe it's waxed. Or he is flat-out bald. Whatever the case, it sets off his very stern yet powerful physique. He is handsome in a much-older, too-many-years-in-Hollywood, crinkles-at-the-corners-of-his-eyes kind of way. Vincent is Bold's Agent in Charge. He not only works with a few clients, but he also manages our various agents.

I wave to Vin as I walk to my chair at the head of the table. I get a few sideways glances at my shirt, jeans, and sneakers, but before I can protest Trinity speaks up.

"Cami came to L.A. late last night for other business. I respectfully requested that she join us for this impromptu meeting, and she obliged."

A few of the board members wipe the shock from their faces and return to their discussions. A few minutes later, our company attorney, Justin Thompson, enters and takes the customary speaker position at the foot of the table, opposite me. He doesn't sit but stands behind the chair. "We have a couple of issues that need to be addressed. First of all, we are in the process of acquiring a new client that will rank alongside Tristan Michaels." My ears perk up just a bit. "However, we are going to have to get involved in a legal battle..."

But I'm no longer paying attention. I am picturing Tristan's face in the headshot in Trinity's office, and the picture quickly morphs into a gorgeous, well-groomed, fit, muscled, beautiful man. The same man that I have fantasized about so many times.

In this fantasy, I'm imagining him in a sparkling blue pool. The sun is warm, and Tristan is steamy sexiness radiating all over my now-blurry vision of a drab conference room.

I'm quickly immersed in a vision of Tristan's sexy, toned body strutting around the pool; showing off his physique. It's almost like watching a slow-motion strip tease. My illusion is like a dream, my desire to touch him, to kiss him, grows stronger and more uncontrollable. I feel myself getting worked up, desperate for his touch, a touch that never comes.

"Okay, so this concludes this meeting. Does anyone have any questions?" Vincent's voice interrupts my reverie. I'm severely disappointed at being brought back to reality.

I stand, feeling a warm, sticky wetness between my legs. My nipples are hard as rocks; I feel them straining against the barbells that run through them. I'm thankful for the overshirt, tank top and bra.

I walk past Rayne and into my office. Taking a seat behind my empty desk, I fold my arms on the desk and bury my head. God, what was I thinking? I can't think about stuff like that in a board meeting about a man I've never even met. This is exactly why I know I'm not ready to be CEO.

I hear a knock on my door and mumble, "Come in." I look up in time to see Trinity and Rayne entering my office. "What's up, ladies?"

"I just wanted to make sure you're all right, you seemed extremely distracted in the meeting." Trinity is very sincere. "I wouldn't have come in, except Rayne was standing at your door debating on whether or not she should enter."

I nod. "Thanks, ladies. Really. I've just been through hell the last twenty hours. I need to get out of here."

Rayne nods. "I called for the limo. It's downstairs, ready to take you wherever you want to go."

"Good. Thank you, Rayne."

"Will you head back to Phoenix?" Trinity asks.

I shake my head. "No, I need to get away from everyone for a while. I'll let you know where I'm going when I get there."

I grab my purse and head down the hall. Rayne is on my heel the whole way. "Thanks again, Rayne," I say as I hit the button for the elevator.

"Anytime, Cami. Please don't hesitate to let me know if I can get you anything." I hear the chime of the elevator's arrival and the doors slide open.

I nod, turn, and step in..

THREE

Calvin, my driver, stops in front of the Hawaiian Airlines section of LAX. I step out of the car, and the warmth of the sun kisses my bare shoulders; I've traded my button-up and sneakers for a tank top and heels on the way to the airport.

I'm blown away by the number of photographers and reporters surrounding the departure area. There are about six of them heading back to the larger group inside the media area. This isn't the first time I've seen this while coming and going from LAX.

As I walk along the terminal, I see several young women with cameras around their necks. My guess is that some major celebrity is expected, so they're camping out. The fandom is unreal. I watch as security hurries over to them. No doubt to tell them to move along.

I make my way through the rest of the departure terminal and into the first class lounge, passing through the security checkpoint there and bypassing the long public lines. One of the many perks of flying first class.

I enter a private room that's reserved for me. The room is decorated in olive green and various shades of brown, surprisingly un-tropical for Hawaiian Airlines. In the center of the room are a square table and four very old-school office chairs. I sit in the one that faces the window overlooking the parking garage, my back to the door. Within a couple of minutes, a lounge attendant brings me a turkey sandwich, pickle, and chips. It isn't much, but I don't care. I'm not that hungry.

As I eat, I browse through the latest online edition of *Entertainment Now* magazine. The contents aren't very interesting, but there is a really nice red carpet picture of Tristan Michaels. Dressed in a suit, he really is stunning. The black skinny tie, white dress shirt, and black pants and jacket really bring out his physique. The caption reads, "Tristan Michaels, outside Nokia Theatre at the premiere of friend Travis Jackson's latest movie *Rebound*, wearing Armani."

"I could have told you that," I mutter to myself. Looking at Tristan's eyes I feel the familiar tingle crawl up my spine, a sensation that makes me feel like he is really looking at me. "Gah!" I mutter, and close the magazine.

If I'm really going to be honest with myself, I'm only trying to avoid the drama of the last twenty-four hours. Especially what happened this morning at the gravesite. Then, of course, my embarrassing daydream during that board meeting. My emotions are all over the place, and I just need to get clear of everything that is driving me insane of late.

Suddenly there's a lot of commotion outside in the lobby: camera flashes going off and a bunch of people talking at once. It sounds like they're asking questions. Very abruptly, the noise is cut off and the silence returns. I shrug and pull out my iPod and headphones. Placing the earbuds into my ears, I am quickly distracted by the sounds of Chris Daughtry, which effectively block out all else.

TRISTAN

Will this madness ever end? I know the answer and it's rather stupid of me to ask myself that question.

"You all right?" I hear Tyson ask.

"Yeah. Fucking people, I swear. They act like they've never seen a celebrity at the airport before. Though the EN reporter was a little too curious about some things. Obviously he was fishing for a comment from me." I take a deep breath.

"Yeah, he was a bit insistent." He turns and looks at the woman approaching us.

"If you will follow me, I have a room down the hall for you. We've made arrangements to have you escorted to the gate once boarding has completed."

"Thank you." I nod as she turns and starts down the hall. We approach a room on the right with the door slightly ajar. I stop dead in my tracks and stare at the woman sitting at the table. Her black hair is up in a ponytail that trails down her back and over one shoulder. The other shoulder is exposed and shows off a tattoo of blue, purple, and silver tones. It looks like a puzzle made of hearts and stars. But what really catches my attention is sprouting from the center of her shoulder blades. Done in some of the brightest ink I've ever seen: black and purple wings – fairy wings to be exact – just visible above the line of the tank top she's wearing.

"Tristan," Tyson whispers in my ear. Slowly I turn toward him, tearing my gaze away from the woman's back.

"Yeah?"

He extends his hand, gesturing for me to follow the lounge attendant.

I look back at the fairy woman one more time and then continue on down the hall.

For the next few minutes she is all I can think about, and a pretty big part of me is hoping against the odds that she's on my flight.

CAMI

As soon as I board the plane, I throw my knapsack in the overhead bin, sit down, and pop in my earbuds to shut out the world. I quickly become absorbed in a book I picked up in the first class lounge that had an eye-catching cover and sounded interesting, so the flight from L.A. to Honolulu passes quickly.

Once in Honolulu, I move quickly to the gate for my flight to Tahiti. I'm not just going to get away, I'm really getting away. About as far as I can without ending up in China. I'm silently hoping that I'll be far enough out there to be out of range of cell phones, emails, and hell even American news.

The flight from Honolulu to Tahiti is just as uneventful as the flight to Hawaii. I watch a couple of movies on my iPad, read some more of the book I started, and even manage to doze off. When I wake from a disturbing dream about the days that followed Bobbie's death, I push it aside and instead call to mind the image of Tristan Michaels. The day keeps dragging, but soon the time change gives me a second wind. Tahiti is far enough behind Phoenix time that it will still be early morning when I get there.

When I arrive in Tarah the next day, I learn that the occupant of the penthouse just checked in last night. I don't do a very good job of hiding my disappointment.

"Will you keep me posted? Once it becomes vacant, I want to move to that suite."

"Of course, ma'am, but there's a good chance it won't be empty for a while."

I can feel myself scowling, though I know it's not her fault.

"How long are you planning to stay?" she asks me.

"Until the penthouse becomes available."

She laughs, but watch me: I'll stick around until I have at least one day and one night in that suite.

As I follow the concierge up to my room, we pass a tall, well-built man with dark blond hair who has an aura of security or protection about him. Not a cop, but he is definitely packing some heat, judging by the slight bow of his arms. Or if he's not packing right now, then he usually is.

"Geez, you'd think the President of France was here," I joke.

The concierge laughs. "No, ma'am, no president." His accent is thick and hard to understand. I wait for him to tell me who in the hotel needs that kind of security, but he doesn't say any more on the subject.

My room is absolutely stunning. Set on the seventh floor, it has two bedrooms, along with a sitting and dining room. The master suite is equipped with the largest whirlpool I've ever seen in my life. The concierge informs me that the tub is small compared to the one in the penthouse. I'm in heaven, very ready to relax and enjoy my stay.

I ask the concierge, "Can you please have a bottle of Cristal 2002 sent up here along with some strawberries?"

"Yes, ma'am. Will there be anything else this afternoon?" he replies politely.

"No, I believe that will be all for now, thank you."

He bows his head and leaves the suite, palming the twenty I gave him.

About ten minutes later my Cristal arrives, chilled to perfection, with two flutes. The server opens the bottle and pours a glass for me. I thank him and pass him a generous tip.

I step onto the patio and look out at my view. The sun is lower in the sky and starting to cast long shadows along the white sand and royal blues of the ocean. The view is beyond amazing, nearly taking my breath away.

While I sit on the balcony, in the quiet, alone, I start to think about some of the decisions I know that I will need to make over the next few months. I'm under immense pressure from Trinity and Vincent to begin stepping into my role as CEO of Bold International, Inc. The argument before the board meeting was proof enough of this fact. I know deep down that the roll of CEO will not be anything near what I fear it to be. I know that a large part of my fear has more to do with the fact that I will be giving up my freedom to do as I please when I feel like it.

Eventually the exhaustion of traveling and the emotional turmoil of the last forty-eight hours overcomes me, and I crawl languidly between the nice, crisp, white linen sheets on the king size bed.

The next day I wake around four in the morning, cursing life because it's so early. I stumble to the bathroom, where I indulge in the eight shower heads. All these shower heads reach places that I didn't even know existed. I don't think I've ever been so clean. I wrap up in a fluffy white bath robe and grab to the bedside phone to order room service.

Once that's done, I sit down on the couch to read through the many amenities the hotel has to offer. I'm pleased to discover that the fourth floor contains several shops, including Gucci, the Gap, a couple of other high-end stores, and a commissary of sorts that sells the kinds of things guests maybe forgot to bring or run out of during their stay. Perfect. I haven't unpacked yet after settling into my room yesterday, but looking at the hotel's amenity list reminds me that I barely packed a thing Tuesday evening on my way out the door. Sticking to a few changes of clothing makes traveling faster and easier, but it also makes a trip to the commissary necessary.

While I'm waiting for my breakfast to arrive, I power up my iPad. Four new emails. Two from Mick, one from Beau and there's even one from Trinity.

They're all wondering what happened and why I took off so suddenly. Mick and Beau let me know they've tracked me to Tarah. I take strange comfort in the fact that they worry enough about me to track me. I reply to all of them, letting them know everything is fine, and I let Beau and Mick know that I will probably be bringing them out to Tarah next week sometime. The thought of spending a weekend with them in Tarah puts a smile on my face. I just need some time alone before I let their invasion begin.

But the questions about what happened and why I left remain unanswered. I've been avoiding thinking about it, but I need to figure it out. Then maybe, with luck, I can explain it to my friends.

I put aside the iPad and pick up a pad of paper and a pen from the desk in the sitting room. I begin by writing down a list.

Reason One: I could not and did not want to deal with Reed and his infidelities, now or in the future.

Reason Two: I was disturbed by the fact that I was turned on at seeing Reed with another woman.

Reason Three: I knew in that moment, when I was turned on and not wanting to make a scene, that I don't love Reed. Reed and I have been on and off again for the last six months. Yes, the sex is amazing but beyond our bedroom compatibility we have nothing in common with one another.

Reason Four: Bobbie.

Over the last week I've felt off, felt wrong about something. Like a change was coming, and it scared me. I know now that change was Reed and whatever we had going. But it's not just that. Over the last year so much has changed, and in such a short time. When Bobbie died, I was angry, and I've stayed angry, but my reasons for being furious with him have changed. Because of him, nothing in my life seems to make sense. I've been given opportunities that most people can only dream about, and yet I waste them. I waste them because it feels like I'm giving in to Bobbie and all of his misdoings. I feel that if I step into the role of CEO, I'll be giving Bobbie what he wanted. But God dammit, what about what I want? What about my wants & needs? Fuck, I sound so selfish. This is not who I am.

There is also the fear of failure. Bobbie knew damn well that I would be fresh out of college and starting out my own life. Okay, he didn't plan to die, but still. Never once did he bring up coming to work for him. Hell, he never even asked if I had applied anywhere. Maybe he had intended to bring me into Bold while he was still alive, and then, of course, when he died, the natural flow of things would mean that I would take over.

There's plenty of time to dwell on that subject while I'm here so I decide that Mr. Amex and I are going to have some fun. I call the spa and make an appointment for an in-suite massage for around five this afternoon and a manicure and pedicure at four. This is going to give me ample time to shop to my heart's content. I make up a list of the toiletries I need; I'll make a stop at the commissary on my way back up to my room. I know full well that I could give the list to a staff member and they would get what I need, but I am not used to being waited on hand and foot and I would rather do it myself.

FOUR

TRISTAN

I am not sure if despair is really in my vocabulary anymore. There is something strange about being locked away in a hotel, thousands of miles away from everything I have come to know. My life has been on the fast track for the last five years, and there seems to be nothing I can do about it.

But out here, surrounded by water, in a hotel that holds everything anyone could possibly imagine, I feel free. My BlackBerry is off, my laptop is stowed, and the weather here is utterly amazing. I cannot even begin to describe how liberating this is, and for the first time, I'm questioning whether or not my life is worth all this madness.

Don't get me wrong; I love what I do. But even the love of acting and the money are small compensation for the madness I am required to endure.

I've realized that I left Hollywood so fast that I forgot to pack toiletries, so I've ventured into the little mall inside the hotel. It's early in the day, so fortunately for me there are hardly any other patrons floating around.

As I stroll through the mall I notice a petite beauty with black hair – several packages in her hands – walking out of the Shoe Shoppe that I just left not moments before. Her skin is pale, translucent even. Her beauty is soft, sophisticated, and natural. She's not wearing much makeup, but her lips are full with a beautiful pink tint.

I slowly follow her from a distance as she strides purposefully into Versace. "Well, that's definitely something you don't see everyday," I mutter to myself.

"What do you mean by that?" Tyson says.

"Someone like her, carrying her own bags and walking into Versace." I chuckle and he joins in.

It has been my experience, with woman especially, that shopping is something that is either done in pairs or with the help of a some poor sap hired solely for the purpose of being a servant. If you sit still long enough along Rodeo Drive in California, you will see the wealthy women walking with poles up their asses and at least one sorry sucker following her with her bags. This little lady strides into Versace, confident, calm, and collected, and minus the stick up her ass.

"Do we know who she is?" I ask.

"Not completely. She looks familiar but not in a way that I can place her. She is definitely not Hollywood."

"Good."

I watch as the Versace matron stops her from putting her bags on the floor. She quickly picks up the girl's bags and bustles off to find the concierge.

My eyes float back to the black-haired beauty. She is standing there talking with the sales lady, and she must be ready to try something on because she takes off the light jacket she is wearing. The tank top she has on underneath is a deep purple, and as soon as she turns to hand her jacket to the sales lady, I see it: the blue, purple, and silvery heart and stars on her shoulder.

"It can't be," I mutter. My knees are growing weak, and then I realize I'm actually shaking as she continues turning around until her back is to me. And there, staring back at me, are the purple fairy wings from LAX.

CAMI

I have been pampered with a manicure, a pedicure, and some much-needed waxing. My in-suite massage was out of this world, and I'm now dressed in the teal blue halter mini dress that I bought from Versace. The dress is accented by the matching Lady Peep Crocos from Louboutin that I purchased specifically for this outfit. The dress is extremely short and barely covers the lace top thigh highs, garters, and suspenders. The dress is comfortable and makes me feel sexy and confident. Stepping into the shoes has really completed the look, and my legs feel long and sleek. Ready to be shown off.

Examining myself in the mirror, I find that I'm dressed to impress, though I'm not sure who I intend to impress on this night. But I'm on vacation, after all, and it's my first night out. Something good has to come from tonight, right?

After finishing my hair and makeup, I head downstairs toward the bar. I pass first through the little casino. It contains a few blackjack tables, roulette, poker, and a good handful of slot machines. It surprises me that it's so empty. I smile. The privacy of this island is really showing its colors tonight.

But as I reach the far side of the room and begin to enter the bar, I quickly realize that this is where most of the crowd seems to be tonight. I pass by the muscular blond man I saw yesterday in the hall. He is standing in a corner, overlooking the bar. Maybe he's hotel security.

The room is huge, consisting of several high top tables, booths, a dance floor, and a stage that's in the process of being set up for a band. The sign next to the stage says, "Country Junkies Live, Friday June 8th at 10 p.m." In front of the stage is a huge wooden dance floor. Pink's "Bad Influence" is playing over the sound system.   There are all manner of people in here, from suits and cocktail dresses to jeans and t-shirts. You name it, it's in this bar. It's easy to separate the locals from the tourists. I chuckle to myself, knowing that I am obviously a tourist, but I feel separate from them. I don't see any other women with black and blue hair who are tattooed and pierced like I am.

Heads turn in my direction as I walk up to the bar. I notice a pretty big group of men and women dressed in suits. Banker types. Wow, nice company to work for if you have conferences on a private island. I finally walk up to the bartender, who eyes my shoulders and smiles. Apparently he appreciates tattoos, because he asks for my drink order in a voice that I'm pretty sure is meant to be seductive. Strange, I've never noticed a reaction like his before.

FIVE

TRISTAN

"It's her," I breathe. My muse, my sign – she's walking into the bar.

I'm pretty sure I've stopped breathing. She gracefully makes a beeline for the bar, despite the five-inch heels she's wearing. My guess is that, without them, she's a full foot shorter than I am. She has on a very short teal dress that fastens at the back of the neck, under her ponytail.

When she walks her ponytail doesn't move; her posture is nearly perfect. She has an air of authority about her. She is not going to let her height and small frame fool people, and she commands the attention of every man in the bar as she starts speaking with the bartender.

The bartender starts to grab a bottle from the well, but she stops him and appears to ask for something else. I watch intently as he turns and grabs a bottle from one of the shelves behind him. Ah, she knows her alcohol. The bottle is filled with a clear liquid, so I'm guessing it's a vodka, but I can't tell for sure.

A group of men gather behind her as the bartender hands her a drink. It's a Cosmo. Of course it's a Cosmo. She seems too loose for a stuffed-shirt-type drink like a martini.

I notice that her wings are more visible tonight, and below them there is something on her lower back trying to peek out from the top of her skirt. Or maybe it's just a trick of the light.

She takes a few sips and starts to turn around, sans drink. I watch as her head bobs up and down to the music that's playing. As she places her elbows onto the bar the song ends and Scott Stapp's "Great Divide" starts to play.

My shoulders slump. "All right, Mum, I get it," I mutter under my breath. It couldn't have been a clearer sign if a spotlight suddenly shone on this beautiful woman.

I take in the head-to-toe image of her. Her skin is pale and in stark contrast to the black of her hair, which is jet black with electric blue streaks running through it. Her makeup is bold: fire engine red lipstick, soft eye colors with bold mascara and eyeliner. Her features are soft, but she has well-defined cheek and jaw bones. Her bangs are short and cut straight across, curled into her eyes slightly. She reminds me of a pinup model from the thirties or forties.

She has a strong hourglass figure with wider shoulders and hips but a small waist. She is well-endowed in the chest. This has my attention for a multitude of reasons, one being that she knows how to accent her best feature, and two, I can see her nipples under her halter top. It was clear from looking at the back of her dress – or rather the lack of one – that she's not wearing a bra. But now I see that her nipples are rock hard. And there's something...is that...?

"Holy fuck, her nipples are pierced." My breathing spikes. Then my eyes finally slide down the contours of her stomach. Her hips are curvy and soft. Her legs are sheathed in sheer black, lace top thigh highs that are peeking out under her skirt. Her legs are sleek and toned.

As I take her in, I watch one man after another approach her. And one after another, she is quickly and effectively shooting them down. She turns and orders another drink.

Now one of the banker-looking dudes who made a show at looking her up and down starts talking to her. She looks at him and smiles. The smile is like turning on a light bulb, bright and friendly. I grind my teeth together in irritation. The gentleman turns to the bartender and points to her glass.

"It's already full, you idiot," I hear myself say. Whoa, where did that come from?

The bartender is speaking to him and he turns toward her. His eyes are wide and she is visibly shaking with laughter at his reaction. Quickly he ducks his head and scampers off with his tail between his legs.

"What the bloody hell is that all about?" I mutter.

I'm completely baffled by this woman. What has these men turning away? "What is it about you?" I say quietly. I need to talk to her somehow. But how? I'm not sure I know how to approach a girl, especially one that has turned down just about every man in the bar. She has an air of confidence that I know can be intimidating to a man, but the last guy appeared to be buying her a drink. I need to figure out an opening line, or maybe buy her a drink. Maybe it's the price of the drink that is turning the men around. Though this hotel is not cheap, so you would think that most of this crowd would be able to afford her drink.

Just then, she turns to her left and catches me looking at her. A puzzled look crossed her features as she studies me. Then she smiles, wide and beautiful, raises her glass and tips her head in my direction.

I feel my cheeks heat at being caught and look down.

Luckily the waitress appears, bearing another drink. Thank God!

"Here you go," she says.

"Thanks."

"Can I get you anything else?" she asks.

A flash of inspiration, and I grin. "As a matter of fact, can you have the bartender make up a Diva Vodka Cosmopolitan for the lovely lady at the bar wearing the teal dress?" Her face falls. "Have it added to my room tab, please."

"Uh...yes, sir." She nods and stalks slowly toward the bar.

Shit, what if she comes over here to thank me? What the hell am I going to say to her? Uh, hi? No, that's stupid. I'm an actor, for God's sake. Dammit, I can't talk to her.

Before the waitress even makes it to the bar, I scurry from my seat and head for the patio doors. Tyson is close behind me. If she's interested, she'll come to me.

CAMI

I turn to Jessie, the bartender, whose name I learned while ordering my third Cosmo, and ask him, "Do you know who that man is, the one in the dark corner?" The man in the booth has eyebrow length dirty blond hair that's falling over his big black sunglasses. He looks gorgeous of course and something about him is familiar, but I can't grasp who or where.

"Not directly, no. This is the second night he's been here and he just sits in the corner and orders from the waitress, who is very obviously trying to get his attention and failing miserably." He laughs.

I smile in return and order another drink, but his attention is diverted to someone at the end of the bar.

"Hold that thought," he says, putting up a finger and walking over to the waitress at the end of the bar. The music changes to Adele's "Set Fire to the Rain" and I can only catch bits and pieces of the conversation between Jessie and the waitress.

"What do you mean he wants to buy her a drink?" I hear Jessie say.

"He asked me to tell you to make her a..." I don't catch the rest of what she says. I lean farther forward, trying to see if I can tell who they're talking about, but the waitress is looking straight at me. Oh great, someone else wants to buy me a drink they can't afford. I roll my eyes.

The waitress leans further toward Jessie and says, "I think he can afford it. His tab is going to room eight." Jessie visibly stiffens at what she's said. It takes him a minute to recover, but he nods, turns, and starts to make a drink.

"Hey, Jessie, you got my drink coming?"

His smile is a little tight. "You could say that."

I cringe. What is this all about? Jessie's movements are careful. But as I watch him pour the vodka, I notice that it's not Absolut Crystal that he's pouring into the glass, but Diva Vodka, one of finest, though not well-known. One of the most expensive bottles of liquor on the market is flowing gracefully into a crystal martini glass.

"What are you doing?" I ask a little too harshly.

He stills. "Making your drink. What does it look like?"

Then comes the Grand Marnier Quintessence. "Holy hell! I didn't ask for this!" I protest.

"Don't worry, you're not paying for it."

"What are you talking about, I'm not paying—" But then it dawns on me. I purse my lips and Jessie notices my discomfort.

"I'm just doing what I'm told to do. Don't shoot the messenger. Please." His smile is sweet, genuine.

"I won't, but my little eighty-five dollar glass just turned into what exactly?"

"Calm down, it's coming from the man in the booth you were just asking me about. He asked Marisa to place an order for a Cosmo with the top, top shelf we have. Which happens to be precisely what I'm doing. Just be glad that our cranberry and lime juice is made fresh in our kitchen, because anything less would be doing this drink a great injustice."

He smiles, widely this time, showing two small dimples that I hadn't noticed before. The dimples give him a cute, innocent appearance, making him quite a bit cuter than he was about three minutes ago. He really is attractive: shirtless, wearing tastefully torn jeans and black boots. His hair is jet black and his skin tone is a beautiful caramel color.

I blush deep red and can feel the heat spread over my entire body as I start to think inappropriate thoughts about Jessie. I'm growing uncomfortable because I'm thinking about Jessie while Mr. Mysterious in the corner has just bought me a really expensive drink. If Jessie has noticed my discomfort, he doesn't comment.

The waitress returns with some fresh raspberries. Jessie adds them to my drink and hands it to me. "Bloody hell! How exactly am I supposed to drink this? It seems like a damn waste."

"Well, you raise the glass to your slightly-open mouth, then tip the glass until some liquid pours onto your tongue." He grins at his own sarcasm. I scowl. Chuckling at me, he continues, "Why don't you start by taking the glass over to his booth, sitting that sexy ass down, and talk to the damn man?"

I feel the blood drain from my face. "Are you serious?"

"It seems like the logical thing to do, given that he just bought you a four hundred and fifty dollar drink."

"Oh, fucking wonderful. Can you at least tell me his name?" I ask.

"Not really. I'm not supposed to reveal the names of other guests. But I can tell you that he's staying in the penthouse."

"That was supposed to be my room," I mutter.

He laughs again. "Well, now you know why you don't have it. He checked in Wednesday night with no check-out date and has spent a good deal of time down here since then." Obviously seeing something in my dumbstruck expression causes him to change his mind about releasing the guest's name. "He's registered as Mr. Rubble."

"As in Barney Rubble? As in the Flintstones?" I bust out laughing. Great, he is either a rich, obnoxious billionaire whose name would be easily recognized or a well-known celebrity.

Suddenly, like a bolt of lightning, it hits me. No wonder I thought I recognized him. Of course!

"Oh man, Jessie, do you know who he is? Full on, no cartoon names included?"

"Of course I do, I don't live in a wet paper bag."

I mouthed his name to Jessie, who just winked in reply.

Holy bloody fuck. Fucking hell. This cannot be happening. Tristan Michaels has just bought me a four hundred and fifty dollar drink. Not only is he the hottest actor in Hollywood, but he's my fantasy obsession. A man who has occupied many of my thoughts and fantasies, especially the last few days. Hell, I was fantasizing about him in a boardroom not forty-eight hours ago and his PR rep caught me doing it! Lest we forget that he's Trinity's – and no doubt Bold's – biggest client. Tristan damn Michaels is sitting in a booth not a hundred feet from me. In a dark corner. Wearing sunglasses. No doubt in an attempt to thwart people from recognizing him. Which probably means he doesn't want me to recognize him. Which probably means I should try to play it cool.

I nod toward Jessie, pick up my insanely expensive cocktail in a crystal glass, and paste a smile on my face, praying I don't look like an idiot.

As I turn around, I slowly raise my eyes to the booth.

It's empty.

SIX

My heart takes a dive. Just then, the waitress who had placed the order for my drink walks by. I reach out and lightly touch her shoulder. She pauses and turns toward me.

"Can I help you?" She says, rather coldly, looking me up and down. There is a hint of unwelcome attitude.

"Where did Mr. Rubble go?"

She raises an eyebrow at me. Looks for a moment like she might try to feign ignorance just so I won't go after him. Then I watch her quick glance at the drink in my hand and at Jessie behind me, and she appears to be changing her mind. "He left after ordering your drink. I think he went outside."

"Oh.....th-thank you."

I turn to Jessie. "Jessie, can I take this outside and then up to my room, where someone can get it tomorrow?"

"Certainly, Ms. Enders."

"Please, Jessie. Call me Cami."

"Certainly, Cami."

I turn around and begin walking in the direction of the patio. I've only been in my suite and the mall since my arrival, so I'm not entirely sure if I'm heading in the right direction until I push through the doors to find a bright, nearly full moon illuminating everything. I'm momentarily taken aback by the wonderful view of the bleached white sand, the dark waves of the ocean, and the wonderfully sculpted back of Mr. Tristan Michaels.

"Bloody hell!" I breathe.

I stand there for a moment, trying desperately to reorganize my now-scattered thoughts and ignore the warm tingling sensation that's beginning to pool between my legs.

Staring at the naked back in front of me, I see what appear to be three tattoos standing out against the pale of his skin. I'm unable to make out what they are because he is facing the moon, throwing his back into shadow.

Holy crap, not only has Tristan Michaels bought me a drink, but he is standing on the beach, not fifty yards in front of me, half naked and tattooed. Can this be anymore of a dream? I want to pinch myself, just to make sure I'm not dreaming, but decide that this fantasy is best served up just like this. My breathing is quiet but ragged. Tristan damn Michaels is standing on the beach but a mere stone's throw away from me.

Slowly I force my feet to move forward. As soon as I step into the sand I remember that I'm wearing very expensive high heels. Leaning over, I quickly shed my shoes and stockings, hook them in my free hand, and begin to close the distance between myself and Mr. Michaels.

As I approach and see the muscles of his back tighten, I can't quite think of the best way to introduce myself. Or at the very least, not make an ass of myself.

"Mr. Rubble," I say, with a small smile on my lips, hoping that he will turn around. He doesn't. I can feel my knees beginning to shake, and my heart is pounding against my chest. Am I really going to talk to Tristan Michaels?

He doesn't answer, but I can see his shoulders shaking slightly. Is he laughing at me?

"Yeah, I guess that's me," he says. His tone is casual, but I notice that his shoulders have yet to relax.

I breathe in sharply at the sound of his voice: sensual, deep. A longing, smothered in sexiness. The heat spreads through my entire body.

"Sorry, I don't mean to bother you. I just felt that I should at least say thank you and enjoy this wonderful drink with you."

"That's really not necessary." I smile at the nonchalance in his voice. "I saw you turning away gentleman after gentleman at the bar, usually after they appeared to be trying to order you a drink." He lets out a low chuckle. "Once I noticed the crystal bottle the bartender was pouring your drinks from, it dawned on me that you were drinking beyond their means."

Wow, I think, he was really paying attention to what was going on with me. "Sounds like you were a little smitten yourself, watching so closely." I blush. Luckily I'm looking at his backside. His nice, perfectly sculpted back and round derriere are right there.

He laughs out loud this time, and wow, that laugh is absolutely panty-busting hot. I feel another jolt of pleasure surges through my bloodstream.

"Yeah, I noticed that you were a bit cold, and thought you could use another drink to warm you up."

"Oh! Shit!" I turn as red as a cherry at that, but what the hell – he was the one looking. "I guess I didn't realize it was that cold in the bar."

He laughs again, and this time I join in. My laugh sounds nervous. "Can you turn around? I'm not a fan of speaking to someone's backside, though I'm rather enjoying the view. Are those dragon wings?" My eyes are more accustomed to the moonlight and I'm finally able to make out a few details of his tattoo. They appear to be veined dragon's wings. Drawn in such a way that they seem to be coming out of his back, almost three dimensional. Trailing down his spine and dipping into his shorts appears to be a dragon's spine. Then, as he turns, I see the rest of his tattoo trailing down his right leg: a tail. I shudder. I can't help myself. When it comes to tattoos, I'm a sucker every single time. Especially when they are on such beautiful, tight, muscled, and flawless skin.

As he turns he leans in toward me and whispers, "You can stop staring at my ass now."

"I bet you get that a lot. Though I would imagine it's not just your ass that they're staring at."

My mouth falls slack as he completes his rotation. On his left pec there is a dragon head that consumes a large portion of his chest. "Wow! Now I understand why you don't do topless or nude scenes in your movies. Shit..." I cover my mouth quickly, remembering too late that I'm not sure I'm supposed to know who he is.

"Ah!" He lets out a breathy sigh, then looks down at his feet and runs his hand through his hair, looking like he's toying with the idea of fleeing the scene.

"I'm sorry, I—I really shouldn't have said that. I didn't really want you to know that I know who you are—"

He raises his hand to cut me off. "Please, it's all right. I should have known that someone, even here, would recognize me. I do hope that you're the only one who's figured this out." He pauses and almost inaudibly continues, "Because after the last two weeks, I really don't wish to cut short my vacation because things get out of hand. I don't get many vacations away from the mainstream, if you know what I mean."

I nod at him, though he doesn't see. I drop my shoes to the sand, and his head jerks up. Extending my hand toward him, I decide introductions are in order. "I'm Cameron Enders. But please, call me Cami."

"Hi, Cami" He nonchalantly points to his chest. "Tristan. But then again, you already know that."

I giggle. "Yeah, I did. Sorry. Again."

He shakes his head at me. "Stop, it's all right. I accepted my fame a long time ago. It comes with the territory of being me." He chuckles again.

"That's a good thing, Tristan, believe me. I'm still making failed attempts at coming into my own reality."

He gives me a quizzical look. "Your own reality?"

"Don't ask. It's a very long and rather uninteresting story to be told another day." Provided I get to see you again after tonight, I add in my head.

"Fair enough, we can discuss another day."

My heart goes pitter-pat at the thought. "So why are you in Tarah?" I ask innocently.

He stiffens at my question but responds. "That too is a conversation for another day." He looks at me, almost as if trying to place me somewhere. "What did you say your last name was?"

Oh no. "Enders," I say wistfully. I'm afraid of his response.

It takes only a moment before the look of recognition crosses his face. "Cameron Enders, as in Robert Enders?"

Yup, there it is. Fuck! "Please believe that your affiliation with Bold has nothing to do with my coming out here." I take a deep breath. "I came out here because you bought me this fantastic drink. I owed it to you to say thank you and to drink it in your presence."

He looks at the drink in my hand. "What's wrong with your drink?" he asks. "Don't you like it?"

Crap. "I haven't tried it yet. I was determined to drink it with you, but you left, and I found you out here." Smiling, I raise my glass in a salute and take a sip.

Oh holy hell. Before swallowing, I roll it around on my tongue for a moment and then let it slowly slide down my throat. A small moan escapes my mouth. "That is amazing. Thank you. But in the future, please don't feel that you have to buy me such an expensive drink."

"Oh, no worries. I knew that you needed to experience a real Cosmopolitan in order to truly appreciate how good they can be."

"Just seems like a waste of hard-earned money."

"Oh, well yeah, I suppose when you put it that way. I'll keep that in mind." He smiles. Holy hell, that smile is amazing. I flush and look down. "Please..."

He places his hand under my chin, lifting it slightly so that I look up into his eyes. "Don't hide your eyes from me. There's nothing to be ashamed of."

I'm suddenly awestruck by his boldness and the tingle that is now rushing through my body from his touch. "I'm sorry, I'm not normally a shy or blushing person. It's just these last couple of days have beat me up emotionally and, well, all those Cosmos are finally going to my head."

"Believe me, I understand completely. I'm exhausted myself. I'd like to see you finish your Cosmo and retire to my room."

Without thinking, I raise the glass to my lips, tilt my head back, and pour the rest of the drink down my throat. I swallow and smile. "Problem solved?" I giggle then because the look of absolute astonishment on his face is comical. "Sorry, I um...told you it was a waste. I'll pay you back."

He shakes his head and laughs. "No need. I would buy you another, just to watch you do that again."

I smile. "Bloody hell"

He's still laughing. "I have to admit, that is my favorite expression and I hear a bit of an accent. Are you British?" He asks. No doubt comparing Bobbie and me. Bobbie was far from British.

"No. I might as well be, however. I grew up in England, under the care of a matron, then in boarding school in Surrey, England. I only managed to convince my father to let me move home about nine years ago." Wow, what is with my mouth running off with all this full disclosure? "I'm sorry, you don't want to hear all this."

"On the contrary, I think I do."

I am quickly realizing that I don't know much about him. But I want to know more. A lot more.

"Tristan—. Can I call you that or would you prefer Barney?" I giggle, feeling the alcohol really starting to mess with my brain. And to be honest, I'm not even sure I'm talking properly. I know that I need to leave Tristan to his evening before I make a complete ass out of myself.

He smiles his big, drop-to-your-knees-for-me smile. "Tristan please, Cami."

"Tristan, I need you to know, more than anything, that I am not out here because of who you are. I came out here to thank you for the wonderful drink and to say hello. Who you are is who you are. It doesn't matter to me what you do for a living." I take a deep breath. I need a minute to get ahold of myself. Tristan's expression is cool and calm, so I continue. "To be honest, the only reason that I know who you are is because I find you attractive and have always been mesmerized by your image – not the stories – on the covers of the magazines in the grocery checkout aisle and nothing more. I've never seen your movies, and I am not going to fall over and grovel at your feet like some crazed lunatic. You don't need that, and frankly, I would probably be liable to do something really stupid to regret tomorrow..." I've lost all the steam I'd built up for my little speech, but there's just one more thing I need to say. "It's your eyes."

So much for getting ahold of myself.

Oh yes, those eyes. The ice blue penetrating eyes that always seemed to bore into me from the covers that grace all the tabloids and even the respectable magazines. They're staring at me now, dumbfounded at my rant.

I decide that it's time to go.

"I'm sorry, Tristan. I just thought that you should know." I take a deep breath. "I'm staying in room seventy-one twenty-one, and I know that you are staying in the penthouse. If you would like to see me again, you know where to find me. It has been a pleasure, Tristan." I extend my hand again. "I hope to see you soon."

He takes my hand and that zing is back. It shoots straight to my heart with a jolt. I've really drank too much tonight. I release his hand. He is slow and reluctant to let go, his eyes locked with mine. For a moment I'm unwilling to let him go, too. The fear of never seeing him again strikes through me.

Realizing that I'm being ridiculous, I pull up my big girl panties, turn, and start to walk away. I feel eyes burning huge holes in the back of my head as I head back to the hotel. I turn my head, just so that I can confirm my suspicions, and smile when I see that he really is watching me walk away. I smile wider when I realize that there is a tent forming at the apex of his thighs.

Suddenly feeling bold, I start to sashay my way to the deck of the bar. When I reach the deck, I bend over very slowly to put my heels back on. Ass in the air, I'm able to see between my legs as I buckle up my heels. He is still staring at me, open-mouthed, and I giggle to myself when I see his cock twitch.

SEVEN

TRISTAN

Skin, the bottom of her dress nearly exposing the round, beautiful, tight ass sticking up in the air. Begging to be touched, caressed. And an opening begging to be filled. My cock twitches again. She strides across the deck and to the door. Her beautiful body on display, wanting. She's trouble personified.

Her black hair with electric blue streaks tells me right off the bat: this girl is different and probably not to be messed with.

Until she came outside and convinced me to turn around, I hadn't yet faced the beauty that is Cami. The tattoos she has on her shoulders are beautiful on her skin. The color contrast is amazing. Both of them have the same hearts and stars mosaic with tribal-style fairies in the center. One is very obviously an angel, or a representation of an angel. The halo and feathery, rounded wings are what make the angel stand out. A good fairy.

Her other shoulder, the right one, is the opposite in color: reds, oranges, and some yellows resembling flames, but without the fire. The center contains a fairy with horns and a pointed tail. The wings are sharp, pointed at the top and bottom. The bad fairy.

And those wings! Like me, she has wings on her back. Fairy wings, done in black and purple. The back of her halter top cut the wings in half, so I'm unsure how far down they go, but after tonight I'm determined to find out.

My eyes shift around the dark deserted beach. My body is casting a very long shadow in the moonlight. The scenery around me is inconsequential when compared to my thoughts about Cami. What forced me into buying her drink was the way she leaned against the bar. Back to the bar, elbows up, with her breasts pushed out. God, she was like a goddess standing there. The finishing touch, the thing that forced me into ordering her a drink, was when her nipples hardened. And popping up on either side of her full, plump, deliciously suckable nipples was hard evidence that her ears aren't the only things she has pierced. My God! Barbells...right through her nipples. AMAZING! I feel the excitement stir in my shorts at the thought of finding what other secrets she holds beneath her clothes. Granted, that dress left very little to the imagination...

She's right upstairs, you idiot, go find out.

I shake my head, trying desperately to clear the images from my mind in a vain attempt to calm down. "Stop it! Stop thinking about it," I start to beat myself up. What exactly would a beautiful woman like Cami want to do with me?

Obviously something, I realize. She followed me onto the beach and gave me her room number. Not to mention the fact that she made a very pointed attempt to get my attention while putting her shoes back on. I feel the smile spread across my lips just thinking about her bent over. Ass in the air, unsheathed from her dress and panties. Nothing but raw naked skin and suspenders from her garter to her thigh highs. Should she keep the shoes on? Yes, yes she should. With her bare back exposed, begging my fingernails to run firmly but gently along her spine. Burying myself deep inside her wet, waiting pussy.

My knees give out and they crash into the sand. Sitting on my haunches, my hands fist, nails digging into my palms as I try and regain some sense of control. She is right upstairs and all I have to do is knock.

Something about this gorgeous girl screams to me that I can't just bed her. She's better than that. She deserves far better than me fantasizing about her on a darkened beach.

I continue to toy with the idea of going to her room, but I know that if I do, it will only end one way - horizontal. That's something I know that I don't want, not yet.

Believe me, I want Cami. But am I really ready to sleep with someone I've just met? I know the answer to that question: no, I'm not.

I've been with women before, and it always seems to end badly. I like to believe in karma, but I can't seem to fathom anything I've done in my past to warrant Layla's betrayal. I trusted her with everything, told her everything. She made me feel like I was really important, that we were made for each other. How wrong was I?

I've never felt so out of place and lost in my entire life. These last few days have been a complete disaster. I ended up in Tarah on a whim because I had to get away and get into hiding before the storm starts. This morning when I checked my email I had six different emails from Trinity, my public relations representative at Bold International, desperately wanting to know where I was, why my voicemail was full, and why I hadn't appeared at the meeting with them on Wednesday. The answer, to me, is obvious: I'm in Tarah and want nothing to do with anything pertaining to Hollywood.

There was even an email from Vincent, which surprised me. He's my agent, in charge of selling my image to perspective buyers in Hollywood. That means directors, producers, and studio executives. I'm quite sure that his email was in response to Trinity's requests to track me down. Though Vinnie and I get along really well, I'm not sure that it extends beyond a professional level.

Turning around to face the moon, I pull my knees to my chest, wrapping my arms around my shins. Staring up at the bright white of the moon and the deep blue of the ocean makes me feel so small and alone. But I know I can't hide here forever. Eventually I'll need to face the music. Trinity can be relentless when it comes to me, my actions, and my decisions. I've come to understand from other actors that Trinity is pretty calm in comparison. She doesn't get worked up over little details, and she doesn't do anything to try and control my life. I'm pretty sure this has more to do with the fact that I make a point of keeping my nose clean and out of trouble. I generally don't have to go running to her with every little thing that doesn't go my way.

Jesus, she is going to fly over the top with this story. When Layla told me about this story, my instinct was to stop it. To call Trinity and put a stop to it. But what would that accomplish? Saving Layla's skin? I'm certain I'm no longer responsible for her, her career, or the outcome of this story.

I was concerned momentarily about the impact this story was going to have on my career. Then, in an instant, I realized that I don't care. While I love acting, I'm certain that I could find something more to do with life than answer to directors and the pretentious actors and actresses on set. Is acting really something I want to do with the rest of my life? That's one of the dozens of questions I need to answer.

I'm concerned about Layla, but how can I help her at this point? She really needs help – rehab or psychiatric help. Neither one of these options are things that she will willingly do on her own. I have no grounds to stand on in making her go. The thought of threatening her or bribing her has crossed my mind more than a few times, but in the end, it will accomplish nothing. It is no longer my battle to fight. She needs to make those choices on her own. About the only thing I can do is get in touch with her dad. Get him involved, and he can take care of her.

I know that eventually I'll need to reply to Trinity, and eventually I need to fill her in on what's going down. Oh, that is going to be a joyful conversation I'm not eager to have.

Before I can register what time it is, or even how long I've been out here on the beach, the sun begins to rise. I start to get this prickling sensation all over my body, the someone-is-watching-me feeling. I look over my shoulder and see Tyson sitting at a table on Blu's patio. The bar is closed and all is quiet on the beach, for now. With the sunrise will come guests to enjoy the beach, so I get up and walk toward him. As I get closer I realize that his back is to me, and I still have that feeling like someone's watching me.

My eyes instinctively scan the beach and the area surrounding the hotel. I don't see anyone or anything that is out of the ordinary. I look up at the hotel. It's beautiful in the fading moonlight. Almost white, though it was more of an orange stucco in the daylight. As my eyes scan the west-facing side of the hotel, they skip past the lower levels and shoot toward the top.

In the middle of the building, a floor below my own, there is a faint light and the silhouette of a person. A woman. A breeze kicks up and I see her hair flare out off her shoulder. Through the pale backlight I catch a hint of blue.

"Cami."

EIGHT

CAMI

"**B**usted," I mutter to no one in particular. For the last fifteen minutes, at least, I've been out here watching Tristan from my balcony. His dragon's wings brilliant against his pale skin. His shoulders tight, head bowed, and his entire upper body hunched forward. His head on his knees. I sit like that sometimes when I'm deep in thought or worried about something. He'd been in that position when I'd gone to bed two hours ago.

He looks up at me a second time, and in the light coming off of the deck I can see he's smiling. I wave, and he waves back. Then he just stands there staring up at me.

"I wonder if he can see that I'm standing here in my birthday suit," I muse out loud. If he can see me, then he'll see I'm blushing at the thought; thinking about Tristan seeing me naked has the warm, ever-present wetness growing hotter between my legs.

After what seems like half a century, he breaks off his staring and looks sharply down toward the bar's deck, like someone's called his name. I can see that he's talking to someone, but I can't see who it is.

I gradually back up toward the door, slipping further into the shadows. All while keeping my eyes on Tristan.

After a very long, hot shower, I towel off and put on a t-shirt and the pair of boxer shorts I love to roam around the house in. While I work the brush through my hair, I pick up the phone and order room service for breakfast.

I'd hoped that something good would come of last night, but the reality has taken me completely by surprise. Tristan Michaels is staying in the same hotel as me. He bought me a drink. He talked with me on the beach.

What in the world was with the magnetism of the evening? I was drawn to him like a moth to a flame. It took everything I had not to turn around and go back to him. I was desperate for his voice, for more conversation, and I'm hoping that we will see each other again tonight. I can't get a grip on the desperation I feel to be near him, for reasons I can't even begin to imagine. All I know is that all night I wanted to be down on the beach sitting with him.

While I wait for room service I decide to pick up my iPad and head for the sitting room. The overstuffed, oversized chair that could probably put me to sleep if I sit still long enough is calling my name. With the iPad in hand, I sit and stretch my legs out to the table and pull up Safari and Google. I enter two words into the search line: Tristan Michaels.

Ten minutes later I realize I've been staring at various images of Tristan. There is a beautiful combination of posed and candid paparazzi shots. The ones of Tristan on the red carpet at various premieres and award shows are stunning. It appears that he doesn't even have a bad side to be photographed.

What I find to be oddly painful are the images of him with Layla Brook. "Dammit! I forgot that he's with her," I grumble. But if he is still with her, then why buy me a drink? Why would he say some of the things he said to me on the beach? I start trying to rationalize the emotions I'm feeling toward Tristan and how I'm going to manage the fact that he's with Layla.

"What am I thinking? There is no way that Tristan Michaels is even slightly interested in me." I'm talking to myself again. "The only reason he bought me that drink was to see if I would reject it like I rejected every other man that tried to buy me a drink. Dammit. Why in the world would he be—"

Just then the high-pitched ring of my BlackBerry shrieks from the bedroom. I jump up and mutter, "Bloody hell."

I take long, slow strides across the room, silently hoping that I will miss the call because the BlackBerry means business – Bold business – and its ringing usually means something is going on and not in a good way. As I reach the phone it falls silent once again. Not looking at the display to see who I missed, I grab it and return to my chair.

As I pull my iPad back onto my lap, I decide that looking at images of Tristan and Layla are doing me no good. So I click on "Web" and look for recent articles instead.

I find Tristan's IMDB profile and am surprised by his short filmography. *Love is Burning* is his only released work. He has a release coming up in three weeks for *Conjure*, a fantasy about a girl who casts a love spell on the man of her dreams, but a different man falls in love with her. Seems kind of cute, but there's nothing else listed.

"Based on his level of fame and Trinity's obsession with him, it seems as though he's done pretty well for himself." I wonder why, prior to the *Love is Burning* movies, he has no history and why the bio portion of the biography is limited and incomplete. I should ask Trinity about it.

Just as I'm about to go back to the search page to look for news articles about him, the wretched BlackBerry starts to ring again. This time I pull the BlackBerry off of the cushion and read the display. It's Trinity. What the hell?

"Hello?"

"Hi, Cami. Sorry to bother you on a Saturday morning."

Considering it isn't even six in the morning. "It's no problem, Trinity, I was already awake. What's going on?"

There is a silence that stretches for more than a casual pause. "Trinity?"

"Yeah...I ah, I'm here. Sorry, Cami, I know that there isn't a whole lot you can do about this, but I felt it was important for you to know that we have an issue with my biggest client."

"Are you talking about Tristan?" I ask. I'm only guessing because of the size of the photograph in her office. All the other images are pretty small in comparison.

Knock, knock, knock.

"Trinity, hold that thought one second. Room service is here."

"Room service? Oh, that's right. You didn't go back to Phoenix. I forgot. I've been so crazy trying to track this guy down. Where are you?"

I open the door and turn to walk back toward the bedroom without looking at the waiter. "Just leave it on the table, thank you."

"Sorry about that, Trinity. What exactly is going on?"

"Where are you, Cami?" Trinity is much more insistent this time.

Not wanting to go into details with her, I simply say, "I'm on vacation in Tahiti."

A small laugh crackles across the line. "Well then I really do owe you an apology for calling so early." There is a small pause followed by another little giggle. "As if I needed to feel any worse about calling you. Isn't it like four or five in the morning there?"

I laugh. "No, try six. But forget it, I was up anyway. Spill it, Trinity. Why are you calling me at six in the morning?"

I hear her take a deep breath and let it out slowly. Wow, it must be really bad. My stomach starts to twist.

"You remember I told you about that client who disappeared from the premiere last Tuesday? Well, I'm still looking for him. There was an argument with his girlfriend that no one seems to know anything about, and as of Wednesday morning his head of security has gone missing as well."

Now it's my turn to take a deep breath. Something is weird and out of sorts about this. Just as I start to mull this over, I hear another knock at the door. That's weird, who can it be now?

"I think she wants it on the table," says a now-familiar male voice. I poke my head out into the sitting room to see a waiter enter my suite, followed closely by Tristan. My jaw hits the floor with a thud. Bloody hell.

"Cami! Cami, can you hear me?"

"What? No, I didn't hear you. Sorry, there seems to be some confusion over my room service."

"Cameron, Tristan Michaels is missing. No one can find him, and he is due in New York in two weeks to do some post-production work for his last movie, *Conjure*."

I bite my lip to stop myself from busting into a fit of giggles. At least it's nice to know I was right, even though Trinity doesn't seem to have noticed. And I know exactly where Tristan is: he's standing across the sitting area from me, appraising my legs, my hips, my breasts. Yeah, definitely lingering on my breasts. Finally his eyes meet mine.

I could solve this problem right here and now, but I'm fiendishly enjoying Trinity's discomfort. "If he's not due for two weeks, why are you completely freaking out right this minute?"

"Because, Cami, that's my job. It is my responsibility to know where my clients are at all times, and at this point I have no way to reach him. I tried to get ahold of his head of security, but I can't reach him, either." The panic in her voice is evident, on the verge of crawling through the phone.

"And what exactly do you want me to do?"

"Tell me that I'm not going crazy, that he's just off on some remote island somewhere with some beautiful woman. Tell me that he will show up in New York in two weeks. I don't know."

I'm biting my lip harder because I want to ease her guilt about his disappearance, but at the same time, Tristan's reasons for being on this island – away from Trinity – are his business, and he needs to decide when to tell her where he is and why he's here.

"Listen, Trinity. I'm sure that wherever Tristan is hiding is for his own benefit. I would imagine that if there is a problem, you will be the first to know. Maybe his fight with his girlfriend has him upset and desperate to get away. Whatever the reason, when the time is right for you to know, I'm sure you will."

Taking a deep breath, I watch as Tristan's face goes through a flood of emotions, finally landing on awe.

"All right, Cami, I will calm down. If you hear anything, will you let me know?"

I chuckle. "Not likely, but keep me posted if he pops up. If you're really concerned about his safety, why don't you get in touch with someone that knows his head of security? Find out if they've heard from him and go from there."

"All right, I can do that. Thanks, Cami."

I'm too busy watching Tristan to answer Trinity. He is standing near the dinning room table with his nearly six-foot, four-inch, muscle-toned, slightly tanned, sexy-as-hell, tattooed body. He's wearing a black muscle shirt and swim trunks that cling to his body in a way that leaves little to the imagination. I can see the tail of his dragon tattoo on his leg, and I remember what he looked like last night shirtless on the beach. Desire, hot and rapid, starts to pool deep down inside. I get a sudden idea.

"Why don't you send me all of his contact information – address, phone and email – and I will try myself to see if I can reach him," I say to Trinity.

"All right, Cami. Will do." Trinity sounds a little surprised that I offered to help. "I'll keep you posted if I hear anything further. Call me if you hear back from him?"

"Thank you, hon. Will do. 'Bye." I hit the end button without waiting to hear her goodbye.

The waiter is finished setting up my food on the table and is waiting for me. I walk toward him, grabbing a twenty along the way. But before I hand it to the waiter, I turn to Tristan. "Would you like anything to eat?"

"Uh, sure. I think you have plenty here, though."

With a small giggle, I say, "Um, no I don't." I turn back to the waiter. "Can you place a duplicate order and have it brought up as soon as possible? Please."

"Yes, ma'am, right away."

"Thank you."

The waiter nods and quickly leaves the room.

I turn to Tristan, pausing a moment to take in the fact that he is standing in my room. "Good morning, Tristan!" He smiles at me, bright pearly whites appearing behind his lips. "To what do I owe this pleasure?"

He smiles wider, if that's even possible. "I saw you out on your balcony. I figured you were still awake because the lights were still on. Imagine my surprise when I knock, you let me in, then walk away." He cocks his head to the left slightly.

I blush bright red. He continues, "It wasn't until you said to set it up on the table that I realized you hadn't even looked into the peephole." He is nearly whispering by the end, and I blush an even deeper red. I begin to turn toward the bedroom. He grabs me gently by the elbow. I flinch at the electric contact between us.

"Where you going?" I try to pull my arm from his grasp. At first he resists. Then he lets go.

"I'm just going to put some real clothes on."

I complete my turn and start walking toward the bedroom. "By the way, that was Trinity on the phone. Care to explain why it is that you're ignoring her?" I say as casually as I can manage. It feels like lightning is running a race from where he touched my elbow through my body straight to my now rapidly beating heart.

Once in the bedroom I take a few deep breaths. Search for and find my favorite pair of pajama shorts and a different, less revealing t-shirt. Not exactly attractive by any means, but I feel it's the respectable thing to do. It's bad enough that my mind is running wild with sexual desire and tension.

Once I'm dressed, I walk back into the main room. He's moved over to my oversized chair, leaning forward, his elbows pressed into his slightly parted legs. God, those muscles. Then I realize he is looking at my iPad. Oh, please, please don't let him be actually looking at the screen.

I look at his face then. He's all tension. His face is tight, jaw straining, almost like he's literally biting his tongue. I need to say something to try and break up this tension.

Just as I open my mouth to say something, there is yet another knock at the door. I make a move to get the door, but Tristan is faster. He walks quickly and purposefully. I hear some chatter in the hallway, and just like that, Tristan is back. His hands now full with a silver tray. His breakfast.

I smile. "Boy, that was fast. Wish I could have gotten my breakfast that fast."

He chuckles. "They usually aren't this fast." He slowly makes his way to the dining room table and places the tray in front of one of the chairs. "Are you going to join me?"

As he turns toward the chair, I'm momentarily lost to the thought of eating with Tristan and to the view in front of me. Tristan has one of those backsides that most women I know would kill to have attached to their own bodies.

Finally, though, I do find my voice. "That depends, are you going to tell me why Trinity can't find you? Obviously you're here with me, but she made it sound like you've fallen off the face of the earth."

Gripping the back of the chair, he drops his head, looking at his flip-flops. "Why would she be calling you about me anyway?"

Oh right. I guess I'd forgotten to mention that part. "So...remember last night when I told you I'm Cameron Enders? Daughter of the deceased Robert Enders? Well, since his death, I've become the CEO of Bold International. The firm that represents you."

There is a very long pause. Tristan tenses multiple times, and at one point I think he is going to bust the chair in two. But he finally releases his grip and starts to pace the room.

I take my seat at the table. "Tristan, are you okay? What exactly is going on?"

While he continues to pace he starts ranting. "How perfect this is? Of all the corners and hiding spots in this world, I just so happen to pick the one that is currently inhabited by the CEO of the one company that I was desperately trying to avoid. The company that holds my career in their hands. Not that the said career is much at the moment, and I'm not sure that I want it to be much more than what it is, yet here you are, on the phone with the one person whose insistence on knowing all the details is capable of driving the sanest of people into the nut house. And here I am in your hotel room – the hotel room of the CEO of Bold International – having highly inappropriate thoughts..." He pauses and looks directly at me. Of course I blush like a school girl. He smiles. "Seems that I'm not the only one having improper thoughts." His grin is tight, but at least he's trying to sport a smile.

I blush a little deeper, but I can't help the smile that makes its way to my lips. HA! I'm not the only one. "Tristan, please, it's all right. Trinity was calling because she felt it important that I know that her star client has gone missing for nearly four days. She's concerned for your well-being. She became increasingly concerned when she was trying to reach your security detail and he too seems to be missing."

"No, I know right where he is. He is standing outside the door to this very room."

Oh shit, are you kidding me? "Why is he standing outside of this room?"

"Because I'm in here and, well, he won't go anywhere without me. I wanted to come here to see you." He pauses. "Now I'm not so sure this was a good idea."

The disappointment swells inside me. Why would being in my room not be a good idea? Is the fact that I have controlling interest in a company that he is involved with going to ruin whatever chemistry seems to be brewing between us?

Please, dear God, no. The fear of whatever has been building threatens my tear ducts. I finally have the man I've fantasized about for years within my reach, and he wants to go. Is he concerned because he has similar feelings to mine? Is he attracted to me? The thought of him wanting me has my heart beating harder and faster.

I can't help but wonder what has him so spooked. I think back to what Trinity told me and start to put it together. "Trinity said that the last time you were seen was Tuesday night at a premiere. She says that you were seen fighting with your girlfriend, though no one seems to know what about. Then you arrived here on Wednesday, or at least that is what I gathered from my conversation with Jessie last night. Right now, I can only imagine that she is the reason that you left L.A...." I trail off. God, this sounds all too familiar.

Tristan goes back to pacing. "Fucking hell! I really don't want to talk about this. I'm sorry, Cami, but the reason why I'm here is because I needed to escape life in general. I left without telling anyone because I need to be able to organize my own thoughts on how to deal with all of this. So please, give me a minute. I've said more than I should have already." He stops and looks around. "Do you have a cigarette?"

I get up quickly from the table and grab the pack I had put on the mantle after Tristan found me on the balcony. As I hand him the pack and my lighter, he continues, "But now I'm guessing I really have no choice, and I know that I'm running out of time."

He continues pacing, and the silence grows between us. I pad quietly back to the chair at the table and sit down. I watch him with my eyes only as he paces, taking long drags on the cigarette he took from my pack. After a couple of minutes I grab the pack and light one myself. His tension is starting to rub off on me and I haven't the first clue why.

I don't press him to talk to me. Mainly because I've learned from my father that once a question is asked, you stay silent until the other person breaks the silence. Gradually his pacing slows. I finish my cigarette, ignoring the food in front of me.

Finally he breaks the silence and starts to talk. "Why are you not eating your breakfast?"

"You asked me to join you. I figured it would be best to wait. To be honest, my appetite is on a mini vacation back in the States." I try to smile, but it's a strained attempt.

He ignores my joke. "I—I can't. I am trying to figure out how best to explain this to you." Finally he stops pacing and sits down in my overstuffed chair, elbows on his knees, looking down at the floor again. With his head in his hands he explains, "Layla cheated on me. From my understanding, it was with half of the staff from the movie she just finished filming."

The angst I felt earlier about seeing the pictures of Tristan with Layla dissolves in an instant. They were obviously having some major issues and are no longer together. Hope blossoms in my heart that maybe, just maybe, this can be more than a professional relationship.

"That's not a reason to go running," I whisper. God, what kind of hypocrite am I? "Though, I, um, ran for a similar reason. I actually caught him in the act."

His head pops up. His eyes, which are normally so light as to be almost translucent, grow dark and hard.

"Well, at least we figured out the first true thing that we have in common. Though of course your sex life will not be plastered all over the headlines of magazines and newspapers." He takes a deep breath and runs his fingers through his hair so violently that I'm afraid he's going to pull it out at the root.

"Cami, there are pictures. Pictures taken by an unknown person and submitted to a magazine that intends to publish the story. This is what we were fighting about. Not about her cheating, but about the effect this will have on her career and mine. I blame her for being so stupid. This was not the first time she's cheated on me, but this is the first time it's going to be made public with proof."

He trails off as he takes in my expression. I'm raging mad. Not at him, of course, but mad is an understatement. Murderous might be a better word for how I feel at this moment.

NINE

My rage is so unbelievably out of control; I can't even begin to fathom how Tristan can be so calm about this. Rage flares for my own reasons, but mainly because Tristan has to face her infidelity publicly and he doesn't deserve it. He needs to put a stop to this, and why he hasn't done that already is a driving force in my rage. "You really need to contact Trinity. Immediately. One, she needs to know where you are, and two, she needs to know what is going on so that she can stop this madness. Whatever it is that needs to be done to get those pictures or keep this quiet, Trinity will do just that, I ca—"

"I'm not entirely convinced that I want this kept quiet," Tristan interrupts. He starts pacing again and running his hands through his hair.

"Why in bloody hell not?" He smiles at me then. His smile is warm, almost seductive. I know he likes that expression, but why the smoldering smile? My head starts to swim. It's no doubt a distraction tactic, and it's working. Dammit. Taking a deep breath, I continue, "Why would you want to let this spread like wildfire? Do you want the world to know that she cheated on you and have your image plastered all over the tabloids under headlines like 'Tristan Michaels Cuckholded' or 'Star of Love is Burning Gets Burned'?"

For a minute Tristan just stands there, hands in hair, elbows out, almost like he's going to start flapping like a bird and fly away. Then he takes a deep breath and says, "The main reason I want to see this story unfold is because Layla is in desperate need of help. She's addicted to drugs and her career is going down the toilet quick. Word has gotten out how difficult she is to work with. If she keeps going this way she's going to end up washed up, homeless, or even dead. The only way at this point that I can see to it she gets help is to see everything she knows come to a crashing halt."

I can't believe what I'm hearing. His girlfriend cheats on him with not just one but several men, and he wants to use his misfortune to get her help. The word selfless comes to mind.

She's obviously hurt Tristan in a big way, and he's standing here talking about helping her? Is anybody really that unselfish? I can't decide whether to cry or shake him. So instead I bring it back to business.

"Tristan, are you at all concerned about the effect of this on your own career?"

"Absolutely not. I don't think you truly understand what the last five years of my life have been like." His voice is raw with emotion. I can see it in his eyes that he is playing with some serious inner turmoil about all of this.

"You don't like being an actor?"

"I love acting. With all my heart, Cami. I would do everything and trade nothing for my career, except..." He pauses. I know where this is going.

"You would happily trade your career for a life free of the fans, the paparazzi, and all of the fame, wouldn't you?" I try hard to smile, but I know the second his eyes meet mine that I'm right. His shoulders slump; they'd probably be on the floor if not for the fact that his spine is keeping him upright.

I can imagine it: the paparazzi chases, the crazy fans, the inability to have a meal without signing a dozen autographs in the course of a thirty-minute dinner. I don't blame him for wishing it away.

"So that is why you're here. In Tarah, away from the madness that is Hollywood. Trying to escape and be a normal human being while all this goes down the drain. You haven't told Trinity or even Vincent of what's going on because you want to let it happen, and you know that they will try to squash it. You also know that Bold will do whatever it takes to stop your name from being dragged through the mud."

"Yup, that about sums it up right there." He finally sits back down in my overstuffed chair. He looks drained, tired. Sadness is radiating from his body and I want to go to him, to comfort him, but before I can get to my feet he says, "I should really go."

What? No. He can't go yet. I'm not ready. "But...you haven't eaten your breakfast." That's the best I can manage, given my state of confusion as to why he wants to leave.

"That's all right. I had it billed to my room, so don't worry about it."

"That is so not the point." I sigh and look away. "If you must go, I understand. But...I really want you to stay. Please?" I can't look him in the eye.

"I...I...ah..." I look up then. He is looking at me like I have actually taken his breath away. "I'm not sure that is such a good idea."

"And why not?" I huff.

"Because." His eyes focus on a spot on the carpet about halfway between us, a smile playing at the corner of his mouth. "Because I'm afraid of what will happen if I stay." He takes a deep breath and changes the subject. "Besides, I should talk to Tyson. Get his take on how I should handle this."

Ah ha! I got him now. I stand up, turn around, and walk straight to the door. Swing it wide open, poke my head into the beautifully decorated hallway. About two doors down is the gorgeous, well-groomed, muscled-up man with military-short, dirty blond hair that I'd seen in the hall when I arrived on Thursday. His piercing grey eyes are staring straight at me.

I flash him my best smile. "It's Tyson, isn't it?" He doesn't acknowledge what I've just said, but I continue anyway. "Would you please join us?"

Just then Tristan comes up behind me and places his hand on the small of my back. A gentle, comforting gesture, but his touch shoots straight through my core and sends involuntary muscle spasms straight to my sex. I try hard to fight against it, but there is something about his touch that is all hot and sexy. My breath hitches in the back of my throat.

Tristan glances at me with a look of "*yeah I feel it too*" on his face. I slowly bring my eyes down from his, past his nose, perfect, his lips, full and delicious, to his chin and jawline. His two-day old stubble helps to accent his angular jawline. His neck – I can almost see the blood pumping through his veins. His tight shoulders hidden perfectly under the Ed Hardy shirt he wears. His pecs are equally on display, followed by his abs, though not as defined but still... Right down to the apex of his thighs. A half smile catches on my lips as I take in the fact that his cock is hard as a rock in his swim trunks. Thick, long, and heavy. I can see the outline of it running from his center all the way to his right hipbone. My God, he's huge.

He chuckles in amusement as my eyes widen momentarily and he realizes I'm staring at his cock. He whispers very quietly, "Now you see why staying is kind of a bad idea. If you keep that up, I am going to take you right here, right now in the hallway, and I don't care who sees, watches, or comes into your room."

My lips part as hot breath escapes in a rush, my heart rate triples, and my breathing becomes irregular. Suddenly that dull ache between my thighs starts screaming with need, desire. Desperate for his touch.

It takes me a minute to peel my eyes away from his erection and direct them back up to his. He's grinning in satisfaction at my heavy, lazy eyes. He knows exactly what he's done to me, and he is taking in pure enjoyment at my discomfort and desire. His eyes are blue. Deep, ocean blue. Warm.

Meanwhile Tyson hasn't moved. Tristan finally breaks eye contact with me and turns to him. "Tyson, if you would be so kind to join Ms. Enders and myself."

I look at Tyson then and think I see recognition in his eyes, though I'm not sure if it's name recognition and the fact that I am more or less his employer, or

"Layla and I started fighting again, constantly, about six months ago. Around the time we finished filming the last *Burning* movie. With the fights came long stays away from the house we lived in. Then about three months ago, she became needy, begging for me to be around more. So I went back, like an idiot, only to discover that she was using drugs."

He looks at me, and sadness fills his eyes. There is something behind this drug-use thing, something that pulls at his heart. While he ponders what he will say next, I vow to find out what secrets hide behind those beautiful blue eyes.

"This is not my mess to clean up and I refuse to argue and fight with her and her PR team about it." He looks at me. "Plus I refuse to pay out god-only-knows how much money to silence a story of this magnitude. This was one of the other reasons why we were fighting the other night. She knows that it's within my power to get this story squashed, but I told her that I refuse, and I stand firmly by that choice."

I'm beginning to sense that the love he once felt for Layla is no longer there. No doubt he cares about her; after spending five years with someone, regardless of circumstances, I would think him selfish if he didn't care at least a little.

My heart soars, warmth spreading throughout my body. If he's free of Layla, then his reasons behind the drink last night become obvious. He really does want to know me more. Well, he did before the whole Bold business came into play.

Oh for crying out loud, what the hell is my problem? I barely know this man. Yes, ok fine, I have been staring at his face and his eyes for years, feeling a connection with him that I cannot even begin to describe. A connection through pictures? Seriously? Yup, it is official: I've lost my marbles. All of them. There is not even a hint of a rattle in my brain right now.

I look at Tristan, who is looking at Tyson, but his eyes keep darting in my direction.

"Okay, but that still doesn't explain why you guys are acting so cagey," I say.

Tyson is staring straight at Tristan. Then Tyson shrugs, and I look back at Tristan.

"Well?" I'm losing patience.

Tristan sighs. "Cami, I'm honestly not sure I'm ready to have this conversation with you. Or with Trinity, Vincent, or anyone else for that matter. When the time comes, I'll pull everyone together and tell you all. Right now, I'm here in Tarah, waiting for the shoes to drop, and when they do, I would rather be here than in Hollywood." He takes another deep breath, and color is slowly returning to his face.

"All right, Tristan. I will respect your privacy on this, just this once. Only because it's obvious to me that whatever this is is very important to you." I make a concerted effort to let this go for now. But there's still the matter of Trinity. "Now. What are we going to do about Trinity?"

Tyson breaks the silence. "I think the best that we can do at this point is warn Trinity of what's coming. She needs to prepare for the onslaught of phone calls and issues that can arise from this story. She'll know where he is," – he nods in Tristan's direction – "but at least he can continue to be here, privately, away from prying eyes and the good old photographers."

"Fair enough. Am I calling Trinity, or are you going to call her, Tristan?" Personally I don't really care who calls who and who does what; it just needs to be done. Now.

"Tristan?" Tyson prompts.

"I'll call her. Cami, does she know where you are?" Tristan looks at me, and I'm surprised to see that his eyes are soft and warm, almost adoring.

"She knows – or thinks – I'm in Tahiti. Mick and Beau, my two best friends, know I'm here in Tarah and that I have no intention of leaving anytime soon. I have my own demons to deal with for a while." Oh boy, is that ever the understatement.

Tristan's expression warms as he realizes that I truly have a purpose for being here. "Mick and Beau?" He raises his right eyebrow at me. If I am being honest, the innocent look on his face is pretty cute.

"Mick is my financial advisor. Beau is my money spender, personal assistant, and best friend. They will probably be coming out here sometime next week. Beau and Mick don't work for Bold, so you don't need to worry about them. Right now you just need to worry about what you're going to tell Trinity."

TEN

TRISTAN

Cami is watching me intently. I get up and grab another cigarette from the pack of Camels she's left on the table. Jesus, what a mess this is turning out to be. I came here to escape Layla and all her bullshit, but that sure didn't last long. She doesn't say anything, but I gather that she knows how hard this is on me. Lighting the cigarette, I turn and head back to the chair. Cami slides the ashtray toward the chair and gives me a hesitant smile. This is not at all how I envisioned meeting someone, throwing half of my life story at her in a single hour-long conversation.

I retrieve my cell phone from my pocket and turn it on. No doubt as soon as I do this, Trinity's team is locking onto my signal so they will know exactly where it is that I'm hiding.

As soon as the BlackBerry loads up, I start receiving emails and missed call notifications. I'm almost tempted to listen to my voice messages.

"Apparently I'm a wanted man," I say aloud.

"Why do you say that?" Cami asks.

"One hundred and seven missed calls." I scroll down my missed call log. "And only a few are from people who truly care. The rest of them are from people that are just trying to cover their ass. Layla and her crew have consumed my call log." I frown. I didn't want this Layla mess to come before Cami, or anyone else for that matter. It makes me feel weak, as though I can't handle a situation, and I don't want to seem weak in front of Cami; she deserves so much better, both from me and from anyone else she has to deal with. "Regardless, what is done is done." I pause and stub out my half-smoked cigarette. "It's time to call Trinity."

"Are you sure you're ready to do that? I can call her if you want me to." Cami's tone of voice is all business again, but something in her warm, steel blue-grey eyes tells me that she is trying to protect me, whether from Trinity or from Layla, I'm not entirely sure.

"No, Cami, this is a battle that I need to deal with." I am cut off by the ringing of Cami's cell phone. I look up as Cami frowns. Her eyebrows pull together as she pushes a button and brings the phone to her ear.

"Hi, Trinity."

I, of course, can't hear the other end of the conversation, and Cami seems to read my mind.

"Trinity, hang on for me." As she says this she brings the phone down and hits another button. "Trinity, can you hear me?"

"Yes. Why am I on speaker phone?"

"Because I don't care to have the phone to my head. Now what's going on?" Cami says.

"Well, we were finally able to pick up a signal from Tristan's cell phone," Trinity says.

Cami rolls her eyes. It's actually kind of comical the way the color of her eye disappears altogether.

With a sly smile and a slight chuckle, she tells Trinity, "You and Mick should go into the tracking business. That didn't take very long, considering he only just turned it on. I'm assuming that you're calling me, instead of Tristan, because it was traced to the Tahiti area, where I just so happen to be, am I correct?"

Trinity laughs. "How do you know that he only just turned it on?"

"Because I'm looking right at him." She smiles at me, her steel blue eyes warm and liquid. "Ironically, he happened to step into my suite as I cut you off from our last phone call. As strange as this sounds, he bought me a drink last night with no clue who I was. So it's all worked out for the best."

Trinity burst out laughing. "Apparently Tahiti is the place for the wealthy-in-hiding. Good morning, Tristan."

"Hi, Trinity." My voice is deadpan. I'm not really sure how to handle the whole situation, nor how to tell Trinity about it. I guess I just have to jump into it. "Listen, Trinity, I would imagine that here at some point today or tomorrow you're going to start getting massive amounts of phone calls from our favorite little magazine."

"I had a feeling," she says as she lets out a deep sigh. "Does this have anything to do with why Layla has been blowing up my and Vincent's phones?"

Wow, Layla must be completely desperate. Either she is looking for me or trying to get Trinity to stop her story. "You got it." I almost smiled. Trinity is a true genius at what she does. "You haven't spoken with her, have you?"

"No, I have this rule about not fraternizing with obnoxious girlfriends, and she's top of that list," Trinity says.

"Listen, Layla was kind enough to give me some advance notice on some things that are more or less coming up to bite her in the ass. More so her than me, other than the fact that I'm going to be portrayed either as the brokenhearted lover or the idiot that should have known better. Either way is fine by me." I pause, and of course Trinity, being who she is and doing what she does, is about a mile and half ahead of me.

"Let me guess, she's been cheating and the paparazzi have more than enough proof to publish a story? Well, Tristan, you know damn well we'll stop this story. Or at least delay it as long as possible—"

"No!" I nearly shout. "Don't. Do not stop this story. Look, this story is going to completely destroy Layla, and I am not at all opposed to letting it happen—"

"But Tristan," she cut me off. "I cannot let her attempt to ruin you like this."

"Trinity, that is absolutely not the point." I let out a long, hard, ragged breath. I have no choice but to let this spill out all over the table. "Look, she has a very long life lesson coming at her. I want to be disassociated with her as fast as possible. Because her life over the next several months is going to be hell enough as it is."

I'm ready to go mad, and at this point, I need to get it all on the table. So here goes nothing.

"Okay here is the bottom line of what is happening. Tuesday at the premiere Layla told me that pictures of her sleeping with the producer of her current project had been leaked to *Entertainment*

Now, who responded by sending her copies of the pictures. She tried to tell me that it wasn't what it looked like in the pictures. But when she showed me cell phone image copies, I'll be damned if it wasn't a goddamn orgy."

I pause to let it all soak in. On the other end of the line Trinity's letting loose a string of profanities no person should really have to hear. Once she quiets, I continue. "Before you start asking questions, let me finish, please." I take another deep breath. "This whole thing happened about seven or eight weeks ago, after the final wrap of the filming. I guess it was their idea of a wrap party. Many of the faces in the images are recognizable. The images are grainy cell phone images, but close enough to make out the producer, two additional actors in the movie, and several of the film crew. All in all there appeared to be nine men and Layla."

"Jesus fucking Christ!" I look up in shock at Cami. She's white as a ghost and has this almost murderous glare on her face.

I raise my hand and with my index finger I gesture for her to come to me. She needs to know that this is really okay. Without hesitation, she stands straight up and comes over to me, bringing her phone. I slide myself back in the chair and pat my leg. She smiles and then wiggles her way between my legs. I begin rubbing her shoulders.

God, her skin is soft, warm, and perfect.

My hand still on Cami's back, I pick up where I left off. "So then Layla surprises me by demanding that I fix her little problem. I refused and she got angry with me. She thought that I would just drop everything and do whatever it takes to keep it quiet. I did think about it for about a tenth of a second before I decided that it wasn't my mess. She made her bed and she needs to lay in it until the storm blows over. I suggested that she take the pictures to all of the men in them and ask them to cover her ass and her career. No doubt they all would have been more than willing to do so, given their own relationship statuses."

I quickly realize that Trinity needs to know all of it if she's going to be able to deal with the press. I look at Cami and silently mouth, "I'm sorry." She is instantly puzzled, cocking her head to the side and raising an eyebrow. I half smile in reassurance as I am about to drop the last bomb.

"Listen, guys, before you go flying off the handle at me, I had nothing to do with this. But in an attempt to get me to protect her from all of this, she told me that she is pregnant." Cami stiffens, and Trinity's gasp can be heard through the speaker phone. "Before you guys get all 'Holy shit' on me, it's not mine. The last time that she and I had any type of sexual contact was some time ago. So I know, without a doubt, that this is a result of her infidelity. Which of course leads me to believe that she has no clue who the father is, and telling me about it was no doubt an attempt to get me back and convince me to protect her."

The wave of relief that washes over Cami is palpable. She smiles tenderly at me. From her reaction I know that she is glad the secrets are out and on the table, and in a way so am I.

"Ultimately, the last bomb is what caused me to walk away and sent me running to Tarah. No doubt she has deluded herself into thinking that it's mine because that is the easiest and safest way for her. She wants nothing more than to try to continue to drag me along with her." Man, this all sounds so bad. But dammit, I'm tired and I don't want to deal with this any longer today. "Look, I know it is not mine, and as soon as it's possible to have a paternity test done, I will be first in line to do so. I will not let her infidelity continue to ruin my life and have her wreaking havoc on my career."

"Cami," Trinity says after a moment's pause. "Is there any reason you feel we should not allow this story to run?"

Cami speaks softly but firmly, the authority in her voice astonishing. "Trinity, I think that it's in the best interest of all that are involved and that Tristan has a point. Layla is obviously trying to use Tristan and his influence to squash this story for her own benefit. If the story is stopped, or even delayed, she will eventually get caught up in something like this again and destroy her own career." She pauses, and I can practically see the wheels in her head turning. "Is there a way that we can cut this story by announcing that Tristan and Layla have split?"

Hm, I hadn't even thought about that. If we announce a split between Layla and me, can we really pull the heat away from me?

Cami continues, "Do we have any idea when the last time they were spotted together was? I know that they arrived at the premiere separately last Tuesday."

Has she been Googling me? The thought makes me smile. She was checking up on me. I'm impressed.

"I'm not sure when they were last spotted together," Trinity says. "They have both been working separately from each other for some time. Are we saying that we want to try and backdate a breakup?"

Cami looks at me to see what I think. I nod, and she continues, "If it's possible, I think it would be best. This way we can wipe Tristan's name from any association with this story. We can spin it so that her little escapade is the reason for their breakup. See what you can do on that. If we can't work it out then maybe we can come up with a different plan, but for the time being, let's try and attack this before it attacks us."

"Wow, Cami, I think that it's time you stepped out of non-active CEO status. You're good, girl!" Trinity is laughing. "You're going to give me a run for my money. Tristan, what do you think?"

I think about it for a moment before finally speaking again. "If we can take some of the attention off me with our own story of a split between us, then let's go with it. But please let's make sure that it's a viable story before we run away with it. It might even be better to wait until the magazines start calling. You could just play dumb about the photos and say that Layla and I broke up."

I realize I'm still rubbing Cami's back. She looks at me, smiles, and for some unknown reason, I feel a strong urge to hug, hold, and kiss her until her lips are red and raw. But for now, I settle for kissing her shoulder. As I pull away, she reaches up and cups my face in her right palm. I lean into it, wanting all of her hand pressed against my face. I reach up and cup her face in both my hands, using my thumb to wipe away the tears that have escaped her eyes.

Trinity's voice interrupts the moment, and our hands fall away from each other's faces. "That's not a bad idea. All right, Tristan, we're all over it. We will let the magazines come to us, and go from there. I'll email you any questions we have and get in touch if it's an emergency."

"No. I won't promise that I'll be available. In fact I'm going to turn off my phone. There were over ninety missed calls from Layla and people from her staff when I turned it on today, and I refuse to be bombarded with more of their bullshit. If you need to reach me then call Cami. She knows where to find me."

"Fair enough," says Trinity.

Cami is sitting on my lap, just staring at me. "All right, guys, we'll be in touch," I say. When the goodbyes are said, Cami reaches over to the phone to press the end button, then turns it off completely. I turn to Tyson, who is standing silently in the corner. "Go take a walk, my man. I'll be here for a while."

Cami stiffens. "Oh hell, I forgot he was even here." She laughs. "Thank you, Tyson."

"My pleasure, ma'am. And Tristan, you know how to reach me." Tyson leaves the suite, and just like that, I'm alone with Cami.

ELEVEN

CAMI

I'm pretty sure that I've never truly wanted to be with anyone more than I want to be with Tristan right this minute. I want to be able to wipe away his sadness, his frustrations. Whatever it is that he can take from my body, I want to give it willingly.

Jeez, Cami, some things never change.

"So, Ms. Enders," Tristan whispers gently in my ear as he continues to gently rub my back. "Now that you know the truth about why I'm hiding in Tarah, what is it that you're thinking about so hard?"

"Well..." I pause, not really sure how to say what I want to say to him. But at this point I don't think that words are going to express it right.

Cupping his face between my hands I bring my lips to his and I kiss him. He stiffens, but then relaxes almost instantly. Our lips begin to move and dance. I'm pulling him in so close, waiting for my opportunity to deepen our kiss and place my tongue along his. He brings his hands back up to cup my face, mirroring my gesture... That's it; I'm done for. I gasp and he beats me to the punch. His tongue enters my mouth, seeking mine.

My head is spinning, my breathing shallow. I can't hardly breathe and I don't care. I am kissing Tristan Michaels!

After a moment of intense kissing, he slowly pulls away, kissing me with little pecks as he does. It's obvious that he doesn't want to stop, but I can tell that he is trying to catch his breath. I smile as he continues his peck kisses, about ten in all. Then he lies back in the chair and closes his eyes. I start to chew on the barbell in my tongue, a nervous habit I have. I'm trying to decide what to do when he grabs my upper arm, smiles, and says to me. "Come here, beautiful."

I smile and blush – of course because I'm your typical blushing fool – and lean in against his right shoulder. He wraps his right arm around me, holding me close. I can hear his pounding heart against my ear. I bring my right hand up and lay it over his heart. "This is nice."

"I have not felt this comfortable in a long time." I can't see his face but I can hear that he's smiling. I lift my head slightly to look. Yup, he is smiling all right. He starts to run his fingers through my hair.

"So tell me something... Why the blue and black hair?" He chuckles and continues to stroke my hair.

I giggle. "Why the dragon?" He laughs. I say, "I don't know, different. It used to be blond and pink, blond and blue, purple, you name it. I am not the conventional type, as if my tattoos, tongue and nipple piercings aren't proof enough." I laugh. "I have more. A lot more. You just haven't seen it all yet." Just then he brings his hand down from the top of my head, through my long, black and blue hair, between my shoulder blades.

"No bra eh?" He smiles.

"Nope. Own them, but rarely wear them."

He smiles wider, his hands continuing their journey down my spine. About two inches below where a bra would normally be, he finds a round platinum ring with a small ball holding it together. "What is this?" he whispers softly.

I smile. It's one of my pride and joy pieces of artwork. "That is a surface piercing. There's another one about four inches to the right." His hand finds and follows the leather thong that connects the two piercings.

"You...you have a corset?" His voice is warm, husky, filled with wanting.

I smile, nearly giggle. "That would be an understatement. Would you like to see the whole thing?"

He doesn't reply immediately, but continues to fondle the leather thong that runs between the piercings.

I have twenty-four piercings on my back, twelve on each side of my spine. There is also a tattoo that the piercings are worked into that takes the shape of a laced up corset in black and purple.

Finally he smiles and says, "I...I would love to see it."

I sit up and reach for the hem of my t-shirt, then wonder whether I should just take the whole thing off. No doubt he's going to want the whole effect of the work. So I stand up and go for the waist of my shorts. The tattoo and the corset extend all the way to about an inch above the crack of my ass, so I have to lower my shorts to be able to show him the whole thing.

He inhales sharply. But it's in reaction to my shorts starting to fall and not because of what he sees; I know the t-shirt is doing a great job of covering my back and butt.

Once I get the shorts low enough to show off the back, I leave them there, nothing exposed yet. Then go back to my t-shirt. I turn around to face him. The first thing I notice is his rock-hard cock straining against his shorts. I smile big, and my eyes follow the contours of his body to his face. He is smiling in anticipation, his eyes locked on my hands, waiting to see what I will do. Slowly I lift the back of the shirt high enough so that the entire piece in the back will be visible. I close my eyes and slowly turn around.

I know the moment that the art comes into view. His breathing speeds up, deep and breathy, then comes a "Sweet Jesus!" At this point I am all smiles, feeling a surge of appreciation for my girl X. She is the best tattoo artist and body piercer on the planet. She and I have spent a lot of time together. Every ounce of work on my body is hers and hers alone.

I feel his fingers graze my back, tracing the outside of the piece, sending goose bumps all over my body. My nipples harden and strain against the barbells. They're so hard and tight I feel like I'm going to snap the platinum rods. A moan escapes my lips. Then both his hands are on me, caressing, kneading their way up my back. He grabs my t-shirt and slowly starts to lift it up.

My nerve endings are on fire, aching for his touch.

"Let go baby-girl," he says. I do as he asks, and he starts to pull my t-shirt up. "Arms up. I'm taking this off." I smile and comply, lifting my arms over my head. He stands up, bringing my shirt with him. "My God, you are beautif—" His breath catches. No doubt the rest of my back has finally registered in his mind. "—ful. Absolutely beautiful."

He releases my t-shirt and it falls to the floor. His hands come up to my shoulders, where my quarter sleeves start, then slowly he moves them across my back, lightly tracing the fairy wings that come together between my shoulder blades. He continues over to my arms and down my sides. His breathing is rough, ragged, and his voice comes to me husky and breathy. "Jesus, Cami, you're so beautiful."

His hands starts to move around to my front, tickling my belly. I long to feel them on my breasts, toying with the barbells through my nipples. "Turn around for me, please, Cami?"

I smile. I've known all along that one day X's genius was really going to pay off, and this moment is it. I've never had anyone react to my body art the way that Tristan is, and suddenly all of the pain of getting pierced, the healing process after getting new ink, and all the time spent in X's chair and shop is paying off in this one reaction.

TRISTAN

Sweet Jesus, I've died and gone to heaven. The artwork is fantastic, and all the tattoos are linked in some fashion, either by color or overall design. Like me, she's spent a lot of time shopping for an artist that wasn't just chosen at random. The ink work is intricate and beyond anything I thought was even possible in tattoo form. And they completely complement her body shape and skin tone. Cami wears her tattoos, not the other way around.

And now as she turns around, she has a model-style stance: back arched slightly, pushing her breasts out just a hair further. They are perfectly round, pert, perky. I stop breathing. Her nipples are a warm pink, accented by the platinum barbells barely visible on either side of her fully erect nipples. The barbells are accented with bright green and purple balls. My cock is throbbing and I can feel drops of pre-cum forming and sliding down my shaft.

Pulling in a deep, ragged breath and licking my lips, I can't stop my hands from trailing up her soft skin from the waistband of her shorts to her luscious pink areolas. She is breathing deep and heavy. Her nipples are so hard and swollen now that her barbells are reduced to the balls on either side. She arches her back, pushing her breasts into my hands. My thumbs graze over her nipples and she moans.

"You're so delicate and beautiful, like a little lily. Begging to open like a flower."

Her breathing spikes. I can feel her heart pounding against my hands, begging me to continue. My hands continue the path they were making. Slowly, up to her shoulders, her neck, her cheeks, cupping her face. I pull her head up slightly and bring her lips to mine. She kisses me back, urgent and excited. I can hardly breathe. This girl is literally taking my breath away.

Then I feel her hands on my hips. Searching for what? Ah, she finds it, the hem of my shirt. She starts to lift it up as I continue kissing her. She pulls upward until she meets the resistance of my arms. I smile against her lips. "Did you want to take off my shirt?"

She laughs, but it comes out hot and heavy, almost a pant. "Yes," she breathes. I raise up my arms, and in a nanosecond, off goes my shirt. She immediately drops it to the floor and takes about a half step back in an attempt to take in the full view of the tattoo on my chest. I watch as she licks her lower lip, the tongue ring she was chewing on earlier showing its bright green ball. Her hands glide along my shoulders, down my pecs; she finds my stud-pierced nipples with her thumbs and rubs lightly. Ah, my God, that...Jesus. "Ah!" I grab her hips and pull her close. Her own nipples press against my stomach, hard and cold. I want so badly to warm them with my tongue.

The idea of my tongue stroking her nipples causes my now-aching dick to twitch. She flinches at the motion and presses further into me. Consuming me. What little restraint I have is being lost. God I want her. I want her so bad. But I have to stop this.

"This feels right, Tristan," she says, like she's been reading my mind. "I can't help myself. I want you." She reaches up to stroke my chin with her index finger.

"Baby-girl, I want you, too, but neither one of us are in a good frame of mind. We have been through so much. I..." How do I say that I need to do this the right way? Somehow, deep down in my heart and soul, I know that Cami is more than any woman I've ever known. She is going to mean more to me. "I want – no not want – I need to take this slow. Have dinner with me tonight?"

"I..." She has a look of hesitation in her eyes. Disappointed maybe? "I would love to, Tristan." She smiles up at me and I kiss her soft warm lips. A chaste kiss.

"Good, I can't wait. Meet me downstairs in Blu at seven?"

She giggles. "Sounds hot! I'll be there. What are you going to do now?"

"Well, first I'm going to kiss you again." I do – sweet, unhurried, but chaste because I know a deeper kiss would crash all the walls of control I have. I pull back. "Now, I am going to head up to my room and take a very cold shower." I back away slightly and shiver at the lack of contact between us. Her body, so warm and pressed against me, makes me yearn for her. "And then climb into bed to sleep. I haven't slept for nearly forty-eight hours and I am dead on my feet."

"Jeez, baby, that is too long. Go get some sleep. I would love to join you, but I am pretty sure that sleep is the last thing that would happen." She laughs then. "I think that I'm going to have a soak in the tub. Talk to Beau and Mick about a couple of things, then maybe do some shopping or take a nap."

"Sounds like fun, Baby-girl. If I can't sleep, I'll track you down. There are only so many places you can hide. How does that sound?"

"Perfect."

I lean in and kiss her again. Then I bend down, picking up her shirt. I straighten it out, gather up the bottom, and gesture toward her. She leans forward slightly so I can gently pull the shirt over her head. I hold it open for her while she gingerly puts her arms in the sleeves.

It's unbearable to have her covered back up again, but it's better this way. At least that is what I'm telling myself in my head as I pull her shirt down over her torso. I then reach into her waistband and pull her shorts up, careful not to snag the fabric on her corset piercing.

"You are the most beautiful woman I have ever met. I am very glad that you're here and that you are so understanding of everything that has happened."

"Oh, Tristan, how could I not be. You have done nothing wrong. I just hope that this has a positive outcome for you."

"Whatever the outcome, it won't matter to me."

"I truly admire that attitude. I should take a lesson from you on self-control, too." She smiles and brushes my chin with the back of her hand. "Go get some sleep, otherwise I am going to put you in my bed." Her tone is light, but there's a pleading in her eyes.

"Baby-girl, that sounds absolutely amazing. But it will do us both more good if I go to my room. I will see you in Blu at seven. I'll make reservations at Caran for dinner." I kiss her again. "Enjoy your day, baby-girl."

I bend down, pick up my shirt and phone, and head toward the door. I look over my shoulder to drink in her beauty one more time. She's standing there with her arms wrapped around herself, almost like she's cold. My heart sinks. She looks so alone. I want to walk back to her and embrace her, hold her. I feel my feet trying to move forward, but my mind is out of the suite and into the hallway. I'm so torn. My head wins, and reach for the door.

"See you soon," I holler as I open the door.

Once outside the suite, I look at my phone and a bitter smile creeps to my lips. Thank the Lord for the silent setting. Ten missed calls in less than two hours. All from Layla. Fuck that! I hit the power button and head to the elevator and to my room.

Once in the elevator I take a deep breath. Cami has proven that she is more than just something good to look at. She has an uncanny no-nonsense business sense, which makes her even more appealing. Being around Cami this morning has taken the sting and frustration out of this whole mess. For the first time since Tuesday night, I finally feel like my life has normalcy to it. I feel that for once I can really just let things fall where they may. The story, Layla, my career – none of it matters when I'm with Cami.

TWELVE

CAMI

Slumping back into the club chair after Tristan left, I realize that this vacation is starting out like a dream. For years and years I have looked into the eyes of Tristan Michaels via news articles, magazine covers, online photos, and whatever else I could find, and I always felt a connection to him, despite the fact that it was just a photo. Sometimes I wondered if I wasn't a little crazy.

Now he is right above me, sleeping, has seen me half naked, and I've felt his desire for me in the twitch of his cock against my stomach. My head swims at the idea that the man I've idolized for the last four or five years wants me. Looking into his eyes today, I felt the same connection that I've felt looking at his pictures, but live and in living color. I can't believe it. I feel like I need to wake myself up because the further into this dream I get, the more disappointed I am going to be when I wake up.

And because of Tristan, I'm starting to feel like I can do something more with my life than live off of my trust. Sure, I went to college. It was because I wanted an education. I loved school and it was something I was good at. I never thought that I was going to be great at anything else. But now, after having dealt with Trinity on a professional level on behalf of Tristan, I feel this almost nervous excitement at the prospect of being in an active role within Bold.

"Gah" I huff in frustration, puling my knees to my chest. Can I really do this CEO stuff? Trinity swears that it is going to be easy, but sometimes I wonder if she is just placating me so that she doesn't have to do it herself. I guess it says something that after a year of doing the CEO thing and maintaining her clients, she's still with Bold, still doing what she does best. Can I really take over Bold and be CEO?

This is something I know is coming, but I never expected that Bold would become a full-fledged portion of my life. For the last year I have been secretly hoping that there would be a loophole out of the terms of Bobbie's will and that taking over as CEO would not be something I would ever have to do.

And suddenly I find myself sucked into it in a whole new way because of Tristan. While I'm supposed to be on vacation, no less. How ironic.

I walk out on to my balcony and sit in one of the wicker lounge chairs. Looking out at the clear, blue, inviting Pacific Ocean, I'm surrounded by a gentle breeze that carries with it the scents of the ocean, sand, and a faint hint of sunscreen. The day is warm – probably the warmest yet – and the beach is nearly full of hotel patrons and guests either swimming or sunbathing. The waves are gentle and the tide is out. The kids on the beach are walking along the wet sand picking up seashells. There is a cute little girl showing her mommy every little shell she finds.

I feel hot, wet tears slide down my cheeks at the sight of all the families on the beach, and I'm quickly reminded that I've never had that experience. Never been able to spend time on a family vacation.

Wiping the tears from my eyes, I give up on that thought process. Dwelling on something that I cannot change will only make the heartache worse. Never truly knowing why my parents didn't want to be close to me is something I came to accept more than a year ago. Bobbie is gone.

I suck in a deep breath in an attempt to clear my mind. What a whirlwind of emotions the last couple of days have been. Thirty-six hours ago I was crushed about Reed's games and bullshit, and now I feel like a woman who has been struck by cupid himself.

My feelings for Reed were always on the brink of going somewhere, even though I knew, deep down inside, Reed was not the man for me. Sure, he was good in bed and he had no problem feeding into my submissive fetishes. But every time I thought that I was giving into my emotions with him, he would do something that would remind me why I couldn't fall in love with him. He was somewhat emotionally abusive in that respect.

But Tristan. Tristan is a whole new ball game altogether. Every time I look at him, something blooms deep down inside. My heart feels like it is swelling beyond allowable limits, and most of all, my stomach flutters at his touch. I've never known these parts to exist on this capacity before; I'm not sure I know how to handle these feelings.

Tristan's touch is electric, a jolt straight to my heart and deep into my soul. I can't quite comprehend the fact that the pictures don't do him justice, but the way he looks at Layla in those pictures tells me that there is something more to be had when it comes to Tristan Michaels.

Not to mention the incredible sexual chemistry. The desire to have him inside me is undeniable. Were it not for Tristan's self-control, I'd be in bed with him right now.

But to Tristan, Layla was far more than sex. They lived together. They carried on a normal relationship. Is it too soon after Layla? Is that why he wants to take it slow?

Then of course there is the fact that he is this ginormous celebrity who is young and gorgeous and has every woman pining for him. The character he plays in *Love is Burning* is every woman's fantasy man. I've never seen his movies – and I don't have any intention to – but I've read the books and know that the character he plays, Dakota, is quite the catch: smart, sexy, rich, and unobtainable. Dakota has been compared to the likes of Romeo and Mr. Darcy, which of course brings out the crazy-obsessed women. It's not really Tristan they want; it's Dakota. They don't know the real Tristan from the guy standing next to them. It's an image. I, however, am getting the opportunity to know Tristan for who he is.

But what if he sees me as just one more of those other women? Does he want to take it slow because he's worried I'm going to turn out to be another fan obsessed with Dakota? Should I remind him that I've never seen any of his movies? Or will that just sound like an insult?

I groan out loud. I'm driving myself crazy. I need to stop thinking about this.

Waking up around five, I quickly realize that I'm just as flushed and anxious as I was before I laid down. Thank goodness for the iPod. Lord knows I would never have slept without the relaxing melodies.

I have about half an hour before I really need to get moving, so I head to the sitting room. The maids have been through, picked up, cleaned up my lunch, and straightened the sitting room. I also notice some packages sitting on the table. I ordered some clothes from Gucci for tonight's date before I lay down for my nap; they must have delivered them while I was asleep. I grab my smokes and head out onto the balcony.

The sun is sitting low on the horizon, but the warmth is wonderful on my skin. The beach isn't as full as it was earlier, but there are still plenty of people milling about, enjoying the sun and the surf. There is a group of about five kids working on what appears to be a huge sandcastle.

The island itself is very small, if islands can be classified as small. From my balcony I can see the ocean on three of the four sides. There are lush tropical trees, and you can hear some of the birds from up here. The ocean water is crystal clear blue. Warm and inviting. Tomorrow I intend to spend the day on the beach, in the water. It's about time I got a damned tan. I laugh out loud.

"What's so funny?" I recognize the voice, but still it makes me jump.

"I...um, was thinking about how bad I need a tan." I turn and look into my suite. It's empty. "What the hell?"

"Look up, beautiful," he says. His voice is soft, sweet, and inviting.

I look up and, sure enough, leaning over the edge of...what is he leaning on? "Are you in the pool?"

He laughs. "I am. Want to join me?" He wiggles his eyebrows in a very suggestive manner. His smile is inviting and seductive.

Trying to catch my breath before speaking, I look at him a moment. "I would, but I have this date with this totally hot, amazing guy that deserves everything I can throw at him – hair, nails, makeup, the whole nine yards – so I should start getting ready." I smile as sweetly as I can manage without giving away my teasing tones.

"Lucky guy!" he mumbles.

"I think I am the lucky one."

"We'll see about that."

"Yes, Mr. Michaels, we shall see about that." I giggle as he blushes the color of a cherry. "I am very much looking forward to our date tonight." I finish my cigarette, putting it out in the ashtray, and look back up at Tristan. "Enjoying the view?" I smile.

"I am very much enjoying the view. Good thing you're not in the pool with me. I'm not wearing swimming trunks. I might scare you." His grin is wicked and knowing.

I laugh out loud. "I highly doubt that. Besides, those trunks leave very little to the imagination." I wink. "See you in a couple of hours." I take two long strides into the suite, and before I manage to shut the door, I hear a grunt and a Tristan-style groan.

"You're killing me, woman!" I hear him shout as the door clicks closed.

I laugh and head for the shower to get cleaned up. I manage to disengage the leather throng from my back so that I can restring it.

Once out of the shower, I put on the panties, garter belt, and thigh highs I ordered from downstairs. I'm going braless tonight because the dress has a fully open back. Not wanting to get makeup or anything else on it, I save the dress for later.

Just over an hour later my makeup is done: in light purples and looking smoking hot. My eyes are accented with diamond-like pasty-gems that bring out the blue in my eyes.

My hair is a curly, messy, up-do style that is swept to my right side. I'm head over heels in love with the way it turned out. The flowers in the sitting room were changed while I slept, and in the vase is a beautiful white with purplish colored trim water lily. I decapitate it and place it in my hair as an accent piece over my left ear.

I lace my corset with black and purple ribbons braided together. Braiding them makes them easier to pull through the hoops, and the two colors look great together.

The dress is made of silver satin with a tank top-style top that has narrow shoulder straps that wrap around my arms. The back is completely open with a small gathering of material that falls just to my hips. The front is loose across my chest.

Standing in front of the full length bathroom mirror, I can see the entire ensemble come together. Turning to my right and looking toward my left shoulder in the mirror, I can see that the top half of my corset is clearly visible, which was the idea. My wings are in full view, except for the outer tips, which are under the shoulders of the dress. The straps of the dress match up perfectly with the top of my shoulder caps. My hair is over my right shoulder slightly.

The dress also came with a beautiful, deep purple lace shawl I plan to bring with me. A smile of satisfaction spreads across my face as I climb into the five-inch purple Christian Loubtin Alti evening pumps. I'm beyond satisfied with everything: the hair, the flower, the dress, the makeup, the shoes – it's the perfect combination. Tristan will be brought to his knees.

With everything in hand and ready to go, I head to the elevator and downstairs, into Blu.

THIRTEEN

From the moment I walk into Blu and see Tristan, I know nothing will ever be the same. He has not yet seen me, but he is wearing a beautiful black suit with a purple silk shirt, accented with a silver tie. Seeing him dressed like this makes my heart skip a beat; my breathing has altogether stopped and my knees start to tremble. I do, however, manage to keep my mouth from falling to the floor.

I'm seated immediately at a booth off to the right of the bar. It's quiet and the lighting is low. Taking my seat, I wait for Tristan to join me. Jessie comes over with a martini glass filled with the same color liquid as my Cosmo from last night. Resisting the urge to roll my eyes, I take a sip. It's so good that a small moan escapes my lips.

As I finish up my drink, it registers that Tristan has yet to join me. Just as I start to worry that he's changed his mind about dinner, I feel a soft tickle on my left shoulder. Looking to my left, I see sitting on my shoulder, in brilliant white, pinks, and purples, a beautiful stargazer lily.

The soft petals on my skin cause goose bumps to rise, first on my shoulder and then beginning to radiate out across my entire body. Lazily my eyes follow the stem of the flower to his hand, arm, shoulder, and finally to a beautiful, warm, inviting smile that is attached to the face of none other than Tristan Michaels.

"Hi," My voice is soft and breathy.

"Good evening, Cami." His voice is soft, sweet. He hands the lily to me and I place it gently on the table.

Turning back to him, "I was beginning to wonder if I should start worrying," I say softly. "Would you please join me?" I gesture to the bench seat across from me. As I do this, he grabs my hand. Bringing it his mouth, he softly brushes his lips against my knuckles, planting a soft, chaste kiss on the back of my hand. Oh my word. If I wasn't getting excited before, I certainly am now.

"I would be honored," he says. I notice with great satisfaction that he does not release my hand as he sits. The gesture, while seemingly small, sends my heart into overdrive.

"Thank you for my drink. Jessie said you had called ahead." I smile remembering Jessie's face, which told me that he was disappointed that I was having a date with 'Mr. Rubble. I think he'd wanted to claim me for himself.

"You're most welcome." He is smiling, practically from ear to ear. No doubt it's a direct reflection of my own smile. God, how has this man made me so weak in the knees in only such a short amount of time? "Did you have a good day today?" he asks, interrupting my admiration.

"I did, thank you. I even managed to take a nap while the Gucci reps went shopping on my behalf." I giggle. "I never thought I would ever say that."

He was laughing a bit too. "Yeah, the idea of being waited on is something that is hard to get used to. I'm not even sure I'm used to it."

"Right! I'm pretty sure that I'll never get used to it. This was never the life I expected to lead. But I'm on vacation after all. It'll go away when I get back to Phoenix."

"Phoenix, huh? I thought you lived in L.A."

I laugh. "No, L.A. and I do not get along well. Phoenix and I, however, are made for each other. The sun, the warmth, the fact that it hardly ever rains."

Jessie brings us another round of drinks and departs quickly. "That may be, but a hundred and twenty degrees is a bit much for my taste."

"You get used to it. Plus as they always say..." In the most obnoxious voice I can manage and with a ridiculous grin on my face I say, "It's a dry heat."

He laughs, surprised. "That is probably the best impression of Walter I've ever heard."

For a moment I'm stunned into silence. I can't believe he knows who Jeff Dunham and all his lovable friends are. Then I bust out laughing. It takes me a minute to settle and catch my breath. "Yes, Walter is by far one of my favorites. Peanut, however, takes the cake."

"Ah, lest we forget our dear friend Peanut." His smile lights up the room. "Jeff Dunham is my favorite comedian. I got to meet him once and was surprised to find out that he is just as funny in real life as he is onstage."

"Mr. Michaels, I do believe I'm officially jealous now." I smile.

He laughs some more. "I'm sure we could arrange a chance for you to meet him. You are, after all, the CEO of the largest PR firm in the world."

"Non-active CEO," I correct him.

"Oh, I think that has officially changed as of today. You were absolutely brilliant with Trinity this morning. I'm not sure I have had the chance to thank you properly for handling that. I have no doubt that had you not stepped up, I would be facing off with her about this story." He shrugs and his smile starts to fade. "I have to admit that having this story squashed was the first thing I thought of when all this went down. I don't like my private life plastered all over every news outlet in the world. But in the end, letting it run seems like the best thing I could do for Layla, as messed up as that may sound."

I can't help but continue smiling at him. I'm completely in awe of the fact that he can take this whole situation in stride and be so determined – no matter what the cost is to him – to let this story run its course. "I hope you realize, if I had it my way this story would die before it even had a chance to blossom. I don't at all like the thought of all those tabloids having a go at you because of something your ex-girlfriend did. However, I will accept the fact that this is solely your decision to make. Should you change your mind, though, we have until noon our time tomorrow to try and stop it."

"Forget it. Not going to happen. Though I am truly sorry that a child is going to be dragged along by a mother that can't seem to make good choices. No doubt, in the long run, he will be the one to suffer. Especially if she never discovers who the father is."

The tone of this conversation has gone from playful to gloomy quickly. "Ok, enough about her and about business," I say. "This is our date and it's time to discuss something else." I smile a genuine smile. "So, we have discovered that we both like Jeff Dunham, what other type of entertainment do you enjoy?"

"I love music, live music especially. I enjoy local unknown bands more than I do the mainstream, or even those with record labels. The passion that comes with the music they play inspires me." I'm happy to see that his smile has returned and his eyes warm again.

"I could not agree with you more on that. I love live music. I do enjoy the mainstream artists that write their own music. Lyrics speak volumes, and to hear them sing something that has been written solely for the purpose of expressing themselves make me the happiest."

"Why is that?"

"Because I usually feel a better connection to the song. Take the winners of those reality shows. Sure, they get singing contracts with a pretty big label, but they are at the mercy of what their new managers and or 'crew' think they should be doing and singing."

"Very well said. Not sure I could have said it better myself. Music is a pretty big passion of mine, personally. Writing music is something I enjoy doing. A lot." His smile has reached his eyes, causing a slight crinkle in the corner. He looks very carefree, younger even.

"Really? I never pegged you for a songwriter, Tristan. A director or even an author maybe, but a songwriter?" I get a little flurry of butterflies in my stomach, mainly because I'm certain that I'm about the only person that knows this about him. "There is a bit of irony in the fact that you like to write songs."

"Oh?" He is looking at me with an intent expression on his face. "Why is that exactly?"

"Because not only do I love music, I play music and sing."

He actually looks surprised at my response. "I think that is something I am going to have to hear for myself."

"Good luck with that." I purse my lips. "I have not sung in front of anyone on purpose since my junior year of high school."

"Why did you stop?" He asks the obvious follow up question.

Shit. Can I tell him this, or do I just brush it off? I'm not sure that I'm really ready to go into why I don't sing anymore. "I'm not really sure you want me to answer that question."

He frowns. "Cami, I wouldn't have asked the question if I didn't want the answer. However, I will respect you not wanting to answer—"

"It is because of Bobbie," I blurt out.

"How does Bobbie have anything to do with you not wanting to sing?"

The question has me wanting to answer. Tristan doesn't deserve secrets. Plus, my hesitation is more to do with not wanting to talk about Bobbie. "It wasn't so much that he didn't want me to sing, simply that he felt I wasn't good enough." He nods gingerly and I continue with my tale. "During my junior year of high school I became friends with a group of girls who, one day, decided that we should start a band."

I take a deep breath, trying very hard to settle my nerves, but then I remember the very expensive

Cosmopolitan sitting in front of me and take a big swig. God it's good.

"I took piano lessons as a kid and continued with them when I went to boarding school. In third grade I received a very nice acoustic guitar, anonymously, and decided to teach myself how to play. I was good. Still am good." Ok stop babbling and get to the point. I look up from my Cosmo and Tristan is looking at me, his eyes warm, almost liquid. A gentle smile on his face, a smile of encouragement that I've never seen from him, or from anyone for that matter. The smile gives me the confidence to continue.

"But anyway, it wasn't until my junior year of high school that I really got to play with other people. Evelyn – my mom – had passed away and I'd convinced Bobbie to let me finish out high school in the States. Some of my friends from school wanted to start a band and asked me to join. We jammed really well together, but when we started rehearsing cover songs we discovered that the girl, Jessica, that wanted to sing, really couldn't sing. Everyone took turns at giving the songs a go. Lisa could sing nicely enough, so I was thinking that they would stop there and just let us continue with her as our lead singer. But after Lisa was finished, Jessica said, 'Let's let Cameron have a try.'"

I'm blushing now, remembering how it felt to put the microphone to my lips and start singing. "I was so embarrassed. I still am, just thinking about it. But I walked up to the microphone and we started to play Shakira's 'Underneath Your Clothes.'" I laugh at that. "God, how things have changed." Waving it off, I say, "Anyway, I was half a verse through the song and the next thing I knew I was the only one playing as all three girls were flat-out staring at me. When I realized this I stopped, but they said 'why did you stop?' They said I was awesome and immediately promoted me to lead singer. Eventually I started to get over my stage fright, and we practiced and practiced."

Deep breath, here it comes. Looking down at the table, I continue, "Then one day we were practicing at Jessica's house and, unbeknownst to me, my father was in the house because he and Jessica's dad had some business to attend to. When you live in Hollywood, everyone knows everyone. Anyway, apparently – and I only found this out later from Jessica's dad – Bobbie got completely sidetracked from whatever they were doing because he could hear us practicing in the garage. According to Jessica's dad, Bobbie was so engrossed in what he was hearing that he just stood there listening. You know Bobbie; when he hears talent, he pounces.

"So, after we finished the song, Bobbie comes out to the garage where we were set up. Starts raving about how awesome we sound, so on and so forth, but he doesn't see me in the room. I was bent down behind an amp. He asked us to play another song, and of course the girls agreed. Then I stood up, guitar strapped to my back, and I see Bobbie's mortified expression. He had no idea that I was part of the band. But he shrugged it off, maybe figuring I was just a guitar player. Every one of us had a microphone to our face because we all usually had some part in a song.

"As soon as we started to play, Bobbie's eyes lit up like Christmas. Then I started to sing, no back up, no nothing – just me, myself, and I. Bobbie's reaction was over the top. His face turned red. He started screaming at no one in particular and it was enough to make us all stop. Bobbie started yelling about how awful of a singer I was and that Jessica and her friends needed to find a new lead singer, so on and so forth. I am sure you get the idea."

Tristan's body is visibly shaking. His face betrays the fact that he's really pissed off. "I cannot believe that asshole. How could he do that to his own daughter?"

"He sent me to boarding school, remember?" I'm upset at telling the story, but also relieved that Tristan, though he's never heard me sing, is angry at Bobbie. It makes me feel important in a very strange way.

"In the long run I figured that it just had to do with Bobbie wanting to keep me from the industry and that he really thought I was a great singer. But as time went on, he proved otherwise. Anytime he would catch me singing or humming around the house he would yell at me and tell me to shut the hell up, though that is putting it mildly. When you put it into the whole picture of my and Mark's lives, he really did despise us on many different levels, especially after Mom passed away."

"Well, I doubt that you have a horrible voice. I would really love to hear you sing sometime." He is smiling now at the idea of hearing me sing. To my surprise, I realize that I actually want to sing for him.

FOURTEEN

TRISTAN

The idea of hearing Cami sing excites me to no end. How can I make this happen? There is the grand piano in my suite, but I'm really trying to behave tonight.

Norah Jones's "Come Away with Me" starts to play. The Goddess of Love is smiling on me. (Love – did I really just think that?) I take my cue, extending a hand to Cami. "Would you dance with me?"

"Uh..." She flushes a little, then says, "Yes."

I stand, her hand still in mine. Helping her to her feet, I walk us toward the dance floor. I turn and pull her into a warm embrace, and we start to move. She's a great follow; her movements mirror mine without her even seeming to think about it. "Is there anything you cannot do, Cami?"

She giggles. "I am sure there is plenty that I can't do, but I love to dance."

Wow. As I start considering the possibilities of dancing with Cami, she leans into me, pushing her breasts against my chest. Dammit! This girl is going to kill my good behavior if she keeps this up. I look down into her eyes. Her face is turned up slightly, looking like she wants to kiss me. Then her lips start to move. It takes me a minute to realize that it's no longer just Norah singing. Cami has started to sing along.

I inhale very sharply. Her voice is breathtakingly beautiful. She sounds a little like LeAnn Rimes; it's wild. I just stare at her. We continue to dance, without missing a beat. Then the song comes to a close.

"My God, Cami! That was absolutely beautiful."

"Thanks, Tristan."

She turns her head to the side, bringing her ear to rest on my chest, over my heart. Looking down, I see the faint flush of red coloring her skin. I hope I didn't embarrass her.

"That's the first time anyone has complimented me like that about my singing."

The music starts back up again with none other than Whitney Houston's "I Will Always Love You." At Cami's urging, we start to dance again. And she immediately starts singing again. Jesus, she can hit the notes with very little effort. It makes me wonder what her true range is.

Her singing is infectious and I find myself singing along, turning it into a duet. This time she's the one that’s staring.

When the song ends, she's panting slightly for air and giggles. "I think if I am going to do that again, I should really quit smoking." I laugh too because she is so damn cute when she laughs that it becomes contagious and I can't help myself.

"There are worse things you could do. Thank you, Cami, for the dance and your singing."

"Me? Man, Tristan. You can act, sing, dance. What other tricks do you have up your sleeve?"

I smile and laugh a little. "Oh, darling, you have seen nothing yet. But our dinner reservations are upon us. Are you hungry?

"Famished."

CAMI

We move away from the dance floor back toward our table, grabbing our drinks. Then we walk over to Caran. Tristan is ever the gentleman when it comes to escorting me through the restaurant to our table. The maître d' beats him to pulling out my chair, and he looks disappointed. It's kind of cute, actually.

We chat all through dinner. About anything and everything: our friends, the things we like to do for fun. I'm surprised to learn that Tristan loves to read books when he has the time. Even more surprising is that he has a degree in English Literature, and before his acting career took off he had full intentions of completing college with a Ph.D. so that he could become a college professor of English Literature.

"My mom had been doing everything she could to put me through college, and when she passed away I was left to find ways to pay for school. I managed school okay, but finding money from one month to the next became difficult when it came to food and necessities, until I found the add for extra's on *Love Is Burning.* I received a rather large advance prior to starting the shoot and was only about two weeks away from graduating. I was able to payoff my student loans, pay back the people that I owed, and make it through my last two weeks of school before filming began.

"I realized quickly, after I'd nearly spent every penny of my initial paycheck, that I'm truly crap with money. I was nearly broke when the filming started."

Laughing, I say, "Good thing you don't have to worry about that now."

"Honest to God, Cami, I can't even tell you or myself how much money is in my bank account right now. I just know when my credit card bills are due and I pay them."

"Sounds to me like you really need to meet Mick." I laugh.

"Who's he?" He's smiling from ear to ear.

"Mick is a financial advisor and planner. Also a good friend of mine. He was also Bobbie's main financial genius and also happens to be dating my best friend, Beau. Beau is, well, Beau. She's my best friend and my assistant who handles my day-to-day finances. She is also a brilliant artist." I pull out my iPhone and show him some of her work. He is duly impressed.

"So are you saying that I can have someone who handles my money for me?" He is positively laughing at this proposition.

"I have a confession." I pause for effect, and he raises an eyebrow at me. "I want to invite Mick and Beau to come out here on Wednesday so that they can spend next weekend with me." His face falls like I've just given him bad news, and my own smile fades in response. "What's wrong, Tristan?"

He doesn't answer right away. Instead he chews on the inside of his cheek, looking like he is mulling over his response. I nervously start to chew on my tongue ring. A long series of emotions flits across his face.

"Tristan, what's wrong? You actually seem upset."

"I just—" He takes a ragged breath. "It's just that next week is going to be a bad week for me. With the story dropping and all."

"Are you worried that Mick and Beau are going to either spill where you are or judge you because of a tabloid?"

"Yeah, I guess you can say that."

Oh boy. "Tristan, Mick used to work for Bobbie. He has been in and around Hollywood for as long as I've known him, though now he lives in Phoenix with Beau. He knows the business and he can be trusted. Beau has not been around Hollywood besides visiting, but she is not the type to gossip, and she would not run to a tabloid and tell them anything." I let out the breath I was holding in a rush. "You have nothing to worry about. Besides, they are a little miffed at me for running off right before my birthday. Apparently I spoiled some serious plans for Saturday night."

He's gawking at me. "Well, don't I feel stupid. I'm sorry, Cami. I didn't realize."

"I wouldn't expect you to know, Tristan."

He takes a long, steadying breath. "To be honest, the reason I'm kind of upset has more to do with the fact that I don't like the idea of having to share my time with your friends."

My heart sputters and a feeling of dread washes through me. Mick and Beau are the two single most important people in my life. After a beat, though, the dread turns to a warm sense of flattery at the fact that he wants to spend more time with me. And I quickly realize that I, too, want to spend a lot more time with him.

"I...I...think we can all four have a great time together. Mick and Beau are some of the best partiers and funniest people I know. I think you'll really like them. And I can almost guarantee that your anonymity will remain intact because they're the type of people that won't care." Though the idea does occur to me that Beau might spill the fact that I've had this obsession with Tristan for the last few years. She's not well-known for having a brain-to-mouth filter.

He pauses, then says, "All right, I trust you."

I release a breath that had gotten caught in the back of my throat at his admission of trust. "Thank you!" is all I can manage to say.

"So," he says gently. "You love the color purple, piercings, music, and tattoos." I raise an eyebrow at him, wondering where he is going with this. He continues, "What inspired your tattoos?"

I'm instantly praying that my face doesn't portray the shock I feel at his question. To be honest, no one has ever asked. Only admired my work. Beau knows, of course. She was with me when I got all of them.

I take a moment to take a sip of wine. "Well, the corset started off as the piercings. I saw one in a tattoo magazine somewhere and I thought it was really cool. Had I known then how much pain I was going to have to go through, I might have thought twice. Fortunately, X, my tattoo artist and piercer, has a very cool contraption that actually completed six of the piercings at a time. So I only had to go through it four times." I watched him wince. "I decided to tattoo it later after X brought up the idea of how cool it would look to fill it in like an actual corset."

Taking another sip of my wine, I move on to the next piece. "Next came the shoulders. Beau actually drew up the design. I wanted to portray good and evil, and she knows my affection for tribal. I'm constantly battling with good verses evil, or bad. Growing up the way I did, I had religion forced on me at the boarding school I attended. I constantly challenged the teachers and priests with their religious logic, pointing out the holes in what they preached. But despite my 'anti-religious' arguments at school, I do still believe in God, or a higher power. So Ariel and Lucy were born and inked." I stop talking, not entirely sure that I can explain the wings.

"And..." His voice is soft, welcoming. "The wings?" he asks.

"Yeah, those."

Pausing for more than a few moments prompts Tristan to say, "It's okay, Cami." He takes my hand across the table. "You don't have to tell me if you don't want to." Taking in my expression, he quickly adds, "I know how hard it can be to discuss something so personal."

Instant respect and gratitude warms my heart at his words. He gently begins stroking the back of my hand.

"It's not so much that I don't want to tell you, Tristan. It's more that..." I feel my throat tighten. "The wings were my first, at barely nineteen. I wanted to fly away, away from life, away from Bobbie, away from my past, and having the wings on my back gave me the freedom I needed." I feel my eyes prick with tears. "I finally felt free of the burden of never really knowing my mother. And of hating my father for the fact that he was never there for me when I needed him. When I was growing up."

I have to stop talking. Bowing my head, I start to chew on my tongue ring again. It's been nearly six years since I've thought about my wings. "I love them, of course. They've become a part of who I am. And every time things get rough, they remind me that I have the power to fly away," I whisper, and Tristan's grip on my hand tightens.

"Thank you for sharing that, Cami. You and your wings are beautiful." Lifting my hand again, he kisses each of my knuckles, slowly, respectfully.

"What about you, Tristan? What about your dragon?"

He instantly stops stroking my hand. Afraid that I've offended him, I peer at him through my lashes.

"Cami...I..." Using his free hand he takes a very large, draining gulp of his wine. He swallows, then wipes his lips with his napkin. His eyes lower to mine, covered in pleading need. "Cami, I..." He stutters again. "I appreciate your sharing your story. And while I want to share mine with you, I'm not ready."

Lifting our intertwined hands, I repeat his previous gesture: I bring his hand to my lips and slowly, I kiss each knuckle, communicating my acceptance of his request to wait to tell me his tale.

After we finish our wonderful meal, Tristan and I take to the beach for a walk along the dark blue waves. In one hand I carry my shoes. My other hand is in Tristan's. He hasn't let go since I told him about my tattoos.

Holding Tristan's hand while walking down the beach feels like nothing I've ever felt before. It is warm and tender, and there is this constant current that keeps passing through our hands straight into my soul. It sparks at my heart and the center of my core, right between my legs. God, I want this man so bad.

"So tell me," I say, as much to take my mind off ripping his clothes off as because I'm curious. "How did you get into acting?"

He ponders his response for a moment.

Taking a deep breath, he begins his story. "I never wanted to be a Hollywood actor. I enjoyed the idea of plays in high school and college. I had performed in several throughout my academic career. My mom passed away during my freshman year in college. She had been my support system, paying for tuition, room, board, and books. When she passed away she left me with enough money to finish out my degree in the necessities, such as tuition, room, and board, but very little in the way of living expenses. She had saved my tuition money, but the money she gave me for living expenses had come from working, so I lost that when she passed. I managed to survive a little, but it got to the point that I needed to take out student loans and grants in order to support myself further. During my senior year, I was broke, horribly broke.

"When I came across an ad seeking extras for a movie that was filming near campus, needing the extra money, I decided to go for the audition. The gig was going to pay enough to get me through the next month until my last round of assistance came through and I graduated. What I was going to do after graduation, I had no clue. But at the time it was going to be enough.

"So I went to the audition, performed my lines, and was asked the questions I now know to be standard about my acting career. Which of course was limited to small-time stage acting. The people I auditioned for were not impressed because I had no on-camera experience, not even a commercial. And Cami, if you want the truth of it, stage acting and camera acting are no different, except that while performing they can yell cut and make you do it over and over and over again." His eyes rolled around in his head as he said this. I laughed at his expression of mock horror. He laughed with me.

"I walked away from the audition feeling rejected. I didn't see what the big deal was; it was only a part for an extra. Around 8:30 that evening I received a phone call direct from one of the movie's producers, requesting that I come back the next morning. I had class, but given that this was important, and I never skipped class, I figured what the hell.

"He was a fast talker but finally cut to the point and told me that he was going to be emailing me some lines from the movie and that he wanted me to practice them and have them ready the next day.

"When I received the email I was confused because the attachment had the lines of the main character, Dakota, and I knew enough about casting that if they were casting extras, the mains were already cast. When I finally just got over it, hoping for an explanation the next day, I started to practice the monologue. It was the part in the movie where Dakota begins to realize that he is falling in love with Alyssa." He pauses, wanting to see my reaction. Is he trying to confirm that I've never seen the movies?

"I don't know about that part in the movie, but I know about it from the first book," I say. "It was a pretty powerful part, and to me it seems the perfect section for you to portray Dakota in an audition."

He nods. "Well the catch to this is that I had never read the books, and most of all, I had little context to go on when reading the lines. By the time I went to bed around three in the morning, I had the lines memorized and I was ready, but overwhelmingly nervous. I laid there in bed, awake, trying desperately to figure out how best to move, how best to bring my whole body into the dialogue. Had I known then what the scene really entailed, I could have done it better, but apparently what I did was good enough.

"Eventually I fell into a fitful sleep, and I awoke around seven, well before the ten o'clock audition. I sat down and did a little bit of Internet research about the movie. I discovered that the guy originally cast was having a hard time with the producers and crew, so he was fighting his way out of his contract. I also gathered from the various blogs that he was not going to be missed by the *Love is Burning* fans. Which of course had me that much more nervous.

"It was very evident to me that there was quite the following for the books and that the fans were eager to see it on the big screen. I should have known then that this was something I should have stayed away from." He laughs.

"Obviously the audition went well," he continues. "I was forced to hire Bold on at the last minute because the day after my audition they called and told me they were going to offer me the part of Dakota. I was forced into an appointment the next morning at eleven to go over the contract. I desperately wanted the job and I knew that if I couldn't meet their demands, I was going to be replaced."

"Is that how you met Bobbie?" I asked. There's a little stab at my heart when I bring my father into the conversation.

"When I called Bold, I told them who I was." He laughs. "Which meant jack shit until I told the person on the phone that I was being offered the part of Dakota for the upcoming *Burning* movies, and then I was transferred directly to Bobbie. Bobbie wanted to speak with me personally, so I agreed to meet him at a café near campus."

"That sounds exactly like something Bobbie would do." I grimace. I can't help feeling hurt knowing that Bobbie would drop everything for the next big thing but couldn't be bothered for most of his life to pay attention to his own kids. I'm somewhat jealous of Tristan's relationship with my father, I realize. I wish Bobbie had shown even half as much interest in me.

FIFTEEN

Tristan must be able to sense my distress because he says, "I never would've imagined that the professional Bobbie and the home life Bobbie were so different. To be honest, Cami – and for this I'm sorry – I didn't even know that he had a daughter. But then again, Bobbie never talked about himself. It was always more important to talk about business."

"That's not a shock to me, Tristan, believe me. I wish it was at least a little. He was always the type of person that couldn't let his personal life clash with business. After I graduated from high school, I had to make an appointment – with his secretary, mind you, and under a different name – in order to tell him that I was leaving for college." In the glow of the moonlight I can see Tristan's face darken. "Mick was the one exception to that rule."

When he calms and the color in his cheeks returns to normal, he asks, "What do you mean?" His voice is tense.

"Mick is the only person I ever had regular contact with who was an employee of my father's. He was the one that took care of my money, invested it, and then taught me the ways of money through a very generous trust fund my father had given me, part of which came to me upon high school graduation, then another part on college graduation, and then—" I come to a sudden halt as realization dawns.

After a beat, Tristan says, "Whoa, Cami, where'd you go on me?" Concern etched his features.

"I just remembered the last part of my trust fund."

"Oh, and that is what exactly?"

I start walking again. "My twenty-fifth birthday brings me the last of my trust money from my father. Provided the trust is still active." Not that another ten million dollars was going to be noticed within my accounts.

Slowly walking down the beach, feeling the wet sand between my toes, thankful that I'd remembered to remove my thigh highs when I went to the bathroom, I'm really starting to think about Bobbie. "Assuming that the trust is still active and that Mick didn't manage to get the balance of the trust after Bobbie's passing, given that I'd already graduated college, my twenty-fifth birthday brings the final installment.

"It's taken me a year to realize that he really is gone, never to return, and the last couple of weeks have made me realize that I will never be graced with fatherly knowledge. For years I'd held out hope that he would come around, that he'd be my dad, that he would be there for me when I needed him, and that's gone."

Tristan grabs my elbow, stopping my steps, and pulls me back to him. He takes in the tears that have started to fall down my cheeks and pulls in a sharp breath.

"Sweet Cami, don't cry."

"I can't help it. I tried for years to hate him, but I never could. Some of the little things he did made me realize that somewhere, deep down, he really did care. Despite the argument we got into the night I found out about my trust, I was torn inside. I said so many nasty things to him, and yet, a couple mornings later, he was there to see me leave for Phoenix. It wasn't until he started to email me while I was at college that I understood that he was starting to come around. He invited me to premieres, including your first, in fact."

He pulls back slightly to look at me. Puzzled. "I couldn't make it," I explain. "It was during finals week, and the timing was horrible." Taking a deep breath, I continue, "Despite the emails, the attempts to see me, to get me to L.A., he didn't show up at my graduation, and he died a couple weeks later." My tears are hot against my cheeks, and they are soaking into Tristan's shirt. Fighting to regain control of myself, I feel that I need to let Tristan ask the questions rather than just tell him everything. His arms are tight against me, and I look up at him. His beautiful face is taught with anger.

"Tristan?" Slowly he looks at me. The adoration and admiration in his face are clear. Something shifts in him as he looks at me. Something that I can't explain or even understand.

"Why—" I start, whispering. "—are you so angry?" I finally manage to get out.

"Cami, I'm angry because of your father. Whether you were you or someone else, it doesn't matter. No child deserves the neglect and anguish you suffer from now. You father should have been there for you, and he wasn't and that angers me. My mother was never rich. She worked hard and fought harder to give me everything I needed in life, no matter what the cost. I know, even though she is gone, that she loved me then and still loves me now." He pauses and I can hear him swallow, hard. His heart rate increases its rhythm against my ear. "No child should ever feel that kind of neglect, and I'm sorry that you have to endure it from now until forever."

He pulls away, lifting my chin so that I'm looking straight up at him, and he kisses me. Softly, gently. A feeling of warm comfort washes over me. The kiss is sensual and far from sexual. Kissing him back, I realize that I've forgotten our conversation of the last few minutes. All I can think about is Tristan and his kiss.

After what feels like an a very long time, he slowly pulls back. Taking a few deep breaths, Tristan asks, "So when do you turn twenty-five?"

"Next Saturday." I say, matter of fact.

"Well then," he says. "I think a true celebration is in order next Saturday." He is smiling now. "I'm sure your friends Mick and Beau would love to help me set up a twenty-fifth birthday celebration for you."

I let out a very strained giggle. "You have no idea."

We walk on in silence for a while, my thoughts drifting from Bobbie to Evelyn. My mother's passing had meant little to me at the time. I didn't know, let alone fully understand, the gravity of her loss until Bobbie had passed and I was twenty-three years old without any parents. Okay, my parents didn't really qualify as parents most of the time. But the bottom line was that even if I wanted them, they were gone.

I notice that Tristan starts falling behind me, and I slow my pace so he can catch up. I look at him as he studies my face for a moment.

"A penny for your thoughts?" he says. He's smiling, but his eyes still show their concern at my tears.

"I have paid a therapist thousands for my thoughts, and you offer up a penny." I giggle and blush. His smile grows bigger, but the concern is still there. "But thank you for that. And to be honest, I was actually thinking about Evelyn."

"Who is Evelyn?" he asks, cocking his head at me. We come back together and stop. He sits down in the sand, stretching out his legs. Patting his leg he says, "Have a seat." Looking at him dubiously, I turn and lower myself onto his lap. He leans back slightly and I turn to my right so that I can face him.

"Evelyn is my mother." He looks at me, a puzzled expression on his face. "She passed away when I was sixteen." He shakes his head. "Don't fret, Tristan. I wasn't close to either of my parents. Evelyn passed away from a cancer that neither Mark nor I were aware of until after her passing." He's stopped smiling. He appears as though he to wants to say something, but can't quite find the words.

"Cami...I...I am very sorry."

"Please, Tristan, it's all right." I can feel my eyes starting to become thick with tears again. I try to blink them back. But the tears aren't for Bobbie or Evelyn or even myself. They are for the look in Tristan's eyes. "Tristan, what are you thinking about? You look like you're upset."

He doesn't answer me, simply reaches up to cup my cheek in his palm. He gently strokes the stray tear from my eye. "Please don't cry, Cami. I'm sorry that I asked. I didn't expect it to be this—"

"Stop. I'm fine." It's more of a plea than an order. "It is the look in your eyes that is bringing on my tears. Please, talk to me?"

"I am not sure where to start. I never knew my father. He was gone long before I was born. My mother raised me by herself. She took pride in caring for herself and me. She loved me exactly like a mother should love a child, and it pains me to see the pain in your eyes at the loss of a mother and father who did not care for you the way that they should have." He's speaking so quietly that it's nearly a whisper.

I can see in his eyes that he has more to say. "Please go on," I tell him.

"She passed away during my freshman year in college. Much like your mother, it seems, mine had been sick for years, but had never told me with what, or why. I could only guess at the pain she suffered from not being able to be honest and tell me. She had always said it was better for me that I not know."

I place my hand on his cheek. "We're both a little messed up, huh?" I say, smiling slightly.

His chuckle comes out a little breathy. "Yeah, I guess we are. Do you miss them?"

That is the million dollar question that I've been trying to answer myself. But I decide to have my best go at it, thinking that if I talk it out I can find a way to understand. "I do miss Bobbie some. But only because he finally started to turn a small leaf after I had left the house for college. It wasn't much, but we communicated via email. He filled me in on how things were going with the business and so on. It was not a great reunion, just simple little things. Now that I get none of that, I miss it."

"I can understand that, more than you know," he says. I smile then.

Both of us coming from parentless situations could be a good thing, I suppose. It is, after all, something we have in common. And we'll never have to fight about where to have Christmas. Wait...did I really just think that?

Tristan takes a deep breath. The energy shifts between us, and I can tell he's about to change the subject. Which is just fine with me. I've had about all the heavy conversation I can take for one night.

"Tell me, Cami, since you're here, and not in Phoenix, what in the world shall we do for your birthday?"

I smile big. It's the perfect subject to lighten the mood. "Well, Beau and Mick will be here. We can hang around the hotel and the island, or we could..." Words fail me for a minute. "I don't know." I giggle. "It's not the birthday girl's job to plan her party."

He is beaming now. "Well, I'm completely confident that we can come up with something."

"Oh, really? Like what?"

TRISTAN

Instead of answering, I lift my hands, grabbing hold of her wrists, and gently pull her into me. Slowly I bring my hands around her back, holding her to me. When we were standing a little while ago, I really enjoyed the feel of her body against mine. Pulling her closer and tighter to my body, I start to rub her back, mindful of her corset and concentrating more on her shoulders.

She lets out a deep sigh. I am so comfortable sitting here like this with her. I kiss the top of her head, content to say nothing for a few minutes.

Listening to Cami talk about Bobbie and about her past nearly broke my heart. I am still very angry at Bobbie for what he did, not understanding why it is that he would act the way that he did toward her. If Cami's mother had anything to do with Bobbie's unwillingness to be a part of her life, then maybe that is why things changed after Evelyn passed away. Cami didn't say much about her mother, but I imagine that she knows very little about her.

Bobbie left this world far too soon, and he owed his daughter an explanation for his actions. She deserves closure, and it hurts that she will never have that. I wish there was some way – any way – that I could give her that. The only thing I know I can do is care for her, respect her, and give her all the things she needs.

Financially she seems pretty set. Though I don't know what her trust entails or has entailed over her previous installments, I know that Bobbie was pretty well-off. I'd been to his house before, and no doubt when he died, that house was worth about forty million dollars.

"You said earlier today that the role of CEO was bequeathed to you via Bobbie. How did that come about?" I ask her. I'm not sure that this is the best time to bring this up, but I'm curious, and I guess I would rather discuss it now, while the emotions are fresh and raw, than try and dig them up later.

"His will. He left Mark and me each fifty percent of his net worth, plus his house. I got the business, and Mark took his money and ran. He and Bobbie never had any type of relationship whatsoever. He was eighteen when Evelyn passed away, so he took his cue and ran off to college."

"But if Mark was older, why did Bobbie give you the business? Clearly it was something you either don't want or weren't ready for." I want to keep her talking, in an attempt to understand her better.

She doesn't hesitate. She pulls back to look at me. "Bobbie had written his will in such a way that if I didn't take over as primary shareholder of Bold, the business would be broken up and sold with all profits going to charity." She starts to chew on her tongue ring again, but after a moment continues. "Trinity, Vincent, and a few of the board members had determined that it would cost more than Bold was worth to buy out of its existing contracts, and no one, not even me, had the kind of capital it would take to do so. We found the loophole that meant that I could be named as CEO and primary shareholder without full-time participation in the business itself. It was decided that I would be the 'non-active' CEO until I decided to step into the role as a functional CEO. Which is something I'm being pressured into by Trinity and Vincent as we speak."

"Why not take over the role?" I ask, trying to understand. "Would it really be that difficult?"

She shakes her head at me. "No, at least that is what I'm being told. Trinity seems to think that it would be more of an image than anything. Bold hasn't pulled in very many new clients because it is starting to be obvious that it is without leadership. If I step into that role, Bold would stand a very good chance of being brought back to the top of its game. The only thing really holding me back is that I have no clue how to run a business, and I'm afraid to give up my freedom."

I smile at her. "Well, I don't know what went on with Bobbie in his office, but he was out in the public a lot, attending events. And a lot of times he was there to support his clients. I have no doubt that if you Google Bobbie's name, a lot of articles and images will come up about his presence in and around Hollywood. Maybe that might help with some insight on what he did."

"Maybe, I don't know. I wanted to be able to get my feet wet in the business, build up to it, but Trinity seems to think that I have a keen business sense and that I can do a lot of good for Bold."

I laugh. "After this morning, I have no doubt that what she says is true." I begin rubbing her back again, attempting to coerce her forward, to bring her head back to my chest and snuggle into me.

She complies and says, "I'm starting to think that you, along with Trinity, are right, and it is another of the reasons why I came out here. I don't need the money, but I need something constructive to do. The work on my condo in Phoenix is nearly done, and I spend a lot of my days doing very little. It's actually getting a little boring." She laughs.

"I can imagine it would get boring after a while."

"I've thought about returning to college for a doctorate, but given that I have an amazing job already lined up, I didn't see the point."

"You don't have to decide today. But it's nice to know what your thoughts are on the idea. When you say you don't need the money, what do you mean?" My heart skips a beat. "I'm sorry, Cami, it's none of my business. I shouldn't have asked."

"Stop, it's all right. I mean that when I received the first installment of my trust fund, it was worth far more than its intended amount. Mick has the Midas touch when it comes to finances, and he has nearly tripled the amount of my trust. Combined with the inheritance, the sale of the house in L.A., my stock with Bold, my condo, and other investments, if my net worth were made public it would land me on the list just inside the top one thousand of the world's richest. Maybe even higher. Mick manages all of that. I have three accounts that are replenished monthly from another source. I use that money for all of my expenses and whatever else I want. But believe me when I tell you that I live modestly. I own my condo free and clear, and I've paid cash for all of its remodel. I drive an Audi Q7 SUV, but I have a toy hiding in the garage."

My mind is spinning over her disclosure, and I'm obviously shocked by the fact that she doesn't hardly know, nor care, what kind of money she has. Obviously, my buying her a drink last night had less to do with money and more to do with how beautiful she was, but the amount of money she has is just...wow. Now it all makes sense: Versace, the first-class ticket, the suite, being here, her own expensive drinks. "You know I don't care about your money, right, Cami?"

She nods. "Yes, Tristan, I know. I don't flaunt it, and outside of Beau and Mick, you are now the third person who knows."

"None of your other friends know?" I feel my brows knit together.

"No. Jolene and Naomi obviously know that money is no object, but they have no idea to what extent.

The Q7 I drive, while it looks expensive, is still less than sixty thousand dollars. The one in the garage and my condo will give me away."

That's the second time she's mentioned the car in the garage. Obviously this is something she is excited to share, so I have to ask. "What's in the garage?"

She laughs. "A custom, purple-with-electric-green-racing-strips Audi R8 Spider."

My jaw drops. I'm speechless. She starts laughing, and the tension of the evening with putting all of our woes out there is instantly broken as she falls off my leg, laughing uncontrollably.

"Holy shit!" I say, joining her in laughter. Slowly she starts to calm down.

She sobers eventually, and I pull her back onto my lap. Wrapping my arms around her I say, "Cami, it means the world to me that you have been so open with me tonight. I imagine that talking about Bobbie and Evelyn is very difficult. Talking about Joanna, my mom, is never an easy thing to do." Pulling her tighter against my body, I kiss her hair again. "Thank you," I whisper.

"No, Tristan, thank you. It's really nice to be able to talk about it. Talking to a therapist is one thing, but to be able to talk about it with you is refreshing, so thank you." She wraps her arms around my chest and squeezes, pulling her body further into mine.

I can feel my heart rate speed up some at her touch, spreading the warmth of wanting through my body, and I feel as though I could sit here with her forever.

I can feel her breasts pressed against my chest, her hands roaming along my back, and I can feel my dick hardening at her body being pressed against mine. My heart starts pounding harder, and I can feel my heartbeat pulsing through my growing erection. I'm slightly embarrassed that after such an intense conversation my little brain decides that now is the time to become hard again. He took a nap once we started discussing Bobbie and Cami's past, but now, he's ready, aching, and searching again. A perpetual hard-on is something I have grown used to in the last twenty-four hours.

Cami is looking back at me, her eyes screaming desire, want, and need. Ready and willing to have me. "Please don't look at me like that, Cami. I know what you're thinking, and trust me when I say this, I want you too, but I'm just not ready. Not tonight, please."

I'm afraid that if we end up in bed before we are both ready for it, this will just end in disaster. Cami deserves to have more than a man who wants her body. While I want her body, I realize that I want her heart and her soul to belong to me.

"Tristan, please don't take this the wrong way, but I understand and I am not ready either."

I nod at her and bring my lips to hers, kissing her. Sweet and sensual, much like before. Desperate to control my breathing, I remind myself that I'm trying to comfort her, not bed her. Not tonight. I feel the head of my cock throb as my brain regains control of my erection. My brain and my heart are being lost to Cami. It's a loss I will gladly take and enjoy.

SIXTEEN

CAMI

What am I doing here? Looking down the length of my body, I can see my nipples, erect and throbbing. A warm sensation radiates out from my sex. Peering past my breasts, I see down between my legs a head of dirty blonde hair. The sensation of warm, wet licks on my cleft. My body shudders in response to a building orgasm. My legs stiffen as my orgasm builds, as the man between my legs continues stroking his tongue along my most intimate folds.

I reach down, intertwining my fingers in his hair, tugging slightly as my orgasm starts to take me. He lifts his head and I'm met with the beautiful, warm, blue eyes of Tristan Michaels.

"Come for me Cami," he breathes across my clit.

And I come.

My eyes fly open. I'm trembling and breathing heavily. "Tristan." There's no response. I look down my body: I'm in my tank top and shorts, the sheets on my bed are askew, and my sex is wet and warm in the familiar aftermath of an orgasm.

"What the..." I trail off, realizing that I was dreaming about Tristan between my legs. My heart lurches at the emptiness I feel thinking about him, wishing he were here. I hope against hope that he will join me on the beach later today. Stretching, I roll over onto my stomach and search for my pillow, begging to go back to sleep. I catch a glimpse of the clock and see that it is ten in the morning. I groan.

Stumbling my way into the sitting room, I see sitting atop the dining room table two dome-covered plates. Padding over to the table, I notice that on my coffee table is a small vase containing one yellow rose in beautiful full bloom. I smile. This has to be Tristan's doing. The gesture is too nice to worry too much about the fact that he sent someone to my suite while I was sleeping.

Lifting the lid off of the closest dome, I see toast, eggs, bacon, and sausage. Lifting the lid off of the other dome reveals a quad stack of pancakes. I lick my lips and take a seat, diving in with gusto as my stomach rumbles.

After eating, I change into my bikini and pull my hair up. As I'm wrapping my sarong around my waist, there is a knock at the door. I freeze momentarily and my heart swells at the idea that it might be Tristan. I call out, "Who is it?" as I reach the door.

"Tyson."

I pout. Then smile because I pouted at the fact that it's not Tristan.

I've been sitting out on the beach since about eleven thirty this morning, getting waited on by a couple of cabana boys. It's been very relaxing. Looking out across the water at the low hanging sun, I debate on whether to head on up to my room to tame my growling tummy or finish reading this sexy scene in the book I'd started on the plane when a shadow appears over my book. I feel the hair on my arms stand on end as the electricity of his proximity sends a current through me.

"How are you not a lobster by now?" His tone is teasing, playful. He walks around to sit on the chair next to me.

I laugh. "It's called sun block and an umbrella." I raise my eyes to the beach umbrella over my head.

"What exactly is the point of sitting on the beach if you are blocking the sun with an umbrella?" I love his bantering.

"Well, if you've been watching me as much as I think you have—" I smirk at him, "—then you have seen the umbrella go up and down throughout the day." I pause to take in the muscles in his neck, shoulders, and his chest; his dragon; his pecs and abs, perfectly defined; and the tiny sprinkle of hair that runs from his belly button into his shorts. Breathing heavier than necessary I say to him, "What took you so long to get down here?"

With a chuckle he replies, "Because, I was having way too much fun watching you. Though I nearly had a heart attack when I watched you untie your top. Plus, I was hoping for a glimpse." He is grinning wickedly now.

"You know, Tristan, all you have to do is ask." My mind briefly flashes back to how I woke up this morning, and I flush.

He chuckles again. "Well, if that's the case, then I'd like a peek."

I start laughing harder now. "I'll show you mine if you show me yours."

"Well, Ms. Enders, given that I'm not wearing a shirt, you can already see mine, so, you know, it's your turn." His voice has gotten lower and taken on a more seductive tone.

I blush at his logic and, as if I was willing them to do so, my nipples harden into tight peaks. Because of my barbells, it's nearly impossible to hide, and it does not go unnoticed. Tristan's grin gets even wider.

"Gah! That is so damn unfair," I mumble.

He laughs. "Why, because I can see your nipples through your top?"

I roll my eyes. "Yes, you get that view and I get what, exactly?"

Just then he stands up, and sure enough, he is hard as a rock. I blush, but am unsuccessful at peeling my eyes away from his erection.

"Feel better, Ms. Enders?"

That breaks my trance, and I throw my head back laughing. "You have no idea how much better I feel."

He smiles and sits back down. "Listen, I've arranged for a sunset boat ride for dinner tonight. Would you like to join me?"

I'm shocked by his casual tone and lack of self-consciousness about the fact that he has an erection. It's all I can think about right this moment, what it will feel like buried deep… I mentally shake my head to clear the thoughts. It's no use getting worked up now. "You say that as if you're hoping I have something better to do tonight than spend the evening with you." He grins at me. "I would love to, Tristan."

"Good. We leave in half an hour."

I gape at him. Thirty damn minutes. He's giving me thirty minutes to get ready for a date? Jesus, I hate men sometimes. "I...uh, should probably run upstairs and change," I say, breathless with irritation.

"No need. It's nothing fancy tonight. It's a nice boat and we'll be waited on hand and foot, but the dress code is casual. You have shorts here, and a t-shirt too. That is more than enough. I'm going in my t-shirt and swim trunks."

I'm speechless. Why in the world would he want me to have dinner with him in a bikini?

"There's a reason for the swim suits and casualness. You'll see," he says. I swear the boy can read my mind. "Want to grab a drink before we go?"

"Uh, sure."

I gather up my stuff, placing my book, t-shirt, water, towel, and sunscreen in my tote. I pull on my shorts and slip my feet into my flip-flops. Despite Tristan's assurances, I'm feeling self-conscious about being so underdressed. I'm sure my hot pink bikini bottoms are visible through these very short white shorts. And my hair is probably frizzy after being out in the sun for several hours. I doubt the half ponytail I've pulled it up into is doing much for me. At least I put on a little bit of makeup before coming down. I don't like going places undone. I usually keep up my appearance no matter what I'm doing, so being forced into going out with Tristan unkempt is a bit of a thorn in my side.

As we walk into Blu he leans over and whispers in my ear, "You look beautiful, Cami."

A smile creeps to my lips. How does he do that?

"It is just going to be you and me tonight, with the exception of a couple waiters and of course the boat captain."

I nod and decide to do everything I can to forget about what I look like.

We make our way up to the bar and Jessie is there.

"Hey, you two. How are you this afternoon?"

"Great." I smile at Jessie. "We're headed off to the harbor in a bit for dinner."

"I heard about that." He chuckles.

Tristan stiffens at my side.

"How did you know about that?" I ask.

"They asked me to bartend for you guys tonight."

Tristan relaxes almost immediately. "So will you be joining us tonight, Jessie?" he asks.

Jessie nods. "I'm just waiting for my replacements to come in. They should be here any minute, and then I will head over there. The boat is already ready to go, just need to take a few things with me. I understand the lady of the boat enjoys Cosmos and the gentleman of the boat enjoys buying her the finest that I can make." He's grinning at me and Tristan.

I look at Tristan, who is grinning like an idiot. He looks at me with an I'm-feigning-stupidity look. "What?" he breathes.

I laugh. "You are so bad. What am I going to do with you?"

Leaning into my ear, he whispers, "Oh, I can think of a few things." His breath caresses my ear and neck, causing shivers to run throughout my entire body. I grin at him.

"Can I get you guys your usual?" Jessie asks, interrupting the sensations and goose bumps forming along my body.

"Yes, please. On my tab." As I say this, Tristan scowls at me. "You look sexy when you're scowling. I should make you scowl more often." He dramatically deepens his scowl and then busts out laughing, unable to hold the deep scowl he was going for.

I join him in taking a seat at the bar while Jessie makes our drinks. As Jessie is wrapping up with our drinks his replacement arrive, and he quickly excuses himself to head off to the boat. Tristan and I sit back, enjoying our drinks and chatting about our day.

"Since you were obviously spending time paying more attention to me on the beach, what else did you do today?" I ask him.

"Talked to Tyson, took care of a few other things, planned our boat ride tonight, took a dip in my pool. Tyson plans to have two additional bodyguards fly out here Tuesday or Wednesday. Mainly because of the story, my anonymity, and of course, your protection."

"My protection?" I say, pointing at my heart.

"Yes. With the story and what I have planned for your birthday this weekend, the extra help will be good."

My jaw drops. "What in the world are you planning for my birthday?"

"You're just going to have to wait and see." He leans in and kisses my forehead. The kiss sends a layer of goose bumps across my skin.

Changing the subject since I know he won't tell me, I ask, "So what's the deal with Tyson? He seems like a nice guy. Are you guys friends?"

"He is probably my best friend. Despite the fact that he insists on calling me 'sir.'" He laughs a bit. "It's his way of keeping a professional image, but he fails most of the time. He is always there for me, and we usually spend a lot of our social time out together. He takes it upon himself to be responsible for me and my safety without hesitation." He's smiling, obviously reminiscing.

"That explains a lot. He does a good job of taking care of you." The wheels in my head begin to turn. "Does he have a girlfriend?" I ask. I try to sound innocent but fail miserably. Anticipating Tristan's reaction, I start to smile. He scowls at me and I laugh. Loudly.

"Why?" He growls.

His growl sends a shiver through me. So carnal. And it does things...down there. I try to laugh it off.

"Well." I put dramatic emphasis on the word and Tristan scowls again. I grin. "He hangs out with you all the time. Does he have someone in his life?"

"No, I guess he doesn't. Why are you so interested in Ty?" He is glaring at me now, so I play it up a bit.

In my best Austin Powers impersonation I let the drama fly from my lips. "Oh yeah, baby, he is so hot and sexy." I grin from ear to ear.

"And what the hell am I, chopped liver?" He starts smiling, so I know he is playing the game.

"No, you, Mr. Michaels, are by far the hottest, sexiest, most beautiful person I know." I blush at my barefaced words. I'm not usually so forthcoming.

But he senses my unease; he takes my hand in his and gently kisses my knuckles. Then he brings his lips to my jaw and plants sweet kisses along it until he reaches my ear. "You're very sweet," he whispers in my ear. I grin. Clearly my words have him uncomfortable or, at the very least, not knowing how to respond.

"To answer your question," Tristan says, "Ty has no problem with women. I just think he feels the need to stay single because of me. I wish he wouldn't because it would make things just a little more fun. If he has to be with me when ever I go out, or when I take you out to dinner, we could double."

I should probably just have this stupid grin tattooed on my face. "I have an idea," I say, enthusiasm evident. "Why don't I bring Jolene out with Mick and Beau? She is a hell of a lot of fun. Her and Tyson might hit it off. Then if they do, the six of us can do our thing and Tyson doesn't have to feel like the fifth wheel."

He is smiling and nodding in agreement. "That might not be a bad idea, though I hate the thought of trying to play matchmaker with him and making him feel obligated to entertain her. What if they don't get along?"

"I doubt that. Jolene is very outgoing and generally gets along with everyone. But, you do have a good point. Maybe we can just make a point to introduce them in a little more casual setting?"

"That might be better. I was thinking about bringing Travis out here, too. He and Tyson get along famously, so they would at least have each other to bullshit with."

"Is Travis single, too?"

Tristan just smiles. I'll take that as a yes and a dodge to my question.

"Then I'll bring Jolene and Naomi, you bring out Travis, and we can see who hits it off. If there is no real connection between the boys and girls, then the girls'll have each other and Ty and Travis will be more than capable of causing their own mischief."

"That's not a bad idea, Cami. I will take care of getting Travis here, and why don't you get Jolene and Naomi squared away. I was going to let Travis stay in my suite, so it sounds like we'll just need one more room for Naomi and Jolene."

"Perfect. I'll make the arrangements in the morning."

Just then Tyson shows up to usher us outside. I smile at him knowingly. I barely know the man and I'm trying to set him up on a blind date for an entire weekend.

I thought of Jolene for him because Tyson is so tall and big. Jolene is six feet tall and a very beautiful woman. Naomi, on the other hand, is short like me. She is the skinniest person I know, but she is beautiful in a tough-and-rugged kind of way. I don't know Travis at all, but I am hoping that in one fashion or another everyone ends up having a great time.

Tristan interrupts my thoughts. "What in the world are you thinking about so hard? I swear I smell something burning."

"Ha-ha, Mr. Funny Man!" I laugh. "I was just thinking about what we were talking about." I throw a significant glance at Tyson's back. I'm not sure how he would take the idea of being set up on a blind date.

"I will bet you a hundred dollars he blushes like a little school girl," Tristan says, and suddenly I'm the one blushing. "Hey, Ty?"

Tyson stops mid stride and turns to us. "Yes, Tristan?"

"Cami is trying to set you up on a blind date next weekend with one of her friends. She thinks that since you'll have to be with me the whole time and I intend to be with her as much as possible, you need a date too."

I am most definitely the color of a cherry as he says this. "Sure, make this all my fault," I mumble.

But Tristan was right; Tyson blushes as red as I am.

"Thank you, Cami, for thinking about me, but it really isn't necessary."

"It wasn't meant to be a set up," I protest. "Just simply thinking that since you have to follow Tristan around all the time, maybe you might want to have a good time doing it. Plus, it bothers me to see you off in a corner all by yourself."

He is blushing a little brighter now. "Is she blond." He says it more as a statement of fact than an actual question. Nothing he could have said would have surprised me more. I laugh out loud.

"Yes, and she is about six feet tall." His smile grows wider then.

"Well, Ms. Enders, you sure know how to pick 'em," Tyson says. Apparently I've nailed his type. Tristan is looking at me with approval.

"Then it's settled," I say, and I know I've got a smug grin plastered on my face. "Tristan is going to bring Travis out to Tarah, and I'll bring Jolene, Beau, Naomi, and Mick. We can have a big old party this weekend."

Tyson smiles and gestures toward a Jeep. "Sounds good to me. We ready to head out?"

"Yup, let's roll," Tristan says.

I climb into the back and Tristan joins me. Tyson hops into the driver's seat and we're off to the docks.

Tristan leans in and whispers in my ear, "I wouldn't have hesitated about them getting along if you had told me she was tall and blond. That's Tyson's favorite."

I giggle just as my cell phone rings. I pull it from my tote bag and check the caller ID. "Speak of the devils." I hit the green button. "Hi, Mick." Tristan smiles.

"Hi, Cams. How's the vacation going?"

"Absolutely excellent."

"I know that voice. You've met someone, haven't you?"

"Jesus, Mick, how can you tell from a two-word phrase?" I'm slightly embarrassed because Tristan is sitting right next to me.

"Because, Cams, I know you all too well and know what gets you excited, so it either means you got a new tattoo or you met a new man. Given that there are no charges on your platinum card for the tattoo shop in the hotel, I can only assume it's a man. So in that case you get my lecture. Be careful! Lecture over."

I start laughing. He really does know me pretty well. "Yes, Mick, trust me, I am."

"Does this have anything to do with the fact that Tristan Michaels is on the same island?"

FUCK! "How in the hell do you know that?" I'm practically shouting. Tyson's head whips around and

Tristan shakes his head at him. He returns his eyes to the road.

"Calm down, Cams. Trinity told me that he was there and that you were actually working at making your paycheck yesterday. She was proud of you and the way you took charge. She even said that it wouldn't be long before they had you as a full-time CEO."

I snort. "Yeah, okay, Mick."

"Don't discount it, Cami. She was really impressed with you yesterday. So, am I right? Is it Tristan Michaels?"

Mick is well aware of my obsession with Tristan, so I'm not surprised that he put two and two together. "I don't need to remind you to keep that little tidbit to yourself, do I?"

"No, you don't, Cams. I signed a non-disclosure agreement years ago that ties my tongue unless it comes to discussing it with the employees of Bold and, well, you, by all technical accounts, own Bold, so that means I can tell you whatever I know." He was being just like the Mick I know and love.

"Good, and you will find out on Wednesday."

"You're coming home?" Hope in his voice.

I giggle. "Hell no! I would move here if it wasn't going to cost me a near fortune every night."

"You can afford it." He laughs again. "If you're not coming home, how exactly am I going to see you?"

"I'm going to bring you, Beau, Jolene, and Naomi out here on Wednesday."

"Oh!" A hint of shock colors his tone, but not in a bad way. "Why?"

I'm laughing. "Twenty-four hours ago you were giving me hell because of my birthday on Saturday. I have decided that I want to spend my birthday here, so that means that you and the girls are getting on a plane and coming out here. So chop, chop! Make the arrangements, would you?" I laugh. Mick hates when I ask him to do things that are usually on Beau's list of things to do.

"Uh, Cams, can't Beau do all that?"

I laugh again at his Oh-dear-God tone. "Yes, I'm just giving you shit because I know you won't. Ask Beau for me, will you?"

"Call her yourself." He laughs knowingly.

"Fine, hang on." I pull up the three-way feature on my phone, hit Beau's number, and connect back with Mick. It's ringing. I roll my eyes when I realize I can hear Buckcherry's "Crazy Bitch" coming through Mick's line. Laughing, I say, "Jeez, Mick, you could've told me she was sitting right next to you."

"But that wouldn't be as much fun."

I pull my phone away from my ear and put him on speaker phone in anticipation of Beau's reaction.

"Tristan Michaels? Are you kidding me, Cams?" Beau squeals with excitement.

Tristan blushes a bright red.

"Maybe," I say back to her.

"Don't you dare hold out on me, Cams, I swear to God I will beat it out of you if I have to." She can no longer hide the fact that she is laughing now.

Tristan holds out his hand and nods toward the phone. I hand it to him, slightly nervous, but knowing Beau, this is going to be funny.

"How dare you threaten to beat my girl?" He is smiling and Beau squeals again. I can picture Beau sprawled out on the floor laughing.

"Your girl, huh?" Beau says, sobering quickly.

"If she will have me, then yes, my girl."

~~*~*~*

TRISTAN

I hold my breath, unsure of her reaction. I know it's moving fast, but I can't help it. I care for her so much already.

"I think we have already cemented the fact that I want to be your girl," Cami says. She's trying to scowl, but a huge grin keeps leaping back onto her face.

I let out my breath and smile back at her. Mick laughs, and Beau squeals again with excitement.

"Cams, you're dating Tristan Michaels?" she asks.

I'm holding my breath, waiting for her reaction. "Yeah, I guess I am. Is that ok with you, baby?" Cami is giggling again as she takes in my reaction. I know my face betrays the fact that I'm suddenly concerned about the fact that Beau might be able to control the outcome of my blossoming relationship with Cami.

Beau suddenly gets very quiet and then serious. "Cameron Enders, if he hurts you I will personally kick his ass. You hear that, Tristan? You had better be good to my girl. She means the world to me and I will not tolerate stupidity from you, you get me?"

The smile that was plastered on my face in an attempt to hide my discomfort falls. Mouthing to Cami, I ask, "Is she serious?"

"I am absolutely serious, Tristan."

I think I might throw up, but Cami just laughs. "I think he gets the point, Beau."

"Good! So I don't know what it is I am supposed to do, but I get the impression I'm gonna be earning my pay?"

Cami smiles, reaches up, and kisses me on the cheek. Whispering in my ear she says, "Don't worry about her, she is harmless. She is just a bit overprotective. We have a long history, and I will explain it later, okay?" I nod and smile, relaxing a bit now that Cami has reassured me of Beau's intentions.

"Yes, you're going to earn your paycheck. I need you to book four tickets from Phoenix to Tahiti on Wednesday. The passengers are you, Naomi, Mick, and Jolene. Tristan and I will take care of your transportation and rooms here on Tarah. Go ahead and set up your return trip for the following Wednesday. There are only certain days that you can get in and out of Tarah to Tahiti and then back to the States."

"Thank you, Cams!" she squeaks out.

"You're welcome. Now get to work and I will see you guys on Wednesday."

"Tristan?" Beau asked.

"Yes, Beau?"

"I look forward to meeting you, and I was only teasing you."

"Me too, Beau. And I know."

"Okay, good. Cams, I will talk to you later. I will email you our information as soon as I have it. Later, guys!"

"Bye," Cami and I say together. Cami is grinning as I hang up the phone.

"She's really not all that bad. She loves me and does her best to protect me. Beau was my freshman college roommate, and we have been inseparable ever since. We both look out for each other. I gave Mick the same speech when they started dating about six months ago."

I can't seem to wipe the smile off my face. My heart is warm with the idea of meeting Cami's friends and with thoughts of our upcoming weekend.

"What?" she squeaks.

"Are you more worried about her kicking my ass or me hurting you?"

"Her kicking your ass." She smiles and pats my leg.

"Good, then we have nothing to worry about."

I don't realize what has come out of my mouth until a moment or two later, and it's far too late to take it back. Also, I realize, I don't want to take it back.

I feel a sudden rush of adrenaline through my system as I realize that she hasn't protested and her mood hasn't changed. Is she really more concerned about Beau kicking my ass than me hurting her? She looks as high in the clouds as I am.

"Come on, our boat is waiting." I start to climb out of the Jeep and turn to take her hand, helping her down.

We head toward the docks and down to the rows of boats. Most of the boats docked here are huge. Ocean cruisers built for long trips on the sea.

We continue down the docks until we come across a boat that is beautiful, glossy black, and very sleek. Looks more like it is built more for speed than pleasure, but boy, she's beautiful. Leading Cami over to the ladder, I urge her to climb up.

"I know nothing about boats," she says.

"Neither do I, and it's not our responsibility to know anything about the boat. We are here to have a good time," I say, reassuring her that we really are not responsible for anything but ourselves tonight.

"Sounds like a great plan to me."

SEVENTEEN

I'm watching her climb the ladder, eagerly anticipating her reaction when she reaches the deck above. The hotel manager had offered me my choice of boats, and I chose this one because it will accommodate the kind of night I want to have with Cami. I really want to show her a good, casual time. Show her that I really can just be a normal guy.

I hear her gasp as she reaches the deck, and I smile, knowing she's seen the hot tub inside the screen-covered bow. We'll ride out to sea while enjoying the hot tub, then have a nice dinner on the deck, near the stern as the sun sets.

Once she's safely on board, I climb up and find her looking around. Her gaze fixes on a table near the hot tub that has been set with a bottle of champagne and fresh, bright red strawberries. I walk up behind her, wrapping my arms around her waist, and whisper in her ear, "Would you like some champagne? It's Bollinger. '99, I believe."

"Oh, one of my favorites. I'd love some, please." She turns slightly in my arms so that she can see me. "This is beautiful. Thank you."

I smile and bring my lips to hers in a chaste kiss. "You're most welcome." I release her, reach for the champagne, and pour us each a glass.

Today while we were apart, I missed her terribly. It was so hard to stay away from her, but I knew that I would make up for it tonight. It didn't take me long to recognize her down on the beach when I decided to go for a swim in the pool. When I looked down at the beach, there she was, lying on her stomach. Her corset and fairy wings were hard to miss, even from eight floors up.

It wasn't hard to stay hidden. Every so often she'd look up and scan my balcony, then look away again with clear disappointment on her face. Cami isn't exactly a poker player. Each time she turned back around, her shoulders would slump just a little more.

In a way I felt bad for hiding from her, but it was a great comfort to know that she too was looking for me. I didn't want to interrupt her time down at the beach. My feelings for Cami are blossoming really quickly, and I know that if I let my emotions get the better of me, I'll push her away. I stayed away until dinner, for her. I was hoping she too would miss me.

"I really missed you today," I say.

She smiles at me as I hand her a glass of champagne. "I missed you, too. I kept hoping to see you up on your patio. I had this weird feeling I was being watched."

I smile at her as sweetly as I can manage. "You were." Her eyes widen at my words. "Well, Tyson was keeping an eye on you from near Blu's patio, and I spent a good deal of time in the pool watching you, too. I saw you looking for me."

She lets out a gasp. "Why?"

"I felt better knowing that you were safe. That, and I had a hard time keeping my eyes off of you. No reasons other than that, Cami."

Her answering smile is comforting. "Okay, I can deal with that. Though you have to realize that no one knows me or who I am."

She has a point, but I am not going to let her use it against me. "That may be, Cami, but people know me and you've been seen with me. I just felt better knowing that there were eyes on you." Also, I know full well what people can be capable of when they want something.

And then, because I feel like the mood needs lightening, I add, "Plus it gave Tyson something to do. Once we had tonight and Friday's arrangements made, he was making me crazy. He doesn't do well with little or nothing to do."

Cami laughs. "Fair enough. Would it make you feel better if I spoke to Trinity about having my own bodyguard?"

Her question throws me off guard. I hadn't even thought that it might be necessary for her to have her own regular security detail. "That may be good once we get back to the States, but I don't really want to talk about that tonight." As I say this I hear shoes clicking on the deck and the captain appears on the other side of Cami.

"All are on board, sir. Are we ready to push off?"

"Yes, captain, we are. Thank you." He bows his head in acknowledgement and leaves Cami and me alone again. Turning to Cami, I ask her, "Would you like to relax in the hot tub while we head out to sea?"

In answer, she sets down her champagne glass and reaches for the button of her shorts. She takes her sweet time unbuttoning them, teasing me. Her eyes are on me, looking me up and down, hooded by her lashes. The look is so seductive that I feel the need for Cami growing hot throughout my body. Slowly she pushes her shorts down, revealing the skimpy string of her bikini bottoms. My mouth goes dry and my lungs devoid of oxygen, but I don't care.

After a few moments she is now sans shorts, and I pull in a long, deep breath. Working my lungs again brings back my focus. I start emptying my pockets. Removing my watch, I place it, along with my wallet and cell phone, onto the table.

Grabbing the bottom of my shirt, I pull it up in a swift, non-seductive manner. Just before the shirt covers my eyes, I catch a glimpse of Cami sneaking her own look. Toying with her, I flex my muscles, taunting her, giving her a show.

Lazy, hungry eyes are raking over my body and she slowly peels them away. A rush of disappointment runs rapidly through my body as she grabs her glass and turns away. As she sinks slowly, deliberately into the hot tub, I notice that her ribbons from last night are gone.

"You seem to be missing something," I tease.

She tenses, and a faint red flush slides over her skin. In a slight panic she looks down and around, like she might have lost her bottoms. "Huh?" she finally replies.

I chuckle. "You're missing ribbons, and your leather is back?"

"Oh!" She turns, smiling at me. "I don't like to get the ribbons wet. They break down and look horrible after a couple of soakings. The leather stands up better, and threading my back is a bit of a challenge, so using leather allows me to thread it once and be done. I can get most of it, but the top couple are a lot harder to reach."

"I see. Makes sense." She really is a perfectionist when it comes to the little things. I like it. What had caught me by surprise earlier was the fact that she had put on a bit of makeup before going down to the beach. These little things tell me that she really cares about her appearance, and I like that even more.

Today she is wearing a hot pink bikini. I'd pegged her as more of the gothic type, and with her tattoos and piercings, it's easy to come to that conclusion. She has a rather eclectic style and seems to wear what she's comfortable wearing. She cleans up nice, but I have no doubt that she could make sweat pants look good.

Coming to the realization that I'm staring at her, I mentally shake my head to clear it up a bit. Just as I'm about to take a step into the hot tub, the lights come on, illuminating her from below. Surrounded by warm, liquid light, she looks like an angel.

As I lower myself into the water I notice that Cami is watching me intently. She starts looking at my chest, at the dragon's head, and it dawns on me that she hasn't really gotten a good look at my ink yet.

"I saw the wings and the spinal work," she says. "I also noticed the tail on your leg. Now a good look at his head on your chest. Is there more?"

"Just on my legs. The tail comes out here." I point to my left upper thigh and lift my swim trunks so she can see the outer thigh. I roll my leg outward so that she can see the inside of my leg where the tail comes out. I watch as she takes in the concept. Then I reach for the other leg of my swimsuit, revealing first my inner right thigh where the tail goes in, then rotating my leg so she can see where the tail comes out the other side. The barbed tail comes out again below my knee and hangs around my ankle, taking up most of my lower leg.

She takes a minute to admire all the work. "It's a very beautiful tattoo, Tristan. Your artist is amazing."

I smile. "I did the drawings myself and he worked his magic. I never thought that it would turn out as beautiful as it did."

"How long did it take?"

"It took about seventeen six-hour sessions to complete the entire piece. I started it after we finished up the first *Burning* movie. While we were filming, I started to shop around for tattoo artists. It took me a while, but I found a great artist in Texas that specializes in dragons. We met, talked. Then about a week later we got started. We traded off the traveling and here it is. It was one of the best decisions I've ever made."

I don't continue the story. I can tell by her expectant look that she wants to know more, but I can't, not yet. The reason behind my dragon is deeply personal and slightly depressing. Not exactly the type of conversation for a second date.

To take the pressure off, I say, "I know you want to know more, and I want to tell you, but tonight is not the best night."

She nods in agreement, taking a seat opposite me. "When Bobbie died, I was so angry that I wanted to just fly away. So Beau and I did. We went to Portland. We stayed up there for the majority of last summer so I would have time to have the work finished." She seems to sense what I was thinking; though we discussed her tattoos over dinner last night, there seems to be a bit more to the story.

"I was crushed when I heard about Bobbie passing away," I say, "and I was unable to make the funeral because of my shooting schedule. By the time I was able to get there, he'd already been buried. I visited his grave a few times in June." I pause. Bobbie had really been a decent person to me. Until I met Cami, I would have thought him to be a good friend, but now it is seeming more like I was his paycheck than a friend.

"You know, Cami, if I had known Bobbie had a daughter, I would have reached out to you sooner, expressed my condolences on his passing. Your father was a good business man and treated his clients well."

"Tristan, my father was a great business man, but as I said, he and I were never close. But believe me, I'm glad that you had Bobbie to turn to when you got thrown into Hollywood. Hollywood is scary, even if it's something that you are after or want. I personally am scared to death of Hollywood. Though it didn't stop me from obtaining a PR degree.

"I got a dual degree, actually, in PR and business management. And graduated with honors. I think subconsciously I wanted to please Bobbie and give him something to be proud of." Her voice takes on a somber tone. "I'll never know, though, if he was proud. I do know that he didn't attend my graduation, so..." She takes a deep breath. "I never even told him what my degrees were in. But I have my suspicions that Bobbie knew because I discovered that his will was last revised about thirty days before my graduation. The only other revision happened within a few months of the death of my mother. I don't know what it said prior to the change, but I suspect that it had something to do with my impending high school graduation."

"Why high school?" I ask her, confused.

"Well, knowing that I would be turning eighteen sooner rather than later, and given what the final will said, I'm assuming the original change has to do either with the business or the property he owned."

My heart suddenly feels so heavy and somber. I honest to God feel like crying right now. Her pain is evident in her voice, and here she is sharing all this with me and I can't even explain my tattoo. "Cami," I whisper. Standing up, I reach out to her, grab her hand and pull her into my arms. "I cannot account for how Bobbie felt or what he knew. But I can tell you that he was a very stupid man for not seeing the beauty in you as a whole. I can't imagine anyone not caring about you. You are such a gentle soul."

I try to sit down again with her in my arms and she resists. I sit anyway, looking up at her, I ask her, "I've been wondering about something since last night." She nods in acknowledgement. "What about your brother?" I ask. "Why wasn't he left in charge instead of you?"

She sits back down, closer to me, but still just out of reach. "Mark has washed his hands of anything regarding Bobbie. He wants nothing to do with the business. Bobbie recognized Mark's separation from him and changed his will to hand the business over to me.

"Mark has a law firm in Dallas with his wife and the twins. I have not seen them since last Christmas, but we talk about once a month or, so and that is about the extent of our relationship. He is only two years older than I am, but we were both raised in boarding schools in two different countries. We never got to know one another. Bobbie of course was responsible for Mark and I being so distant. It's something else that bothers me about Bobbie. But that's a whole different story."

I nod. I figure that she's told me more in the last two nights than maybe even Beau knows about her life before college. I feel like I need to share some information about me and my past with her to reciprocate.

"As I told you last night, I was really close to my mom, but she passed away during my freshman year of college.

I never knew who my father was. Still don't know to this day, and frankly, it doesn't really matter to me."

"Why?" she asks.

"Well, to be honest, what can he do for me now? I'm an adult, and the time that I needed him was when I was younger. But my need for him was never about me, it was always about my mom. I watched her struggle with multiple jobs, working insane hours, doing everything she could to give me everything I needed. One of my biggest regrets in life is that I was never able to take care of her." My heart aches and I absentmindedly rub my chest. A habit I have then I'm hurting inside.

Cami cocks her head, a million questions in her eyes, but she doesn't ask them. She just admires me from across the hot tub. I decide to continue talking, let her come to me when she is ready.

"Shortly after I hired Tyson, some random guy showed up, claiming to be my father. The man did look a little like me. For all I knew he was the real deal. But Tyson proved his loyalty to me by screening him and getting a DNA test done before I really got involved in the situation. When the results came in, Tyson told the man that I was not his son and later had him arrested for harassment and stalking. The guy kept tying to get close to me, insisting he was my father. He had no idea that Tyson had managed the DNA test until he got arrested and charged with harassment and Tyson appeared in court on my behalf. I would've gone myself, but the prosecuting attorney told me that there was no reason for it, and it would only bring further attention to me. But by the time the trial rolled around, it had become evident the guy only wanted money."

"The nerve of some people." She scowls, and I see in her face what she saw in mine earlier, and I chuckle.

"It was shortly after the *Top Paid Celebrities of 2010* list came out. The first of the three *Burning* movies had been released, and my life was no longer my own. If you've seen the list before then you know that the article publishes your earnings for the world to see. At the time my net worth was roughly fifty million dollars because of the *Burning* movies and all the promotions that came with it, and I made the list."

She laughs. "I've seen the list. But I'm curious about something. There don't seem to be a lot of interviews or videos of you out there. Why is that?"

"I don't do interviews, mainly because so much of what I say gets twisted into something more than what it really was. Plus, they are a waste of time because no one listens to what you have to say anyway. Especially my fans. They just want to know about my love life." I laugh. "Which I guess includes you now."

She is giggling, "Trust me, I don't mind falling into that category." She takes another swig of her champagne and sets her glass on the edge of tub.

My heart skips a beat, then picks up in double time at her words. Grabbing her hand, I pull her toward me. "Come here, you." I pull her into a warm, comforting embrace. She is so tiny that I swear I can wrap my arms around her twice over, but I really liked the feel of her body pressed against mine. "Thank you, Cami."

She looks up at me, puzzled. "For what?"

"Oh, I don't know," I say conspiratorially. "Joining me for dinner tonight. Talking so openly with me about Bobbie. I imagine that is not something you do with just anyone."

She smiles. "No, I don't. Mick knows because he was around for a good portion of my teenage years with Bobbie. But as a general rule I don't talk about my family or background with my friends. Beau knows some, but I don't like to talk about Bobbie with her because it always brings up the subject of money, and that's kind of a sore spot." She giggles. "Beau is no longer the poor girl I met in college, but that's because she is my 'personal assistant,'" she says with air quotes. It's cute, actually. "She handles just about everything for me. I love her to death, and we have a rather interesting relationship."

I let out a strained laugh. "Yeah, I could tell while she was on the phone."

"Oh jeez, I suppose I should explain that. Beau and I are ex-lovers."

EIGHTEEN

I'm sure the complete shock running through my body is evident on my face. She's bi?

"Sorry, I didn't mean to catch you off-guard."

"No, no it's ok. Just not something I expected to hear. When you say ex, what do you mean, exactly?"

She blushes. I'm getting so used to the sight of her blushing that I rather enjoy the idea of making her do it as often as possible.

"Well, exactly what I said. We dated in college, but it was an interesting kind of relationship. We slept together, did just about everything else together, but we always went on date hunts. Neither one of us got jealous of the other when we found someone else to be with, but when it all fizzled out, we would find ourselves back in bed together. We haven't slept together in over two years. We just kind of grew out of it, I guess."

I am unsure what to say, mainly because I find that I'm actually turned on by the prospect of Cami with another woman. Though I don't know Beau, I am more curious than ever to meet her.

"Seems as though she is a little protective of you."

"She is. She and Mick are both overprotective of me. It doesn't bother me. But I think because of the fact that both of my parents are deceased and I have more money than I could possibly spend in a lifetime, they feel like they have to keep eyes on me. I can't let it bother me because I know that if it did, I wouldn't be able to have the type of relationship I have with them."

"Well, I'm looking forward to meeting both of them. And I'm really hoping that Mick can help me out with my finances. I'm crap with them, and I'm bothered by the amount of money I do have. I've done very little to earn it. There are some days I wish I could do it for free. Then there are other days I feel that I am not paid anywhere near enough. It's an overwhelming burden sometimes. I'm guessing you know how that feels."

She nods. "Yeah, that I do understand. I make more money then I can possibly spend." She sighs. "I worry sometimes that having money will turn me into a pretentious bitch."

I laugh. "Well I vow to do my best to not let that happen."

Smiling at me, ignoring the suggestion in my words, she continues, "I wasn't raised with money. Bobbie gave me a meager allowance, and it wasn't until I graduated high school that I was handed the first portion of my trust fund."

I nod. "I would love to do what I do without all the money and the fame that comes with it. Nothing is more annoying than going to the pharmacy and being followed around the store by crazed fans demanding autographs or touching me. It's gotten to the point that I usually send Tyson or someone else out to do my shopping, and trust me, that gets old. I don't like being confined to my house or hotel because of the fans."

"I can understand that to a point. It's not something that I've ever had to deal with. I suppose that's something

I do have to thank Bobbie for. He kept me out of the spotlight. I know that he made the tabloids more than a few times."

I grin. "Yeah, I suppose you do. You're his best-kept secret. Although, if you should decide to take over the company, I would imagine that would change pretty fast."

"I imagine that being around you alone will change that status pretty fast."

Shit! "Good point," I say simply. She's smiling. "What's so funny?"

She ponders her answer for a second. "Honestly?"

"Of course."

"The thought of hanging around with you."

"Why is that funny? It's not a bad thing, is it?"

She shakes her head. "No, it's intriguing. Kind of like what you told Beau on the phone. Did you really mean what you said to her?" she asks.

"Yes, although I'm curious as to what part you are referring to."

"All of it, but more specifically the 'if you'll have me' part."

"Yes." I look at her, pulling her closer and tighter. A line comes into my mind from a movie I saw some million years ago. I've always wanted to use it on a woman, and it feels right with Cami. "Can I keep you?"

She blushes and about ten different emotions cross her face, but all of them seem good, so I'm not concerned. She doesn't answer me out loud. Instead, she wraps her arms around my neck, pulls me tight into her body, and brings her lips to mine, cementing our relationship with a kiss that's passionate and full of promise. Her body fits against mine perfectly, despite our difference in height.

Her tongue gently seeks entrance into my mouth, I let her in easily, eager to feel her tongue against mine.

Kissing Cami is the ultimate. Her taste and flowery scent cause a great single-minded desire to pool deep down in the pit of my stomach. To have her close to me. I'm not sure if it's Cami or the hot tub making my head swim. But as much as I want her in this moment, I am going to behave myself. She deserves better than this hot tub for our first time.

Tyson comes into my peripheral vision and clears his throat. "Dinner will be ready in about ten minutes."

I look up at him, barely able to pull away from Cami's kissing. "Thank you, Tyson," I try to say clearly, but it comes out husky with desire. It's very obvious to me that Cami has caught the tone in my voice because she squirms a little in my arms. Tyson nods to me and retreats back to wherever it is he's been hiding.

"Should we get dried off for dinner?" I ask.

Without waiting for an answer, I stand up with Cami still in my arms. She weighs next to nothing, and it partially satisfies my desire to have her in my arms. I carry her out of the hot tub, my arms wrapped around her ribs and her feet hanging straight down. Her corset rings are warm against my arms. I gently lift my arms up a little bit higher, hoping that I'm not rubbing or pulling on her piercings.

As I step up out of the tub I can feel her feet bumping against my shins. I let out a chuckle.

She gives me a puzzled look. "What's so funny?"

"It wasn't until your feet bumped into my shins that it dawned on me just how short you are."

"Ha-ha!" she says, sticking her tongue out at me. I laugh, then suddenly her face lights up into a huge smile. "You know, Tristan?"

"What do I know?"

"Great things come in small packages." She giggles and squirms against me, brushing against my erection.

Feeling playful, I quickly loosen my arms like I'm going to drop her and she squeals. She quickly has me in her clutches; she grabs tight onto my hair and pulls.

"Ah!" I growl and look down at her. She is still smiling. "You think so, little lady. Keep that up and I can't promise to control myself." No need to directly mention the fact that her hair-pulling move has made my already painful erection throb harder. "For the record, I like what comes in this small package," I say, kissing her forehead.

I can feel her breasts and hard nipples pressing against my chest. All it will take is one quick flick and I can have her bikini undone and her breasts falling out of her top.

She pulls my head down and kisses me with fervor. I meet her ferocious kissing with my own tongue. I pull her lower lip between my teeth and tug. She moans into my mouth.

Without breaking the kiss, I set her down on the deck near the table and pull her tighter against my body so I can feel every delicious curve pressing against me. I steady her, then my hands caress her back, slowly sliding down until the tips of my fingers meet with the top of her bikini bottoms. She stands on her tip-toes so she can deepen the kiss, rubbing her breasts against my chest.

My fingers trail along the waist of her bikini. She shivers at my touch but kisses me even harder. I slide my hands around her hips to her stomach and then up to the underside of her supple breasts. Slowly my thumbs graze, feather light, against the hard peaks of her nipples.

She moans and her hands move down my body and skim across my ass. Her fingers continue gently along my hips before diving into the waistband of my shorts. My erection is aching, throbbing for her touch. Her fingers are cool when they finally find me, stroking me slowly and gently, a sweet teasing torture. She gasps as her fingers take in the surprise she finds along the shaft of my erection. I moan back into her mouth and my thumbs both begin rubbing more firmly against her nipples.

My want is quickly turning to need as she continues to stroke along the shaft of my cock. I want desperately to take her back into the hot tub and strip her of her tiny bikini, but I know I have to stop this for multiple reasons, one of which is the fact that I'm not ready to go there. Also, the hot tub is hardly the place for our first time, and lastly, Tyson has come back around the corner to let us know dinner is ready. I can see him out of the corner of my eye.

He is smiling as he looks at me. I can tell that he is happy to see me this happy.

I kiss Cami a couple more times, each kiss becoming more chaste. I reluctantly pull my hands away from her nipples. She follows my lead, releasing my erection and taking her hand out of my shorts. She brings her arms around me and hugs me, looking up at me through her lashes with an expression that's sensual and full of lusty promise. A promise I so desperately want her to fill.

"If we keep this up, Cami, you're going to strip me of every ounce of strength I have in place to control myself." Her face falls just a little bit. "Believe me, I want you, but I'm not so sure I'm ready for that tonight."

She looks at me and smiles a brilliantly white smile. "I do love a challenge, Tristan."

"Not a challenge." I smile and lean in to whisper in her ear. "I want to be buried deep inside of you, in every imaginable position. But not here. Not now. And not tonight." I pull back and add in a normal tone of voice, "Besides. Dinner's ready."

NINETEEN

~~*~*~*

CAMI

As we walk toward the stern of the boat for our dinner, Tristan's trying desperately to make subtle adjustments to his erection and failing miserably. Knowing I am the one causing that makes me want to giggle like a school girl.

I was very pleasantly surprised by the four piercings running along his shaft. A Prince Albert and three frenums along the shaft of his cock. Feeling that sent a shiver through me, desire hot and heavy running through my body.

I know what a challenge it is to wait; it's taking every ounce of strength I have to not rip off his shorts and take him right here on the deck. I've never encountered someone of the opposite sex wanting to hold out. Were it not for his erection, I might feel self-conscious about how much I want him, but it's comforting to know that Tristan and I are both having a hard time controlling our urges to bed one another. To know that this means more to him than getting laid is a bit heady.

Now that I'm out of the hot tub and we're out on open water, I'm a bit chilly, so I slip on my t-shirt. Tristan's face falls as I cover myself up.

"So, let me guess. You would rather enjoy having me for dinner in the buff?" I tease.

He blushes. "Is it that obvious?"

I blush in response. "Sometimes. But just now I noticed that you looked a little disappointed when you saw my shirt. Then you perked up when you realized it was going to be just as revealing as the bikini." I giggle. "Don't worry," I whisper. "I like it."

His returning smile practically lights up the evening sky. "Good, so do I."

He lifts his elbow in a gesture for me to take his arm. I take it, and he leads me through the cabin to the deck on the other side. The view is spectacular. The captain has turned the boat so that our table is quite literally backlit by the beautiful setting sun. I gasp as the view takes my breath away. The sun is huge, sitting low in the sky, and it has lit up the water in a beautiful array of reds, oranges, blues, and purples. It looks like the clouds are in the water.

"My God, Tristan, this is beautiful," I say as I look up at him. He's not looking at the sunset, but rather at me.

"I couldn't agree more."

He pulls out my chair for me to sit. "Whoever said chivalry is dead was dead wrong," I giggle out. "Thank you."

"Chivalry, in my book, is far from dead. A man should always hold a door and pull out a chair for a woman."

Oh my, my! I cannot believe he just said that. At least now I know not to be surprised by the gesture going forward. "I will keep that in mind."

"What are your plans for tomorrow?" he asks.

"Tomorrow morning, around eight, I have a video conference with Trinity. That is where I earn my paycheck." I smile and continue, "I expect that tomorrow will be filled with a lot of talk about you."

He scowls. "Why would you be doing that?"

Before I can answer, a gentleman dressed in livery brings out our dinner salads and a bottle of white wine.

"Well, we need to figure out our plan of attack for Tuesday. Bold is going to be completely bombarded with phone calls regarding the story. We need a plan in place when it comes to who all will be involved in the situation."

Trinity had emailed me earlier today regarding the story. Attached was the unreleased copy. It was a very well-written article, and Tristan was painted rather favorably. Even so, the stories that are going to follow will be harsh as far as Tristan is concerned.

As we begin to eat our salads, Tristan looks as though he is mulling something over.

"Penny for your thoughts?" I tease.

He flashes me a brief, tense smile. "I'm just not looking forward to all the negative attention on Tuesday."

"But you won't have to face the fans or the press until you go back to the States. The only people who know you're here are Trinity, Mick, Beau, and me."

"That's not true. I was recognized downstairs today. I signed autographs and let them take some pictures in an attempt to stop them from being vindictive. I asked the girls to wait a couple of days before telling their friends." He takes on the task of pouring our wine. "I'm not sure if it'll work, but I did my best."

Crap. Well I guess it's inevitable that he'll be recognized, even all the way out here. "Hm. In that case, I suggest that once this story comes out, you drop from sight. Change the name on the hotel room to something a little less common."

"Tyson is on it."

"Good." I have this overwhelming desire to protect him as best as I can. "I want you to come out of this in one piece. Stories like this can completely destroy a person emotionally."

He frowns. "I know, but frankly, at this point, once the promotional events are done for the movies I have already completed, I'm not entirely sure that I care to get back in front of the camera."

I sigh. "Is that because you no longer want to act, or is it because you're afraid this will destroy your career?"

He does not respond right away. I watch an array of emotions cross his face and his body. Anytime he is tense or anxious, his entire body tightens up. When he finally does respond, I'm amazed by what comes out of his mouth.

"Cami, I love acting. There is nothing more that I want to do in this world than continue to pursue the career as far as it will take me." He pauses, taking a very large swig of his wine. When he drains the glass, he refills it and drinks about half of the new glass before continuing.

"I am scared to death that Layla has destroyed my credibility with all this negative publicity. I know it's an irrational fear. I didn't do anything wrong in this whole mess. But my name is going to be dragged through the thickest of mud regardless of what I do." He takes another drink of his wine. This one is slower and smaller. "The contracted production schedule for the films prevented me from taking on very many new roles. I was able to take two additional roles and completed the production of those films outside of Burning, but the last few months have been pretty dry on scripts, and I'm concerned that my career is coming to an end and not because of Layla." He takes a deep breath.

I'm puzzled because I'm not exactly sure what he's referring to. "What do you mean, 'not because of Layla'?" I ask.

"I haven't received very many new scripts. The ones that I have received were either poorly written or they were B movies with unreasonable production schedules." He takes a bite of his salad. "I've been wondering if it has to do with my acting ability or if it's just the movies that I've done. A lot of my popularity stems from the character I play, not necessarily my acting abilities."

Our waiter returns to clear our salad plates and bring us our main course: blackened duck, roasted potatoes, and mixed vegetables. I pick up my fork and knife and slowly slice into the duck. It's tender and juicy.

Before I take my first bite, I say to him, "Vincent has four scripts sitting on his desk – at this moment – waiting to be released to you. He's just waiting until we have a final production schedule and tentative contract in hand. From my understanding, he holds the majority of your scripts until he has more information. He tries very hard not to bombard you with scripts that turn into nothing or with demands for production that you can't meet."

His expression changes from grim to slightly excited.

I take my first bite, and it's delicious. Mouthwatering. I swallow and take a sip of the wine, which tastes crisp after the rich meat.

"You'll be able to pick and choose or possibly do them all," I continue. "According to Vinnie, the tentative production schedules would not overlap, and you could meet the timelines on all of them."

Watching his reaction intently, I see how his body shifts from bent over and tense to a looser, straighter position. A smile spreads across his face, and his eyes warm.

We eat in silence for a few minutes as I mull over the fact that I haven't told him everything I know, and it's nagging at me. Finally I take a deep breath and speak up, bracing myself for his reaction. "I've seen the article."

"Wha...? When? How?" He's pretty cute when he's flustered, actually.

"Trinity sent me the article today. She received it yesterday but waited to forward it to me until the pictures were validated. There's also a video, but that won't be released to the public. It confirms that it's her, though, without doubt."

"She admitted to cheating."

"Right, she did. To you and no one else. At least that we know of. Validating the photos is standard in scandal stories because if they're faked we would fight it and file a law suit to stop the story. In this case, the pictures are pretty good quality. They haven't been altered or enhanced."

"Well, I guess that's something," he sulks.

"Tristan, the article tears Layla apart, claiming that this is not the first time she's done this. Though the source requested anonymity in the article, the magazine did receive written permission to disclose their information you and to Bold."

He looks at me, completely puzzled. "You know who took the photos?"

"No, I don't know who took the pictures. But I know who sent the pictures to the magazine, and I also know why the source chose *Entertainment Now* to release the story to." I had never considered who the source might be until it was brought to me. The source's anonymity is being protected by Bold until Tristan decides he wanted to know. I am hoping that the person who sent the pictures will reveal themselves to Tristan in their own time.

"Why EN?" he asks. I can tell that he is doing all he can to calm himself. But surprise washes over me that he asked this question and not who.

I take a rather large drink of the wonderful wine. It seems like a waste to gulp it, but I am suddenly feeling the need to steel myself for the rest of this conversation. "EN was chosen because they have a reputation for verification. Also, they only publish once a month, and they tend to sit on the stories until the person or persons involved have a chance to respond. They do all that so they can fully attempt to verify the validity of the claims. The creators of the magazine feel it makes for better magazines if they report the truth."

The waiter interrupts us with another bottle of wine and our desserts. I take a sip of my wine, thank him, and watch him disappear back into the cabin.

Tristan is pale. His gaze is locked on the table.

I really want to reassure him. I take a stab at what might be bothering him the most about all this. "EN has given Trinity ample time to submit a statement, but per your request, she has not. Fortunately for you, EN hasn't been pressing Trinity for a response. They understand that you had very little to do with this and that you are truly a victim in this situation."

I watch as his face relaxes some, but his eyebrows are still furrowed. "I'm trying to decide if I want to know who sent in those pictures. From the way you're talking, it seems like you think I know this person. Which makes me wonder why they didn't just come to me with the story."

"I think I can answer that without telling you who."

"Go on," he encourages.

"My best guess? The pictures were released to EN rather than you personally because they wanted her to be painted in the light that she deserves to be painted in. This person probably knew that if you got the photos, it would end your relationship with her but you wouldn't make Layla's betrayal public. You told me yourself her career was already in jeopardy after the *Burning* movies. I'd say it's deader than dead now."

"I guess I can't say I'm surprised. She always caused so much trouble on set, and the constant coaching was awful and painful to have to watch and listen to. She really is a horrible actress." He takes a bite of his dessert and a sip of wine before continuing. "It would not surprise me if she slept with someone to get the part of Alyssa." He pauses, seemingly deep in thought.

It suddenly strikes me like a freight train going ninety miles an hour. "That's why she slept with you, isn't it?" I ask, completely breathless. The revelation has knocked the wind right out of my lungs. Suddenly my heart aches for Tristan.

The corner of his mouth twitches. "It would be logical. She kept me close to her so that she could have me on her side, both on set and in her battles with the production company. She was constantly fighting with them, and it was natural that I would stand up for her." He seems to sober as he speaks about this.

"The bottom line in all of this, Tristan, is that Layla used you to further her career. When she realized that your success was not helping her any, she took matters into her own hands."

We've barely touched our desserts, but I feel full, and now I'm struck by the urge to be close to Tristan again. I get up and walk around the table. Squirm my way onto his lap. I sit straddling his legs, my arms wrapped around his neck, looking squarely into his eyes.

He smiles. In his eyes I see desire, affection, lust, need. I snuggle closer into his body, and he starts rubbing my back in a very tender gesture.

"Are you ready to know who sent in the pictures?"

~~*~*~*

TRISTAN

Do I want to know who sent in those pictures? Absolutely. But not right now. All this heavy talk is a bit much. Tonight is meant to be about Cami and me.

I shake my head slightly. Kiss her nose. She blushes deeply, which sends my blood flying through my veins. The erection I had from before dinner comes back with a vengeance. She is so beautiful. Her makeup is very subtle, natural almost, but, like before, it shows me that she cares enough about herself and her appearance to take the effort. I won't compare her to anyone, but it is very nice to see.

"Let's go back to the hot tub," I whisper, and she nods. She starts to get down from my lap, and I hold her tight. "Nuh uh, you're not walking." I let out a chuckle and stand. She really is light, and I have no problem carrying her back to the hot tub. As we pass by the waiter I say, "Can you please bring us some more champagne? Then please have Jessie make us a round of drinks?"

"Of course, sir. Will there be anything else?"

"No, thank you."

Once we make it to the tub I set her down in the chair and reach for the hem of her shirt. She lets me pull it over her head, which leaves her in shorts and bikini top. She's smiling coquettishly at me.

Then she stands, kicks off her flip-flops, and starts to undo her shorts. She is purposefully trying to make a show of taking off her shorts again. It's working, and I grin wickedly at her as she turns ever so slightly and slowly lowers her shorts to her ankles, bending at the waist.

With her ass in the air, perfectly smooth, she steps out of her shorts, batting her eyelashes in a vain attempt at innocence. I smirk at her. She takes two steps in my direction and reaches for the hem of my shirt. But before she gets a grip on it, I grab her hands, intertwine my fingers with hers, and bring them out to the side, forcing her to take that last half step that brings our bodies together.

I can feel her breasts pressed against my diaphragm, and I bend down, finding her lips, and I kiss her. The moment our lips meet, I feel the sweet sting of the electricity that flows through us, and the strings of conscious thought are lost. All I want is her. Here, now! But I can't.

I pull back and, slowly opening my eyes, I see her peering at me with her coquettish grin. "Oh, dear, sweet Cami. The things you make me feel." I smile at her. It's true; she makes me feel alive.

I start to pull my shirt over my head, but as the shirt covers my eyes, I hear her sharp intake of breath, then her hands are sliding up my stomach along my abs to my pecs and then up around my neck. With the shirt still covering my eyes, she tugs my head in her direction and I let her.

Her lips crush into mine. My body lights up like a live wire. With my sense of sight cut off, everything seems that much more intense.

Her hands release me and she starts tugging at my shirt. I let her remove it the rest of the way and embrace her. I pick her up again, further deepening our kiss.

Slowly, I walk us toward the tub and gingerly climb in. The water is warm. It sends shivers through my body and into Cami's. We both let out a breathy laugh. I sit down on the submerged bench that runs along the tub's sides.

The acknowledgement of my desire to wait is there in her eyes as she looks at me. Something else passes over her face, and I feel the now-familiar tingle of emotion run through my body, knotting my stomach in a very good way.

We both know that tonight is not the night, but I don't know how much longer I can hold out. I suspect that she, too, is about done cooling her heels for me.

Slowly we pull back from each other. With her straddling my lap, I pass an Eskimo kiss over her nose. We stay like this for most of the rest of the night.

TWENTY

~~*~*~*

CAMI

As my eyes begin to flutter open, the first thing that comes to mind is an image of Tristan, wet and warm from our hot tub escapade last night. The memory of his hooded, lust-filled eyes is warming my insides and forming an unsatisfied ache between my legs. Tristan's self-control has me weak in the knees; I don't know how much longer I can resist him. I roll onto my side in an effort to stop myself from giving into this urge to go upstairs to his room.

I think about satisfying the ache myself, but when I look at the clock I see I've slept in. It's seven; I only have about an hour before I'm supposed to talk with Trinity about Tristan and the story, and I still have to shower, eat, and get dressed.

I clamber into the shower thinking about last night, trying desperately to avoid thinking about our wonderful make-out session. I'm barely keeping it together as it is.

After such a short time I'm afraid of the feelings that are beginning to blossom deep down when it comes to Tristan. While we were discussing Layla last night, I realized that Tristan's selflessness knows no bounds.

Regardless of all the pain that Layla has put him through, he still wants to help her. Today when I talk with Trinity, I'll suggest that she get in touch with Layla's PR people so that they know about her drug use. Layla's team needs to be aware of the path that Layla is headed down. Maybe they can help her.

The pregnancy, of course, complicates things, but I would hope it would give her the necessary motivation to get cleaned up and back on the right path. I don't know whether or not she is fully addicted to the drugs she's using or if it's recreational, but if she's pregnant, she needs help no matter what.

I was a little surprised that Tristan decided he wasn't ready to know who sent the pictures, but I have a gut feeling that it won't be long before we have that conversation. Unless the person who sent them speaks with Tristan first, which would be my preference.

But right now our biggest issue is maintaining Tristan's anonymity in Tarah and keeping him away from public scrutiny. This is definitely something I'm not ready to handle on my own. I'll be grateful for Trinity's advice on that today.

As I put on the fluffy white bathrobe, I hear a knock on the door. The timing is such that it makes me wonder how long they've been knocking. When I reach the door I peer through the peephole and see what appears to be a hotel staff member carrying a huge bouquet of flowers. I smile to myself and reach for the door handle.

"Good morning, ma'am." He nods as he makes his way past me and into the room. "Where would you like your flowers?"

"The coffee table, please." I gesture to the table where my phones and iPad are sitting. Then I notice he's carrying more than just flowers.

He places the flowers in the middle of all my electronics, then turns to me to ask, "Are you familiar with a MacBook, Ms. Enders?"

I giggle. The one thing that I didn't bring with me was my MacBook. Shortly before I'd left Phoenix it had met the floor in a not-so-nice way. I hadn't gotten around to picking up a replacement. I had noticed an electronics retailer with an Apple logo in the mall downstairs, but I wanted one of the latest models and doubted they'd carry them.

"Very familiar. Is that what you have in your hand?" I say, pointing to the box he is holding.

My level of annoyance rises within. No doubt this is the work of Tristan, and after all I've told him, I hope he realizes how unnecessary this gesture is. It's so over-the-top for an expense for a blossoming relationship.

"Oh. Yes!" He stutters slightly. "Compliments of Mr. Rubble. I believe there is also a card inside the box."

I nod because I'm not sure I can keep the irritation out of my voice. Buying me a Mac is hardly necessary. I'm more than capable of purchasing one on my own. From the looks of the box in the gentleman's hand – George, I can finally see his name tag – I'd been wrong about the store not carrying the most recent models. This is the fifteen-inch, two-point-six gigahertz model with retina display.

"Thank you, George." I paste on a smile and turn toward my purse.

"No need, ma'am," he says. "Mr. Rubble took care of it already. Also, your breakfast is on its way up."

"Well, thank you kindly, George. You have a wonderful day."

"You as well. Thank you again," he says and leaves.

I walk over to the table to read the card attached to the flowers. It says:

Good Morning My Sweets,
I do hope you enjoyed last night as much as I did.
I look forward to seeing you again. Tonight? 6:30 in Blu?
I hope each time you look upon these flowers today you will think of nothing else but me.
Have a fantastic day!
Tristan

My, my! Mr. Tristan Michaels wants another date with me tonight? Of course, how can I say no after these flowers?

The arrangement is mostly yellow, white, and pink roses. I can spend hours breaking down what this means, but mixed in with the roses are stargazer lilies. Stargazers are by far my favorite flower. The center coloring of these is so bright and vibrant they must have opened up this morning. They're beautiful.

Before getting into the box that George placed on the table, I need to let Tristan know I received his flowers and thank him for his delightful gesture. I pick up my iPad and email him, knowing he'll be able to read it from his phone:

Good Morning Yourself Handsome,

Sweets, huh? I have a feeling I'll need to get used to that, but no worries, I like it. Your beautiful flowers have taken pride of place upon my coffee table so that while I'm busy working today, I can be distracted by their beauty while thinking of yours.

The MacBook box is a little more daunting and I've yet to open it. So for now, I thank thee for my beautiful flowers.

Yours, Cami

While I'm waiting for Tristan's response, there's another knock on the door. I'm about halfway there when my BlackBerry chimes, letting me know I have about ten minutes before my Skype meeting with Trinity. I reach for the door and open it.

It's a server with breakfast. A breakfast I didn't order. Regardless, it smells divine. Sitting on the cart is another, though significantly smaller, vase containing purple irises and purple daisies. I have to give him credit, he has great taste in flowers.

My BlackBerry chimes again, indicating that a message has been received. Odd. I'd sent my email to Tristan from my iPad.

As the server finishes laying out my breakfast on the dining table I ask, "How can I place a flower order for hotel delivery?"

"Dial star one nine nine on the phone and you will be connected directly to the flower shop."

"Perfect. Thank you so much." I go for my purse again and am quickly shot down. It's apparently already been covered. I nod and he leaves.

I return to the coffee table, where my flowers and the ominous box are sitting. Grabbing my two phones, I return to the dining table, take a seat, and uncover my plate.

Under the warming cover are two pancakes, two slices of whole wheat toast, two sausage links, two strips of bacon, and two sunny side up eggs. Tristan obviously paid attention Saturday morning. I pick up the syrup and cover my pancakes, grab my fork, and dive in.

"Mmm," I moan around a mouth full of pancakes. These are so good.

I pick up my BlackBerry, clear the alarm notification, and see the email that has come in. It's Trinity telling me that they are running about twenty minutes late. Realizing I have more time before my meeting, I slow down my breakfast a bit. It's only about a quarter 'til, so this means I have about half an hour. Normally I might be slightly annoyed at Trinity's tardiness, but I can't, not today. I have breakfast and a very overwhelming silver box to open.

I finish the eggs, bacon, and pancakes before picking up my plate and heading back to my chair. I can munch on the toast and sausage while I get set up for the meeting.

Now that I have some additional time, I grab the Mac box. Placing it on my lap, I lift the flap. Inside is a shiny silver machine with a light-up Apple on the top. I slide it out of the box and open the laptop. Sitting on top of the keyboard is an envelope with the hotel logo. I hit the power button and open the envelope.

While the Mac boots up, I read Tristan's note:

My Dearest Cami,

This is my gift for you. The idea of you working so hard for me from your iPad gives me overwhelming anxiety. I thought maybe you could use something more substantial to work with.

Thank you, Cami, for all that you have done for me and all you plan to do. Please accept this gift as a token of my appreciation.

Yours, Tristan

P.S. Your password is 4MysWeet&

Can I really fall for this man? Yes, yes I can.

I look at the now powered-up and ready-to-play Mac. No wonder it wasn't wrapped in plastic or anything; Tristan's already set it up for me. The login screen has Tristan's picture as my login icon, but the name underneath is neither mine nor Tristan's: it says "Sweets." I guess I really do need to get used to the nickname.

I type in my password. Immediately, iMessage pops up with a message from Tristan.

Tristan: I see you.

Sweets: I see you too. Good Morning Handsome! I see you have labeled me as Sweets everywhere.

Tristan: It suits you very well.

Sweets: It would suit you too, but I think I would get confused by seeing 'Sweets' on both sides of this conversation. LOL!

Tristan: LOL! Yes, it would make it more difficult to follow. When you come up with a nickname for me we can change it.

Sweets: What if I already have?

Tristan: LOL! Sweets does not count Cami.

Sweets: LOL! <Pout> Fine if I cannot name you Sweets2 then I'm going to come up with a name that suits you best, eventually. :)

Tristan: Fair enuf.

Leaning back in my chair, I mull over the idea of Tristan calling me "Sweets." Sure, in a way I guess it fits, but it's been three days. Is he trying to tell me that his feelings are blossoming as fast as mine are? Or is it truly an endearment for how he feels about me?

I decide to ask.

Sweets: Why did you choose Sweets?

Tristan: Because it's short for Sweetheart, and you have proved to me on more than a few occasions that you are a sweetheart, so the name fits.

I smile, liking my nickname better now that I know the reason behind it. I never thought of it as sweetheart, but it works. I have more than a couple of ideas for nicknames for him, but I'm not sure that I'm ready to share.

Tristan: Aren't you supposed to be in a meeting right now?

Sweets: LOL! Yes, but Trinity is running late. I have about 3 minutes before my iPad starts ringing.

Tristan: Ok, so I have you for three more minutes. First thing's first. I have loaded your Macbook with a music playlist I created for you. Whenever we are near each other and our machines are on, it will sync to mine automatically. Your iCloud, me account, iTunes and the App Store are all set up under the email address Sweets4Me@millennium.com.

Sweets: You know this is really not necessary.

Tristan: No it's not, but I wanted you to have something from me to thank you for all that you have done and are doing for me.

Sweets: You do realize that what I'm doing or have done is part of the job that Trinity and Vincent are trying to get me to do regularly, right? But I have a feeling that I should not be arguing with you, and simply say Thank You?

Tristan: LOL! Yeah, that would be good. You will lose the argument.

Sweets: Fair enough.

Man, he has me all in knots. He wants me to have something that reminds me of him, and it just so happens to be a MacBook that I will be using nearly every day. I'm not really sure how I feel about this right now.

Sweets: I need to run and put some clothes on real fast. You going to stay online?

I wait for a response for about ten seconds and I don't see one. Maybe he's walked away from his computer. I head off to the bedroom for my clothes. As I come back out, my iPad starts ringing. Sprinting to the table, I grab it and press the green button, and I'm being connected with Trinity via Skype.

An hour later I'm finishing up my Skype call when there's a knock on the door. I say my goodbyes to Trinity quickly and get up to answer it. As I approach the door I can hear two men talking.

I peek through the peephole and see two hotel staff members standing with a cart in between them. I can't quite see what is sitting on it, but I have a feeling Tristan isn't done sending flowers. Unlatching the door, I swing it open.

"Good morning, gentlemen. To what do I owe this pleasure?"

The one in front speaks first. "We have a special delivery for 'Sweets.'"

I smile. "Well, that would be me, I guess. Come on in."

"Yes, ma'am." They speak and nod in unison. I step out of the way to let them in. They reach for the cart behind them, and I gasp in shock. There are no less that six dozen long stem roses in all different shades: red, yellows, whites, some orange, some Fire and Ice, and some even silvery in color. They are breathtakingly beautiful.

"Um, I'm not sure where you can put all of those."

"No worries, Ms. Enders, we have our instructions."

I nod at the gentlemen as they go to work. I turn to close the door and stop short. Tyson's standing in my doorway.

"Hi, Ty! Great timing, I just got off a call with Trinity." I'm glad he's here. It'll give us a chance to talk.

"Cami," he says and nods, but he's looking over my head at the two men who just came in with all the flowers.

I smile because it had taken a lot of persistence yesterday during our impromptu meeting before I went down to the beach to convince Tyson to call me Cami. He finally relented.

"Something the matter, Ty?"

"I just came to check on you."

"Oh!" I try to hide my surprise and fail. I smile at him as I speak. "Tristan didn't send you down here, did he?"

"No, ma'am!" I scowl at him and raise an eyebrow at the same time. No small feat, but years of practice have helped me perfect the expression. "Cami, sorry. Old habits die hard. I was on my way up to Tristan's suite and I thought I would do a hall check here. I saw the two men waiting outside your door and just wanted to make sure that all was well."

I'm surprised a little at his protectiveness. "They seem like normal staff," I say.

"All the same, I would like to come in and make sure."

"Of course, Ty." I let him into the suite. "Is there something going on that I don't know about?" I ask. Between Tristan's insistence on protection yesterday and Ty checking my hallway today, it seems like they're concerned about something.

Tyson shrugs. "No, Cami, nothing directly to be concerned about, but both Tristan and I are a little concerned about the story. When people start to understand that Tristan is single, they'll have a tendency to get a little weird. It's just a precaution."

I try hard to take comfort in his words. I have no reason not to trust what he has to say, but it still makes me feel a little uncomfortable.

Looking around, I notice that the flowers are now scattered all throughout my sitting room. I look at Tyson, and he is shaking his head back and forth.

"He is completely smitten with you, isn't he?" A genuine smile spreads wide across his lips. Tyson really is beautiful. There is no other way to describe it. Jolene is going to go bat shit over this one.

The two men finish arranging the flowers, bow, and leave. Good, here's my chance.

"Ty, we need to talk about something."

"How's business?" he asks, and I can see he knows what I want to talk to him about, and he's trying to avoid it.

I sigh and give in. Just for the moment. "Great," I say. "Trinity says hi. She says Tristan's been keeping them busy. I told her about the girls that Tristan ran into downstairs and she wanted to know if you found out anything about them."

"I did," he says, and relaxes a little because he thinks I've let him off the hook. "They actually left this morning. Checked out of the hotel. The manager said that the man who rented their hotel room was part of a small business conference that was here for the last week or so. The girls came in on Thursday and left with him today. They've never been here before, so I'm guessing the cell phones they used to take Tristan's picture were not international and didn't have the ability to send out from here. That gives us a day or two cushion before they'll be posted to the Internet, provided the girls are going back to the States now." Tyson's so professional. I'm in awe of his abilities.

"What security measures are in place to avoid unwanted guests?" I ask. Another of Trinity's questions.

"Well, that's a whole different story. They're limiting those to the island that have reservations at the hotel, so we will know who will be arriving and when they are expected to check in. I am not privy to names, but they have been notified of who the red flags are. Layla and her entourage are on the list, and we are to be notified. Unfortunately we cannot give them the name of every reporter, and many of them use aliases anyway, but I have given them the names of our biggest concerns."

"Sounds like you have things sewn up pretty tight around here. Thank you, Tyson, for all your hard work."

"That's why Tristan pays me the big bucks." He's smiling now.

I'm opening my mouth to bring up the other subject when there is a knock at the door. Dammit.

Before I can react, Tyson's at the door. I watch as he checks the peephole, then opens the door.

Tyson is huge. I can't see around him until he steps aside. It's Tristan. At the sight of him, my heart rate quadruples. He walks into my suite with great purpose, straight in my direction. When he reaches me, he wraps his arms around me in a tight, warm hug.

He whispers in my ear, "I missed you, beautiful." And I blush beet red.

"I missed you, too."

Obviously I'm glad to see Tristan, but I still need to talk to Tyson. Without Tristan around. I guess I'll have to track him down later.

TWENTY-ONE

~~*~*~*

TRISTAN

I'm really beginning to enjoy having my arms around Cami. Though I can't decide what's more exciting about it, the fact that I feel like I'm protecting her, or the way her body warms, flushes, and presses into my own. I'm going to have to go with a toss-up.

I was a little dumbstruck when Tyson answered the door. What is he doing here? Cami showed genuine excitement when she saw me, and I'm not suspicious of anything, but it seems a bit conspiratorial. Cami has given me no reason not to trust her. Do I?

"What do you want to do with your friends this weekend?" I ask in an attempt to pull my thoughts away from the idea of Cami and Tyson alone together.

"I don't know. Head back over to Tahiti, hang out in the hotel, hang out in your suite with the pool, go shopping, party like rock stars." She giggles. "Or ginormous celebrities."

I throw a mock scowl at her, and she laughs harder. I can't help but join in.

Eventually she adds, "Here's an idea. Why don't you plan something and let me know?"

I nod in agreement, pondering the wide range of ideas that are now running through my head. Cami had mentioned Bora Bora earlier, and we can plan to spend a day or so in Tahiti on our way out of the area. Hm, so many ideas to ponder.

As much as I'd like to, I can't linger in her suite. I need to get in touch with Trav and make sure he is free for Wednesday and the weekend.

I kiss Cami quickly, not wanting to start something I'm no longer sure I'm capable of stopping anymore, and I take my leave.

Tyson follows. Thank God for that.

During the elevator ride up to my suite, I entertain the idea of having Cami join me in New York next week. Am I ready to show her off to the world at the airport and the premiere?

Upon returning to my suite, I grab my iPhone and call Travis. I haven't talked to him since the premiere, and we have some catching up to do.

Travis is my best friend. I've known him for a couple of years, and there is something about our friendship that keeps us close. He is like the brother I never had. I can tell him anything, and he can see all the things I'm not telling him. It's weird. But it works for us.

"About damn time you call me, ass-hat," he says as he answers the phone.

"Har-har!" I retort. "I've been a bit busy, what can I say?"

"Busy my ass. I know you've been off, and yet no one has heard from you. What gives, bro?"

I let out a sigh and start in on my story. "At your premiere, Layla decided to inform me that EN has some pictures of her naked and getting effed."

"By you?!" he practically shouts. I know he is worried about me in all this, and this is one of the reasons I love him like a brother.

"Uh, no. Try the producer and a whole slew of the crew on her last movie."

"No effin way!"

"Not something I would joke about, bro. But yeah, she brings it up, expecting me to cover her ass, and well, I basically told her where to shove it." Travis laughs. "Then she tried to pull the pregnancy card."

I hear him let out a growl.

"Calm down. Even if she is pregnant, it's not mine. We haven't had sex in over six months."

"Thank fuck for that. Please tell me you are not getting your PR people involved in this?"

I laugh. "No, Trav, this is on her shoulders. Trinity is involved only because you know how vulturistic reporters can be. They are going to try and dig up anything they can on me, or at least seek a reaction from me, and right now, I choose inaction and am hanging out in Tarah."

He whistles. "Nice digs, man. When you coming home?"

"Never," I say, joking.

"Whatever," he says.

"Actually, that's why I called. You tied up this week?"

"No, free. Don't have anything major until after the first."

"Nice, wanna come to Tarah?"

"Hell yeah! When?"

"Wednesday? Stay through Wednesday? I have to be in N.Y.C. Thursday next week for voiceovers and the *Conjure* premiere."

"Ah, that's right. You still want me there?"

"That's entirely up to you. I think I'm gonna bring Cami, though." I know this will elicit a what-the-hell style response.

"Whoa! Who?" There it is.

"Cami. Well, Cameron Enders."

"Who..." He pauses. "Why does that name sound familiar?

"She's not Hollywood, if that's what your worried about."

"Huh, I could swear I've heard that name before."

Not sure that I want to explain all the details of my relationship to Cami right this minute, I tell him, "Don't worry about it. You can meet her on Wednesday. She's bringing out a few of her friends to spend the weekend with us. You all might even be on the same flight. From my understanding, Jolene and Naomi are single, and Beau and Mick are together."

"Tristan, are you trying to set me up on a weekend date?" He laughs.

"Yeah, maybe I am. You got a problem with that?" I tease him.

"Hell no!" He's still laughing. "I think I'm a little flattered actually."

I laugh harder. "Well if it works out, you will be good to go. If not, Tyson will be here. Though I think Cami believes that Tyson and Jolene are going to hit it off, and then you might be left to your own devices."

"Yeah, 'cause that has always been a problem." He laughs again.

I laugh with him. Travis can be a bit of a womanizer sometimes, but when he finds someone he is really interested in, he zeros in on her and nothing else. I don't know Naomi from any other woman, but it might work for them.

Travis interrupts my thoughts. "So. Tell me about Cami?"

I smile at the mention of her name and my insides tighten. If it hadn't been Trav asking the question, it might have sparked something in my pants. "Ah, Trav. She's beautiful, she's inked, pierced, smart, I can't stop smiling when I'm around her..."

"Dude, you sound like you've been hit by cupid."

"Yeah, I think I have."

"Whoa, man, when did you meet this girl?"

"Friday night, at the bar downstairs."

"But, it's only Monday," he says, matter of fact.

"Yeah, I know. But there is just something about her. She's different. She's engaging, honest, open, and she makes me feel so comfortable. She helps me forget everything." I sigh.

"You sleep with her yet?" I knew that question was coming.

"Not that it is any of your business, Trav, but no, we haven't"

"All right," he says, resolved. "I trust you to trust your own judgment. But just be careful."

"Thanks, bro. I'm doing everything I can to do this right." My comment is met with silence for more than a few heartbeats. "Travis?"

"Yeah, I'm here. I'm just...I don't know. I've never heard you like this before."

"It's all right. I've never heard me like this before. I'm a little awestruck and not sure what I should do other than ride this wave."

"Okay, that's all I need to know. So I get to meet her Wednesday, huh?"

I laugh. "Yeah, Wednesday. Take care of your flight. Forward me the deets and I will send the money ov—"

"Shut the hell up, Tristan. I'll pay for it."

I shrug. "All right, be that way. See you Wednesday?"

"Wednesday. Later."

"Later, Travis."

He hung up first, no doubt as dumbstruck as I feel right now. I don't talk about girls with anyone, and it's kind of trippy. Travis of course knows about Layla; we've talked a lot in the past. It was kind of hard not to when I ended up crashing at his place after a Layla fight or when I didn't want to deal with her.

Tyson walks into the room. "Tristan, Cami has requested penthouse access."

I smile. "Well, what are you waiting for? Give it to her."

"I already did." He laughs. "She's waiting in the foyer."

"Let her in already, would you?" I can't believe how much I want to see her again already. It's only been an hour since I left her downstairs.

I hear her come into the room, and I stand up from the sofa and turn to find Cami in a lime green bikini top and a wraparound sarong at her waist. She's carrying the tote that she had last night.

I smile at the sight of her. Her skin is still pale and glowing slightly from the natural light entering the room from the open patio doors.

"I'm going to go down to the beach and I was wondering if you wanted to join me," she says.

I smile. "How was your massage?"

She grins. "It was perfect. I feel nice and relaxed. Thank you." After a brief pause she adds, "But you really don't need to keep buying things for me."

I know my face falls. She really has a hard time accepting gifts and I need to break her of that. I have more money than I know what to do with, and spending a little here and there on her to make her happy is just part of the whole Tristan package. "You work hard at what you're doing for me; you deserve far more than what I am giving you."

"That's really not the point, Tristan. I'm not interested in what's in your bank account." Her eyes move up and down my body, taking in my tight t-shirt and shorts.

"I know you're not interested in my bank account, Sweets, and it has nothing to do with why I've done the things I've done today. I felt it was important to show you, some way, that I truly appreciate what you've done for me, and on your vacation no less."

She just nods. I can tell that she is lost in thought – about what I have no clue. She continues to rake her eyes over me from head to toe. It's almost an absentminded thing she seems to be doing, but it gives me an idea.

"Instead of going to the beach, I have a better idea. Why don't I have Tyson call for some room service? I'll change into my suit, and we can use the pool up here."

She beams at me. "I like the sound of that."

"Good, then make yourself at home and I'll go and change." I start to turn and call out, "Tyson?"

He appears before me about ten seconds later, "Yes, boss?" I frown at him. "Tristan," he corrects himself.

"Cami and I are going to go hang out on the patio and indulge in the pool. Would you mind calling room service for some champagne and finger foods?"

"Of course. Any particular kind of champagne?"

"Bolli, please."

"Got it." He nods, turns on his heel, and heads back into his room.

"You're welcome to join us, Tyson," Cami calls out in his direction.

"Thank you, Cami," Tyson shouts back, but I know better than to expect him to join us.

"I'll be right back. Make yourself at home, Sweets."

I change into my trunks and head out to the pool. When I get there, Cami's already in the water. The way she moves is almost stealthy and cat-like. She's leaking sex appeal all over the pool. I drop my towel and dive in next to her. When I surface, she's staring at me.

"What?" I ask, curious as to what's on her mind.

"Nothing, really. You're just extremely sexy. It's hard to look away."

Well then. "I can say the same thing about you." She smiles. I slowly prowl toward her. By the time I reach her, she's giggling. She pushes away from the wall and embraces me by wrapping her arms around my neck and her legs around my waist. She is too short to reach the bottom of the five-foot deep part of the pool comfortably, and I'm more than happy to have her body wrapped around mine as tight as a glove. Her body is pressed so tight that I can feel every contour of her body against mine. Including the warmth radiating from her sex. Against the coolness of the water, it's very warm.

"Hi, beautiful," I breathe.

"Hi beautiful yourself," she whispers as she begins to gently rub her nose against mine. I match her movements.

"I love Eskimo kisses." I smile and kiss her gently but swiftly, trying hard to behave myself.

"Have you seen the view from the edge?" I ask. She shakes her head and I wade over to the pool's edge. The view is fantastic from up here, made that much better now that I have Cami to look at as well. It's very close to – if not after – noon, and the sun is high in the sky. The ocean is electric blue and crystal clear. You can see the outlines of the reef that surround most of the island.

"It's beautiful," she breathes.

"I've made arrangements to have dinner downstairs tonight, if that's okay with you?"

"It's fine with me," Cami says. "Though I was kind of hoping to stay in tonight."

"I am never opposed to staying in. However, I wanted to take you downstairs tonight because after tomorrow I plan to stay hidden from view. The less chance of people seeing me here means the more likely I'm going to be able to stay out of the public eye." I look into her eyes. "All I want is to keep this as private as possible – for you, for me, and for all of our friends who will be here on Wednesday."

Her response is a look of pure adoration. The small, quiet "thank you" that follows is completely unnecessary; it's all there in her face.

"My world outside of this hotel is a madhouse, Cami. I will do whatever I can to protect you from that scrutiny." I speak softly and she nods.

"I'm willing to take the chance, Tristan. I am not made of glass."

"I know, Sweets, but I will not have them attempting to drag your good name through the mud." I smile at her, though in my chest I feel a fierce protectiveness.

"And for that I respect and commend you," she whispers as she starts to kiss me. This kiss is different: deeper, sensual, and so full of desire that I instantly become hard as a rock.

Cami senses my desire, and I feel her tongue on my lips, seeking, wanting entrance. Mmm, it feels good, but not ye—

Just then she flicks her hips at me and I moan as her sex grinds against my now throbbing erection, and her tongue is on mine. My head is swimming and I'm lost to her touch. Every inch of skin connected with hers is on fire, sending shivers through my body.

I slowly slide my hands up her back, careful not to catch her corset, until I find the back of her bikini top. Sliding my fingers along the string, I find the knot, and I hear her gasp.

Her hands fist into my hair, tugging hard, and I feel her pull her body up higher on mine, pushing her breasts closer to my mouth. An invitation?

I tug on the end of one of the strings and it comes undone. The water quickly pushes her top up and off. I feel one of her hands release my hair as I start seeking the strings that create the top of her halter. She beats me there, quickly pulling, and in an instant, her breasts are bare and pressed against my chest. Her barbells are cold, and my own nipples harden and my cock twitches.

I pull back to take in the sight of her, sucking a sharp deep breath between my teeth. "Jesus," I growl, and she pulls herself up higher and it's right there: a glorious, rose-colored nipple. I can't resist; I flick my tongue across it.

"Ah!" she moans. The sound is so hot with desire that my dick lets loose a gob of sticky pre-cum into my shorts. I lick again, this time pulling her nipple into my mouth, and she writhes against me. "Don't...ah...don't stop," she breathes, hot, heavy, and needy.

I pull my lips away from her nipple and lick again, kissing my way up from the swell of her breast to running kisses along the hollow of her throat, her jaw – I nip it with my teeth and she groans. Finding her lips again, I pull her tighter against me, pressing her breasts against my chest.

I kiss her, breathless and wanting. "Not—" I say, still kissing her. "Here." I kiss her again. "Not now."

She catches my meaning and ever so slightly backs off the ferocity of her kiss, but she doesn't stop. It sends a shudder through me to realize that it won't last too much longer. I can't keep holding back. But not in the pool.

Sometime later that evening Cami and I manage to untangle ourselves from one another and head downstairs for dinner. Cami looks stunning in her mini skirt and backless top. It doesn't seem to matter what this woman wears, she always wears it with pride and looks stunning.

During dinner we talk about music, and I'm surprised to find that we like a lot of the same artists. She asks me to tell her something that she can't find out about me on the Internet, and when I tell her I'm a huge football fan, it turns out we're both Baltimore Ravens fans and absolutely hate the Steelers. We both decide that we should try and get to a Steelers versus Ravens game this fall. The idea of fall plans excites me more than anything. It makes me hopeful that she really wants this to continue after our vacation together.

Emboldened by this, I ask her about coming to New York.

She takes a sip of her Cosmo, compliments of Jessie just a few moments ago. "Why do you want me in New York?" she asks.

Because I'm pretty sure that I will be an anger ball without you there, I think. Out loud I say, "Well, most of all, I want you there because something about being with you calms me. I don't feel anxious about anything, and I find it truly difficult to be nervous around you."

"I have a hard time picturing you as nervous." She smiles reassuringly.

"Well, I am not usually the nervous type. But I'm not a fan of crowds, and these premieres bring them out in droves." I sigh. "The girls get crazy, and all the screaming and hollering just gets overwhelming."

"I can understand how that would bother you. The idea of it scares the hell out of me. I've been to a couple of premieres before, but never via the red carpet. Bobbie used to walk the carpet all the time, but mostly after Mom passed and usually on the arm of some woman he was dating. If I was invited, I was brought in the back doors."

"You know, it's interesting. Bobbie did a lot to try and keep girls and people at bay unless he thought they were of some benefit to me. Directors, producers, casting directors, and the like. He had a way of instilling fear into me in regards to people outside of Hollywood. Girls and women in particular. He said that all they were ever after was my character and money, not me and who I am. It didn't take long for me to realize that he was right. It started after the first movie came out." I roll my eyes. "At first it bothered me, but then it became second nature. People loved me for the role I played and not really who I was."

"The only reason I knew who you were was because of the supermarket tabloids and the pictures that they would print of you. It was strange the way that those images made me feel. And then my reaction to the headlines. I'd get really worked up over some of the nastier ones." She takes a sip of her Cosmo and clears her throat. "I knew that none of them were true. Or at least they were getting twisted to the point of out of control."

"Why would you get upset?"

"Because they were running a perfectly good person through the ringer for no good reason other than to sell magazines!"

I can't help but laugh. She's the anger ball here. But it warms my heart. Something she said about getting angry sends a thrill through me, knowing that before she even met me four days ago, she was defending me.

"That is about the reality of it," I say. "Some stories had some true undertones. But the majority of them were blown way out of proportion."

"Do you really need me there in N.Y.C. with you next week?" She says as she sets down her silverware and looking at me.

The abrupt change of subject surprises me, but I don't hesitate. "Absolutely."

"All right, I will come with you to New York. I will coordinate with Trinity to see what I can do besides be your arm candy."

"Cami, you will never be arm candy." My tone is sharp.

She looks at me, wide-eyed at my reaction. The thought of her thinking of herself like that makes me ill. It is in this moment that I begin to realize that there is going to be so much more between Cami and me than there ever was with Layla. My eyes sting slightly, looking at her is like looking at an angel and I quickly realize that she is exactly the person I need beside me. Guiding me wherever I go. My desire for her spikes anew.

"Would you like to take a walk on the beach?" I ask, hoping that a change of scenery will help cool my desire a bit.

She smiles. "Absolutely," she says, and drains her glass.

Standing, I reach for her hand and she takes it. I can't help drinking in the sight of her as she stands. I take in her shoes, then her shins, her knees, her skirt. Then my eyes slowly wander up past her stomach and breasts, shoulders, neck, jaw, then, looking straight into her eyes.

As we walk through the doors onto the deck, I quickly realize the mistake of being on the beach. It's deserted.

TWENTY-TWO

~~*~*~*

CAMI

We walk along the surf until we reach the opposite end of the island from the hotel. While the hotel is visible behind us, it's peaceful and quiet over here. The moon is high and bright, lighting up the beach, which is mostly deserted; there are just a few couples milling about. Most of them are heading away from us, back toward the hotel.

It's getting to the point of no return, desire turning to need. I'm so afraid that I will end up hurting myself emotionally, that I'll end up trying to be with a man even if the feelings are not reciprocated. But something about his reaction regarding the arm candy comment tells me that we are both in similar places emotionally, and about this I'm overjoyed.

Both of us are quiet now, thinking. I want to ask Tristan what's on his mind, but I think it's better if I just leave him to his thoughts. I don't want to pry, and when he's ready to talk to me he will. I have no doubt.

Suddenly Tristan comes to a stop, tugging on our linked hands, pulling me into him. Then he releases my hand and reaches up to grab my arms. Tightening his grip, he pulls me into his chest, wrapping his arms around me so tight he's nearly crushing me. But I don't mind. I like being this close to him. My ear is pressed against his chest. I can feel his heart pounding out a rhythm, faster than I would have thought just from walking. My own heart is starting to push the blood behind my ears so fast it's starting to match the pace of his.

Gently he places one hand at about the middle of my back and the other cups my face. His thumb starts to gently stroke my cheek.

I feel his erection against my stomach. My sex heats from deep, deep down, heating my blood as it spreads throughout my body. I feel like I'm going to burst into flames.

I look up and our eyes meet. His beautiful, warm blue eyes. "Kiss me, Tristan," I whisper, and even I can hear the lust in my voice, but that doesn't stop him. He leans down. Slowly, painfully slow. His lips inching ever nearer mine. It's like a tease.

Stepping back slightly, I bring the length of my body into full contact with his. My back is arched, my breasts pressed into his chest. I hear his sharp intake of breath as he registers that his erection is pushing at my skirt, begging entrance into its warm sanctuary.

A mere hairsbreadth away from my lips, he stops.

"I have an idea," he says.

He moves his right hand from my face down to my chin, my neck, my shoulder, down my back, until it finds that sensitive spot where my butt meets my thighs. It tickles, and I squirm. He lets out a breathy chuckle and begins moving his fingers, forcing me to squirm some more, and I start to giggle.

"I love that sound," he says, though I can barely hear him over my fit of laughter.

Then, out of nowhere, he grabs my butt with both hands and pushes up. I squeal.

"Wrap your arms around me, beautiful, and hang on."

Blushing again, I do as I'm told, but before I have a firm grip on him, he picks me up off the ground. For a moment, terror grips my body, and I tighten my grip reflexively. Then I realize what he's done and start to giggle again.

"What are you doing?" I'm smiling so hard my cheeks are starting to burn.

"Kissing you," he says.

My fingers grip his hair, and I pull his lips to mine with a crushing force. His lips meet mine in blinding passion. They are soft, warm, and sensual against my own, and we quickly find a rhythm. Conscious thought eludes me as my head begins to swim. My heart is racing. My breathing becomes ragged. His own breathing mirrors mine, but he doesn't pull back, and I pull him tighter to me.

His tongue caresses my lips, seeking the perfect opportunity to enter my mouth. I feel his teeth graze my upper lip, then the lower, trying to tug. It feels so good I don't want to let him in. He grunts in frustration. It has to be one of the cutest sounds I've ever heard, and I smile. He senses he's winning, so he grabs my ass cheeks, squeezing hard. I gasp, and he steals the opportunity. With my distraction comes his warm, wet tongue, stroking against my own. I feel like I can't breathe. His kissing slows, and I notice that he, like me, is gasping for air. I feel him start to sway and his grip tighten. He slowly lowers himself to a sitting position in the sand, taking me with him.

During our decent, our tongues never stop. I feel him lift me slightly as he sits, and as he brings me back down,

I quickly realize why: his cock is rock hard against my labia. It's the perfect spot. The slightest friction against his erection and I'm going to be a quivering mess. I giggle again because I can tell that he is smiling through our kisses. I flick my hips ever so slightly, grinding my clit against his erection. A moan escapes his lips. The sound heats my core, and in an instant my sex is absolutely soaked. I grind again. This time I moan. I feel his cock twitch between us. Slowly I pull my mouth away from his, disengaging our lips and tongues by degrees.

Starting at his chin, I kiss and nibble my way along his jawline to his ear. He groans again and falls back into the sand, bringing me on top of him. He releases his hold on my butt and gradually drags his hands to my hips. He tugs at my hips so that my clit rubs against his cock again.

"Keep that up, Tristan," I whisper in his ear, "and you're going to make me come."

He smiles and does it again, this time pressing me onto his erection just a little bit harder. He pulls and pushes, pulls and pushes, and I let out a whimpered moan against his neck. His moan in response is enough to set off the tightening of my sex. The contraction of the orgasm has me stiff and whimpering against his neck. I bite my lip to try and stop it from consuming me.

"Let me hear you, Cami. Let me hear you come." His words have my orgasm at its peak. My eyes close and he pulls my sex against his and the bright white flashes of pure pleasure are visible behind my eyelids. Days of torture and I come unglued with friction. I release my lip and moan unabashedly against his neck. I'm panting, desperate for the air my lungs seem to be lacking.

I lie across his chest, and my breathing slowly returns to normal after a few minutes of heavy breathing. Tristan seems content to let me recover, and my heart warms at the subtle consideration for me.

I feel his hands release my hips and start stroking along my outer thighs until he feels my skirt end, a touch of skin, and the top of my thigh high stockings.

"You're wearing stockings!" he growls.

I smile and whisper in his ear, "A garter, too."

"Jesus fuck, you're trying to kill me here, aren't you?"

He pulls the hem of my skirt up, exposing my ass, and I laugh again. "I'm wearing a thong too, you know," I whisper wickedly.

"Fuck me! You are going to kill me."

"I don't see what's stopping you."

He hesitates just long enough that I finally look at him. His eyes are closed, his face turned up toward the stars. Still he says nothing and doesn't move.

All my years of insecurities wash over me. Something has stopped him and I have no idea what it is. I start to sit up, but then his hands are on my back, holding me in place.

"Please don't move."

"What's wrong, Tristan?" I say quietly, trying hard not to let the flood of emotion crush me. I don't fool him. His eyes fly open and he looks straight into mine.

"I'm scared, Cami." He's whispering so low that I can barely hear him.

What in the world is he scared of? I look at him with a puzzled expression.

"For two reasons," he says. "One, I was with the same woman for five years and I want you so much more than I ever thought possible, it scares me." He pauses briefly, then goes on. "And reason two, it's silly, but I'm afraid of hurting you."

Still puzzled. Okay, granted, the same woman thing, I get that. There's nothing wrong with being apprehensive about your first time with someone. I have my own apprehensions. But is he trying to say I move too fast? That I pushed him into something he's not comfortable with?

"I was just going with the flow, Tristan. I...I'm sorry if I did something to—"

He cuts me off, "You did nothing wrong, Cami. I want you. Believe me, I want you more than anything."

I'm really trying to trust him, but I have never actually been denied before, and this feels a lot like rejection. Trying to change the subject, I go with the easiest question I can think of. "Why do you think you will hurt me?"

He smiles at me and lets out a breathy laugh. "Give me your hand and slide back just a bit."

I do as I'm told and he takes my hand, turns it palm down, and brings it down on his erection. He starts at the junction of my sex and his, because a good portion is still underneath of me. His finger, seemingly accidentally, strokes my clit through my thong. I moan at the contact and he smiles again.

"Hmm, this could be fun," he says.

I'm completely lost in the sensation that begins to radiate throughout my body. My clit is still swollen and excited from only a few minutes ago. The contact instantly has me warmed right back up. But instead of continuing, he ignores my clit and begins to slide my hand up the length of his huge cock.

"I can do that," I whisper, and he releases my hand.

Slowly I push back down to the base of his cock, and then I slide my hand back up to the tip. I watch as his eyes roll up and under his eyelids. His head falls back to the sand and he moans again. I'm really beginning to enjoy the sounds he makes.

"So by hurting me, you're concerned about this big boy making its way deep inside me?" As I say this, I continue stroking him. He's huge and thick.

"Cami, I'm hung like a horse. We're on a beach, in public, which seriously hinders me from taking the time I need with you. This is hardly the right place for our first time." He is watching my hand stroke his cock through his pants.

"Your room or mine?"

He smiles but says nothing.

My self-consciousness floods back, threatening to completely destroy this entire moment. I slowly pull my hand away and maneuver myself off of him. I turn a hundred and eighty degrees and sit in the sand, knees pulled up to my chest, head resting against them, looking away from Tristan. The abrupt lack of contact has me feeling cold. I shiver.

"Cami?"

I don't answer. How can I explain this to him without sounding like an idiot? Frankly I'm already beginning to feel stupid for climbing off of him.

He sits up and slides closer to me. "Cami?" He takes a deep breath. "Cami, what did I do?"

"Nothing."

"Don't you dare pull that bullshit with me." I can tell he's trying to get my attention. Then I feel the tug on my left wrist, trying to pull my arm away from my shins.

"I'm sorry," I say, still looking away.

"Why are you sorry? Please, Cami, I'm in the dark here."

"I know, I'm sorry." I pull in a ragged breath and turn my head toward him. He tugs at my arm again, and this time I let him pull it away from my shins. He takes my hand in his, intertwining our fingers. Our hands fit perfectly. I feel my heartbeat increase. They fit so perfectly, like they were made for each other to hold. This isn't the first time we've held hands, but it's the first time I notice them like this.

"Tristan, this is going to sound so stupid. It's embarrassing on many levels."

"Try me."

"I..." I hesitate. "I've never been rejected before. I didn't know what—"

He cuts me off. "Cami, I'm not rejecting you. You saw it, and you felt it. I want you more than anything right now. I'm still rock hard and not walking away. So please believe me."

"It's hard for me to believe, Tristan. I ask you whose room and you don't reply. I'm not sure what to think..."

"Cami, I didn't reply because, believe it or not, I have some self-control." I try to interrupt him, but he cuts me off. "The only reason I'm using any self-control is because I have so much respect for you. And most of all...most of all," he repeats and pauses. I look at him, willing him to continue what he was trying to say. He sits silent for a minute.

Shame washes over me, sudden and so strong I want to get up and walk back to the hotel. Shame because he's just barely broken up with his girlfriend of five years, who disrespected him in the worst possible way, and here I am practically forcing myself on him.

He looks at me, and I know he can see the sadness in my eyes. He seems to be wrestling with his own shame.

"Cami, you deserve so much better than me, than being bedded by me so quickly. I don't want to ruin whatever chance I may have with you, so I need to do this right."

The words are sweet and my heart swells, but also the statement confuses me. "What exactly are you trying to say, Tristan?

He looks out at the water. "What I'm trying to say..." He pauses. "I mean..."

After what seems like an eternity I ask, "Tristan?"

"I'm trying to say that I am scared to sleep with you because I don't want you to feel like a rebound from Layla. I don't want to think of it like that and I'm concerned that if we sleep together too soon, it will become just sex. A weekend fling, a..." He pauses again. "I'm trying to tell you that I really like you, Cami. More than I should, given that I hardly know you." He smiles at me, a tentative smile. "I really want to get to know you, for you and not just for your body."

I'm completely taken aback. I suck air into my lungs so fast that I might pass out. After a couple of deep breaths I say to him, "I really want to get to know you, too." How can I say this? "Tristan, the only way I know how to be close to anyone is through sex." It's true. "I've never been in a relationship outside of the bedroom. The only way I know is my body. I'm sorry I pulled away from you. I don't know how to handle rejection. I really do want to get to know you, for you."

"I hope so, because I feel like we really need to do this right. I'm not sure how or why, but I've felt this way since I saw you in the airport in Los Angeles on Wednesday. I saw you again in Honolulu, and again shopping in the mall on Friday, and then finally in the bar Friday night."

"What do you mean L.A., Honolulu, shopping? Why didn't you say anything before?" I'm out of breath, shocked.

He's smiling again, but he looks down as though embarrassed. "Yeah, I saw you in the first class lounge Wednesday. Well, actually, I really only saw your wings." He pauses. "When I saw them, I saw them as a sign from my mother, a sign that things were going to...work out. I saw you again on the plane to Honolulu. You were so wrapped up in some book. You had your ear buds in." How in the hell did I not notice this? "Then, when we landed in Honolulu, I tried to follow you, but I was swarmed by a bunch of teenage girls."

"That was you?" I gasp. I saw the commotion, but at the time, I didn't think anything of it.

"You noticed that?" he asks. I nod. "Yeah, that was me. By the time I became untangled from them, you were gone. Tyson was dragging me off to my connecting flight to Bora Bora."

"I got on the Tahiti flight," I whisper.

"That would explain how you ended up here. I got into Bora Bora on Wednesday and was able to get here Wednesday night."

"Yup, you stole my penthouse." I try to laugh, but I'm so completely taken aback by the fact that Tristan saw me first, not just in the bar, but in L.A.

"It wasn't reserved when I got here," he says with a light teasing note in his voice.

"Yeah, I know. I never got around to making a reservation. Didn't think I would need to." I playfully push at his thigh. He laughs.

Our fingers are still intertwined. His thumb slowly starts to stroke the back of my hand.

"Then, Friday, I saw you shopping. I was following you, sort of, until you went into Versace. I didn't realize that it was you until you took off your hoodie and I saw your shoulder." He leans over and lightly kisses my left shoulder. "And then you showed up in the bar Friday night. I seized my opportunity." He places another warm kiss on my shoulder. "Yeah, I admit I was a bit of a peeping Tom at the mall."

"I can't believe you were watching me shop." I blush.

"Don't you dare be embarrassed, Cami. I enjoyed watching you shop. You looked so happy and carefree. Then when I saw you in the bar wearing the Versace outfit from the window, I realized that you were someone I had to talk to. And not just because of the price tag on that outfit." He laughs.

"So from the moment I walked into the bar Friday night you were watching me?"

He doesn't reply, just nods. He slowly brings my left hand up to his lips and gently kisses each one of my knuckles in turn. He lets out a sigh when he's done.

"A penny for your thoughts?" I whisper.

He smiles as I turn his line around on him, but he doesn't answer. Just keeps looking out toward the water. His brow is furrowed in deep concentration. My brain is going about a mile a minute sorting through all the possibilities of what could be on his mind.

"Tristan, please, what's bothering you?"

TWENTY-THREE

~~*~*~*

TRISTAN

So much has changed in the last few days. I feel like I've barely begun to grasp it. I said I wanted to wait, I want to prove to her (and maybe to myself) that she's not just a rebound. But right now, in this moment, watching her out of the corner of my eye, I begin to realize that Cami could never be just a rebound. She is more wonderful than anything I could have ever imagined.

Suddenly I can see it, the vision that's haunted me for years: a beautiful blushing bride; a woman's belly swollen with our child; the same woman playing with our child, smiling and happy. I've had this vision before, but this time, instead of a nameless, faceless woman, it's Cami I see.

Now, if only I can figure out what all of this means.

"Tristan, please?" Cami whispers. Her voice is strained. The desperation in her tone makes my heart stutter as if it wants to stop. I look over at her, and those gorgeous blue eyes are looking intently at me, betraying the same emotion as her voice. How can I explain to her what I don't yet understand?

"I'm not sure what to say. There are so many things going through my mind that I don't know where to start," I say, my voice husky. I reach up and move a lock of hair that's fallen onto her face back behind her ear. Cocking my head to the side slightly, hoping that she sees the gesture as comforting, I cup her face, and her hand reaches up to cover mine, holding it there.

After a beat or two she releases my hand, and I slowly pull back and run my fingers along her shoulder, down her side until my fingertips trace the lace across the top of her thigh highs, find the garter strap, and follow her upper thigh toward the hem of her skirt.

She lets out a soft moan. My erection throbs, threatening to explode against my pants. I groan.

"Cami?"

"Tristan?" She looks straight into my eyes, like she's trying to read what I'm thinking. She could not be more wrong. "We don't have to do anything you don't want." She lowers her voice. "I respect your choice to wait. I'm just not sure I have such self-control."

"Would you think of me as anything less than a gentleman if I carried you to my room?" I half growl at her.

Her cheeks heat. Her eyelids lower slightly, hooding her eyes as a look of sheer seduction crosses her face. I'm going to explode any minute and I need to do it in her, with her. I can't take this anymore. I'm past the point of no return, and my ability to be a gentleman is flying out the window at the speed of light.

"No."

No. She said no. Wait... "Do you mean no you won't come to my room, or no you won't think me less of a gentleman?"

She laughs. "I would never think you less than a gentleman, and I thought you'd never ask."

That's it. That is all I need to hear. After the conversation we just had, I was afraid that I might've scared her away from me. I do really want to wait, but I'm thinking that I'm trying to wait for all the wrong reasons.

I stand up, bringing her with me, pulling her to her feet. I bend down, grab her around her thighs and hoist her over my shoulder. She squeals and protests my movements by squirming. I realize she's in a position that's far from ladylike, and I can't resist the urge to bring my free hand up to her butt in a quick slap. She lets out a soft hiss and a moan, a sound so seductive that for a second I think I might just come in my pants.

"You keep that up and I will take you right here, right now on the beach, and I don't care who watches."

She giggles again, and then I feel her shoulders shift, and her hand comes down hard, square on my ass. I hiss and spank her again. But before this can become an all-out spank war I shift her in my arms, without breaking my stride, bringing her to the front of my body. She sticks out her lower lip in a cute pout but wraps her legs around my waist and her arms around my neck.

Lucky for me, little brain has shifted to the right and is no longer pressed between us. I'm not sure that I would make it back to the hotel, let alone up to the room, otherwise.

"Do you have any idea how hard it is to walk while staring at you?" I chuckle and tighten my arms under her butt. It takes me all of half a second to notice that her bare ass cheek is cradled nicely in my left hand. I began to caress her skin. She smiles and lets out a rushed breath.

"Do you have any idea how hard it is to be carried, out of control, and more than willing to try and tackle you to the ground, right here and now? Keep caressing my ass and it just might happen." She lowers her lids at me again. Her stare screams lust.

"Oh, believe me, if it weren't for the fact that there's a group of people walking out of the hotel and in our direction, I would have taken you back there about a hundred yards. You can be a good girl and wait until we get to my suite."

"Yes, sir."

Oh, wonderful. She has a damn sense of humor, doesn't she. Just for that, I pinch her ass cheek. Lightly, but firmly enough to make her yelp. She's glowing and smiling at me. A look that says, 'Okay, you get that one, but I will do better to earn the next one.' My hand stills, and she squirms in my arms.

"What's the matter, Cami? Did you want me to go back to what I was doing?"

"Yyyessss," she breathes, and I smile.

But at this point we're nearly to the deck at the back of the bar. As much as I don't want to let her go, I put her down so she can walk into the hotel on her own two legs. I'm more than a little satisfied to see how shaky those legs are. I'm glad I'm not the only one.

We cross the lobby to the elevators. I reach out and push the call button. She groans.

"The elevator." Looking up at me she continues, "You know what they say about elevators?" I grin wickedly at her. Her eyes widen and she says, "I have a feeling I am getting myself into trouble already."

"Yes, I think you are, considering this elevator opens right up into my suite. If we are alone in there, there will be absolutely nothing stopping me from tearing off your clothes."

She moans quietly at me again. Apparently that idea really appeals to her.

I finally let myself imagine what it'll be like to be inside of her, to feel her bare skin against mine, to have her surrounding me.

And then I remember the other reason I wanted to wait. Dammit.

"Cami?"

"Hmm?" she says lazily, no doubt thinking about the same thing I was.

"There was another reason I wanted to wait." I watch as a look of disappointment colors her face at my words, but I try hard to ignore it. Leaning into her ear I whisper, "It's because I don't have any condoms."

She stiffens slightly. "I use birth control and I know that I'm clean. I don't usually have sex without a condom. It's my number one rule." Her voice gets quiet at the end. Contemplative.

"It's my number one rule, too. However, I can tell you that I too am clean. But..." God it's hard for me to say this; I want her so bad right now. But I'd hate myself later if I didn't give her the option. "Cami, we don't have to do anything tonight."

"I trust you," she whispers and looks deep into my eyes, into my soul. Her expression reiterates the words she's just spoken.

Stepping into the elevator, I wonder if there is any way to keep it empty all the way up.

TWENTY-FOUR

~~*~*~*

CAMI

The elevator arrives and we step in. We're alone. He swipes his room key and punches number eight.

Looking into his eyes, I see fear, although that's not the dominant emotion. He's hungry for me, wants me and only me. I have no doubt that my face and eyes are showing that same emotion because it is all I can think about.

My feelings for him have grown so quickly, and I know that if we sleep together now, that feeling will only intensify. And frankly, it scares the hell out of me.

"I don't know if I am ready for this, Tristan," I whisper. I can see in his eyes that he's not going to disagree with me.

He says, "Would it be okay if we just spent the night together? No expectations?" There is slight disappointment in his voice, but the smile on his face tells me another story.

Each night, being taken to my room and left alone has been painful. I hate to be away from him, and now he is giving me the chance to stay with him.

Smiling back at him, I tell him, "I can live with that."

His lips meet mine. The kiss is strong and passionate but extremely gentle. Loving, really. He pulls back a little and then kisses me along my jaw to my ear where he kisses that tender spot just below my lobe. Then he licks my earlobe, pulling it toward his mouth.

"I've had a marvelous time tonight," he whispers softly. His hot breath caresses my skin and sends shivers down my spine.

In the short time I've known him, he has managed to incite feelings I never knew I was capable of, and I would do anything to keep feeling this way.

"Tristan, today and tonight have been amazing. Thank you," I whisper as I reach up and cup his face. With a little bit of pressure against his cheek I coerce his mouth toward mine and kiss him.

I faintly hear the ding of the elevator over the sound of the blood rushing and pulsing through my ears. I realize I'm not breathing. His hand on my jaw exerts gentle pressure to lead me forward. Not until the elevator closes mere inches behind me do I realize that we've entered the foyer of his suite.

I reach up and grip his hair, pulling his mouth to mine in an aggressive kiss. I feel his hands on my back, seeking a zipper. In contrast to mine, his motions are slow and calculated. Like he is trying to make sure that this is what I really want. "Want" is no longer a word in my vocabulary. I need him.

I pull away from the kiss and bring my hands slowly down his neck to the top button of his shirt. Slowly, one by one, I start to undo his shirt.

As I slowly undo each button, little visual pleasures come into view. His chest is cut to perfection. His abs are chiseled. As I unhook the last button, his shirt starts to fall away from his shoulders. A good portion of the dragon on his chest comes into view and I take a moment to breathe in his scent His scent is like heaven, and my body heats. He is gorgeous.

Opening his shirt brings out the sexy, well-defined V that accents his hips. My breathing spikes and my mouth goes dry. His pants are hung low on his hips in such a way that I would be surprised if he was wearing anything underneath.

Reaching up, I push his shirt off, drinking in his nakedness. I'd seen him shirtless before, but not like this. Not with the eyes of knowing that tonight everything changes between us. Once we start, it is going to be impossible to stop going forward.

I continue pushing his shirt down his arms. His biceps are beautiful, toned, and tight. Perfectly contoured, thick and strong. His skin is very warm to the touch with a slight hint of a tan. When the arms of his shirt reach his wrists, they stop and go no further.

"Cufflinks," he whispers against my lips, ready to kiss at a moment's notice, his breath hot. I stare into his eyes as my fingers go to work releasing the cufflinks from his shirt. I could be faster, but my eyes are lost in his. Finally I hear the cufflinks clatter to the floor.

He chuckles briefly, then just like that his lips are on me. I let out a breathy laugh since his kiss has interrupted my undressing of him. His fingers move up my sides, feather light and warm, causing strange tingling sensations to radiate through my body. The motion sends chills across my skin, the shiver of anticipation heats my already hot sex further, and my now painful nipples swell even more. The pain is such that only his warm, wet tongue can soothe. I feel the wetness of my sex starting to seep down my leg.

His hands continue their ministrations against my skin, moving up to the fine sheer strap that covers the back of the bra I'm wearing. I feel his fingers move from my arm across the back of my neck, sweeping my hair to the side. Trailing fingers slide down my back, right along the nape of my neck, down between my shoulder blades, and a new wave of desire surges through my body as his hands seek the hooks holding my top together.

He's leaning closer to me, and I nip his jaw, and in an instant his lips are back on mine. The tingle of contact opens the flood gates in my body and I sway as he steals my breath away. My lips are becoming raw, and the pleasure of his mouth on mine drives my desire even higher.

My head is swimming with his scent: fresh air, salt water, Armani, and a scent all his own – musty, warm and sweet, almost like chocolate.

"How do I get this dress off of you?" he growls against my lips.

I giggle, trying hard to catch a breath; he keeps stealing them from me with every touch. "The right side of the back strap." I pause to take the deep breath I so desperately need, subconsciously noting that his breathing is just as ragged as mine. Something tells me that his desire is quickly becoming necessity, just like mine. "It unhoo—"

Before I can finish I feel my dress and bra start to fall away. Tristan takes a deep, sharp, quick breath as my breasts and fully erect nipples come into view.

"Now the zipper. Top of the skirt," I breathe.

His hands move down and find the top of my skirt. He unhooks the small clasp, and his touch brushing along my back sends a shiver through me. His mouth roams my jaw, neck, shoulder, and back again, each pass getting lower and closer to my breasts. Each kiss a big, open-mouthed, sensual kiss. His tongue caressing my skin.

I arch my back, hoping that he takes the hint. He does, but chooses very quickly to ignore it.

With the zipper undone and nothing to hold up the dress it slips down to the floor in a hushed rush. It pools silently around my heels and I'm momentarily trapped. Tristan seizes the opportunity and takes a half step back. His eyes rake over my body from top to bottom and back again, settling on the garter, thong, and thigh high combination. Air audibly rushes into his lungs and his mouth falls open. His tongue peeks out, hungrily licking his lower lip.

He stares through hooded eyes for more than a minute. I want to unhook my garter straps so that I can slowly remove my thong, but his expression changes. A huge smile lights up his face. Giggling at the expression, I start to imagine what it will be like to have Tristan devouring me, licking and biting along my body.

"Enjoying the view?" I settle my giggles. His brilliant smile turns into a toothy grin. "I will take that as a yes. But you should ask me to turn around so you can enjoy the view from the back."

"Turn around, Cami."

In response to the command my blood surges through my veins and I smile. For a moment the sound of my pulse is all I can hear.

I start to turn slowly to my right, keeping my eyes on Tristan as I do. I'm desperate to see his reaction as he takes in the full effect. After a quarter turn, I can no longer see him, but when my backside comes into view, sans bra and other hindering objects, he lets out a gasp of pleasure.

His reaction doesn't disappoint. I feel his hands slowly gliding along the curves of my wings, my shoulder blades, and down my sides. Looking over my right shoulder I watch as his eyes go from lustful need to a bright ice blue, and then he laughs.

Touching the dimple of my right butt cheek, he asks, "Who the hell kissed your ass?" And his voice is so light and carefree that I nearly forget that I am, for all intents and purposes, naked.

Laughing, I ask him, "Are you sure you want to know?" He nods. "Are. You. Sure?" I say, emphasizing each word. He smiles, laughs, and nods, this time with gusto. "Beau."

Suddenly the room is filled with nothing but the echoes of Tristan's laughter, and I can't help but join in.

I reach out my hand to his and he takes it, bringing it to his lips and planting gentle kisses on each knuckle. A gesture that I'm quickly finding is highly enjoyable.

"How about a drink?" he asks.

"I would love one." The moment is broken, for now.

He steadies my elbow and points to the dress at my feet. "Step." I step out of the dress, careful not to catch my heels, and bend to pick it up. "Leave it," he says. "We can get it later."

I stand up, and as I reach my own full height, I catch a sparkle coming off his chest, a reflection coming from the eyes of the dragon. Reaching my hand out as if to touch them, I ask, "Dermals?"

"Yeah, they're about five weeks old."

"I've thought about those. Even replacing the corset hoops with dermal piercings. I just can't find the right attachments."

He cringes slightly. "I would rather have my tattoos done a hundred times over than have more dermal piercings done. They are positively the most painful thing

I have ever felt." Then he smiles an I-have-a-secret smile. "Well, almost the most painful."

Oh my. I wonder if he is referring to the piercings in his cock and nipples, or if it is something else entirely.

~~*~*~*

TRISTAN

I can't get over how beautiful Cami is. And so uninhibited, standing here talking to me, completely topless and with only a few scraps of material covering her most intimate parts. Those eyes, the blue of the South Pacific sky, are sharp and miss nothing. Her facial features are soft, round, and inviting. Her lips are beautiful, luscious, a small natural upward curve at the corners giving off the impression that she is always smiling. The smooth lines of her neck and shoulders. The curve of her collarbone. Obviously she works out because her arms are trim and lean, and she has a four pack in the abs department. Strong but also sensual. Ardor is running hot and ramped to the point that I can barely keep my feet from pulling me in her direction.

Shaking myself mentally, I remember that I asked her if she wanted a drink. "What would you like to drink? I have a pretty full mini bar, or we can order up some room service."

She blinks a couple times. Is she trying to clear her head, too? Looking up and into my eyes, she says, "Wine would be great."

"Red or white?"

"White, please."

"Coming right up." Walking over to the bar, I fish a bottle of white wine out of the fridge, pop the cork, and pour her a glass. Returning the wine, I grab a Blue Moon off the shelf and head back to her. "I don't know anything about wine, other than this is white."

She giggles and takes the glass from me. "It is probably the same sauvignon blanc that I have in my room. Great stuff. You should try it sometime."

I let out a low chuckle. "Yeah, maybe. I am a beer and whiskey kind of guy usually, but I'll consider it."

"Fair enough."

She starts to wander the room, seeming to forget that she's topless. I can't take my eyes off her. The curve of her backside as she walks away is almost like Aphrodite in the flesh. Her hair is falling down her back, almost to the top of her corset, in long loose waves. Her supple curves are on display. My cock twitches and lust burns hot and bright through my body.

"I'm curious about something," I say.

"Oh? Ask me anything."

"If I asked you to be completely naked right now, would you?" I smile at her, hooding my eyes to show her a small taste of the desire I'm feeling.

She doesn't miss a beat. "With or without the heels?"

I smile bigger. "Without," I whisper. Though I love the heels, I want her completely naked.

She doesn't hesitate. After she sets her wine glass down on the nearby table, she reaches for one of the hooks on her garter. When she has released the three straps, her hands go to the top of her thong and she begins to slowly but deliberately move the material down her thighs. She pauses when the top of her thong is flush with the top of her pubic bone and spreads her legs so that the panties are stretched tight.

I know where this is going. She is going to tease the living hell out of me with a strip tease. I reach for my iPhone, pulling up the Bluetooth, and hit play on "Porn Star Dancing" by My Darkest Days.

She smiles wide and starts to move her hips from left to right while rubbing her hands up her body, across her stomach, up to cup the bottoms of her beautiful, full tits. She pulls her nipples between her thumb and forefinger and rolls them between her fingers. Her nipples, which are a beautiful, deep pink, get even harder with each roll.

I'm ready to come undone right now. My knees are going weak and I'm pretty sure I'm going to fall over. I back up into a chair and plop down in a very ungraceful move. My eyes never leave her body.

Her hands, spread wide, make their way back down her stomach to the top of her garter belt, and she slides it down her hips and thighs, leaving her thong in place. When the garter belt hits the top of her thigh highs, she turns around, moving it further down her legs, and she bends over to remove it. Her beautiful, round ass becomes the center of my attention, the view interrupted only by the small triangle of her thong. As she pulls her right leg free from the garter belt, she spreads her legs wide and I can see her between her legs.

Her eyes are closed and I can see the small red flush across her cheeks. But she is smiling, so I'm not concerned that she's embarrassed by my brazen request to be naked for me. God, she is practically naked. Biting my lip to hold back the groan that's threatening, I watch as she raises her head, smoothing back her hair, and she rises slowly, the muscles in her ass tightening and smoothing in the most delicious way.

My breathing is uneven, and I'm sure my mouth is hanging open. At this point I wouldn't mind if the song lasted all night.

Cami stands up straight, turns back around, and starts stalking toward me in nothing but a thong, thigh highs and heels, crossing one foot in front of the other in a slow, seductive walk. The chair I'm sitting in is an oversized club chair, big enough for two, so I spread my own legs wide in invitation. She turns around again, slowly lowering her sex to mine. I bite my lip again as she slowly starts to grind against my swollen and aching cock.

She stands up again and goes to work pulling her thong slowly down her thighs, repeating the earlier show. This time there's nothing left to the imagination. I clearly see her sex, glistening with arousal and aching to be touched. I moan.

She finishes removing her panties and turns toward me again. This time she straddles my lap. Reaching up, she runs her hands through my hair. Gripping hard, she pulls my head toward her. I'm fully prepared to kiss her, but it turns out that is not on her agenda. Instead she brings my head to her left nipple and rubs the hard tight bud against my lips.

As the song comes to an end, she lets up on the grip she has on my hair. Afraid she might break the moment and get up, I place my hands on her back and release a hot breath across her nipple.

"Ahh!" she moans, arching her back. I take full advantage, dragging a hot, thick, languid tongue across her nipple. She moans out a semi-coherent "please." At the realization that she wants more, my cock lets go of the pre-cum it's been holding as I flick my tongue hard against her nipple. Her hands move from my hair down my neck to my shoulders as I slowly lick and kiss my way across her chest, over to her right nipple, which I pull into my mouth. The barbell piercing her skin is cold against my hot tongue.

Her fingertips find my nipples, and I let out a grunting moan against her breast. As I suck harder and faster she starts to squirm, and my own hips start to move with her. Lost to the sensation of my sex against hers, desperate to repeat her earlier orgasm, I note that her fingertips are lightly stroking across my chest and stomach, and then she reaches the button on my pants.

I shake my head against her breast and look up to meet her eyes. She sticks out her luscious lower lip, disappointment clear in her eyes. She's actually pouting at me.

I smile and release her nipple from my mouth. "Hold on to my neck, like before," I say. I cradle her ass in my arms and stand up. And then, by way of explanation, I say, "Not here, in bed."

She smiles wide at me then. I move my lips to hers as I walk across the sitting room and into the bedroom. I lower her gently onto the bed, holding her close to me with both hands wrapped around her. "You are beautiful, you know that?"

She blushes, smiling shyly at me. "As are you." Her slight accent has me smiling. I feel hands traveling down my back to the waistband of my pants again, then they slip inside, moving around to the buttons. This time I make no move to stop her.

TWENTY-FIVE

~~*~*~*

CAMI

I'm doing my best to make quick work of the buttons on his pants, desperately needing to spring his cock from its confines, which have a not-so-small wet spot on the crotch. Jesus, he is gorgeous. His body speaks of sex and more sex. He has me so turned on that one tiny flick of a finger or tongue across my clit will have me exploding.

I finish with the buttons, kick off my heels, and bring my legs tight around his waist, pulling his erection into my now drenched sex. He pulls his arms out from underneath my body, careful not to pull against my piercings. He rears up slightly, placing all his upper body weight on his left arm. From the corner of my eye I see his bicep flex at the exertion, but he doesn't falter. Slowly he trails his right hand down my side to my hip.

I'm breathing hard as his right hand comes across my stomach to my left leg, then back again, lower across my pubic bone. I squirm. He pulls himself up, placing his knees under my thighs, and I can feel the head of his cock press against the entrance of my body.

As he pulls himself up, he lets his left hand glide across my shoulder and down my breast, catching my nipple. I shiver, sending goose bumps across my skin, my nipples hardening further. They burn for his tongue, but he continues moving his hand to my leg.

Bringing his hands together on my right leg, he very slowly and seductively pulls the thigh high down, his fingers caressing my skin as the nylon travels down to my knee, shin, ankle, toes. He gently grabs my ankle and pulls my foot, now bare, to his lips. He lightly and playfully bites into the pad of my big toe.

I moan loudly and call his name. He smiles against my foot and then continues kissing and licking up to my ankle, then the inside of my calf, up to the back of my knee, where he circles his tongue. With my leg pointing straight to the ceiling, I feel his teeth graze the back of my knee. He doesn't bite, but the sensation is enough to cause another moan. I feel his lips spread, and I begin to watch him watching me. Our eyes meet, and I have a feeling that I'm about to get paid back for my strip tease a few minutes ago.

He continues up the inside of my leg, sliding his body back so that he can lay on his stomach. He is kissing, licking, and nipping his way up my thigh, and my sex is burning with the need to come, and come hard.

I feel my orgasm spreading throughout my body, so I slam my eyes shut, knowing that watching him is helping my orgasm build. On the verge of orgasm, I feel that he's reached that sweet spot right where my sex and thigh come together, and I know that if he bites me, right there, I will explode. Sensing his hesitation, I nearly shout, "Do it, Tristan!"

In a rush he bites down. The bite hurts, but the pain quickly turns to pleasure, and I come loudly as he slides two fingers deep inside me. I shatter into a million pieces. He continues to milk my orgasm for every ounce it's worth, sliding his fingers in and out of me as I moan and writhe against his hand.

As my orgasm subsides he slowly pulls his fingers out of me one last time and releases the now painless grip his teeth have on my skin. Sitting up, bringing his knees back under my thighs, he brings his fingers to his mouth and licks. His eyes darken and close in a silent groan as he tastes my arousal.

Finding strength in the need I now feel for him, I sit up, reaching again for his pants. I want to see him, feel him, and taste him. Realizing that he has his pants bunched under his ass, I push on his shoulder and he falls dramatically to the bed. I start to pull on his pants, and he lifts his ass.

His cock is hard as a rock, a healthy glob of pre-cum sliding down his shaft. I'm beginning to wonder if he will even fit inside me. But it's not his size that surprises me the most. It's finally catching a glimpse of the piercings I felt earlier.

He has four total, a Prince Albert that is currently occupied by a small gauge, open-sided silver ring. Below his PA there are three frenum piercings running down his shaft, each about an inch apart. The first one is about an inch below that sweet spot on the bottom side of his thick, mushroomed head.

"Oh, my!" I whisper with a smile. I push his pants to his knees, but can't make them go any farther. "Take those off," I say, and he does.

"Was it worth the wait?" He's smiling ear to ear. I watch his thick, swollen penis bounce while he finishes undressing. I absentmindedly remove my other thigh high.

We're now both completely naked, and I reach out for his erection.

"I want you in my mouth."

Still smiling, he lays back onto the bed. I take his erection in my left hand and begin to tease the head of his cock with my tongue. I lick and kiss the length of his shaft, and then I watch his eyes darken as I pull him into my mouth. My tongue ring clicks hollowly against his piercings, my mouth locked tight around his erection.

His cock is so thick that I can really only get a few inches in, and I'm struggling to keep my teeth sheathed by my lips so I don't hurt him. When I reach the second barbell my jaw is stretched so far that I doubt I'll ever be able to get him far enough in to activate my gag reflex.

He moans, his eyes closing with pleasure. "Cami..." He is out of breath. "If you don't stop, I'm going to come in your mouth." I smile against the head of his cock and continue sucking and licking his fully erect sex. He moans again and I take him in as deep as I can, sliding back up then down again.

On my fourth thrust down he barks, "Holy shit, Cami, I'm coming!" Desperate to make him orgasm the way I did when he bit me, I don't stop. I feel every muscle in his legs lock up tight. His hands curl into fists in my hair, and a very thick, hot shot of cum slams against the back of my throat. I pump his cock with my mouth as the salty sweetness hits my tongue. I continue sucking hard, milking his sex for every last drop. After several shots down my throat, he finally stops squirting his orgasm into my mouth. But rather than stop, I simply slow. He groans and twitches as my tongue grazes the underside of the head.

Though he came like a rocket down my throat, he is still hard as a steel pipe. I smile and pull back just a little. "Is this normal?"

He chuckles, and in a barely coherent voice he replies, "For you, yes, I am pretty sure this will be normal." He props himself partway up on one elbow and tugs gently on my right arm. "Come here."

I follow his lead, and he pulls me on top of him. His hand moves from my arm to my cheek as he pulls my face down so he can kiss me.

"Straddle me, baby-girl," he breathes against my lips. On hearing the endearment, I feel desire surge again, hot and hard. I throw my leg over him, lining up his cock with my entrance. "Slowly," he breaths, and I do as I'm told. His erection is still so hard and standing up at full mast. His sex brushes against my wet pussy, and I can feel the head of his cock seeking the entrance to my sex. A warm delicious shiver runs through my body as I slowly start to lower myself onto him.

He is staring straight into my eyes. Something is happening between us. There is a charge that fills the air as the sweet smell of our arousal comes together.

As my sex slides past his PA he groans. "For fuck's sake, you're so tight." I continue sliding down. "And soaked." I feel the first barbell pressing against my opening and I clench down on the head of his cock. He swallows hard, his eyes beginning to roll back into his head.

Lowering myself further and unclenching against his erection, my body is stretching, kneading him as he slides further into me. I feel the second barbell push past the soft barrier and then finally the third.

I pull myself back up, allowing my arousal to soak his own. He groans as I pull off of him until only the very tip is buried inside me. I slide back down, this time a little faster, until I feel the tickle of his balls against my ass cheeks. I stop as a shiver of satisfaction rocks through me and every nerve in my body comes alive.

Tristan lets out a soft moan of satisfaction. "Dammit, baby-girl. Go very slow, please. I feel like I am ready to explode again."

I smile and slowly start to grind my hips against his. I can feel his sex buried deep within my core. My clit is rubbing gently against his pelvic bone, and with this fullness inside, coherent thought is lost as I feel my next orgasm warming from that special spot. I bite my lip to help slow the onslaught because I'm determined to take as long as I can with him – tonight and every night.

I close my eyes, let my head fall back, and arch my back. My pussy tightens against his hard-on. I moan rather loudly, and he reaches up to cup my breasts in his hands. "Ahhh," I breathe, and then suck in a loud, harsh breath as his fingers pinch my nipples. My hands go to his chest, bracing my body so that I can really start sliding up and down.

I tease him by bringing my pussy to the point that I can feel him start to slip out, and then I slide back down, hard and quick. He moans. I do it again. And again. When he is completely sheathed inside me, I flick my hips against his, and I feel the head of his cock massage my g-spot and my clit grinds against his pubic bone.

His hands come down from my chest to my hips, and I feel his fingers press into the soft flesh, urging me to lift, and I do. Once I'm back to the head of his cock he slams his hips into me and I moan. I hear his rush of breath at the exertion and disappointment of coming back out, but he doesn't go far before he slams back in.

Sweat covers his body and mine. I watch as he watches me. His eyes are dark and dilated, but they never swerve from mine. Looking into his eyes and his persistent pounding into my sex causes my heart to flutter, and the sweet sensation of warmth rises from deep inside my very core.

My clit is throbbing with each contact with his skin. "Tristan," I say as my eyes roll back into my head, breaking our connection. My arms start to shake and become weak. I shift so my arms are above his shoulders, next to his head, and I bring my mouth to his, kissing him with ardor. He instantly starts kissing me back and my body goes limp against him. His hands glide up my sides, and he cups my face while he continues to slide in and out, slower now but still solid against my sweet spot.

His hands work into my hair, and my legs become stiff. My toes curl against his thighs. He pulls me harder against his lips, and my orgasm boils over. I pull away from his kiss as the orgasm overtakes me, taking me to a place of pure ecstasy. "Trriiiiiisstan! Ah!" I moan as I come harder than I ever have before.

My sex grips hard onto his erection, and his motion slows. His hands come free of my hair and are on my hips in an instant. My sex is pulsing, coercing his cock into orgasm. Gripping my hips he pushes me down hard. His cock meets the resistance of my cervix. He pulls back and slams down again. And again. His jaw tightens, every muscle in his neck stands out, and his nails dig into my hips. His cock pulses within me. On the fourth thrust he stills, and I feel the first shot deep within my core.

The sensation of his cum entering me brings me to another immediate release. Every pulsing shot of his orgasm pushes me further and further over the edge.

"CAMI!" I hear him cry out.

I collapse onto his chest, completely spent, both of us breathing hard. Our hearts beat out a fast, chaotic rhythm in our chests. His hands release their grip on my hips and slowly slide up my back. I feel the tension on a few of my piercings, but the sensation is lost as he engulfs me in an embrace that is so sweet and tender. I can feel his eyes on me, but I'm beyond the point of comprehension and I don't look up.

His cock twitches inside me, and the motion causes another moan to escape from my lips. As my moaning registers on him, I can feel his erection growing inside me again.

I smile. I'm tired, but I've had nowhere near my fill of him.

"What are you doing to me, Cami? Apparently I can't get enough of you."

I giggle, and the motion causes my hips to move slightly. Tristan groans.

One second I'm laying on his chest, and in the next I'm on my back, beneath him. His sex never leaves mine as he rolls us over.

He slowly starts to move in and out of me, looking deep into my eyes. There's wonder and tenderness and significance there, and I stare back at him, hoping my face shows that I'm feeling the same. He seems to find what he's looking for, and his motions increase slightly, picking up the pace.

I'm so wet. He's sliding in and out of my tight pussy without resistance, smooth and sensual. I'm dying to feel him bury himself deep inside me while coming, and I start to move my hips against his once again.

~~*~*~*

TRISTAN

She is already starting to moan while I move slowly in and out of her. I lower my head to her chest and start to sweetly lick her right nipple. Her head pushes back against the pillow. Her eyes are closed tight.

I pull up off of her nipple and sit back a little. I lift her left leg, effectively halting her motions against mine. I hold her leg straight up and slowly slide in and out of her. I'm in so deep now, deeper than when she was on top of me. I can feel every inch of her sex surrounding my rock hard erection.

I lick and kiss along the leg that's in the air. She is moaning again and I feel her pussy tighten. She is going to come again, but I'm not ready for that. I'm amazed to realize that if she comes again, so will I. I can feel my orgasm at the head of my prick, desperately trying to escape.

I lower her leg, twisting her so that her ass cheek is meeting my pelvic bone. Her ass is perfect and round and jiggles ever so slightly with every slow thrust. She adjusts the top half of her body so she's laying on her side.

"Can you get your arm under you and lift yourself up?"

She nods her response and turns more onto her stomach. As she lifts herself up, I sit straight up, bringing her hips with me.

"Now get your right leg under yourself. I want to take you from behind."

She knows exactly what I mean, and she pulls her leg up, lifting herself off the bed, placing calf along my leg.

I'd stopped thrusting while she turned over, but now I pick back up again, and she rocks gently back and forth on her elbows and knees. The view of her ass sliding along my cock is probably the most beautiful sight I've ever seen. Her head is turned to the side, eyes straining to see me. To maintain eye contact with me. Her hair is sweeping to her left and I can see her hands intertwined with it. Her wings are in full view, taunting me to touch them. Her corset is laced with a purple ribbon tonight. I can see her breasts swaying slightly beneath her, and I place my left hand on her hip and grip, sliding her back and forth against my cock.

I let out a moan and start to pick up my rhythm. She arches her back downward, and I feel my cock slide in deeper and her pussy tighten. She's sliding along my dick with effortless motions.

My right hand slides along her corset, careful not to catch a ring, and reaches for the open end of the bow at the top. I tug gently, untying it, and she moans as the ribbon tickles her skin. I slowly start to pull the ribbon through her corset. I watch as the muscles in her back twitch when the last bit tickles across her skin.

"Ahh,"

Hmm, I seem to have found a very interesting turn-on. Once the ribbon is free of her corset, I let it tickle along her back, and she writhes. I can see goose bumps forming in its wake.

When I bring the ribbon down along the small of her back, her pussy tightens around my cock, hard. She stiffens. and I can feel the heat building up in my spine. My orgasm's imminent as her pussy tightens even more against my erection.

"Cami," I say, and she knows what I mean and her pace increases, our hips slamming together, harder and faster. I'm meeting her thrust for thrust, pushing myself harder and deeper inside her. Her pussy pulses and tightens with choking strength, and her entire body becomes hard and stiff.

She cries out my name as her orgasm takes her. Her body becomes boneless as she twitches beneath me, her pussy milking my cock. My cock twitches. She moans, my cock hardens as my balls tighten, and my orgasm forces my eyes to close. It peaks and I feel my cum shooting into her, hot and hard. I shout her name as I explode inside of her yet again. She doesn't stop coming until I do.

I collapse against her back. No doubt I'm heavy, so I slowly lean to my left, bringing Cami with me. My cock is still semi-hard, but I have nothing left to give, and Cami seems to have nothing left to take.

I slide my left arm under her neck, and my right arm snakes around her stomach. I pull her in tight. My chest presses against her back and my erection, though thoroughly tamed, is still inside Cami, and I know that we're both going to fall asleep, just like this, for many more nights to come.

TWENTY-SIX

~~*~*~*

CAMI

My bladder is going to explode. The thought stirs me awake. As I register the feeling, I realize that there is a warm sensation building through my body, and it's not my bladder. An orgasm?

I'm wide awake now, but I keep my eyes closed. A moan escapes my lips. Tristan is slowly sliding in and out of my sex. Did we really sleep like this all night?

His hand slides up over the curve of my hip, up my side, as he moves inside me. His pace is slow, passionate, with unhurried anticipation of the orgasm he knows he's leading me toward. I let out another moan as I roll my head in his direction. He is leaning over me, smiling.

"Good morning, beautiful," he whispers.

"Good morning beautiful yourself," I reply with a smile as big as his. His hand has reached the soft swell of my breast. His finger glides over my nipple, teasing it into a hard, tight, deliciously sore peak. I moan again. "I could get used to this, you know?"

His breathy laugh sends a thrill through me. "So can I," he whispers into my ear. "When I woke, it took me all of two seconds to realize that I was still buried inside you." Reaching my lips with his, he says, "I couldn't resist."

His lips are on mine, soft and tender. My breathing slows to huffs with each thrust of his hips. He lowers his hand from my breast past my stomach, and he finds my clit. I lift my right leg, hitching it around his thighs, opening myself to him.

My head is swimming with the overwhelming sensation of his tongue on mine, his fingers circling my clit. My orgasm comes on quick. Every muscle in my body clinches, my sex kneading and milking his. He moans into my mouth.

"Come for me, baby," he orders softly.

In response my pulse quickens, my pussy tightens further, and my orgasm bubbles from my core. Building and building as I moan louder and harder. I reach the cliff and I come. Hard.

"Tristan!" I scream as my body quivers.

My mind is gone, lost in the sensation of my climax, which is taking me to heights I never knew existed. I start to come down and realize that he hasn't stopped. He is still sliding in and out of my freshly soaked pussy.

He tugs lightly on my hip, urging me upward. "Ride me, baby. Please?"

I hook my right leg higher over his hip for leverage. My muscles are weak from sleep and sex. I'm determined to pull myself up without losing the delicious full feeling.

He helps to lift me up and lowers me back down on his erection. I feel his barbells slide along my pussy. It's painful against my tender, swollen sex in a good way.

I'm riding him backwards, facing his feet. I stretch back, placing my hands on his firm pecs, and start to slide up and down his rock hard shaft. I know I'm hitting the right spot when he groans. The sound is so carnal and wanton that I start to move faster. I moan, biting my lip as he starts to match my thrusts. His ups meeting my downs. Hard.

The need to make him come spurs me on. I feel his erection get harder and shift slightly inside, straightening. My sex gets tighter.

I feel the crushing weight of climax and my own motions slow, but he doesn't stop.

"Don't stop," he growls, and I pick my pace back up, holding onto my orgasm because I need to come with him.

"Come, Tristan. Come inside me."

He starts to pound harder against my sex and I lose it as his balls hit my clit. My orgasm explodes, sending white hot fireworks off behind my eyelids. I can barely hold myself up. The fireworks ignite once more as soon as his cock twitches inside me and the first shot of hot cum fills my core.

"Jesus fuck, Cami!" he howls as he comes hard inside me. His nipples harden under my touch. I start to trace my fingers around the buds and pinch his nipples and he jerks once, twice, and yet a third time inside me, and he groans again. "Ahh! Fuck."

Did I really just make him come twice? I smile widely at the idea. His hands release their grip on my hips and fall back to the bed. His whole body goes limp and softens underneath me.

"Tristan?" I say, a bit worried that he's passed out on me.

"Hmmm?" he mumbles incoherently, and I smile.

"Did I really give you two orgasms back-to-back?" I'm smiling so wide, I would be amazed if he actually managed to understand me.

"Mm hm," he mumbles again.

"Are you even on the same planet as I am right now?"

"Nuh-uh."

I giggle. Here I thought I was bad after sex. But my head is swelling at the idea that I did this to him. Talk about a trip.

And he is still rock hard inside me. Ready and wanting more.

I clench the muscles of my sex around his erection and he groans. I let out a soundless chuckle.

"What do you think you're doing there, little lady?"

I am on cloud twenty-nine at this point, so I clench my muscles again. "I want you."

"You have me." His voice is warm and sweet, and I think I understand that he really means that if I want to take him again I can, at any time, anywhere, and in any way I want him.

I sit up straight on his hips, the head of his erection reaching deep into the very core of my body. The sensation is amazing, slightly painful, but oh so delicious. I lean forward and place my hands on his thighs. Arching my back, I start to slide slowly up and down his thick shaft.

If he's not done, then neither am I.

~~*~*~*

TRISTAN

Her ass is gloriously riding the length of my shaft, up and down, slow and deep. I can feel the walls of her entrance tightening and releasing as she glides with very little effort up and down. Her pussy is soaking wet and warm, the evidence of all our activities.

Knowing that she is slick with us has me more turned on. I watch as our orgasms leak from her sex, pooling onto my groin and sliding onto my balls. I wish I had a camera to capture this.

She's moaning at her own movements, and I'm simply laying here, watching the action. She lets out a moan and starts to thrust harder. The sound is quieter, muffled, and I can tell she is moaning against her lip.

"Tristan, I'm gonna come," she whispers.

She quickens her pace. Her right hand comes off my thigh and goes straight to her clit. I reach up with one hand, take her right nipple between my fingers, and I twist.

Her orgasm explodes all over my cock, sending a rush of warm creamy cum all over my head and shaft and I lose it. My own orgasm tightens my shaft, the fresh warm of my cum mixing with hers.

I drop back to the bed, sated – for now – exhausted, breathing hard and heavy as I feel my heart slow back to normal. I'm ready to go back to sleep.

I don't want to leave her body; I want to stay here forever, but I know that I need to take care of what woke me in the first place. I have to pee like a motherfucker and all this bouncing on my bladder isn't helping.

As if she read my mind we both say, "I have to pee" at the same time.

She giggles. "So that's what woke you up, huh?" I can hear the smile in her voice.

I laugh. "Yeah, it was. But I found something warm and wet and thought that would be more fun."

She sighs, content. "I thought that my building orgasm was my bladder screaming at me, until I realized I was on the verge of coming and that you were sliding in and out of me. I decided that was more important than my bladder."

She shivers. I'm still hard inside of her, but hopefully she will understand that it's not an invitation for more.

She slowly lifts her hips off of my cock. The rush of cool air sends shivers through my own body as I watch her stumble toward the bathroom. She flips on the light and turns to look at me.

In that moment, with the light shining behind her, she looks like an angel. I let out a gasp as she smiles at me. She is absolutely gorgeous and she is all mine...if she will have me.

After Cami exits the bathroom, it's my turn. I give her a quick kiss as I pass her.

Heading into the bathroom, I take stock of my body. I feel like I've been run over by a freight train, but in a very good way. My eyes are bright blue, portraying the high that I'm running on.

When I leave the bathroom, she approaches me. "Feel better?" she asks.

"Much." I kiss her lightly again.

"I'm gonna go freshen up a bit." She strides past me and I watch her naked form retreat into the bathroom. I sigh inwardly. What have I done to deserve this beautiful girl?

When she emerges a couple of minutes later, I am sitting on the edge of the bed. She saunters toward me and comes to stand between my legs. Between the height of the bed and my own six-foot-four frame, we are at the perfect height for a nice, warm, deep kiss.

I reach up, cup the back of her neck, and bring her toward me. She smells minty.

I chuckle. "Did you use my toothbrush?"

She smiles against the lips she has yet to kiss. "Close. Your mouthwash." I laugh. "I didn't want to kiss you with bad morning breath."

"In that case, I am going to go freshen up a bit."

But Cami isn't having that. No, her hands sink into my hair, gripping my head and pulling me to her, crushing my lips against hers in a deep, powerful, and sensual kiss.

The kiss ends far too soon.

"It doesn't bother me," she says. "But I could use a shower and some clean clothes. I also need to get my iPad and my other phone. No doubt Trinity is blowing it up already."

I sigh. Today's the day of the big Layla story. It's strange that I don't really care.

"Grab my phone, would you, baby?" I ask Cami. She walks over and grabs my phone.

But instead of handing it to me, she places my phone between her supple round tits and squeezes them together, wanting me to dig my phone out from between them. I smile, pull her close, and lower my head between her breasts. I lick the crack they've created and her nipples harden immediately. I lick the left one, then back to the crack again, and then the right.

"Okay, fine. You can have your phone," she says with a breathy laugh.

I laugh and dial a number. "Ty?"

"Hey, Tristan. What can I do for you?"

"Can you run down to Ms. Enders's suite and bring up her chargers, her other phone, some clothes, and her iPad, please?"

"I already did, sir. I also informed the hotel that you were checking out today and that Ms. Enders could have your suite. I had the contents of her room brought up and placed in the living room. The hotel knows that you're staying here but the room is changing hands. Ms. Enders still has her suite downstairs if she doesn't want to really stay here. I figured in the interest of being inconspicuous, this would be best."

"Nice work. Thank you, Tyson." I pause. "One more thing. Where are you?"

"I moved my stuff to the third bedroom. Do you need something?"

"No, just stay there. I'll come get you shortly."

"Yes, sir" he says, and he disconnects the line.

"What was that all about?" Cami asks.

"Well..." I pause. "Tyson was kind enough to collect your things from your room. He also arranged to check me out of my suite." Her jaw drops. "I'm not leaving, so don't worry." She pulls her jaw back up but still has a look of concern on her face. "This way it appears that I have checked out. In the event that my location is leaked, the hotel has plausible deniability that I'm no longer staying here. They have transferred the suite to your name. So effective immediately, this is your room. You can finally stay here. And I can stay in the second bedroom or take your suite downstairs."

"Why not just stay here, in this room, with me?" She asks the question I was hoping for, but I didn't want to make assumptions and I wanted her to make the choice.

"If that's what you want, Cami, I would love to share this suite with you."

She smiles approvingly at me, and all traces of concern are gone from her face.

"That is exactly what I want. When Beau and Mick get here tomorrow, they can have my suite downstairs or stay in the second bedroom."

"That sounds like a great idea. There are actually three other bedrooms in this suite besides this one, room enough for all, if they're willing to share."

"I guess that will depend on how well everyone gets along. Where's Tyson now?"

"He's in the third bedroom until I go and get him. You're free to go get what you need from the living room."

She grins. "Good. I need some clothes and to get in touch with Trinity."

"What about that shower you wanted?"

"That, too. Will you be joining me?"

I grin a wicked grin. "Of course!"

~~*~*~*

CAMI

Hoping that Tyson really does stay in his room, I grab my chargers, my new Mac, the iPad, and my BlackBerry and head back into our room. Tristan is there to shut the door behind me.

As I set everything down on the desk, I catch a glimpse of Tristan from the corner of my eye. He's watching me intently, and it dawns on me that I'm still completely naked.

I turn toward him and smile. "Enjoying the view, Tristan?"

He blushes. "What do you think?" he grumbles.

I look down at his lap, and the answer is obvious. He is hard as a rock yet again. I grin.

As I finish plugging in my electronics I make an obvious effort to put on a show for him, bending a little too far forward so that my ass is in the air, my legs spread to reveal the lips of my sex. When I'm done I walk over to him, grab ahold of his shaft, and lead him into the bathroom by his cock.

"Oh you think so, little lady?"

I really enjoy that he calls me that. I continue to lead him into the bathroom, and he shuts the door behind us.

TWENTY-SEVEN

~~*~*~*

TRISTAN

About an hour later Cami and I finally emerge from the bathroom, squeaky clean and weak-kneed. We help each other dress with minimal distraction, and then Cami heads over to the desk to check her email while I open the door to the living room to see about ordering some food.

To my surprise, Tyson is sitting in a chair watching the bedroom door. His face is a stony mask.

"What's wrong, Ty?" I ask.

"Trinity has been blowing up my phone, trying to reach you and Cami."

No sooner has he finished his sentence than Cami shouts my name from the bedroom. Her voice is laced with horror, and for a moment fear surges through my body.

"Cami, what's wrong?" I ask. She's sitting at the desk, one hand covering her mouth and the other frantically trying to dial her phone. "Calm down, Cami. Breathe, Sweets. It's all right." Her panic is contagious.

I walk around the desk and stand behind her. She's looking at an image on her computer. In the sidebar the email program icon is bouncing up and down with new emails.

"I texted Trinity and told her that you guys would be in touch shortly. No doubt she is blowing up Cami's phone and email," Tyson says from the bedroom door.

I look back at the computer and it only takes half a second to realize what she's looking at. It's a house, or what used to be a house. The charred remains of a house. Something about the picture strikes me as odd, familiar even.

"Are there more pictures, Cami?" I ask.

She clicks to the next one. A press shot, crystal clear but at some distance, and from that angle I immediately recognize the building. It's Layla's house. The house we had shared for the last two years of our relationship.

"Jesus fuck!" I shout, and Cami jumps. "How the fuck did that happen?" I'm struggling to catch my breath. I whisper, "Layla?"

Cami's hand comes down slowly from her mouth. "I don't know anything else yet. This is the first email I clicked on." She clicks out of the picture and moves back to her email inbox.

Just then her Skype lights up. It's Trinity. She pushes the button to answer the call. Within seconds Trinity's face pops up on the screen.

"Please, dear God, tell me that Layla is all right?" Cami says.

"From what we know, yes. She's fine. We were told that she had been staying somewhere else since the premiere." Trinity speaks very matter of fact.

"What the fuck happened?" I practically shout at the laptop.

"There are mixed reports right now, but the majority of them point to a disgruntled fan that went off half-cocked once the story was posted. I sent you a video. The girl in the video calls Layla a slut and several other unflattering names and claims to have set the fire in retribution for how she treated 'Dakota.' Clearly not a stable person."

Someone, some deranged fan, burned down Layla's house because of what she did to me. If it weren't for the fact that this girl is obviously in serious need of professional help, I might have thanked her for sticking up for me.

"Supposedly the arson was recorded, and the police are investigating it," Trinity continues. "The fire is out, obviously. You can see from the pictures. The police seem to be pretty confident that no one was inside at the time."

"Thank God for that," I bark. "Where was her security team when this went down?"

"That," Trinity began, "is why we are pretty sure Layla was not on the property." She stops talking and looks away from her monitor at what I'm assuming is a cell phone or a tablet of some type. She's reading something. Several different emotions cross her face, and she gasps at a couple of different points.

"What, Trinity?" Cami's the first to attempt to break the tension.

"It's a tentative press release from the Orange County Sheriff's Office. Apparently there is some speculation that Tristan was in the house at the time of the fire, and there are reports surfacing of his disappearance. They intend to address in their press release that they do not know where he is and that his last contact with Layla was a week ago. They are also saying that while Tristan had full access to the home, they're unsure of whether or not he was in the house at the time of the fire."

Her phone rings in the background. She holds up one finger at us and answers it.

"Yes, Vinnie? Yeah, I have them both on Skype right now. Yes. All right, hang on." She lowers the phone from her ear and presses a button, and Vinnie's voice comes over the Mac.

"Hi, guys!" Vincent sounds almost chipper.

"Hi," Cami and I say in unison.

"Listen, here is what I know so far. The police are concerned for Tristan's well-being. Until they hear from Tristan directly, they are going to proceed as if he is a missing person."

I hear Cami gasp and look over in time to see her facial expression change from shock to determination. "We have to stop that from happening, Vin."

The business side of Cami that made its first appearance a couple of days ago is about to have it's own PDF file; she's no longer Cami but Cameron Enders, CEO of Bold International.

"Can we release a statement without Tristan needing to talk to the police?"

"No, Tristan needs to make contact with the Orange County Sheriff's Office. We have already tried on his behalf, but OCSO won't go for anything less than Tristan himself contacting them."

"Jesus fuck! Why the hell do I have to call them? I don't need or want to have my location revealed to them or anyone else," I nearly shout from across the room, which I've been pacing. "Short of showing up at the police department, how am I supposed to prove who I am?"

"That's actually the easy part. You can Skype in. We told them that was the only way that you'd be able to make contact with them because you are not presently in the country. Of course that raised more than a few eyebrows. I'll send Cami the Skype info on Deputy Peterson."

"I can handle Skype, but I will not contact him from my account."

"You can use mine, Tristan," Cami chimes in. She looks paler than normal, if that's even possible.

I mouth to her, "Are you okay?"

She nods, only slightly, not wanting to tip off Trinity to her stress. This whole situation must really be getting to her.

"Is there anything else I need to know right now?" I ask. I just want the whole thing over with. Trinity shakes her head.

"When we're off of Skype with Deputy Peterson," Cami says, sternness in her voice, "I'll write up a press release to forward to you. We're now left with no choice but to release a statement, and I will inform the Sheriff's office of our intention so they don't go running to the press with the fact that they have talked to Tristan. I'm sure they're already working on something based off of your conversations with them."

"We can write up the press release on your behalf. You don't need to do that."

"Trinity, I appreciate your wanting to handle this, but this is affecting me in ways I never thought. Cami and I will put it together, in my own words, and forward it to you. From there you can change whatever you think necessary, but it has to come from my own mouth."

"We'll take care of it, Trinity," Cami says, her voice strained.

"All right, you two. Get in touch if you need anything further, and I'll let you know as soon as I know more.

"Oh. And Tristan?"

"Yeah."

"Don't be surprised if it comes out that this was Layla's own scheme to take the heat off of her. The Internet is abuzz with both stories, but the news is focusing on the fire more than the article."

The crazy thing about what Trinity just said is that I agree with her. Layla is manipulative enough to have done this on her own. "She is just that naive to think that she can get away with this," I say.

Trinity just nods. "All right, Tristan, I leave you in Cami's hands."

"Thanks so much," Cami mutters.

Trinity chuckles and disconnects.

I turn to Cami. I'm concerned about the strength it has taken to handle this and what her reaction is. She looks to be a wreck.

"Cami, what's wrong?"

She looks up at me, and her eyes are glassy with unshed tears. Her silence is almost more than I can handle.

"Baby-girl, it's all right."

I reach out for her hand, she takes it, and I pull her from the chair into a hug. Her shoulders start to shake as soon as she is in the protective barrier of my arms.

I turn to Tyson and nod. He bows his understanding and silently leaves the room.

"It's just you and me, Sweets," I whisper, and as if on cue she lets loose what I didn't realize she was holding back. Her body shakes harder with silent sobs, and I can feel her tears soaking into my shirt.

I pull back, just enough so that I can reach her chin to lift her face toward mine. When she's looking up at me, I bend down and softly kiss away the tears.

"Don't cry, baby-girl," I whisper.

"I...I'm sorry. I'm not sure what's come over me."

She's so unbelievably beautiful. All her walls are down and crumbling, and in this moment I know that it will break my heart to ever let this girl go.

"Tell me," I say, speaking softly. "Why are you so upset?"

She hesitates for a moment, then says, "I'm sorry. I just got so overcome with the idea that you could have been in that house. That you could have been killed, kidnapped, or hurt. I know you're safe. I feel you in my arms, but the idea that someone would try to harm you..." She doesn't need to finish her statement. I can see in her eyes that she's truly shaken up by the idea of losing me.

"Oh, Cami. Please, don't cry. I am here, safe, with you. The only place I need or want to be." I hug her tighter to show her that I really am here.

"I'm really sorry about your stuff."

At first I don't understand what she means. Then it dawns on me.

"I had nothing in that house that cannot be replaced. A few pairs of shoes and a few pairs of jeans, at best. The one thing I learned early on was to keep minimal possessions and to keep them with me at all times. I travel with what's most important to me, and the rest is expendable."

"That's good," she says softly.

I lean down and lift her up. She wraps her legs around my waist and her arms around my neck. I kiss her. A chaste kiss, meant to be comforting. Deep kisses will just lead us right back into bed, and we have work to do.

For a moment we stare into each others eyes, communicating without words. With her eyes she lets me know that she is very happy and that she, too, feels that this is a turning point with us.

Cami says, "We have work to do."

"Just one more kiss, then I'll let you down." I smile against her lips and kiss her again. And then again, more deeply, dancing dangerously close to distraction.

Cami giggles against my lips and squeezes me closer and tighter to her body. I can feel her nipples, hard as a rock, pressed against my chest. So not helping, I think. I have been dying to lay her back out on this bed since we left the bathroom.

"All right, back to work, my little bear," she says.

I blush. "Bear, huh?"

She grins. "Yes. Bear."

I smile at her blunt statement. "Where does bear come from?"

She blushes now. "Papa bear, teddy bear, cuddle bear, you growl like a bear, and most of all, I find a comfort in your arms that I never knew I needed."

"I love it."

I kiss her again. She giggles and tries to squirm from my grasp, but I have no desire to let her go. I sit down in the desk chair with her straddling me.

"You know what happened the last time we were in this position," she says.

Ah, yes. I remember very clearly.

"Go ahead. I can work distracted," I tease.

"I'd like to test that theory, but I'm afraid of my inability to control myself. I don't want to end up distracting us both so we get nothing done. Because believe me, I would capture your attention."

Oh, how right she is.

"Too late," I tease her back, and she giggles.

She reaches around me and grabs her iPad off the desk.

"You use the laptop, and I'll do what I need to on the iPad."

She squirms her way off of my lap. Just before she walks away, she reaches out and runs her hand over my sex. A promise of more to come.

~~*~*~*

CAMI

I climb up on the bed and prop my head up against the headboard, bringing my knees up so that I have a place to rest the iPad. When my email comes up, I have seventeen new messages, all either from Trinity or Vincent regarding the stories about Layla's affair and the fire at her house. My heart constricts again to think that he might have been caught in that fire instead of safe here with me.

An email from Vincent catches my attention, completely different in tone and content than the rest. As I read it, a huge smile spreads across my face.

Tristan, who must not be doing a very good job of getting to work, asks, "What has you smiling so much, Sweets?"

"Oh, nothing. Just you."

He snorts. "What about me?"

"I received an email from Vincent about ten minutes ago with some very good news for you."

"What does it say?" I can tell he's trying to keep his excitement in check.

"Well, Vincent has not only received clearance to send you a script, but he has received four additional requests to schedule auditions."

I watch as the smile on his face spreads wider and wider until he's literally grinning from ear to ear.

"Cami!" he shouts. "Are you fucking kidding me?!"

"That depends, Tristan. Should I be kidding?" My smile is just as wide as his.

"Do you realize what this means?" he says. "It's not over. It's not over. Oh my God, Cami, it's not over!" He's shouting now, his legs bouncing up and down in his chair. "I'm not done. I can keep doing this?"

I nod, and he leaps up off the chair and runs toward the bed. He dives on top of it like it's a pool, hitting the bed with such force that I shoot straight into the air. I squeal as I bounce back down.

"Come 'ere, woman!" he growls as he grabs at my arm to pull me close to him. He pulls me around so that my face is upside down under his, with my feet resting on the headboard.

"I could kiss you right now."

"So what's stopping you?"

It takes us the rest of the day to get things straightened out with both the police and the press. We order a late dinner up to the room, and afterwards decide to go for a swim. The sun has set and the outside lights flicker on.

The pool is illuminated with LED lights that change color between blues, greens and purples. It's stunning to watch, and even more stunning to be swimming in when they change.

While Tristan's changing, I find Tyson in his bedroom. I knock lightly.

"Come in," I hear him say.

Turning the knob and peeking my head in the door, I watch as he puts down the book he's reading, only catching a small glimpse of the title on the cover, which is bright orange.

"Hi, Ty," I whisper. He's surprised at seeing me. "Sorry. I don't mean to bother you."

"No worries, ma'am...Cami. What can I do for you?"

"First of all, you can relax. I would like you to join Tristan and me out at the pool."

"That's really not necessa-"

I cut him off. "I won't hear of it. You've been working around the clock for the last week and then some. Take a load off. Nothing will happen to us up here, and you'll be closer to us anyway. I'm going to order a couple bottles of wine and champagne. Anything specific you enjoy?"

"Apple juice." He smiles like he's hiding a private joke.

"With vodka?"

He laughs. "No, Cami. I don't drink."

Did he not understand? "I want you to relax and have a good time with us. There must be some type of alcohol you like."

"No, really, Cami, I don't drink. On or off duty. Apple juice will be fine, and I will happily join you guys."

"All right, Ty. I'll have some apple juice, wine, and champagne brought up. Anything else?" He shakes his head. "See you in a bit."

When I finish the room service order, I call down to front desk to see if I have any messages. The concierge informs me that two messages were delivered to my suite downstairs, one first thing this morning and one just a couple of hours ago.

Odd. Anyone who knows where I am has my cell phone number.

"Can you have the concierge who delivers my order to the penthouse grab the messages from my suite on his way up?"

"Certainly, Ms. Enders. One more thing while I have you on the phone. I was the one that took the second message not that long ago. I informed the caller that we had no guests by the name of Ms. Enders, and she was quite insistent that I was mistaken. When I refused to transfer her call to any of the rooms, she grew aggressive. I just thought I should warn you."

My heart stops.

TWENTY-EIGHT

~~*~*~*

TRISTAN

I'm sitting on the pool's edge, patiently waiting for Cami to join me. The water is warmer than it was yesterday afternoon, no doubt due to the warmth of the day. The lights emanating around the sides give a great ambient glow. I'm excited to see Cami's porcelain skin glowing elegantly under these lights.

I hear a noise behind me and I turn. I'm surprised to see not Cami but Tyson in his swim trunks.

"Hey, man, what's up?"

"Nada. Cami pretty much ordered me to join you guys tonight." He looks rather sheepish in his explanation.

"Good. You need a night off."

"You had no idea she was going to do that, did you?" He smiles.

I chuckle. "No, I didn't, but I don't care. She's welcome to do as she pleases, and I'm happy to have you hanging out. Where is she?"

"She was ordering room service. Wine, champagne, and apple juice, I think."

"You and your apple juice." I chuckle. "One day soon I will get you drunk."

He laughs, shaking his head. "Don't hold your breath on that one."

"Watch me," I tease.

I know that Tyson never drinks, but he never drinks because he's always on duty. I'm going to make a point of giving him some much-needed time off once the other two bodyguards get here tomorrow. They can keep an eye on us, and Tyson can enjoy himself.

"Are you excited about tomorrow?" I ask.

Cami had shown me a picture of Jolene from her Facebook page. She's quite the looker, with some big, beautiful green eyes. Six feet tall, too, which is still shorter than Tyson. She looks like she needs someone tall and strong to hold her.

Tyson just shrugs. He takes a step into the pool and slowly wades into the water. "I'm trying not to get my hopes up."

"I can completely understand." I pause for effect. "I saw a picture of her today."

His head whips around to look at me in complete surprise, "Oh yeah? Care to share?"

"Nope!" I laugh, throwing my head back.

He gives me a dubious smile. "You're an ass, Trey."

I laugh harder. "No, not an ass. Just letting your imagination run wild for another twenty-four hours. I must say, I don't think you will be disappointed." I smile knowingly and he blushes slightly.

"In all honesty, I'm more nervous than anything. It's been years since I even considered entertaining a woman, let alone dated one." He looks down, a bit shy. I must say, a shy Tyson is a bit of shocker.

"You'll be fine. Just be yourself and that will say it all."

I hear the clinking of glasses behind me. Tyson perks up a bit, and I turn my head to see Cami. In one hand she's carrying three champagne glasses upside down between her fingers. In her other hand are three bottles, one that looks like Cristal, one a wine bottle, and the third plain old apple juice.

I smile at her, but the smile she gives me in return is strained. Something's off. Then I notice a couple small pieces of paper in the hand holding the glasses.

"Hi, baby. You all right?"

"I need a drink first."

I nod as she comes over to me. I take the bottles from her and she sits down next to me, dangling her feet in the water. I look for the corkscrew and see it's hooked into her bikini top. Hmm, guess she ran out of places to carry it. I reach over and grab it, brushing my hand against her nipple.

She gasps. "Behave yourself," she breathes.

"Impossible," I retort.

I twist open the apple juice, grab a glass from Cami, and pour. Tyson sloshes over to us, and I hand him the glass.

"Thanks," he says to me, then turns slightly toward Cami. "Thank you, Cami."

"Of course, though I wish you would have some champagne or wine with us."

Tyson chuckles and shakes his head. "No, thanks."

When I pop the cork on the champagne it goes flying toward the center of the pool. I chuckle as I move the pour-over to run onto Cami's lap. She starts laughing and I bring it up higher so that it runs over her breasts. She tilts her head back, and I pour some into her mouth. She's laughing as she tries to swallow, and I watch the blush spread across her cheeks. No doubt because Tyson's watching with interest.

"There," I say. "You've had your drink, now what's bothering you?"

She holds up the pieces of paper I'd noticed earlier.

"There were two messages delivered to my suite downstairs today, one this morning and one just a couple of hours ago. The concierge downstairs took the second message and felt it necessary to warn me that it was rather rough." She takes a deep breath. "I haven't read them yet. I brought them with me."

She hands me the two pieces of paper.

"You want me to read them?"

She nods. Taking the corkscrew back from me, she opens the bottle of wine and pours some into a champagne glass, then pours me a glass of Cristal.

I look at the folded pieces of paper. On the backside of each are the date and time of the message.

I open the one from this morning:

Gentleman caller for Cameron Enders. Caller informed no such guest is staying at the hotel. Caller insisted that I was mistaken, aggressively advised me to transfer him to Ms. Enders immediately. When I refused several times, caller requested a reservation for Wednesday, June 13th. When told there was no vacancy, caller hung up. Call was routed through Hawaii, indicating a call originating in the U.S.

"Sweets, besides Mick, do you know of any other men who know you're here?"

"I know a few men, but only Mick and Vinnie know where I am. There is Reed, of course. I suppose he could have tracked me down. Why?"

I tell her what the note says.

She looks puzzled. "Reed's the only one I can think of who might seek me out here, but he has my cell phone number. And besides, there's no way he would have tried to make a reservation. He can't afford the last-minute flight, let alone the price of a room at this hotel. So the chances of it being him are slim." She paused. "What about the other message?"

"I haven't gotten there yet." I unfold it and hold it out to her. "Do you want to read it first?"

She just shakes her head.

I look at the note and realize quickly that someone is onto us.

Female caller, very distraught, first asked for Tristan Michaels, then when I informed her that no guest existed by that name, she started spouting off various cartoon names. I denied each one. She grew increasingly more upset and finally asked for Cameron Enders. She was informed that no guest was here by that name. Growing more agitated and said, "I'm gonna kill that bitch," and "That bitch stole my man." Swearing and ranting continued until I politely terminated the call.

"Fuck!" I shout.

I'm so unbelievably angry. How dare she threaten Cami? Not to mention I'd made it very clear that we were broken up. Layla had no right to claim me as her man.

"What?" Cami and Tyson say in unison.

I read them the note. "I swear to God, this has to be Layla. But how in the hell did she find out where I am? And how in the fuck does she know about Cami?"

Cami and Tyson look at each other, complete shock on their faces.

"Those girls? With the autographs?" Cami asks.

"It's entirely possible," Tyson says. "Though where would they have seen you together? They were too young to be in the bar, and I don't remember ever seeing them in the restaurant downstairs. And even if they'd seen you together, they wouldn't know Cami's name. The hotel would not release any names to anyone regarding their guests."

"Staff? Like Jessie or the waitress in Blu last Friday? They would've had access to hotel guest names," Cami suggests.

"Truth is, it could've been any member of the staff that knows Cami and myself. Though I'm not registered as Tristan, it's not hard to put two and two together. But how would it get back to Layla? There's nothing in the papers regarding my whereabouts. That is the only way I can think of that Layla would have had a direct line to where I am." I take a deep breath. "Maybe it wasn't Layla. Maybe it was some other woman, like the crazy one in the video about the fire. Or maybe the call came from within the area, and it was really a staff member. This note doesn't have routing information on it like the first."

Tyson chimes in, "To be honest with both of you, until we have a real threat to worry about, not a phone call that is subject to interpretation, I'm not taking this very seriously. Hell, for all we know Mick and Beau are playing pranks on both of you. Male first, this morning, then the female this afternoon. It's possible."

Cami shakes her head. "Not something that they would do. I personally really don't care who it was. All I care about is Tristan being able to relax without the fan bombardment."

Someone threatens her and all she cares about is that I can relax?

I wrap my arm around her waist and pull her close to me. Kissing the top of her head, I whisper, "You, my sweets, are one amazing woman."

She blushes and ducks her head. I lift her face to mine.

"Don't ever be ashamed of a compliment, Cami. You will be receiving them from me often. You surprise me at every turn." This is true on so many levels. "I stand by what I said this afternoon, after we finally got off that awful sheriff's office call. I would be honored to have you as my PR rep or even my agent. And you will make an amazing CEO when and if you decide that you want to step up and take control. No doubt, once people can see what you do, it'll bring even more people to Bold."

She nods but says, "I rather enjoy my freedom and ability to do the things I want without having to be tied to an everyday office job."

"That may be true, baby, but you would be CEO, and your working hours would be entirely your choice. You have proven today that you can effectively handle a crisis no matter where in the world you are."

"I never thought about it that way." She seems pensive. "I work well with Trinity and Vincent, and I enjoy working for them. I'll think about it."

"Good! Now, let's have some fun."

I get up and head to the box on the side of the patio, where I'd found some fun pool toys the other day. I find the beach ball that I am after and toss it with speedy precision at Tyson. It bounces off the side of his head and lands on the far side of the pool. Cami and Tyson both start laughing. I cannonball into the pool, effectively soaking Cami.

She's still laughing as she drops into the pool, swimming after the ball. I reach for it, but she beats me to it and turns to toss it to Tyson. My plan backfires when it becomes a game of keep-away from Tristan, but we're all laughing and having a good time.

Finally around midnight, Tyson calls it a night, leaving me and Cami with half a bottle of champagne and the pool to ourselves.

Once Tyson is out of sight it takes me all of two seconds to embrace her and start kissing her lips, nudging her cheek with my nose, and caressing her body with my hands. She responds immediately, her breathing becoming harsher and deeper. The moans that escape her lips bring about the desperate need to be inside her.

I grab at the bows of her bikini and pull. The material floats free of her breasts and I groan. She wraps her legs around my hips, rubbing her pussy against the tip of my dick through my shorts, even as her heels work at pushing them down. My cock is already spitting out desire for Cami, so I help her get my shorts off. As soon as I'm naked I feel Cami seeking to line up my stick with her entrance.

We're up against the side of the pool, the champagne bottle within easy reach. As she slowly slides herself onto me I take the bottle and whisper, "Look up, baby." She does, opening her mouth, and I pour.

I miss, catching her breasts. She moans as the cool champagne hardens her nipples. I lick at the champagne. She thrusts down, swallowing me whole in one thrust and coaxing a moan from both of us. I clean off her breast with my mouth, paying special attention to her nipple, licking and sucking as she starts to slide up and down my erection. I pour more champagne, this time closer to her mouth so I don't miss. When she has her fill she turns her head. But I'm so distracted by the sensations along my dick that I just let the rest of the bottle pour out all over her neck and bare breasts. I lick and suck my way around her body.

She quickens her pace against my dick. I feel her pussy pulsing and quivering hard around my cock. She's close to coming and her orgasm is going to release mine in a hot messy rush.

I drop the bottle in the pool and grab tight onto her hips, taking over. Her moans get shorter, louder, and more frequent. Her body stiffens.

I'm fighting with every ounce of willpower I have to stop myself from exploding, but the tip of my cock is beginning to pulse.

"Come for me, Cami. Now!" I growl, and she lets loose at my command.

Her sex tightens and pulses harder and I come unglued. My orgasm rocks through me. The relief is amazing. I feel my cum mixing with hers, warmth overwhelming my body as she continues milking me, sucking me in deeper.

As my orgasm slows, she twitches her hips and I instantly become harder than I was before. I can feel my orgasm building again.

"Jesus, Cami, you're going to make me come again."

She doesn't slow down and I instantly understand why. She, too, is on the verge of yet another orgasm.

As she thrusts with abandon I latch onto her left nipple, lightly using my teeth. She digs her nails into my shoulders.

"Fuck!" she groans. "I'm coming—"

Her breathing is rough and ragged, and when her orgasm finally hits she screams my name. My name coming from her lips during the heat of passion is my undoing again.

TWENTY-NINE

~~*~*~*

CAMI

I wake up at one point during the night and quietly pad into the bathroom. Upon my return, I reach down to pull back the covers and Tristan's eyes pop open. I can just make out his silhouette and the whites of his eyes in the glow from the moonlight coming in the window.

"You okay, Sweets?"

"Uh huh," I mumble. "Just had to go potty."

He pulls back the covers, inviting me underneath. I settle in and he wraps his arms around me. I feel protected like nothing in the world can hurt me. I hug him tight and he nuzzles my hair. I fall back asleep almost immediately.

Later I wake up to Tristan kissing my shoulder. His hands are seeking, rubbing, caressing.

"Good morning, beautiful," he whispers against my shoulder.

It's light out now, but between the emotional roller coaster of yesterday and all the sex with Tristan, I'm still exhausted. I snuggle deeper into my pillow, mumble something incoherent, and fall asleep again.

A few hours later my eyes begin to flutter. The bed feels strangely cold, and I realize quickly that I'm alone. Through that strange connection we share, I can sense that Tristan isn't even in the room.

The next thing I notice is the delicious achy feeling racing throughout my body. For the first time in two days, I actually feel fully sated. The irony behind that is I know the minute I lay eyes on Tristan, that feeling will vanish faster than I can blink.

The thought of getting to see him is what springs my eyes all the way open.

Sitting on the table next to the bed is a glass of something resembling sparkling water and a note. The writing is rough, yet strangely elegant.

Good Morning Beautiful Sweets, I do hope you slept well.

I grab the glass and take a long, delicious drink. Cool black cherry flavored sparkling water. My favorite.

I stretch, head to the bathroom, and climb into the shower. Right as I'm reaching for the nozzle to start the water, I hear Tristan's voice. It seems to be coming from the bedroom, but I don't hear him call for me, so I assume he's talking to Tyson. I think about going out to say good morning but decide I can wait ten minutes until after I've showered.

The water's hot and steam starts to fill the bathroom. I climb in and let the water consume me. It's warm and relaxing, and it makes me think of the hot tub out on the patio. Seems like a great place to spend tonight with Beau, Mick, Jolene, Naomi, Travis, Tyson, and Tristan. I smile to myself as I name the last three, the Triple Trouble.

Over the sound of the shower I hear a knock on the door.

"Cami?"

"Yes," I shout back.

"You okay, baby-girl?"

I peek my head out of the sliding, steam-covered glass door and smile at the sight of Tristan. He's back in his swim trunks and nothing else. I inhale deeply as my eyes devour him head to toe.

No doubt sensing the desire quickly building in me at the sight of him, he starts to saunter toward the shower. His eyes are dark, pupils dilated. He has a look of deep, dark promise as he reaches me, and he quickly brings his lips to mine.

The kiss, though, is surprisingly soft and chaste. Perhaps he's trying to gage my reaction, unsure of whether I'm up for it after falling asleep on him earlier.

In answer to his unspoken question, I reach my hands up, grip the back of his neck, and pull his lips closer and tighter to mine. An involuntary moan escapes my lips, the rush of warmth flooding my core. There's a rush of cold air as the door slides open and Tristan steps into the shower.

He slowly backs me up against the wall, his hands first finding my hips, then caressing the curve of my butt. He lifts up, coercing me to wrap my arms around his neck so that he can pick me up. I wrap my legs around him. I'm wedged between the wall and Tristan, spread open for him, at his mercy.

He begins tracing kisses along my jaw to my ear, where he gently licks the lobe. My nipples harden to sharp peaks, the barbells making them ache.

As if Tristan can read my mind, his warm, wet mouth finds one nipple, then the other, licking, caressing, warming. Satisfying the ache within them. I'm writhing under his touch, quickly growing warmer with each passing caress.

He slowly lowers me until my feet touch the cool tiles. Without any prompting, Tristan grabs my poof hanging on the wall and lathers it with the lavender scented body wash on the shelf. With his arms wrapped around me, he begins gently washing my shoulders, my back, my butt. He is careful not to rub the poof along my corset, but squeezes it so that warm soapy bubbles slide down my back.

He lowers himself to his knees, washing my right thigh, taking careful measures, I notice, to avoid my now-aching clit. He slowly washes down my leg to my knee, my calf. After a gentle tap on the back of my ankle, I lift my foot so that he can wash and gently massage the arch and balls of my feet.

I throw my head back in satisfaction. "That feels so good," I murmur.

When he's done with my right foot, he slowly places it back on the tile and gently taps my other ankle. Shifting my weight, I lift my leg and he repeats the process.

When he's done with my foot, he slowly works his way up my leg. But this time, my clit is no longer a safe zone. Bringing the poof between my legs, he rubs gently against my sex. I moan as he rubs from front to back, again and again.

Suddenly I feel the poof hit my ankle as it falls to the ground. My eyes are closed, heightening the sensation.

Tristan's hands are on my hips, pulling me forward and further under the water. Warm water rushes down all over my body, washing away the soapy film. Then his hand is between my legs, gently caressing my clit for a moment before sliding away to explore. I moan and silently beg his fingers to find my entrance. His thumb presses against my clit, and my knees shake.

"Ah, Tristan, don't stop," I mewl.

I hear his light chuckle, and the next thing I know his hand is gone. I whimper at the loss. Both hands clamp onto my hips again, and then I feel the warm wetness of his languid tongue moving across my clit, firm but soft, in circular motions that send me into a state of pure ecstasy.

I'm only vaguely aware of his hands moving up and down my body. One finds my breast and the other gently works the entrance to my sex. Teasing strokes to bring me to the edge.

I feel fire ignite within me and I know my orgasm is closer than I thought. My body begins to shake. So many sensations all at once. My legs stiffen as Tristan thrusts his thumb into my sex and I explode, burning fireworks going off all over my body.

But Tristan doesn't stop; he continues working all my center points, and one of his long, sleek fingers toys gently with the tight bud of my anus. Before I even know what's happening, the gentle pressure forces another screaming orgasm from my body.

"Tristan," I whisper. "I am going to fall over if you don't stop."

He slowly retreats from my body, first the hand that's caressing my nipple, then his tongue. But he kept his thumb and forefinger in place.

He looks at me with eyes screaming wanton desire, eyes that beg me to give him anything he wants. "I want to play with this." He moans as his finger taps against my ass. I moan because every nerve in my body is alive and blazing. "But not right now," he continues. "I have plans for that, and right now I need to be buried so deep inside you that I don't have the patience to play here."

He slowly rises to his feet, lightly running his mouth and tongue along my body as he finds his way to my lips. His kiss is hot and quick. In response I pull him closer and put all the passion I feel for him into this kiss. His mouth tastes like a sweet mix of him and my arousal, a heady combination that has my sex on fire once again.

He reaches behind me and the water stops. He slides the door back and grabs my towel, wrapping me up nice and tight. He uses a second towel to dry my hair as best he can. He shivers.

"Are you cold?"

He chuckles and shakes his head. "No, I'm thinking about burying my cock deep inside your warm, dripping wet pussy."

I blush. He can be so crass and unguarded sometimes. I love it.

I turn to leave the shower, but he touches my shoulder. I turn back to see that he's naked, his swim trunks in a pile on the floor. His erection is causing the towel he has wrapped around his waist to tent. No doubt cool air is rushing up his erection because he shivers again.

"I'm going to carry you," he says, then bends down and scoops me up in the firm grip of his arms.

He walks cautiously across the bathroom floor, but when his toes hit the carpet of the bedroom he picks up the pace.

He's gentle laying me out on the bed. Then he slowly begins to unwrap the towel, like he's unwrapping the ultimate Christmas present. I giggle at his expression. His eyes are alight with excitement.

"What's so funny, baby-Girl?"

I smile. "The look on your face. The excitement in your eyes. I'm giggling because it's pretty hot."

He chuckles, and from there we instantly become lost in each other.

About an hour later we surface to reality. Sated and excited for tonight, I start to get dressed, but Tristan stops me.

"Just your robe, Sweets. I have a massage waiting for you on the patio. After you're done, we'll have lunch."

I gape at him. "What?" I whisper. I'm completely shocked by his gesture.

"Well, with all the stress of the last thirty-six hours, and the roaring excitement of your friends coming in tonight, I thought maybe you could use an hour or two relaxing with someone else taking care of you." He looks at me with such devotion, But his eyes are crinkled in the corners, worry? "What's wrong, Cami?"

I don't respond right away. The fact that he was thoughtful enough to order another massage for me really has sent my thoughts into a tailspin.

"I am just not used to..." I pause, not sure how to say what I want to say.

I hesitate too long and Tristan finishes my unspoken thought. "You're not used to someone else caring about you, are you?"

Emotions well up in me so strong I don't trust myself to answer, so I nod. He comes around the bed to me and wraps me in his arms. His embrace is warm and comforting. Tears prick my eyes, but I don't want him to see me cry again, not over something as trivial as this.

Growing up in the Enders household meant that you were left to your own devices. Parents that shipped you off to boarding schools on the other side of the world. Parents who died, leaving you to face the fact that they claimed to love you and wondering whether, in some strange way, they did.

Wrapped in Tristan's warm, protective embrace, I begin to hope that maybe I really can be loved and that I, too, can love in return.

The revelation brings the tears to overwhelming thickness and they spill over. I'm pressed so tight to his naked chest that it takes only a matter of seconds for Tristan to realize that I'm crying.

He tries to lift my chin to look at him. I fight it as best I can; I don't want him to see me like this.

"Cami, baby, please don't cry. Why are you crying?"

I sniffle a little bit, searching for the right words so that he will know how much I appreciate the gesture and what it means to me.

I take a long, deep breath. And another. "I am very flattered, overwhelmingly so, that you would do something as sweet as getting me a massage because I've been stressed." I take another deep breath. "Tristan, I've never had anyone that's cared about me, put me before themselves, or even took the time to listen. The idea that you want to do all of that is so overwhelming that I'm not sure how to handle it. I was mistreated by my parents for my entire life, and when they were gone I was relieved and then mocked by their willingness on their deaths to attempt to prove that they loved me. Something I, to this day, cannot fathom."

He peels himself away from me and sits on the bed. I shiver at the loss of his warmth and comfort from my body. He looks up at me. His eyes are swimming with a need to convey something.

He reaches out for my hand, and I take a step toward him to stand between his legs, looking into his smoldering blue eyes.

He takes a deep breath and... "Sweetie, I am deeply sorry that your parents were not what they should have been. You are a bright, brilliant, beautiful, strong woman, and your parents are the ones that realized far too late what a gem you really are. I will always do my best to put your needs before myself and before anything to do with me. The massage is because of all the stress I know I have put you through these last few days with my own personal drama. It kills me that you had to get involved in all of this."

I open my mouth to protest, to tell him that I volunteered to help him and am doing it because I want to. But he holds up his hand to silence me.

"Let me finish, love. I know that you came here last week to get away from all the drama in Phoenix and you met me. Something I hope is a good thing and not a damper on your vacation."

I shake my head. How can he think that? He's the very best part of my vacation.

"Then I bring my life down on you at blinding speed. I'm beyond grateful" –he brings his other hand to his chest, over his heart— "that I met you, and I wouldn't change anything about this week, except..." He pauses just long enough to catch his breath. "Except that I would not have had all the drama of Layla to come along with me.

"Cami, I need you to know that you are very important to me, and I want to see you well taken care of, no matter what the price. No matter what it takes.

"So please, go. Enjoy your massage. Relax and unwind for a while. When you're done we'll have a late breakfast delivered and adjust so that we can have dinner with our friends tonight. I would take you to Caran or Blu, but I can't go downstairs. There have been some new arrivals today." Tension fills my body. "The hotel assures Tyson that their reservations were made long before the story, but some of the women have been overheard discussing the story and me."

I know that this is the part of his celebrity status he hates, and it's easy to understand, especially now. He has to limit his own movements, and with that, mine.

"They're all in their early twenties. No doubt they know who I am, and I do not want to subject myself or you to the maddening fandom."

I place my finger to his lips to silence him. He's starting to babble, and I already understand what he's saying.

"Tristan, you are who you are. I will go with you regardless. I will endure whatever public scrutiny you will be faced with as a result of your celebrity or this stupid story. All that said, I'm more than okay staying in the suite with you."

I lean in and place my lips on his. The now-familiar electricity zings between us.

Our recent post-shower escapade has left me sated and somewhat exhausted, and the massage is sounding better and better. I'm tense for obvious reasons, but I'm also sore because the man I'm kissing is nothing short of an animal in bed.

When the kiss ends, Tristan says, "That doesn't stop me from wanting to protect you, but your words are nice just the same. I'll do my best to remember, but please don't get angry with me if I forget."

"Fair enough," I say, and I kiss him chastely again and reach for my robe.

Tristan finishes dressing in a t-shirt and khaki shorts, sans underwear. Yeah, 'cause I need the reminder that he's wearing nothing under the shorts. My sex warms.

Will I ever get enough of this man? The answer between my legs is no, no I won't.

THIRTY

~*~*~*~

TRISTAN

***H**earing* commotion inside the suite, Cami and I head out of the bedroom to find Tyson, Mike, Sasha, and Leroy standing in the sitting room. Cami's gaze quickly meets mine, confusion in her eyes.

"I told Tyson on Monday that we would need a female bodyguard here for you and your friends. She blends in nicely so that when you ladies desire some unaccompanied shopping this weekend, you can take her with you."

I've been expecting her to be angry, but instead her eyes widen slightly in fear, the reality of the situation crashing down on her in a rush. Then her expression goes from fear to adoration in a nanosecond.

"Thank you," she breathes.

"I just want to know you're safe. After those calls yesterday I really feel it's necessary to ensure you guys don't have any issues when you're away from Tyson or myself."

She just nods, and I proceed with the introductions.

"Cami, this is Mike." I point to the shorter and stouter of the two men.

She reaches out to shake his hand. "Nice to meet you," she says.

Then I point to Leroy. Don't let the name fool you, the man is a beast. Standing at six feet, seven inches, he looks a lot like a body builder. He reminds me of Shaq or Michael Clark Duncan.

"This is Leroy."

Cami's eyes widen slightly at the sight of him, but she says, "Pleasure to meet you," and reaches out to shake his hand.

I have to stifle a laugh at her pale skin against Leroy's dark skin and the fact that his hand is about as big as her head. When Leroy lets the handshake linger a little longer than necessary, I grow a little uncomfortable. She doesn't seem to notice that he's hanging on a little too long, and that warms my heart. I hope I don't ever have a reason to show my jealous side to Cami.

She turns next to Sasha. Sasha has a gymnast's body: broad shoulders and hips, toned to perfection, and silent muscles that you really can't see, but no doubt if she flexed you would be immediately intimidated. She has a very butch style haircut that has me wondering about her sexual orientation. All in all she is not unattractive.

"And this is Sasha." I say.

"Yes, Sir." I frown. She extends her hand and Cami takes it. "It's a pleasure to meet you." She has one of those ultra-raspy, I've-smoked-too-many-cigarettes-in-my-life voices. It's strangely a bit sexy.

"Likewise." Cami's accent comes out on the word and I feel sensations deep down, tugging at the already present erection. Walking around with a hard-on is something I'm getting used to. Cami just has this effect on me.

"Since Mike, Sasha, and Leroy have arrived, why don't you fill me in on what you've found out about the new guests?" I say.

Tyson glances briefly at Cami, and I give him a tiny warning glance. We had discussed this earlier while Cami was sleeping. Anything Tyson has to say regarding Cami's or my safety is to be discussed in front of her without hesitation.

Tyson nods almost imperceptibly and says, "Six women, all in their early to mid-twenties. There's no indication that they know Tristan is here."

Sasha adds, "We spoke with the manager on the way in. He informed me that the reservations were made early Tuesday morning, but we confirmed that their flight into Tahiti was purchased several months ago. Their reservations are good through Saturday morning, and they have requested transportation back to Tahiti at eleven that morning."

"Sounds like they just decided they wanted a weekend getaway in a place a little more remote than Tahiti." Cami is ever thinking and countering. This is why I want her to know all of what is going on. She adds some pretty good insight to a situation.

Mike is next to speak. "I ran through the names on the guest list. None of them stand out as photographers or reporters."

"They're out on the beach now," Tyson adds. "You can see them from the balcony if want a look for yourself."

"No, thanks." I have no desire and no need.

"Speaking of balcony." She turns to the three bodyguards. "It was a pleasure meeting you. I'm sure I'll see you guys later." Then she turns to me. Reaches up on her tiptoes. I lean in to shorten the distance, fighting a smile. "Thank you," she whispers and kisses me. A chaste, appreciative kiss.

She turns on her heel and heads to the open doors. I watch her walk away until she turns to climb onto the massage table.

Turning to Tyson, I say, "Are our guests on schedule?"

"Yeah. Logistics are all taken care of. ETA is around ten thirty tonight. We've set them up downstairs in Cami's other suite. With the two bedrooms and pullout couch, I think they'll be comfortable."

I look to the trio and they all nod. I look back at Tyson. "Thank you, Ty." I smile, feeling true appreciation for all he has done. "Anything else?"

Tyson clears his throat. "Trinity was looking for Cami earlier. She said it was important, but not an emergency. I told her I'd have Cami get in touch when she got up."

"It is probably time that I checked my email, huh?"

Tyson nods. "That might not be a bad idea. You have been MIA for a week now. Well, not completely MIA, but you know what I mean."

I laugh. Yeah, I guess I do.

To the three new bodyguards I say, "I do my best not to be demanding. You all know what your job entails. Sasha, I have you here more for this weekend. I have no doubt that Cami will want to go shopping or even hang out at the beach. I would just like you to be here in case anything comes up."

I don't feel her presence is truly necessary, but I have a feeling that once we get to our destination on Friday morning, the press is going to be quick to find me.

"Yes, sir!" she acknowledges.

I roll my eyes. "Please do not call me 'sir.' I am not old enough to carry that label with any dignity. Tristan, Trey, or T will suffice."

"I'm sorry s— Tristan."

I smile. "Thank you. If any of you need anything, please see Tyson. He knows what my guidelines are and what I expect from you all. If it's not within his jurisdiction he'll discuss it with me. Fair enough?"

They all nod. Then Leroy pipes up. I can't be sure, but I think he might be blushing. "I am just wondering if...if I...could ask..."

I know the routine well enough to know what he's after. I smile, maybe even laugh a bit. "Is it for you, Leroy?"

Yup, he's definitely blushing.

He shakes his head. "No, my niece. She gave me a list of all the people whose autographs she wants provided I get to meet any of them. You're the first on her list."

"I'll take care of it for you. I think I have a few publicity stills around here somewhere."

"Thank you, Tristan." I notice he's careful not to address me as 'sir.'

I look over at Tyson, who's trying hard not to fall over with laughter. I understand why. I'm having a hard time fighting it myself.

"What?" Leroy asks, a little embarrassed still.

I laugh, unable to hold it in any longer. "You should have seen your face."

"Yeah, yeah. All right, you two, very funny. It's embarrassing, but I love my niece so I had to ask."

THIRTY-ONE

~~*~*~*

CAMI

As Alana works her fingers deep into the muscles of my back, my mind keeps wandering back to Tristan's steamy sexiness. The way his body moves, the way he embraces me, kisses me...

Dammit Cami, stop that. Think about something else. Something not hot. Like Bold. That's about as not hot as it comes.

It's a short leap from thinking about Tristan to wondering whether my sudden interest in taking a more active role in the company is due to my relationship with him.

The question lingers in my brain. No, it's not entirely due to my relationship with Tristan. It has more to do with the fact that I'm about to turn twenty-five and I need to find something to do with my time. Do I have to work? Absolutely not. But do I want to work? Yeah, I think I kind of do.

These last few days have been highly enjoyable on a professional front. They've shown me not only that I could be really good at this, but that I might even find it fun. I'm excited about New York, and I think I'm more excited about helping Tristan do what he does best than I am about walking a red carpet on the arm of America's hottest, sexiest man in Hollywood.

I also know now that I can do what I need to do with the business without being tied to L.A. At least that's something. I detest L.A. and refuse to live there. Bold owns its own plane that would be at my disposal whenever I needed it, which would make traveling much easier.

Even so, I'm not ready to make a final decision just yet. At least not about stepping into the CEO role. But I do want to be more involved in the business. I have no doubt that Tristan will support whatever decision I make.

It's that thought that leads me to finally take a minute to break down the feelings that are blossoming. Feelings that I would have never believed possible until last Friday are growing deep quickly. Every time I see him, my heart skips a beat and excitement pools down in my belly.

And the sex is utterly amazing. I have never felt more worshipped than I do when Tristan and I are tangled up in the sheets. Or the pool. Or the shower.

I squirm slightly at the memories and then remember that it's Alana's hands all over my back. Must settle down.

Am I falling in love with Tristan? Absolutely. Of this I have no doubt. The way he looks at me tells me that he too is beginning to feel the same way.

At least, this is what I think some of the looks he's giving me mean. I'm terrified to ask him. What if I'm misinterpreting his looks, his actions? Is it possible we could part ways next week and he'd never give me a second thought?

The idea causes me to tense up again. Alana notices and the pressure of her fingers increases. This massage is getting to the point of painful.

My body's reaction to the idea of losing Tristan tells me that I'm falling head over heels in love with him. With this revelation my heart swells and warm sensations fill my body. I've never really allowed myself to feel what it's like to love someone. I'll need to keep my emotions in check until I know, truly know, that he's on the same page.

Plus, I can't be the first one to say it.

I see Tyson come out on the balcony and light up a cigarette. I've never seen him smoke before. He's either really good a hiding it, or it's a stress-related habit. I know mine comes from boredom and stress.

"Hi, Ty!"

"Cami, you all right?" He actually looks a little concerned.

"Perfect, you?"

He shrugs. "I think so. I'm a little worried about our guests tonight. Worried someone will recognize Travis and follow him to the island. Or that someone will uncover Tristan's location." He pauses as if not sure whether to say more. "Actually, I'm pretty nervous about meeting Jolene, too." He blushes and I smile. It's pretty cute to see a man as big and brawny as Tyson blush. He takes a drag and continues, "Tristan told me he's seen her picture. He's pretty sure that I'll like her, so I guess that gives me some hope." He's still blushing.

"Well, as far as Travis being followed, the only thing we'll need to worry about is whether the hotel name is on the helicopter from Tahiti to Tarah, and from my understanding it's not. And I don't know how anyone would discover Tristan's location after all the trouble you've gone to." He smiles at that. "As for Jolene, she's a beautiful blond woman with big, beautiful green eyes. She's tall, too. Could pass for a Rockette. So on that note, thou shall not worry." I giggle as his smile grows wider.

"I do love the blonds," he says, teasing.

"Good thing I am not a blond then, huh?" I tease him back.

Alana finishes her massage. "Do you need anything else, Ms. Cami?"

"No. Thank you, Alana. I feel wonderful." Despite her added pressure to get me to relax, I actually feel like jelly pooled on the table.

"It was my pleasure. Please call again." She bows and leaves the balcony without a backwards glance.

"Ty, can you turn around, please?" I ask. He obliges quickly and I pull my robe back on.

"Can I have one of those?" I point to the pack of cigarettes in Tyson's hand.

He turns around and looks where I'm pointing. "Sure" He hands me one, and holds the lit lighter out for me.

I take a deep drag. "Thanks. Can I ask you something, Tyson?"

"Anything, Cami."

I take another drag off of the cigarette and slowly exhale. "Why haven't you talked to Tristan about where *Entertainment Now* got those photos?" This is the conversation I'd been trying to have with him on Monday morning in my suite, before Tristan interrupted.

After taking a drag from his cigarette, he looks at me. Raw fear in his eyes. "I'm scared."

"Of?" I ask.

"His reaction. I'm afraid he'll fire me. I'm afraid that he will see red at what I've done and it'll be over. I care for Tristan a great deal, Cami. He's my best friend and I would do anything for him. Including take a bullet for him." His eyes are so sincere, and I finally begin to realize why Tyson does what he does.

I hop down off of the massage table and take a couple steps toward Tyson. I gently place my hand on his shoulder. "I think your worry is unnecessary. He trusts you and your judgment. I believe he'll understand."

~~*~*~*

TRISTAN

I see Alana leave, so I head toward the patio to check on Cami. But as I come around the sitting room, I see Tyson and Cami standing close together, talking. Cami is smiling and has her hand on Tyson's shoulder.

Rage starts to build.

They're talking. They are only talking, nothing more. She's not flirting with him, nor he with her. I try to calm myself.

Their voices are low and I can't hear anything they're saying. Tyson leans toward her a little. She smiles at him again, laughs a little, then blushes.

I'm torn between running out the door away from them and running full-tilt toward them.

No! Dammit. This isn't happening. I'm reading too far into this. They're just talking.

I take a few deep breaths to steady myself. My knees are weak. Only a few minutes ago I felt desire, love, and tenderness for Cami. Now this.

Suddenly it becomes clear. Clearer than anything else I've ever felt in my life.

~~*~*~*

CAMI

"Talk to him, Tyson. He'll understand. And who knows, he might even be grateful for what you've done."

He pauses to think it over, and I'm relieved when he asks, "When?"

I smile to reassure him. "Now is as good a time as any. I'll go grab him, okay? Hang tight."

He nods. I pull away from him and head into the suite.

As I cross the threshold, I notice Tristan sitting with his back to me in one of the overstuffed chairs in the sitting room. His forehead in his hands, fingers gripping his hair. His shoulders are tense.

I'm barefoot so my touch makes him jump, but he doesn't look up. My heart starts to pound, and my palms sweat. I have a horrible feeling about this.

"Tristan?"

"What?" His voice is harsh, angry.

"What's wrong?" I scowl. I'm perplexed by his sudden change in mood. What's happened?

"I..." he stutters. "I saw you flirting with Tyson."

What the bloody hell? "What?" I come around to face him. Still he doesn't look up.

"On the patio, just a couple minutes ago."

Oh dear. My building anger fades away into understanding and recognition. "Tristan, Tyson and I were just talking about a couple of things. About you, mainly. He told me he's never seen you as happy and as alive as you've been this past week. He said that he has me to thank for the change in your attitude, for how happy and carefree you seem."

I watch as his shoulders slump. The fight is gone.

"Jesus, Cami." He looks up and his hand touches mine. "Jesus, I'm an idiot."

I feel the breath whoosh from my lungs. He tugs on my hand, maneuvering me between his legs. He wraps his hands around my thighs and brings his head to rest against my stomach.

"I'm such an idiot," he says again.

"You're not an idiot, Tristan." I lower myself to my knees so that I can look him in the eye. Once I'm there, he rests his forehead against mine. "I'm sorry if I gave you the impression that I was flirting. I wasn't."

This is it, this is my answer. If he didn't care about me, he wouldn't be jealous, right? He must be falling in love with me.

We stay like this for a few more minutes. Finally I speak. "Tyson would like to talk with you. Do you mind joining him on the patio?"

He doesn't speak, just shakes his head. I kiss his nose and get up. Taking his hand in mine, I pull him to his feet. He wraps his arm around my shoulders, pulling me in tight.

"I have a feeling I'm not going to like this, am I."

"I think everything will be fine. Come on," I say, pulling him toward the patio.

THIRTY-TWO

~~*~*~*

TRISTAN

"Cami said you wanted to talk?" I ask Tyson as we step onto the patio. His eyes slide to Cami, and in an instant my earlier jealousy surfaces. Then he looks back at me and nods. "What's up, Ty?"

Cami's arm snakes around my waist, and she pulls me tight against her side.

"There's something I've been wanting to tell you for a while now," Ty says. "Um, Cami said that she told you she knows who leaked the pictures. But that you weren't ready to know." Cami's grip gets a little tighter as Tyson continues. "I..." he stutters a bit. This is unusual for him. "I...I'm not sure that this is the best time to discuss it..."

I shake my head at him. "Ty, if you know what's going on, please, for the love of all that is holy, tell me. Was it you? Did you leak the pictures to EN?"

His silence is my answer. His body is rigid. His eyes are cast downward, looking away from me as best he can. His usual mask when discussing something important with me is gone, and his eyes are leery, afraid.

My breathing falters. I feel lightheaded and my anxiety level is creeping up on me. All I can manage is, "Why?"

"Remember when you asked me to keep an eye on her?" I nod and he continues. "I talked you out of it because I didn't feel it was necessary. I was hoping that you would find your own distance from her and move on. She was making you utterly miserable. But I asked Layla's bodyguard to report anything significant to me. Chanty and I are closer than we let on. She was witness to and told me about a lot, if not all, of Layla's infidelities. This was my final straw." He takes a ragged breath. His shoulders slump. For once he's dropped his guard. He looks like a normal, terrified person. "But I wasn't responsible for the pictures. Chanty was fed up with Layla's bullshit and wanted her own out. She's the one that took the pictures, and then she forwarded them to me."

"Why then didn't you come to me? Or even Vincent or Trinity, for that matter?" I ask.

"I should have come to you first. I reacted on impulse in an attempt to protect you and to give you the freedom you needed from her. I received the pictures last week Tuesday. EN pounced the moment I offered the story. In exchange for the story, EN agreed to paint you in a positive light. As soon as the contract was signed, they went after Layla to force her confession." He begins to pace. "I had intended to tell you. But within two hours of me submitting the images, Layla was telling you about it at the premiere. I had expected her to sit on it, wait until the last minute, or at least go running to her team of people."

I don't respond for some time. I'm pondering my next move. I want to be able work this out in my head before I start babbling like a moron. If he received them last Tuesday, that means that Chanty waited until then to send them off to Tyson. Was she waiting for some type of blackmail opportunity? Well, to be honest, that was obvious. But why now? Why not right after it happened? What changed?

"I would like to be able to talk to Chanty about all of this. I don't want to hear the gory details, but I need to know why in the hell she waited so long to send them to you. There were at least six weeks between the time it happened and Tuesday last week."

He nods at me and then looks to Cami. She nods at him and I pull away from her.

"Wait a goddamn minute!" I'm angry now. Furious. I turn to Cami. "You knew all of this?"

"Yes." Her response is quiet, shaky.

For fuck's sake, is everyone conspiring against me now? Tyson didn't talk, and Cami knew and didn't tell me. I feel betrayed.

"Look, it wasn't intentional." I glare at Tyson, he continues before I can say anything. "Originally Chanty had no intention of releasing the pictures or video to anyone. Personally, I think she wanted to use them to blackmail Layla. But a week or so ago, Chanty overheard Layla discussing a pregnancy, and from the conversation she concluded that Layla was talking about herself. She heard what Layla planned to do." He goes back to pacing. I'm pretty sure I know what Layla's plan was. "Layla wanted to use the pregnancy to trap you and at the same time blackmail the men. I am pretty sure that you don't need me to outline what she expected to gain from you and from the blackmail."

Shock. Pure, unadulterated shock is all I can feel in this moment. I'd known almost instantly, the night she told me, that the baby isn't mine. But if she hadn't told me about the story too, if she'd told me about the baby under sweeter, more intimate circumstances, I would've been blindsided by the situation. Would have fallen to bended knee. By the time I came to my senses and realized the truth, it might've been too late.

I grab the pack of cigarettes off the table, light one, and walk over to the railing. Look down at the beach. It is so quiet out here, peaceful. Completely at odds with the turmoil inside me.

I want so badly to be angry at Tyson for not coming to me first, but I'm taken aback by his desire to protect me. I haven't felt anything like this for years. When my mom died, my whole world changed. I never realized how much I leaned on her until she wasn't there to lean on any longer. For the last ten years, despite my friends, I've felt lost and alone in the world.

When Layla came along, I was hooked at first. I thought I'd found someone who could relieve that loneliness. I would bend over backwards for her. But I quickly saw that the emotions were all on my side. She was colder, detached. Our relationship seemed to take a long time to kindle. For as long as it took to kindle, it took a matter of minutes to fizzle out. I realized she never had feelings for me. It was all an illusion. Even when I was with her, I'd always been alone. I had started to think I'd always be alone.

But hearing what Tyson and Chanty have done to protect me makes my heart ache. For the first time since my mom's passing, I feel like I have a family in Tyson.

Suddenly the hairs on the back of my neck stand to attention and my heart starts racing. I know it's because she's behind me. I feel her tiny hands on the small of my back. I flinch. I'm tempted to be comforted, but I know if I don't nip this in the ass now, it will eat me alive.

"If you ever keep something from me, something as important as this, I swear..." Words fail me. I quickly realize that the jealousy I feel is nothing compared to what it would be like without her in my life.

"Tristan, I didn't withhold anything deliberately. Yes, Tyson and I talked. Yes, I knew about him sending in the pictures. But in all fairness, I gave you ample opportunity to ask me about it, to find out from me who it was. I wanted Tyson to be the one to tell you because I knew that if I told you, your anger would be directed at Tyson." She pulls her hands off of my back, and the lack of contact has my emotions soaring. "And believe me, Tristan, I would much rather have you angry at me for not telling you than have you mad at Tyson for what he's done. That man will do anything to protect you, including risk his own life for you. He is devoted to you and only you. I'm sorry if that conversation made you jealous earlier; it was never my intent."

"That's the other part you guys were talking about?" I ask her.

"Yes. It was the reason I was touching his shoulder, it was the reason I was so close to him. If I've ever given you the impression that I was flirting with him, or with anyone else, I'm sorry. It's not something I would ever do intentionally."

Sweet Jesus, it's official. I've crossed over the asshole line. She has given me no reason, none whatsoever, not to trust her, and here I am, getting jealous of something that doesn't exist.

"Tristan, I can't not talk to Tyson, not when your relationship with him puts us in such close proximity. You have to understand this. It's you." She places her hands back on the small of my back and I feel her start to stroke up to my shoulders and back down to my waist. I grab her wrist to bring them around front. Catching my intentions, she embraces me in a bear hug. Her touch is electric. It's almost like hitting delete on a long script and all I can think about is her. I can't think about everything that's just been brought to my attention. It's me?

"Tristan, you are all I want. But you have to be patient with me. I've never done this before."

My shoulders slump and I cover her hands with mine. My heart feels like it's expanding and contracting at the same time. I want to express the inexpressible. I want Cami to know and understand all the feelings roiling around inside me that I can't name. I want her to know that I love her and trust her deeply.

Hot, wet tears start to stream down my cheeks, and I realize that the last time I remember crying was at my mother's gravesite as they lowered her casket into the ground.

"Cami."

She slides around me, an expectant look in her eyes. "Yes, Tristan?"

I take a deep breath. Here goes nothing. "You asked me the other night about my tattoo."

I hear her intake of breath and I look into her beautiful blue eyes as I pull her in front of me. There is an undeniable trust and devotion that I've never seen before.

"She called me her little dragon. My mom." I pause, just a second. "When I was a kid, she told me the story of Beowulf and Grendel. I fell in love with the dragon in that story and I was more upset that the dragon died. She taught me to fight for what I believe in, no matter what. One of the things she said when I was about twelve was that there was a dragon inside of me, begging to be set free."

I look at Cami then. Her eyes are warm yet sad. She understands, better than I could have hoped, what it means to be telling her this story.

I continue. "She said that one day that dragon would be set free. Free to protect, to defend, and to guard the woman I love. At the time she told me all of this, I thought she was crazy because I was twelve and girls still had cooties." I laugh a little. "As I grew older, though, the story stayed with me. When I reached my senior year in high school, I felt that she was right. I felt as though the dragon was fighting to be freed.

"When my mother died, my dragon was released. A piece of him went with her." I turn my back to Cami and lift my shirt. I don't explain. I don't have to. If she is looking for it, she will see it.

I feel the warmth of her touch run along my spine up to where the spine of the dragon stops. Her hand pauses, and I hear her small sob as she traces it.

Starting at the top of the dragon's spine is a V. She traces the line of the inside of the right wing up and around to the inside of the left wing and back to where she started. The heart is complete.

"It's on fire," she breathes.

From the inside of the bottom, blending into the browns and oranges, are flames. There is a raggedness to this part of the wings that gives them the appearance that something is missing. The detail is so subtle that, unless it's pointed out, no one would know.

"The space matches up with that of my own heart. When my mom died, I thought I had lost everything I ever knew of love." I turn around and embrace her. "Until I met you."

I stroke her cheek – "When I touch you," – I kiss her – "when I kiss you," – I look deep into her eyes – "when I look into your eyes, the sparks fly, the electricity ignites, and my heart swells.

"When I decided to finally get my tattoo, everything in my life seemed so surreal and mythical. Very little made sense. I spent all my time in Hollywood. I had no time for myself. At one point, I felt myself slipping away. Away from who I was and who I am. My tattoo brought all of that back. Brought me back to my mom, back to my roots. Out of the clouds and back onto solid ground. It brought forth my sense of reality, self-preservation, and safety. When the tattoo was done, I vowed that no matter what I would stick to three things."

I hold up my finger. "One, I would look to my mother within myself when things went wrong." Another finger comes up. "Two, I would never let my life get away from me like that again, and three," – I add another finger – "I vowed to protect everyone and everything I love."

I take a deep breath. "The night I found out about the story, I put my hand over my chest and begged my mother for a sign. Something that would set things right."

Cami looks on the verge of tears.

"My sign came. And when it did, it was you, in LAX."

She gasps. "What do you mean, me?"

"I saw you. In the first class lounge. Then on the plane to Honolulu. I followed you from the plane into the Honolulu airport." I stroke her cheek lightly with my index finger. "Then finally, after I thought I'd lost you for good, you strode into Blu."

She doesn't respond right away but stands there, looking at me.

"I would never have paid any attention to you whatsoever if it hadn't been for these." I reach around her shoulder and gently trail my finger along her wings. "This is my sign."

THIRTY-THREE

~~*~*~*

CAMI

"Lunch is here," I hear Tristan say through the bedroom door.

"I'll be right there," I say back.

Until Tristan told me about his dragon, I hadn't realized that I'd felt incomplete when it came to him. His story stirred emotions deep down inside that are so foreign to me that I'm not sure how to take them. But the resounding sense of completeness overshadows any level of doubt I had about how I feel.

Knowing this makes the jealousy that he felt over my conversation with Ty a little harder to handle. I've never given him a reason to not trust me. But I have to remember that he's been scorned pretty bad. I know now that I need to be mindful of my flirtatious side, a side that has been a part of me for so long.

Couple that with a serious jealous streak in Tristan and we will have further issues. However, I'm confident that after today we will be able to work through it, no matter what.

I finish with my shorts and t-shirt and head for the door. But before I open it, I hear Tristan.

"No, I'm not mad at you. Though I wish you would've come to me sooner. But all the same, I understand and appreciate why you did what you did."

I assume he's talking to Tyson. I don't want to interrupt.

Tristan continues, "Are Leroy and Sasha on their way over to Tahiti with the helicopter?"

"Yeah," Tyson says. The rest of his answer is muffled and I can't make it out.

"Great, thanks," I hear Tristan say.

Sensing that their conversation is over, I open the door. Tristan's back is to me, but I can see Tyson and the smile that spreads across his face when he sees me. I can see now why Tristan gets worried about flirting.

Tyson's smile alerts Tristan to my presence, and he turns toward me. The smile on his face is even bigger and wider than Tyson's.

"Hey, beautiful," he says, and I'm pretty sure that I blush.

"Hey beautiful yourself."

He chuckles. "That's become our greeting, hasn't it."

I laugh. "I suppose it has."

Over Tristan's shoulder, Tyson's still smiling, but he's shaking his head.

"Ready to eat?" Tristan asks me, and I nod.

"You guys enjoy your lunch and I'll see you both in a bit," Tyson says.

I shake my head. "You know, Tyson, you can join us for a meal once in a while."

Tyson smiles and heads toward his room. "I've got a couple things to do. Besides, you two look like you need some time alone."

My jaw drops as he closes the door.

I turn to Tristan. "Are we really that bad?" We both start to laugh.

~~*~*~*

TRISTAN

"Come 'ere, Sweets," I say, extending my hand.

I escort her onto the patio, where, sitting on the table, two domed place settings holding our lunch await.

"I thought you could use something to eat." She sits as I pull back the domes. Underneath there are pancakes, sausage, bacon, and eggs.

"Mmm, that smells wonderful." She takes a drink of orange juice as I sit down.

She cuts into her sausage then spears it with her fork. An invisible shudder runs through my body as I watch her bite down.

I can't think about that now. I need to convey something to her. "Thank you, Cami."

"For what, Tristan?" She looks at me, puzzled.

"Well, mainly because for a long time I've felt like nothing has been in my control. The fallout with Layla and the story, but also..." I sigh. "Doing what I do requires me to relinquish control to those involved, mainly my agent, my PR rep, and of course the production and promotion teams for whatever movie I'm filming or promoting. Having you here to help handle Trinity, Vinnie, the police, the press conference, all of it, means a lot to me and I realize that I haven't properly thanked you for all of it. I'm finally starting to feel like I have some control back in my life. So thank you."

Cami doesn't respond and I look at her, perplexed. "What is it?"

I watch as she blinks rapidly, wide-eyed, looking as though she is fighting back tears. "I just feel a little overwhelmed."

I set my fork next to my plate and bring my fist up to rest my chin on it. Looking into her eyes I say, "Explain, please?"

"Well, I came here to get away from Reed, and to just escape life. And my escape has led me straight to you. I'm afraid that I'm becoming emotionally overwhelmed, but in a very good way." Pregnant pause. "I—I'm worried about where we will go from here."

"We, as in you and I?" She just nods. "Well, I will tell you where I see us going from here." I pause and take a sip of my juice. "When I picture New York next week, I see you by my side. When I picture the following press tour for *Conjure*, I see you on the red carpet with me. And most of all, when I picture the worldwide press tour for *Love is Burning*, I see you touring Europe with me." I pause. This is it. This will either be the nail in my coffin or an open door. "In other words, Cami, I see you, everywhere I go, alongside everything I do."

The tears she was fighting now slide silently down her cheeks. I don't say anything, just let her absorb my words.

Finally she speaks. "What are you saying, Tristan?"

Can I honestly, after only five days, tell her that I'm on the verge of falling in love with her? Can I be completely honest with myself and fully embrace the fact that it's true? But what if she's not in love with me?

As the silence stretches out, the hope in her eyes turns to worry. Jesus, she is falling in love with me.

Watching the raw emotion on her face, I know without a doubt that I will protect and cherish this smart, beautiful, sexy goddess that sits before me. She is everything I ever wanted in a woman.

"Please, Tristan, just say whatever it is you're thinking." Her eyes plead for a response.

"Cami," I breathe. "I can't imagine leaving here without you or going about my life without you. It has taken me twenty-eight years to find you. I'm not about to let you go."

I stare at her, trying hard to show her with my eyes what I'm not yet ready to say aloud. We need time to grow. To learn one another.

I lean across the table to kiss her, slowly, passionately. Unhurried. When I pull away I say, "You're beautiful, Cami. Never forget that."

Reaching up, she caresses my cheek. Leaning into her touch I realize I barely know her, but I will spend every day for the rest of my life getting to know her.

After our very late lunch Cami took care of some *Bold* business. Answering emails and such. Despite what she thinks, I think she's ready to take over her father's company. If she thinks for one minute that Trinity, Vincent or I will let her fail, she has another thing coming. I will not, after these last few days see her give up on something she is so natural at.

Watching her work has me in awe. Her level of concentration is amazing, and she looks so damn sexy in her reading glasses that I hadn't seen until now.

When she's done she goes into the bedroom get ready for our friends' arrival. She's been in there quite a while, and I'm starting to worry. After everything that's happened today, I'm afraid she may be rethinking getting involved with me. She may have been willing to put up with the fans and paparazzi, but I don't think she expected my being so protective of her.

My thoughts are interrupted by Tyson striding quickly into the room with a look of sheer horror on his face.

"What's eating you?" I ask.

He just stares at me, lost in thought, like he's unsure how to say what he needs to say.

"Spill it, maestro."

"We have a pretty big problem," he says.

"Whatever it is, we can handle it."

"Right. Well, yeah, I suppose we can, though you might want to get Cami in here first."

My brow creases. "Why?"

"It involves her, too."

"What involves me?" Cami's voice is clear and coming from behind me.

I turn to look at her and she looks utterly amazing. Her hair is up, curly and swept to the side. Highlighting the blue streaks across the top. Over her left ear is a purple flower. Her makeup is subtle but beautiful, and her skin reflects the glow of the sunset outside. She's wearing a purple halter top that matches her purple pumps perfectly. Her legs are clad in white skinny jeans that accent the curve of her hips. My mouth falls open like a drooling fool and she stares back at me.

"You like?" She smiles a seductive, secret smile and turns around.

I hear my sharp intake of breath. The back is open except for a silver chain keeping the two halves together, and it's immediately evident that she's not wearing a bra. Her corset is strung with white and purple ribbons. It's impossibly hard to pull my eyes away from her sexy, nicely rounded derriere that my hands twitch to caress. The twitch in my pants is all the proof I need that I'll never get enough of this beautiful woman.

"I..." I stutter through my response. "I—I think you look amazing," I finally manage to sputter.

Her smile is warm and genuine.

She finally looks away from me and toward Tyson. "What's going on, Ty?" she asks, real concern coloring her tone. I turn to face Tyson expectantly.

"We had a large group of about eight women check into the hotel about an hour ago. They were asking for the penthouse suite, and one of the women threw a ginormous fit when the concierge told her it was currently occupied."

I interrupt him. "What exactly does that have to do with us?"

"Mike was in the lobby when all of this was going on. He was unable to see who was causing the altercation; however, it was not the woman arguing that caught his attention. Two of the women appeared to be bodyguards, dressed in black, standing back in a semi-protective stance from the woman throwing the tantrum."

"Okay," Cami interrupts this time. "So it's someone famous. Or at least someone that feels the need to be protected. What exactly does that have to do with Tristan, or myself for that matter?"

Tyson takes a deep breath, "I'm getting there." He shudders. "Mike sent a cell phone picture to Sasha, wanting to know if she could identify either of the bodyguards." Tyson has turned back into Mr. Professional.

"And? Did she?" Cami asks Tyson.

I'm pretty sure I already know the answer.

"Yeah, Sasha knows one of them. They used to work together."

"Well?" Cami barks.

I find my voice. "It's Chanty, isn't it."

I feel Cami stiffen immediately. When her voice comes, it's lower than a whisper. "Layla."

For fuck's sake, how in the hell does this happen? First, the main reason for fleeing to Tarah shows up in the form of Cami, and now the real reason I ran shows up in living color.

Dammit all to hell. Cami is not going to put up with this insanity, I know it. Why should she?

Cami manages to pull herself together far faster than I can even begin to comprehend. "What impact is this going to have on us? Our guests arriving? Travis?"

Jesus, she's not running?

"None, if I can help it. We can maintain radio silence from within the hotel. Though I suggest making contact with Trinity. Fill her in."

My head snaps up. "We will do no such thing. I can handle this, and if I can't, then I have complete faith in Cami's ability to handle this."

"Uh..." she stutters. "Tristan, I..."

She has so much self-doubt about her abilities. I need to find a way, some way, to help her see that she can handle this if the need arises.

"Cami, if it comes to it and we need to call Trinity, we will. But right now, Layla blowing my location blows her own. No doubt she's here for similar reasons as both of us. She's not going to go running to the press."

I turn to embrace Cami and she has a very leery look in her eyes. Looking down at her I say, "You asked me today to trust you, said that you've never given me a reason not to. So I'm trusting you, and trusting your ability to handle this if the need arises."

She smiles slightly and nods. "All right, Tristan, I will do what I can, if it becomes necessary."

"That's my baby-girl," I say, caressing her back.

"What does this mean for me?" she asks Tyson, pulling back from me but not letting go of my waist. I wrap my arm around her shoulder, holding her close.

"It only means anything if she knows who you are. The likelihood of that is relatively slim." Tyson is cool and professional.

Cami nods and moves to sit down on the couch.

I'm anything but cool, calm, and collected. What kills me the most is that I'm trapped within these four walls when right now I want nothing but to flee the room. I feel so lost. Cami and I have come so far, only to have Layla come between us after all.

I've started pacing the room without fully realizing that I'm doing so. Cami sits silently on the couch, staring down at her hands, lost in her own thoughts. I have to find out what's in her head.

I cross the room and kneel down at her feet. She doesn't move to look at me, but she also doesn't move away. I turn to Tyson and nod toward the door. He nods back at me and leaves the room.

"I want to touch you, to hold you, but I'm afraid you're going to reject me," I whisper.

I look up to look into her eyes and I see tears forming in the corners. Not spilling over just yet, but I know they're close. I reach out tentatively toward her to cup her face. When my fingers reached her cheek she leans into my gesture. My heart soars. I use my thumb to stroke away her tears.

She looks up then, staring at me. "You're not going to get rid of me that easily."

I gasp. She brings her hand up to mine against her cheek, pressing to hold me there.

One sentence is all it has taken for me to want to admit that I love her. I love this woman. I have fallen in love with Cami.

I open my mouth to tell her, but before I can speak her eyes grow wide, and in a very small voice, almost like I'm not meant to hear, she says, "I was scared that I was the only one."

I cup her face in both my hands. When our lips meet, I'm lost to sensation, to the warmth in my heart spreading throughout my body. My love for Cami bringing me back to life. I know in this moment that I will die without her. I need her like I need air to breathe, water to drink, and food to eat. I know I will do anything for her, including forego my career in favor of our love and our relationship.

My kiss becomes more demanding, but just as sweet and sensual. I put into it every ounce of the love I feel for her. Cami is my angel. She is my saving grace and my guiding light.

THIRTY-FOUR

~~*~*~*

CAMI

Tristan, Mike, and Tyson are all waiting patiently in the sitting room for everyone to arrive, but I can't sit still anymore.

Layla is somewhere downstairs, hanging out with her girlfriends, doing God knows what, and I have this awful feeling that this is not going to end well. Having all of this coming down around me is something I know that I need to get used to. It's a part of who he is. I try hard to tell myself this.

I've wandered out onto the deck near the pool, overlooking the beach below. The sun is well below the horizon, but there is still a faint blue glow in the distance. It's something I've noticed the last couple of nights on the beach.

Despite the darkness, I can still see a few people milling about on the beach in the light of the moon and the hotel. There is a group of women about twenty to twenty-five yards from Blu's deck. From this distance, it's impossible to tell who's down there. It could be Layla and her group, or someone else entirely.

Off in the distance, I hear the whooshing of helicopter blades. Looking in the direction of the sound, I see two red lights and one white search light heading right toward me.

"They're here," Tristan says from behind me. I look over my shoulder to see him walking in my direction.

"Stop," I say, and his face falls. "There's still a group of about eight women down on the beach. I don't want them to see you."

He shakes his head at me. "It's impossible to see up here from down there."

I smirk at him and close the distance between us.

"Hey, beautiful," he says as he grabs my arms to pull me in closer.

"Hey beautiful yourself," I say, and he smiles.

The helicopter is getting louder and closer, but rather than descending to the helipad below, it's rising. We both watch as the helicopter makes its approach. I look in the direction of the roof and see that there are lights shining on top of the hotel.

"There's a helipad up there?" I ask Tristan.

"Yup, that's where they're headed. Tyson redirected them so that they can come into the hotel undetected. Well, sort of."

The wind picks up and my hair starts flying around. Tristan pulls me toward the door to the suite. I reluctantly follow, mesmerized by the way the helicopter moves.

Inside, Tyson is talking to Jessie, the bartender from Blu.

"Hi, Jessie," I say. My tone might be a little too friendly because Tristan stiffens a bit.

"Hi, Cami." He walks toward me, hand extended, and we shake.

Then he turns to Tristan. "Mr. Rubble," he says. Tristan and I both laugh, and Tristan takes his hand.

"I trust that you know full well who I am?" Tristan asks. His brief moment of jealousy seems to be forgotten.

"I do, Mr. Michaels. However, we like to afford our guests as much privacy around here as possible."

Tristan nods. "Great. Then feel free to call me Tristan. But only while we're in this suite, if you please?"

"No problem. Where would you guys like me to set up?"

"How about the patio, near the table? I believe we will be dining al fresco this evening."

"Perfect. I'll have drinks flowing in a just a couple of minutes. Would you two like your usuals?"

I smile at Jessie. He sure knows how to make us feel welcome. "I will. Tristan?"

"Beer for starters, thanks, Jessie."

Jessie nods and off he goes. I lean in toward Tristan's ear. "Relax, love. All is well and I'm just being friendly. No flirting, Okay?"

"I know, just habitual." He leans in and kisses me. Softly at first, but soon we forget that Mike and Tyson are in the room with us and it turns passionate. My head starts to swim. My arms wrap around his neck and my hands grab fistfuls of his hair.

"Get a damn room, would you two? Jeez, we're not even in the door and ya'll are already making out."

I know this voice immediately. My lips still locked with Tristan's, I turn him so that I can see over his shoulder. I open my eyes and wink at Beau. A huge smile spreads across my face, bringing an end to the kiss.

Tristan growls.

"And you wonder why I call you Bear," I tease him.

He growls playfully again and I release him.

No sooner are my arms free than I'm engulfed in hugs from Beau, Jolene, and Naomi.

"Gah! I missed you guys!"

"Apparently I wasn't much of a distraction," I hear him huff.

"You are the best distraction," I say to him from within the circle of bodies.

Finally the girls release me and Mick wraps his arm around me.

"Tristan Michaels, meet the one and only Mitchell Bast," I say.

Beau laughs. Mick hates to be called Mitchell. He tightens his arm around me, a playful, unspoken threat to squeeze until it hurts.

"Fine, fine. Whatever, Mick. Mick Bast."

Tristan laughs and extends his arm. Thank God Mick has to let me go to shake his hand. I squirm out of his grasp and take in the sight of my three best friends.

Naomi is still short, sassy, and extremely sexy, but she now has a big streak of purple in her platinum blond hair.

"Purple, huh?" I ask. Naomi nods. "I like it."

Just then, Travis – though I've never met him, I wasn't born yesterday – comes over and wraps his arm around Naomi's shoulder, and she blushes bright red. Evidently they've already become acquainted.

I extend my hand to him. "Pleasure to meet you, Travis."

Tristan laughs and I look in his direction.

"Pleasure to meet you, Travis," he repeats, mocking my English accent.

"Har-har!" I glare at him. "Hi, sista!" I say to Jolene, who has also changed her hair. "How are you?"

"I'm great. You look amazing! Getting some sun I see."

Tristan snorts and Jolene laughs. After a week in the sun I'm still pale as a ghost.

"Very funny, you two. You dyed your hair red. What on earth for?" I giggle.

She shrugs. "Something different. I wanted to try being a redhead."

"Well that puts a damper on my plans," I say teasingly.

"If you're referring to the sexy man over there in the corner staring at me," – I look over my shoulder and sure enough, Tyson is all but drooling at the sight of Jolene; my insides start bouncing with glee – "then I don't think you have much to worry about." I laugh, she's probably right.

"Hi, sexy!" I say to Beau.

"Hi yourself!"

Tristan laughs. "Now I know where you got it from."

Beau laughs too. "No, I stole it from her."

I introduce my friends to Tristan, Sasha, Leroy, and Mike, and then we split up so the new arrivals can get settled in their rooms.

The phone rings. Mike is quick to grab it. "Dinner is coming up," he says. Perfect timing.

After an amazing dinner, we are all sitting around the table on the patio. Jessie is on top of everyone's drinks and we all seem to be getting along well. Everyone is talking, laughing, and having a good time. Travis is a riot of jokes and laughter. He about had me spewing Cosmos all over the table. Tyson and Jolene are talking quietly, and something tells me that Travis and Naomi will be sharing a room this entire trip. I'm in complete awe of the fact that neither Travis's or Tristan's celebrity has had any bearing on the conversation. I'm relieved that no one's mentioned Hollywood or the stories that broke this week.

Suddenly Tyson is interrupting us with this horrified look on his face. I hadn't even realized he'd gotten up to answer the phone until now.

"What's doing, Ty?" I ask. Tyson's expression lightens a bit as he looks from Tristan to me and back again.

"Someone is requesting access to the penthouse via the elevator on the seventh floor," he says. I can tell he's fighting to keep his voice calm.

"Who is it?" I ask, but the phone starts ringing again. Tyson looks from me to Tristan and then turns on his heel and strides quickly into the sitting room. I see him square his shoulders and stand just a little bit taller as he shifts from relaxation mode to business mode.

I call after him, "Ty, just let Leroy handle it and come back to the party." He stops mid stride and I watch as his shoulders visibly relax.

Leroy picks up the phone.

Tyson has turned around and is now looking intently at Tristan. "I'm not sure letting her up here is such a good idea. We don't know what her intentions are."

My heart sinks into my stomach and I feel Tristan stiffen, tension instantly rolling off of him in waves.

"I'm sorry, she's mistaken. There's no Mr. Jackson in this suite."

Travis! I scream in my head.

I stand up and make a beeline for the sitting room. I reach Leroy and put my hand on his shoulder. He jumps a little.

"Let her up," I whisper in his free ear.

He raises his eyebrows at me and mouths, "Ma'am?"

"It's all right. She's just going to keep trying if we don't let her up. Let her up. I'll handle this."

"Ms. Enders says let her up," Leroy says into the phone.

I sidestep Leroy and begin making may way toward the foyer. Sasha steps into the hallway ahead of me. "She does not come past the foyer," I say to Sasha. "Keep her at the elevator." I'm thrown off internally by the authority in my voice. Now that Tristan's pointed it out to me in reference to dealing with Trinity and Vincent, I'm beginning to recognize it.

I feel something grab my elbow. Tristan pulls me around to face him. "What are you doing?" He's pissed.

"Getting rid of Layla before she causes a scene bigger than we have the ability to handle." His eyes are cold, angry, and distant. In response, I get calm. "Tristan, if I don't squash her now, she'll be bugging us all night long. I want to enjoy my evening. Please, let me handle her."

"Oh no you don't, Cami. I will handle her."

I vigorously shake my head at him. "Like hell you will, Tristan. She has no clue that you're here. She thinks that Travis is here and might know where you are. She's fishing for information, so let me handle this. She doesn't know me from Eve. Sasha is here. Mike can come with me or stand by if necessary." My words are finally starting to register and his gaze softens.

"All right," he says. "I trust you."

The words coming from his mouth have me shaky and turning to jelly.

He leans in and kisses me. When our lips meet, my hands immediately force their way into his hair and I pull him hard and tight against my body, kissing him back with ferocious intensity.

Someone clears his throat behind me. "She's here." It's Mike.

I peel myself away from Tristan and look him square in the eye. "I've got this, baby. Please." He nods.

I turn around and Mike is between me and the hallway. As I walk around him I whisper, "Stay close." I get closer to the door and I can hear two women in a slightly heated confrontation. One voice I easily recognize as Sasha's. The other, I know, has to be Layla.

THIRTY-FIVE

When I open the door, the bickering immediately stops. One word rings out, "Travis," and it comes from Layla.

"Who's Travis?" I ask, looking directly at her.

She looks exactly the same as in the photos from my Internet search on Tristan, only in the flesh. Her chestnut-colored hair is curled slightly. Her dark brown eyes look almost black in the light of the foyer. She's standing near the elevator, seeming a bit flustered.

"Travis is a friend of mine. I know he's in your suite." The words are confident, but her voice comes out hesitant.

I purse my lips at her in annoyance. "What makes you think that your friend Travis is in my suite?"

"Um. Because I saw him come down here from the roof."

She has to be joking. I tilt my head sideways, staring at her in disbelief. There is no way she could have seen Travis on the roof from anywhere but on the roof.

"Well, I don't know. You may have seen your friend, but let me assure you, he is not in my suite," I state firmly.

As she opens her mouth to speak, loud laughter erupts from the suite. Obviously everyone has come back inside.

"Now if you will excuse me, I have a suite full of people and a party going on."

"Oh? My friends and I love a good party. Can we join you?"

I cringe internally at her desperation, and then again at the idea of having her in my suite.

"You know," I say, adopting a confiding tone. "It's a bit like having Ellora's Cavemen in there. Hot, steamy, and some seriously sexy fun." I pause for effect, and her face lights up. The odds of her knowing who Ellora's Cavemen are stand at pretty slim, so it's the idea of men that captures her attention. "I'm pretty sure that I don't want to share that with you or your friends," I say, and watch with satisfaction as her face falls.

I let my amusement show on my face as she racks her brain for another way to get me to invite her in. Nothing like inviting your unwanted self to a party.

"We can bring our own booze," she tries.

"That's good, because I'm positive that we're keeping the best bartender in this hotel busy up here. So you can keep your booze downstairs because you're not invited to join us."

Suddenly her expression goes from tentatively friendly to positively pissed. "Do you know who I am?"

Ah, here comes the snarky bitch. "What does who you are have to do with anything?"

Out of the corner of my eye I see Sasha perk up just a bit as I get snippy with Layla.

"Everything! It would be to your benefit to have me at your party. I'm just trying to do you a favor. When you have friends like me, you can go places, become someone."

I can't help but bust out laughing. A deep, no-holds-barred laugh that is going to cause tears. Layla turns fifteen shades of red. This of course spurs me on, and what keeps me laughing is that she doesn't head for the elevator. This woman has no dignity. I finally start to calm a bit and became capable of semi-coherent speech.

"Hey, Sasha, did you hear that?" She nods and I look back at Layla. "Layla Brooke is offering to be my friend." I chuckle a bit longer, then step up to Layla. With me in my heels and her in flip-flops, we are eye to eye.

"First of all, Layla, do not believe for one second that just because I'm on a private island in the middle of the Pacific I'm unaware of your little story yesterday. I would think twice about threatening or promising me something you can't deliver, little girl. Your pants are not big enough to play in my world." I point my finger at her chest and Sasha stiffens, on high alert. I hear the door open behind me – oh shit, not Tristan – but I don't look around. I stay focused on Layla. "Your career hangs by a precious little thread, and believe me when I tell you that I am your puppeteer."

I watch as Layla steels herself and takes a half step forward. Sasha isn't having that; she moves in our direction. I put my hand up to tell her to stay put. I can tell by Layla's body language that we're not going to get physical.

I hear a couple of heavy footsteps behind me and Mike comes into my peripheral vision. Layla's eyes go wide as she realizes that there are not one but two bodyguards in the room.

"Who are you?" she asks, surprise evident in her voice.

"Someone you should learn to play nice with because fucking with me will only damage what little chance you have left in Hollywood." I pull in a long breath. "Your little stunt yesterday with the fire is a true credit to the type of person you really are." I pause for a second, but she doesn't deny it. Rage flashes in me again. "Not to mention the fact that the alcohol on your breath tells me that you have no respect for yourself or for the unborn child you're carrying. Unless you were lying to smooth things out with Tristan."

She retreats a couple of steps.

"What were you expecting, Layla, that he would fall to his knees with open arms for you?" I look over at Sasha, whose mouth is slack with surprise at my speech.

Layla has turned white as a ghost. "He's here. I knew it!" she exclaims. Of all the things to pull from what I'm yelling at her about, she decides to jump to the conclusion that Tristan is here.

"What the hell are you talking about?" I snap back.

Her eyes dart from me to Mike to the door and back again. "Tristan. He's here, isn't he."

"Hell no, he's not here."

"Then how do you know all of that? About me?" Her voice is mousy and weak.

"Because I am privy to all of my clients' most personal and private details, whether he wishes to share or not."

"You're not his lawyer."

I laugh. "You're really dense, aren't you." She scowls at me. "Did you see his press release yesterday?" She just nods. "I wrote that press release. Tristan is one of my company's biggest clients. So yes, Layla, I am fully aware of all your little stunts, and I do have the power to destroy you. So be a good little girl and go back downstairs.

You're not welcome here." I take a step back and Sasha visibly relaxes.

"I—" She stutters a little. "I never meant to hurt him." Her voice is still small and weak. "Please," she says, "if you talk to him, I really need to speak to him."

My heart lurches at her expression and anger washes over me.

"Don't hold your breath. I'm pretty sure the two of you have nothing to discuss." I turn to Mike. "See to it that she leaves my suite and returns to her own." He nods and I move toward the door to the sitting room.

"I'm not pregnant," she says behind me, and my rage fires again.

"Bloody hell! What do you mean, you're not pregnant?" I ask without turning around.

"I—"

"Please do not tell me that you had an abortion, because you will win no points with me," I say through clenched teeth.

"No. When I told Tristan I was pregnant, I only thought that I was."

"Oh, now that's great. You knew that was the one thing that could possibly get Tristan to his knees and you used it against him." I turn slowly, rage seething in my veins. "That was a low blow, Layla, and you know it." My voice is strained as I fight for control of my anger. I want so badly to hit her, or at the very least make her cry. "You are an insensitive, selfish bitch. What in the world would possess you to do something like that?"

"I—I don't know. I was scared. I didn't want to lose Tristan."

I shake my head. "No, Layla, you didn't want to lose your supposed career. But what you really need is help. Professional help. You are not cut out for Hollywood.

You're too caught up in yourself, drinking, and drugs, and that combination will only do one of two things. It will get you kicked out of Hollywood or get you killed."

She slumps in defeat. No doubt this is the last thing she expected to have happen when she came up here tonight.

I get in her face again, and Mike and Sasha are instantly at my side. Tears are forming in Layla's eyes. Her pitiful look makes me want to smack her and wake her up to the reality she has created for herself. "Hollywood is no place for little girls," I rage. "Get your shit together and get out of my suite."

I turn, and walk toward the door. To no one in particular, I say, "Get her out of my suite."

~~*~*~*

TRISTAN

"Get her out of my suite."

I can tell from her voice that she's angry, which matches my own sentiments regarding Layla right now.

She's not pregnant. God dammit, it really was a ruse to get back at me. She knew that would be the one thing that would make me crumble to my knees.

"Jesus, she's manipulative" I mutter to myself.

On the plus side, the news that Layla isn't pregnant is a huge relief. I'd felt guilty that Layla was facing a pregnancy alone with all her issues. I don't think that's something any woman should have to go through alone. And I was worried about the long-term effects of being a single parent on top of her other issues. Any child deserves love and affection, and I'm beginning to believe Layla isn't capable of providing either.

I'm completely blown away by what Cami's just said to Layla. I'm not thrilled with the idea that she revealed to her that she knows more about Layla than maybe she should, but at least Layla still doesn't know who she is. For now. I suppose over the coming days and weeks it will quickly become a well-known fact as to who Cami is, and Layla, if she is paying any attention at all, will quickly put two and two together. Oh to be a fly on the wall when Layla sees the pictures from New York next week. She'll know I was here, and that will chafe her hide more than anything. Though I wouldn't say I want revenge on Layla, per se, it would be nice to watch her squirm just a little bit.

I hear the door open and close, and instantly all my angst about Layla washes away like the tide of the ocean. I'm hiding around the corner, and I can't see her, but I can hear her heels clicking against the hallway tile. As she passes I slip behind her, grab her by the arm, and spin her around. She squeals and smiles as she lands in my arms.

"Hello, beautiful."

She blushes and a big smile spreads across her face. "Hello beautiful yourself."

I lean in and lick the bottom of her earlobe, and she lets out a breathy chuckle in my ear. "Behave," she breathes, but I can't help but nibble a little at the lobe because I know it will drive her nuts.

"Kiss me," she says and I happily oblige.

The sensation of our lips touching sends shivers down my spine and straight into the erection I've been fighting. Kissing Cami is like nothing I have ever felt before. Each contact, each stroke, each sensual touch is like an electric shock through my entire body, straight into my heart. Each shock stranger than the one before.

I pull back ever so slightly. Her lips follow mine, not wanting to lose the contact between us.

"You are possibly the bravest woman I know. I'm in awe of you, Cami."

We stare deeply into each other's eyes for endless minutes, communicating wordlessly, and I realize that my life will never be the same. Regardless of how our relationship plays out we will always be a part of one another. Imagining Cami as anything other than my other half twists my stomach into an uncontrollable knot.

"Thank you," I whisper, and her eyes never leave mine but I can see the puzzled expression cross her face. Rather than wait for her question, I say to her, "Thank you for what you did in there, with Layla."

"You were listening?" The shock is not lost on me.

"If it hadn't been for Tyson I would have been through that door in a nanosecond. I wasn't going to allow her to talk to you like that. When she told you about the pregnancy, Tyson actually had to hold me back from charging the door. I was so angry with her. One, for lying, and two, for the fact that she has some real nerve inviting herself up here. It just proves to me how unstable she is and incapable of respecting anyone." I take a deep breath. "I'm finally beginning to see all of her games and regret the fact that I have spent the last five years with her."

She wraps her arms tighter around me. Without breaking eye contact she whispers, "Never regret the things you do in life, Tristan. Layla is the one that will suffer in the long run from all this nonsense. She doesn't deserve what a wonderful man you are, and what you are capable of." She pauses. "Neither do I for that matter."

For the first time in the last few minutes she drops her eyes from mine and lowers her head. I try to let her words sink in. Try hard to understand why she would say such a thing. She certainly deserves to be loved by a great person. Why in the world would she think otherwise?

"I don't deserve you, Tristan." I can hear the pain in her voice.

"Cameron Enders, what on God's green earth makes you say such things?"

"Tristan, I—" She is fighting for the words. "I don't know love. I don't know what it feels like to love another or be loved by someone. I'm scared."

My heart lurches and my stomach twists. "Then let me show you," is all I can say, and her eyes, full of unshed tears, open wide to look deep into my own. "Please, Cami, don't cry. Let me show you."

"I don't know how," she breathes. Her unshed tears threaten to fall down her cheeks.

"There is nothing to know. It just comes naturally. You'll see, I promise." I plead with my eyes.

"I'll try. I will try, Tristan."

"That's all I'm asking."

We're interrupted by Beau, who calls to us from the patio. "Come on, you two. Let's go swimming."

"We'll be right there." I speak up so that Cami can try and compose herself without answering.

"Are you guys okay?" Beau asks, her voice getting quieter and closer.

"We're fine, Beau. Give us a minute?"

"Sure." She walks away.

I look back up at Cami. "Are you all right?" I ask. She nods her reply. "Can we continue this conversation later?"

"Yes," she breathes. "I didn't mean to cry."

"Shh. Please, Cami, it's okay. Never be afraid. Please?" I bring my hands to her face. "I'm not going anywhere," I say with emphasis on each word, and as I say them, their truth becomes evident.

"I'm trying, and I will continue to try."

For the moment, it's enough. I have patience to wait for the rest to follow.

I start to kiss her, softly, but her hands quickly find my hair and she pulls me into her. My answering kiss is hard and insistent, my desire for her building with each second. I want her right here, right now, and nothing's going to stand in my way.

"You do know that there are four bedrooms in this suite, right?"

Dammit, Travis!

THIRTY-SIX

~~*~*~*

CAMI

"**C**an I use your bed?" Tristan asks Travis, and I blush from head to toe.

"Hell no. You have your own room. Unless of course you're planning on sharing."

I stiffen and giggle nervously. Is he joking?

"That might not be a bad idea," Tristan says, and I go still. Travis immediately notices my discomfort and lets out a low chuckle.

"But you have to bring Naomi along too," Tristan says. "You can't be the only one having all the fun." I smack Tristan on the shoulder. "Ouch!" he exclaims, then busts out laughing.

Oh thank God he's joking.

"I'm thinking Cami disagrees with our idea."

I scowl at him, then decide to tease him back. "I think that Naomi is rather straight, boys. Get Beau, then we can talk."

"What about Mick?" Tristan asks.

I giggle. "I'm pretty sure he wouldn't mind joining the party."

Tristan gazes at me, the expression in his eyes a mixture of playfulness and concern. I wink at him, and the concern vanishes.

"Why don't we all get naked and skinny dip?" Tristan says.

Now it's Travis's turn to look a bit nervous, but there's some excitement in his eyes too.

"Sure," I say. "Then we can have a penis contest."

I burst out laughing because Travis is doing a perfect impression of a cartoon character whose eyes are bugging out of his head.

"I'll go get the girls, and you can grab the guys and get naked. We'll climb on the couch and judge." I start walking toward the patio but don't get very far before Tristan scoops me up. I squeal and laugh out loud.

"Oh, no you don't," Tristan says. "There will be no penis viewing for you!" The smile on his face practically lights up the room. He carries me toward the patio doors.

I cross my arms. "Hmph. Talk about spoiling a girl's fun." I give him my best mock pout.

As Tristan crosses the threshold onto the patio he takes off my shoes. "You don't need those."

Everyone else is already outside, and before Tristan or Travis can ruin my fun, I blurt out to Beau, Jolene, and Naomi, "The boys want to have a penis contest."

Beau raises her eyebrow at me, a move I am certain I taught her. "A penis contest, eh?"

I proceed to burst into a fit of laughter that has me nearly in tears. "It sure as hell wouldn't be a boob contest." I look very pointedly at Beau because she's clearly the biggest chested in the group. I squirm to get Tristan to put me down, but he holds on. "Why don't we all just grab our suits and go swimming?" I ask.

"Who says you need a suit?" Tristan says into my ear. I blush again.

"You want me to go swimming naked?"

He laughs. "Hell no!" He takes two big steps toward the pool before I figure out what he's doing.

"Oh no you dooon—" And before I know it I'm flying through the air, the lights of the pool getting closer and closer. I squeal and land butt-first in the pool. Had I been more prepared I would have cannonballed.

I breach the surface of the pool and look at everyone standing on the pool deck staring at me. "Why am I the only one—"

The next thing I know all seven of them jump into the pool at once. I'm tossed around for a minute as they surface. I'm laughing because the only one in a swimming suit is Tristan, but no one seems to care.

As the water settles, Tyson and Jolene gravitate toward each other. Travis and Naomi are laughing and looking carefree. But it's Mick and Beau who really catch my attention. Something about the way they embrace each other reminds me of Tristan and me. As I watch Mick looking at Beau, I recognize the look in his eyes. Mick's gaze is filled with love, affection, and longing for Beau. It makes me smile.

"What's so funny, Sweets?" Tristan asks. I turn to look at him. It's there; the look that Mick has on his face is also reflected on Tristan's. Almost an exact replica. Only seeing it on Tristan's face makes my insides quiver in anticipation of his touch.

He doesn't disappoint. He cups my cheek lightly in his palm, subtle and sweet. I lean into his embrace, and the electricity of the contact sends sparks through my body. Blood races and my heart pounds as the fireworks go off inside my head.

I know that he loves me and that I'm going to love him back.

We stay in the pool for what seem like hours. Jessie keeps our glasses full, which helps keep the conversation going. As usual, Naomi quickly becomes the life of the party. I watch as Travis is frequently taken aback by Naomi's boldness, but he keeps up with her. He seems more surprised maybe that they have similar personalities. Beau regales everyone with stories from our college days. At some point Jolene initiates a game of volleyball. Tyson and Tristan are rather quiet, which concerns me at first, but they're smiling and laughing a lot, so I decide that they're just taking a step back to allow us girls a chance to have some fun.

At around two-thirty in the morning things start to wind down. Jessie comes by and asks if we need anything else, but I think we're all beyond done at this point. It may only be two-thirty in Tarah, but it's about five-thirty in the morning back home and everyone's exhausted.

Tristan and I eventually retire to our room, and we explore each other's bodies with newfound desire and a desperate need to be close to one another.

Thursday finds us girls on a major shopping spree downstairs, Sasha and Mike trailing after us. We see Layla and her entourage of people and bodyguards, but she wisely keeps her distance. Thank goodness for that because Beau is just the type to open the can of worms Tristan and I are trying desperately to avoid.

After our shopping spree, we all spend a few hours in the spa getting buffed, waxed, and massaged. It's really nice to have some serious girl time.

Upon our return late in the afternoon, we enter the suite to find that the men have put out champagne and roses. The gesture is very sweet, but it's odd that the boys are nowhere to be found. Inside each of the bouquets of roses are cards with each of our names on them. Quickly opening mine, I find Tristan's ruggedly elegant script.

On our bed you will find an outfit I would like you to wear tonight. At precisely 5:45 this evening a group of women from the salon will come by to help you and your friends get ready. See you at 7:15. –Tristan.

I hear the squeals as the other girls read their cards. We all scatter to our rooms.

Laying on my bed is a beautiful Gucci strapless dress with large pink, red, white, and green flowers. The material is full and the dress soft. When I pick it up and hold it to my chest it reaches the ground and then some. Next to the dress on the bed are two boxes. One obviously contains shoes, but the other is more of a mystery. The shoes are Jimmy Choo peep toe pumps in suede black. Also in the shoe box are stockings, black lacy boy-shorts, a garter belt with suspenders, and a sheer lace strapless bra, all of which are my size.

At the bottom of the box is an envelope addressed to me, inside which I find six satin ribbons – three pink, one red, one green, and one lavender – and a note.

My dearest Cami, please have someone help you string these. –Tristan

I smile. They match the dress almost perfectly and are more than long enough to be strung through my corset.

The other box is wrapped in pink wrapping paper. Written on the paper is another note:

This is on loan from downstairs.

On loan? I shrug it off and rip open the paper.

"Oh! That's why."

It's a black velvet jewelry box that contains a choker: an elegant set of platinum rings intertwined with a black ribbon and studded with diamonds. Front and center on the choker is a bow. There are also a matching bangle and platinum hoop earrings with diamonds hung in the center. The diamonds on the earrings have to be at least half a carat. They are beautiful and will match the dress perfectly.

I admire the jewelry for a few minutes before heading into the bathroom for a shower. I open the door to find candles surrounding the bathtub, more flowers, and a card addressed to me.

Think of this as the start of an epic birthday weekend. Sit back, relax and enjoy a nice long bath.

As I put the card down, I see that the water has already been run. It's steaming slightly in the coolness of the bathroom. I quickly strip out of my jeans and tank top and climb into the tub to enjoy some relaxation time.

At precisely seven o'clock Leroy enters the suite to find the four of us dressed in outfits that look better suited for the red carpet than whatever it is the men have planned for us. Naomi and Jolene look amazing with their hair done up, and the dresses they're wearing are very flattering for their figures. Naomi is rocking a cocktail-length, leather contoured dress with studded accents and shoes that have the same studs. Jolene's dress is a strapless number, white with a black lace overlay, that accents the curves she has. She really is beautiful with her gorgeous green eyes and soft lines. Beau is something else entirely. She had presented herself last night as rugged in her jeans and v-neck shirt, but tonight her hair is pulled up, makeup's on, and she's wearing a floor-length, high-slit dress topped with a modified halter top that comes over her right shoulder in a thick strap. It's held over her left breast with a silver chain strap that matches the belt around her waist. The shoes peeking out from under her dress match perfectly, too.

"Ready, ladies?" says Leroy, who is smiling at us. I take it as a good sign.

We all nod or say yes in unison.

Leroy nods in return. "Now, if you will go down to the lobby, you will find Sasha and Mike awaiting your arrival," he says.

We dutifully follow him to the foyer, where the elevator is already waiting for us. We file in and Beau hits the button for the lobby.

"I wonder why all the mystery," Naomi says as soon as the doors close.

Beau answers before I do. "I would imagine it has to do with keeping Tristan hidden from the public. Having Layla Brooke in the hotel certainly isn't helping that at all," she says. She's absolutely right of course. No doubt the boys left the suite at a time when they wouldn't be seen and have been hiding out ever since.

"Why isn't Leroy escorting us downstairs?" Jolene asks.

"That's a good question," I say. "I'd imagine because we haven't yet been seen with him, and Mike and Sasha have the market on our escort services." I laugh and everyone joins in.

"Honestly, Cami. Is all this really worth it?" It's Beau asking the question.

I know what she's implying. She knows what kind of life comes with celebrity, and I think she's questioning my motives for wanting to be with Tristan. Being thrown into the spotlight of Hollywood for being someone's girlfriend has never been high on my list of priorities in life.

I shrug.

Thank heavens we've reached the ground floor and I have an excuse not to continue the conversation. The doors open, and Mike and Sasha are standing in front of the elevators.

"Good evening, Sasha. Mike." I step out first, followed by Naomi, Jolene, and Beau bringing up the rear. "To where do you have the pleasure of escorting us?"

Mike's shoulders shake with laughter. "Dinner, á la Tristan," he says quietly, but his voice is dripping with humor.

I blush and look at the girls, shrugging. They all laugh.

We start walking toward the entrance of the hotel. As we get near the doors I can see two white Jeeps, much like the one Tristan and I were in the other night.

"What in the world?" I ask aloud to no one in particular.

Sasha is the one to respond. "Your chariots await." And she ushers us through the doors and into the Jeeps.

THIRTY-SEVEN

~~*~*~*

TRISTAN

"**T**hey're close," Tyson says.

"Oh, thank God." Travis's voice is exasperated.

"Oh please, Trav. You have been waiting for all of ten minutes," I jab back at him.

"Trey, you and I both know that I am not a patient person. Ten minutes is like an eternity in my book." He is laughing and he's right, he doesn't do patient well.

Although, this whole evening is his idea and on his dime, I told him what my plans were for Cami's birthday, therefore providing the opportunity and he acquired the means of how to get there.

We're back on the boat that Cami and I had taken out a few nights ago, only this time it's lit up with stings of lights and lanterns. The hot tub is covered, at least for now. Unbeknownst to the girls, we have packed each of them an overnight bag, and Leroy is staying behind to make sure everything in our suite is packed up.

I'm extremely nervous about Cami's reaction to my birthday idea. She brought it up once before, but we never discussed it further. I'm sure she'd been thinking were going to spend her birthday quietly in Tarah.

Headlights approach the parking area, and the two white Jeeps come to a stop. I watch as the doors open and, one by one, they all get out. I look around at Tyson, Travis, and Mick, and the looks on their faces say it all. We have done well. Tonight is going to be amazing.

When Cami climbs out of the car my heart immediately starts sending blood racing through my body. The electricity that has always sparked before is present again. Her hair is pulled back into a vertical bow with curled tendrils framing her soft face. Her tattoos are on display in glorious elegance. Her dress is so long that when she walks the toes of her simple black Jimmy Choo's can be barely be seen.

The girls turn and take in the size of the boat. Cami catches me staring and smiles, and her smile is like turning on a lamp that lights up the whole world. Okay, maybe just my world, but a world nonetheless.

The girls start to make their way toward us along the dock, careful not to catch their heels in the planks. One by one, Travis, Tyson, Mick, and I step off the boat and line up to greet them as they approach. The air is charged with energy and excitement as they walk toward us. As soon as Cami's within reach, I grab her arm and pull her close to me.

"You look stunning," I whisper in her ear. I kiss her cheek.

"Me?" she says. "Look at you, all dressed up." She smiles. "So, what's this all about?"

I speak a little louder so that all the girls can hear. "We wanted to treat you all to a nice dinner, and we figured the best way to do that privately would be to take the boat out."

Jolene laughs. "Then swimsuits would have been appropriate."

Tyson joins in her laughter. "Yes, they would have, and we have those too, but for now your dresses will do."

"Ladies and gentlemen," says the captain from above us on the boat. "If you would be so kind as to climb on board, dinner is ready and we will set sail."

I turn to lead Cami onto the boat, but a movement catches my eye. I do a double-take. Oh no.

"Ty," I growl through clenched teeth.

Tyson instantly places Jolene behind him, and I do the same with Cami. Then Tyson shifts, bringing Jolene with him, in an attempt to shield me.

"You son of a bitch!" shouts the woman charging toward us along the dock.

"Please, good lord, tell me she is unarmed," I say through my teeth.

In an instant Mike is in front of us. Sasha intercepts Layla and grabs her in a bear hug, clamping down on her arms.

"Let me go!" Layla shouts.

"What are you doing here, Layla?" All I can see is red, bright red, as rage washes over me. I feel Cami grip my arm, and Tyson stands further in front of me.

"I knew it. Last night, I knew you were here. Your little girlfriend back there did a mighty good job of covering for you. But I knew you were here."

"So what, Layla. We're done, we're through. There's no reason whatsoever for you to be stalking me."

"Tristan, I'm sorry," she says to me, and the change in her tone of voice is so sudden it momentarily throws me for a loop.

For a second the red falters, blinks, and then rages on again in full force.

"You're sorry? You're sorry?! If you were sorry, Layla Brooke, you would have loved me. You would have been there for me. But you weren't. You were too busy fucking for your next role. Too busy caring about no one but yourself. Now that you have nothing, that you've washed it all down the drain, you want to come crawling back to me? Forget it. I'm done."

Layla stops struggling against Sasha's hold. I step out from behind the line of people protecting me.

"Tristan, don't," Cami pleads with me.

"It's all right," I say over my shoulder.

I stroll up to Layla, Tyson on my flank. As I get closer to her, the lights from the boat reveal that her pupils are dilated. She's high on something. Figures.

I lean in close to her ear, and when I speak my voice is pure venom. "Get out of here, Layla. Do not come back. Go home, Layla. Go home and get your shit straight. Clean up. Do not let me see your face again." I straighten up. Tears are streaming down her cheeks. "Go home, Layla." I repeat.

I nod to Sasha. "See that she gets back to her suite. Find Chanty and have her get Layla's shit together and get her back to the States. You'll have to rejoin us tomorrow with Leroy."

"Yes, Tristan," she says and turns, taking Layla, still in a bear hug, with her.

I walk back to the boat. Cami comes back to my side in an instant, taking my hand in hers. I look at her, and she at me, and in her eyes I see the closure that is reflected in mine. I finally got to say my piece.

Slowly, Travis helps Naomi up the ladder, followed by Mick and Beau. Tyson helps Jolene climb up, then turns to Cami and me.

"She won't be able to follow us," he says. "Odds are she'll make another attempt on the suite, but I'll text

Chanty and tell her what happened. Once she knows you're here, she'll persuade Layla to leave."

Cami nods, but doesn't say anything. Tyson looks to me. I nod hesitantly, and he turns to climb up.

Once he's reached the top, I turn to help Cami. "Are you all right?" she says before I can even open my mouth.

I give her a half smile. "Is it bad that the only thing that's bothering me is that I'm worried she's put a damper on our evening?"

She smirks, then laughs. "She certainly likes to try to do that. But I'm fine, so long as you're okay."

I smile at her and raise my elbow so she can take it. As her hand slides into the crook of my arm, I say, "I've never been better." And it's true. The weight I've been carrying for days, maybe even years, is finally lifted from my shoulders. I'm free of Layla at last.

We make our way to the bar, where Jessie has two glasses of Bolli waiting for us.

"Jessie, do you ever sleep?" Cami asks.

When I'd spoken with the hotel manager about taking the boat again and having one of his bartenders accompany us, he told me that Jessie was more than willing. I tried to give the poor man a night off, but the manager insisted that Jessie wanted any and all available opportunities to assist us.

Jessie laughs. "No, Cami, not with you guys around. Though I'm really beginning to enjoy bartending your parties."

"Good." She smiles at him in appreciation.

The maître d' emerges and addresses us. "Due to the cooling temperature and increased winds on the open waters, dinner will be served inside this evening," he says. "If you all will please follow me."

We follow him through the sliding double doors of the main cabin. Inside is a large table set for eight with wine glasses, porcelain plates, and elegant white linens and garnished with two small vases of white and yellow roses. Unlike the hull of the boat, which is black, the cabin is white with dark wood accents. There are five plush chairs and a comfortable-looking bench seat.

Once we are seated, two servers bring us our salads and some white wine. I don't catch the label, but it has a unique tropical fruit taste to it. My guess is that it is a locally made wine. It's delicious.

We all carry on the conversation at dinner without much effort. Everyone is getting along really well, laughing and joking and having a good time. I'm grateful to see that Layla's interruption hasn't spoiled the mood for the night.

After dinner we sit around the table talking and drinking wine, champagne, and eventually our own favorite drinks. Jessie is attentive enough to make sure our glasses are never empty. Eventually we feel the boat slow. I look at my watch; it's nearly eleven. I'm guessing we're at about the halfway point of our journey.

"Are we back at the dock already?" Naomi asks.

None of us men can hide our smiles.

"Why don't we go take a look?" Travis says. He nudges Naomi to slide off of the bench.

Escorting our ladies through the door, we all step toward the railing, looking out into the darkness.

"Oh, wow," Cami says. "It's gorgeous out here."

The moon is high and huge against the blackness of the ocean. The lights strung around the boat reflect off the water. All the other lights are off outside except for two very large spotlights under the water, gently illuminating the boat from below, softening the blackness.

"How would you ladies like to sleep here tonight?" I ask.

Jolene is the first to speak. "Um, I am not sleeping in this dress."

Tyson chuckles. "No, baby, you can sleep naked for all I care, but we have some clothes and bathing suits for each of you in your cabins."

I feel Cami lightly smack my arm. "You are too much sometimes, you know that?"

I turn to her and look squarely into her eyes. "No, not too much, just thorough." I watch as she smiles.

Speaking loud enough for all to hear, but intimately enough for Cami to capture the unspoken meaning, I say, "We are not returning to Tarah until after a weekend in Bora Bora." Cami gasps. "The boat will take us there in the morning," I tell her.

Her smile stays on, but I sense her hesitation. I think I can guess why. "No worries, Sweets, Leroy is getting all of our things packed up. He'll have them brought over in the helicopter." As I tell her this she relaxes and her smile grows wider.

I watch as she visibly starts to bounce, and the excitement is palpable. She throws her arms around my neck, almost throwing me off balance, and crushes her lips to my cheek – once, twice.

After a moment she pulls back. "Thank you, Tristan. This is turning out to be a fabulous weekend," she whispers.

I lean into her ear and whisper, "Anything for you." And then I kiss her.

It's not until our lips meet that I realize how much I missed them, how much I long for them. Her hands snakes into my hair and she pulls me in tighter.

The effect is instantaneous. My breathing goes ragged and I fight the urge to pin her up against the railing. I'm lost in Cami's kiss, so soft and sweet. My cock hardens further.

"I want you," I say quietly against her lips.

"Take me," she whispers back.

I step back, grab her hand, and pull her toward the cabin and our stateroom.

"Hey guys, we're, um...gonna go put our suits on," I stutter. I hear chuckles from Ty and Trav, but I don't care.

"Sounds good to me," says Mick, and he grabs Beau's hand and starts to follow. As do Tyson and Jolene. Travis and Naomi seem lost in each other too.

THIRTY-EIGHT

~~*~*~*

CAMI

As soon as we enter the cabin, I start trying to pull the zipper on my dress, but Tristan stops my hand.

"Oh, no you don't," he says from behind me. "That's my job. I want to unwrap you."

His words make the blood pump faster and harder through my body. My body temperature begins to rise in anticipation. I feel his body come closer to mine, and then his lips are against my neck as his hands work at unzipping my dress. His finger tracing along the inside of my fairy wings sends shivers down my spine and throughout my body. My nipples are instantly hard, pressing against my bra and begging to be freed from their confines.

Finally he gets the zipper all the way down and the front of my dress falls away from my chest. Tristan pulls the dress down my legs and lets it fall to the floor of the cabin.

I hear Tristan take a sharp breath through his teeth as he takes in my corset. Beau helped me intertwine the ribbons he left for me and it turned out pretty cool. His fingers trace around the outside and then across the ribbons, tracing their path through the hoops. The sensation tickles slightly and sends more goose bumps through my body.

Then his hands follow the line of my garter belt around to my sides, his soft touch sending shock waves of pleasure into my very core. My sex warms in anticipation, and I wait to see what he'll do next.

His hands continue around to my stomach, his touch warm and sensual, and then they are sliding their way up toward my breasts. I lean forward in anticipation of his caress.

I hear his breathy laugh behind me.

"What's so funny?" I'm trying to hide the smile on my face and failing. He chuckles again.

"Eager, aren't you?"

"Can you blame me? I haven't seen you all day." I bring my hands behind my back and feel around until I find his erection through his trousers.

"Oh, no," he says, pulling his erection from my hands. "We are doing this my way."

I pout, and he laughs as my shoulders slump. He spins me around and cups my face. He crushes his lips to mine and I'm lost to the sensation. His kisses get more intense each time our lips touch.

My body responds with urgency. My hands find the lapel of his jacket and he helps me by shrugging it off. Then his tie and his vest are all but ripped from his body. I'm impatient to have his naked chest pressed against me.

"Do you care about your shirt?" I ask against his lips, and he shakes his head.

I grab the shirt and rip it open, sending buttons flying to the floor.

He grins against my lips as his hands find the clasp of my bra. He unfastens it with great fervor, freeing my breasts of their confinement, and he wraps his arms around me, pressing me to him.

His kisses intensify. Our tongues dance with each other.

His hands slowly slide down to my buttocks, cupping and caressing. It tickles slightly and I squirm. He goes to unhook the suspenders holding up my stockings and I laugh.

"That tickles," I squeal, and he does it again, and again.

I'm starting to laugh uncontrollably and hardly notice that he pushes me toward the bed. He continues tickling me until I sit down.

"Now that's better," he says.

I unbuckle his belt and then unbutton his trousers. Hooking my thumbs in the waistband of his boxers, I pull down. Once his pants are to his knees, I lick the purplish head of his rock hard cock. He shivers at the contact. I moan as I take his head into my mouth, licking and sucking and working him in further, deeper.

His hands touch the back of my head and the flower that is holding my bow tie ponytail. As he undoes the tie, my hair quickly falls down my back, and his hands grip hard and firmly into my hair.

I continue licking and sucking, slowly sliding him in and out of my mouth.

I move my hands to cup my breasts, and my own touch sends a jolt of excitement through my sex. My clit hardens, begging to be touched. Slowly I slide my hands down my body and into my panties, and I find my clit with my fingers.

I moan as the sensation washes through me. I look up at Tristan through my lashes, slowly stroking his cock with my mouth as my hand continues its slow, sensual assault against my sex. Tristan moans.

Finally he can't take it anymore, and he pulls back until I nearly lose my balance trying to keep him in my mouth. His sex pops free, audibly, and he grins at my pouty face.

"I was having fun with that," I mutter.

He lowers himself to his knees. "I know. But now it's my turn."

He undoes the last two suspenders holding up my stockings and quickly bares both my legs, removing both stockings and shoes. Then he's back to remove my black lace boy-shorts and matching garter belt.

Before I can blink, I'm naked and Tristan's tongue is buried against my sex, licking, stroking, and caressing me with ardent excitement. I feel the warmth of an orgasm building deep within my core. My legs stiffen and he slows, but only for the briefest of seconds. Before I even realize he's no longer kneeling, he is slamming his cock hard and deep into me, and I explode.

Fireworks, white stars, an indescribable sensation.

"Tristan," I all but scream as my orgasm rips through me.

"Shh, baby," he whispers.

Just then I hear Beau letting out her own orgasmic release, giving ironic context to Tristan's comment.

"Well then, I guess we're not the only ones vying for the loudest orgasm," I say.

He shakes his head and slowly begins to slide in and out of me, pulling back until he's practically falling free and then slamming back into me.

Tristan leans down and kisses me, warm and sweet, sensual.

And there is something else. Something about the slowing of his motions in time to the beating of my heart. I place my hand on his chest and his own heart beat is in sync with mine. Beat for beat.

I look into his eyes, and there's a warmth, a depth to them that I've never seen before. He's biting his bottom lip, perhaps in concentration or in an attempt to hold back his own orgasm, as he continues to slowly slide in and out.

An unbelievable sensation washes over my entire body. Warm, caressing, and comforting. Not a pending orgasm, but something else. Something that feels like it's going to burst out of my chest.

"I love you, Cami."

That's it!

As my orgasm pulls me into bliss I can no longer keep my eyes open. "Tristan," I breathe. "I'm going to...ah!" I moan.

"Let it go, Cami. Let it out," he breathes against my lips. There is a double meaning to his words.

"I love you, Tristan."

Then his lips are on mine, a hard, passionate kiss.

Finally the string snaps. Tears form in my eyes as my orgasm washes over me. A sensation so intense that I hold my breath. The orgasm envelops my entire body, and I feel like I'm falling apart at the seams, melting into Tristan as our bodies and souls become one.

THE END... For Now.

Acknowledgements:

Words cannot express the gratitude I feel towards you for reading Finding Love's Wings.

So Thank You to each and every one of you. In conjunction with thanking all of you, I need to thank some brilliant individuals.

To my true inspirations... Barb, Rachel, Natalie, and Jolene. These beautiful ladies are my Beau, Rayne, Naomi and Jolene. Ladies, I hope you enjoy your alter-egos. Your encouragement, love and support without you guys, well, this story would still be rattling around in my noggin. So Thank You!

The Girls, Crystal, Angie, Marata and Ronin, your enthusiasm and support of my first novel knows no bounds, I heart you all!

TweetiePie, I cannot forget you and your undying patience, I can't wait to come to England, you owe me a cup of tea!

The Undead Duo and Crew, you all know who you are, you pushed me beyond my limits and for that I give you all big HUGE tackle hugs!

Okay, I think that covers everyone. My beautiful editor Sione got copyright page billing. :-)!

STAY TUNED FOR MORE IN THE LOVE'S WINGS SERIES!

FOLLOW ALONG AT

WWW.ZOEYDERRICK.COM,

WWW.TWITTER.COM/ZOEYDERRICK OR

WWW.FACEBOOK.COM/ZOEY.DERRICK.

Zoey Derrick

I cant wait to see you there!

About The Author:

It is from Glendale, Arizona that Zoey Derrick, a mortgage underwriter by day and romance and erotica novelist by night, writes stories as hot as the desert sun itself. It is this passion that drips off of her work, bringing excitement to anyone who enjoys a good and sensual love story.

Not only does she aim to take her readers on an erotic dance that lasts the night, it allows her to empty her mind of stories we all wish were true.

Her stories are hopeful yet true to life, skillfully avoiding melodrama and the unrealistic, bringing her gripping Erotica only closer to the heart of those that dare dipping into it.

The intimacy of her fantasies that she shares with her readers is thrilling and encouraging, climactic yet full of suspense. She is a loving mistress, up for anything, of which any reader is doomed to return to again and again.

www.ingramcontent.com/pod-product-compliance
Lightning Source LLC
Chambersburg PA
CBHW070634180626
46817CB00006B/2116
* 9 7 8 0 9 9 0 3 2 6 4 1 0 *